Flesh and Mind

The Time Travels of
Dr. Victoria Von Dietz

Valerie Bentz

Credits for Cover Images
For the Nazi Insignia: File:Parteiadler der Nationalsozialistische Deutsche Arbeiterpartei
Image of George Herbert Mead: http://web.lemoyne.edu/~hevern/nr-theorists-photos/
mead.jpg
Image of Martin Heidegger: phillweb.net (edited by Richard L.W. Clarke)
link http://www.phillwebb.net/History/Twentieth/Continental/Phenomenology/
Heidegger/Heidegger.htm
Image of Woman:favim.com *link* - http://favim.com/image/17312/
Image of Alfred Schutz: Paul Roebuck, PhD
link - http://www.roebuckclasses.com/people/thinkers/schutz_a.htm

ISBN-13: 9781492167235
ISBN-10: 1492167231
Library of Congress Control Number: 2013915546
CreateSpace Independent Publishing Platform
North Charleston, South Carolina

Dedication

To George Herbert Mead and Martin Heidegger, the philosophical loves of my life. To Jane Addams, sister and friend to all, pioneer for peace and women's suffrage. To SPHS, the Society for Phenomenology and the Human Sciences, where I came to revere Alfred Schutz, and to know Helmut Wagner, mentor and friend. To all those who suffer from oppression and tyranny and those, like Addams, Schutz and Wagner, who fight against it.

Acknowledgements

I am grateful to Dr. Stephen Figler, novelist par excellence, spouse, editor and friend. Special thanks to members of the Novel Idea writer's group of San Luis Obispo, who critiqued and encouraged me. I appreciate artist Marshall Hamachi for cover design ideas and Catharine Macdonald for editorial help. I alone am responsible for the content.

Disclaimer

This is a work of fiction. While some of those portrayed are real historical characters, my rendition of what they said, did and thought are completely from my imagination. Similarly, I morphed dates, places and times, family members and events to fit the demands of plot and emotional coherence and events are not intended to bear the weight of historical scrutiny.

Flesh is the entire world, past, present and future, in which our bodies and minds are uniquely entangled.

"The flesh is at the heart of the world."
—— Maurice Merleau-Ponty

PRELUDE: APPROACHING HITLER'S CHAMBERS

My footsteps echo through the long marble corridor of Charlottenberg Castle as I come closer to Adolph Hitler's chambers. The dagger hidden between my breasts has grown hot from my pounding heart. My twin sons bounce on each hip, happily gurgling and smiling, oblivious to my anxiety. I kiss each on his smooth, cool forehead, fearing for each one's life whether I succeed or fail.

The boots of the guards click in syncopation behind me. When they came to escort me, they insisted I bring the babies. Der Fuhrer's orders.

I am not a violent woman. To the contrary, I've devoted much of my life to peace and justice. I was never sure whether I owed my professorship to my accomplishments or to my famous husband. But since then, my theory of overlapping time has earned my own recognition. It was this work that brought me to Adolph's attention.

I hoped to change Adolph's mind once he became intrigued with me. First because of my work, then because of my striking resemblance to the one woman he had ever loved, his niece Geli, killed by gunshot when she tried to leave his estate. I hope to dispel his anger, to lead him to rethink his ambitions, which I have so far failed to do. Maybe today. If not, with each step I'm closer to becoming his killer.

PART ONE
CHICAGO, 1970s

Chapter One
Martin Luther Looks In

For every nail that pierced Christ, more than one hundred thousand should in justice pierce you, yes, they should prick you forever and ever more painfully!"
Martin Luther, *A Meditation on Christ's Passion*, 1648

"Kathy, turn off the television and do your homework!" Tom's booming voice jolted Victoria out of a late afternoon slump over her desk in her upstairs bedroom/office. "Oh, please, not more snow," she said to herself noticing the snow flakes out her window. If it kept on that would mean yet another morning up before dawn to shovel out the driveway.

"Mr. Rogers' Neighborhood is almost over, Dad," came Kathy's high-pitched response from downstairs. "Witch Hazel has Sarah Saturday by the throat!"

"O.K., a few more minutes," said Tom.

Victoria was grateful for Tom's watchfulness over Kathy. Until their marriage several years ago, Mr. Rogers on T.V. and her father, Grandpa George, had been Kathy's father figures.

The musky haze of Tom's pipe tobacco wafted over the Persian hallway rug into her study. Why the change to this fragrant, almost intoxicating one? Lately, Tom had been going to more night meetings at the college, staying away late. Victoria held her queasy gut. Suspicions swirled in her head as if she drank a martini. She shook her head.

She couldn't let herself think about her troubled marriage. Victoria sighed, looking at the stack of term papers and her unfinished research application held under her typewriter. She took a breath and straightened her shoulders.

The first term paper she picked off the stack was that of a student who she suspected of plagarism. When she had questioned him about it he seemed arrogant and dismissive. The word had come down from the president's office that his father had contributed a million to the college endowment fund. He needed to pass Victoria's class to complete graduation requirements. She placed this paper at the bottom of the stack.

Victoria was up for tenure this year at Athens college. Either you got it along with a promotion or you were out. Despite gaining international recognition for her publications on the theory of time, Dean Schenk was like a pit bull after Victoria's ankles. She recoiled at her memory of his harsh words at her pre-tenure review. "Your involvement in peace, feminist and other imprudent causes detracts from your role as an Athens professor," he had said with his jaw tight. Not only was her career at stake, but since Tom had only a part time job her income was essential. Victoria was nauseated at the thought of losing her income, her home and Kathy's place at the private academy in which she was thriving.

She had not been able to buddy up to the silver haired men who made up the tenure committee. These full professors found the time to dominate the faculty lounge with the latest football scores or hunting escapades. Victoria stopped having her lunch there after she attempted to engage them in conversation about Nixon's escalation of the Vietnam war. Their response was cold scowls and "we should bomb them into the stone age".

Maybe she should take Gladys Bentley, her department chair's, advice. "Just go there for coffee, be nice, smile at the old geezers until after you get tenure. Then you can say what you want," Bentley had said. But Victoria was never one to play politics. She was a woman of principle.

"My student evaluations are high. If I just continue to do a good job, I'll be O.K.," she tried to reassure herself. She took another paper off the pile. A ray of the setting sun spotlighted the huge image of Martin Luther in the stained glass window on Reformation Lutheran church across the street from their two story framed house.

Luther, wearing his monk's robes, held up the ninety-five grievances he had nailed to the doorway of Wittenberg cathedral in 1648. He seemed to gaze directly at Victoria as she looked up from her desk. His piercing glare told her he was aware of her lack of concentration.

She could also see Martin Luther through the parlor windows downstairs, or rather, it seemed he could see in. Was she dusting her furniture, cooking proper meals, doing her wifely duty, being a loving mother?

She recalled the years in school, memorizing Luther's Catechism. God's judgment rained on any who had sex outside of marriage. The celibate life was what He preferred, but for those who were too weak to harness their animal urges, marriage was the only alternative. All sins came from Eve and her juicy apple. Adam and the power of God the Father couldn't keep women from making trouble.

The Holy Ghost, appearing as a lovely white bird, was the only part of the trinity Victoria really liked. Named "Sophia," this holy spirit had mystery and grandeur. God the Father was a stern old man looking down from the sky for chances to ventilate his anger and aggression. Even his own son had to pay for all the bad things everyone else did. She closed the drapes, hiding Luther's gaze. The snow came down faster, turning into sleet as the sun set. She rubbed her hands to remove the chill, and then sat down at her desk.

Yoga and meditation would help. She sat cross legged on her mat trying not to think of anything but openness. She practiced her breath of fire, forcing the air out of her lungs, breathing in, breathing out.

In the background she noticed the full length photograph of her favorite philosopher, George Herbert Mead. He seemed to look back at her. She had cut the picture from the front cover of his book, *The Philosophy of the Present*, and placed it in a carved frame. Here was someone she could admire, a thinker with depth and vision. Mead believed that the past and the future existed in each moment. Although he died in 1938, Mead was a significant person to her. She spent years devoted to his work, writing her doctoral dissertation about his philosophy of time. Victoria saw the world through Mead's eyes.

She came out of meditation, disappointed that she had not been able to make her mind completely empty. But at least she had been able to transcend her troubles with the dean, her marriage, for a moment.

As she stood, Mead seemed to look back at Victoria with loving admiration. She wondered if he would have appreciated her long blond hair, her ample bosom, her long shapely legs. Did the side of his moustache tilt upward as she pulled her skirt down over her knees? His face was handsome, aquiline, hair graying. Though the photo was black and white, she thought his eyes might be blue, like her father's, another George. Her nipples tingled. One of Mead's hands was in his pants' pocket, pushing his tweed jacket aside. A man who stands like that is comfortable with himself, a master of knowledge, a man who might even challenge the evils of the world. Was she carrying this too far?

She mused about her arousal from Mead's picture. She and Tom rarely had sex anymore. She was hurt when Tom had insisted right after their wedding, now almost three years ago, that they have separate study/bedrooms. Now she was indifferent about it. George Mead had excited her mind and her passion even before she met Tom. In fact, it was his resemblance to Mead that first attracted her to him. Like Mead, Tom wore three-piece suits with pocket watches.

She imagined Mead taking her in his arms. She smelled his pipe tobacco and the fabric of his English wool suit.

"You are my life," she said softly to Mead's photo.

Familiar running sound on the stairs brought her focus back to the present. It was Kathy and Snuggles, their golden lab.

"I've finished my homework, Mom. . . except for math," Kathy said, Snuggles put his head down on Victoria's lap. Kathy climbed onto the day bed under the window still wearing her school uniform. "Why do you have the drapes shut, Mom," she asked.

"I just got tired of looking at Martin Luther," said Victoria, smiling.

Kathy laughed, "I get tired of him too."

Kathy slid off the day bed and came towards Victoria, her head tilted to the side. Victoria grabbed Kathy's hand, then kissed Kathy on the cheek.

"Why do you have Herbert George Mead's picture on your desk?" said Kathy. She pulled her long brown braids out to each side of her face.

"George Herbert Mead, sweetheart. He's a great philosopher."

"What's so great about him?" Kathy wiggled back and forth from one foot to the other.

"Well, he started the League of Nations, he helped get laws against children working in factories, and he supported women's suffrage," said Victoria.

"What's good about women suffering?" said Kathy.

"Suffrage, Kathy, meaning the right to vote. Women weren't allowed to vote until 1920," said Victoria.

"Oh, Mead's a pretty good guy, I guess," said Kathy, "but why don't you write about Grandpa or Daddy? Because they're not famous or because they're not dead?"

Victoria laughed, "Probably both, sweetie."

"Why don't you write your own philosophy, so you could be famous too?"

Kathy's question hit Victoria, like only a child's fresh insights can.

"I'm working on it, sweetie, but you have to start somewhere. Noone will read you unless you work from an known philosopher and they are mostly men."

"But Mom, you tell me I can be whatever I want."

"Go do your math with Daddy. That will take you a lot farther than philosophy in this men's world."

"Ugh. I like talking ideas with you better, or even practicing the violin," said Kathy. She picked up her math book and tromped into the hall.

"It smells different up here," said Kathy.

"Do you girls like my new tobacco?" said Tom from his study down the hall. "Come here and we'll work on your math. But first go down and get me a cold beer."

Victoria's stomach churned as she inhaled the brandied, exotic scent. She pictured Tom at his desk, his dark brown hair parted on the side, his aquiline face, deeply intelligent eyes looking through round wire glasses like Steppenwolf's, white shirt, now tieless. His ever-present vest would be hanging open, beloved pocket watch attached. His good foot under his desk would be wearing a brown leather slipper, his prosthetic foot and leg from the knee down lying beside his desk like a deserted puppet. And the ever present empty beer bottles.

Kathy, followed by Snuggles, raced down the stairs. Victoria was irritated by Tom's asking Kathy to fetch his beer. Yet she couldn't justify her feelings on reasonable grounds as she thought Kathy should be helpful. With Tom's artificial leg the stairs were burdensome.

Tom does love me Victoria thought. He tells me often enough of his admiration, his esteem for my work, calls me "beautiful". It was already clear that he felt diminished by the circumstances of his only being able to secure a part time position as an instructor while she was an assistant professor.

Victoria looked at Mead's picture again. She was enchanted with his world. Mead was not just an intellectual sparing partner to her, as he had been to the guys in her graduate seminars. She picked up the blue notebook on her desk. Gazing at Mead's picture she wrote:

He is the master of a vast territory. He is a man of power. His words make things sparkle with clarity. His face brings peace and hope. He is a god-man. Now he looks directly at me, like he never looked at me before.

"Your mustache, stylish though it was at your time, must go. I will trim it for you," she whispered to him.

Startled at the sound of her own voice, she thought, "in my inner mind I'm married to Mead".

His eyes shone with love and appreciation. She heard Mead respond, "Yes, I've known you, Victoria, all these years, I've been with you the whole time, I've loved you, and only you, you are my wife, my lover, my delight. Only you, of all those who have read my work and have written about me, understand my soul."

She heard him say, "Will dinner be ready soon, dear?" It was not Mead's voice but Tom's from across the hall.

"I love you, you are my darling gazelle," Tom called.

She trembled as she rose and closed her notebook.

"Did you hear me, Victoria? I said I love you?"

"I love you too," she shouted back, staring into Mead's eyes.

Chapter Two
Bluebeard's Castle

Durations are a continual sliding of presents into each other.
— George Herbert Mead, *The Philosophy of the Present*

After finishing a chicken and rice dinner Victoria had prepared early that morning, Tom read Kathy a new French rendition of Bluebeard's castle. She was proud of Kathy, who was studying French, only asking for a few words to be translated. Through Tom's dramatic flair and exaggerated inflections, the horror of the trusting wives murdered, then buried alive behind the walls of the house seemed more bloody and sinister.

"The moral of the story is, don't ask the forbidden question, " said Tom at the end. "The wives were happy until they asked."

"What's the forbidden question, Dad?" asked Kathy. Tom leaned on the back two legs of the chair, loosened his tie and pulled his pipe out of his inner jacket pocket.

"Lovely dinner, darling," he said.

Snuggles, enjoying the chicken scraps in his bowl, barked in agreement.

"Dessert?" Victoria asked, going to the kitchen with the dinner plates, wondering if he was going to ignore Kathy's question.

"We have pineapple upside-down cake, Dad. I made it," said Kathy, beaming.

"That's worth putting off my pipe." He placed his favorite burl on the table.

When they were all seated eating desert Kathy again asked Tom what question Bluebeard's wife asked. Tom said:

"The point is not what the question is, but what happens to those who ask." Tom sounded as if he spoke from a pulpit.

Victoria mused on how Tom intensified his Oxbridge accent, when he wanted acquiescence. At more relaxed moments, the West Virginia tones of his childhood showed through his acquired aristocratic aura.

Kathy squealed, "I know what happens, Daddy! Bluebeard puts them behind the wall and they die!" She spread her plaid skirt over the Queen Ann dining chair. Her legs swung from under it like a rag doll's. "He's a scary, bad man," she shouted.

"Ladies don't kick their legs at dinner, nor do they raise their voices," said Tom frowning. Kathy sat up straight and prim in her chair. If nothing, else, Kathy is learning excellent manners from Tom, thought Victoria.

He picked his pipe up from the table, filled it. "A bit of cognac would be nice, my dear." He placed his hands on the side of his chair to push himself up.

"I'll get it, darling." Victoria anticipated his grimace of pain when he stood. Her feet and back hurt from the long day, preparing dinner ahead of time, teaching, then picking up Kathy. A long evening of lecture preparations lay ahead. The snow was now thick sleet, blurring the image of the neighbor's house nextdoor to the dining room.

"We'll have to get up early again tomorrow morning to shovel," said Tom.

Victoria sighed and went to the antique sideboard and poured the cognac into large snifters, just a few sips for her and nearly full for Tom. Tom reached into his pocket for his lighter. He engaged in the familiar pipe lighting ritual, which always brought a glow to his face. The unfamiliar tobacco scent filled the room, causing Victoria to break into a cold sweat. "New tobacco?"

"Can't a man change tobacco without his wife questioning? I made a change, that's all. Now back to Bluebeard, off of me. Don't be critical of Bluebeard. He wanted simple proof of loyalty, of love, of trust from his wives."

"But surely someone does not deserve to die for being suspicious of a serial murderer!" said Victoria. The security she thought she had with Tom seemed to burn with his tobacco.

"Bluebeard's creepy, creepy" said Kathy.

The phone rang. Victoria jumped up, her heart pounding, as it may be a call from the hospital where her father had been since his recent diagnosis of pancreatic cancer. Her mother's usually abrasive tones were floaty and vague. He was to have surgery the day after tomorrow. "Ma, do you really think the surgery is a good idea? Dr. Kramer says the odds are not good. . . are you listening to me Ma?"

"George should have every chance possible." Her tone changed to her usual crabby sense of righteousness. "You'd better come up for Friday."

"Yes, Ma, I'll come up . . . ," thinking she'd still need to miss class as it was a ninety mile drive up to the hospital in Milwaukee. Victoria felt like she was going to loose her dinner.

Until a week ago her father had been active and seemingly healthy, young for his age of sixty-three. Tears came to her eyes at the thought of loosing him. Even more so, it pained her to think of Kathy loosing her grandpa. She swallowed to push back the tears.

"Is Grandpa O.K.?" Kathy's voice was an octave higher than usual. Victoria caught her breath. She sat down, taking a sip of cognac. Tom raised his eyebrows. Outside the front window, the setting sun sharpened the image of Luther gazing back through the sleet.

"Yes, Sweetie. Grandpa is O.K. just now. But they will be doing surgery to try to take away his cancer," said Victoria.

Kathy jumped down from her chair and buried her head in Victoria's lap. She stroked Kathy's back.

"Now, Kathy, its time to practice your violin," said Victoria. "That way you'll have a new piece to play for Grandpa."

"But I have to do the dishes."

"Dad will do them, as usual," said Victoria. Tom insisted that he do the dishes as payment for his lack of cooking skills. This, in addition to letting Victoria pay the household bills was his testimony to belief in women's rights. She resented having had to pressure the bank to put the house in her name as well as Tom's, even though she made the payments. "What happens if you get pregnant?" the loan officer asked her. "What happens if you get pregnant?" she replied. Finally she got the deed of trust in both their names, only because of the recent passage of the equal rights amendment. And yet she mused, though I'm a feminist, I feel much like a slave. I have to do it all—career, wife, mother and I'm exhausted.

"But Dad isn't feeling well tonight," said Kathy.

"Kathy, go practice," said Tom, getting up stiffly. With a grimace he limped toward the kitchen, the uneven rhythm of his feet on the hardwood floor echoing off the high ceilings.

"I'll be in my study," said Victoria. "When you're done practicing, come up for your bath."

"O.K. Dad, will you read me more before bed?"

"We'll continue with Bluebeard."

"Not Bluebeard! Beauty and the Beast. The beast looks ugly but he is really a prince. Not, scarey like Bluebeard," Kathy took her violin out of its case and carefully tuned the strings. Her long brown braids hung over the violin as she practiced the Vivaldi concerto. This sweet sound merged into the bathtub water running, and then into little feet coming upstairs for her nighttime story.

Snuggles decided against following Kathy into the bathroom. He shook himself out and walked into Kathy's study.

"Not taking any chances on getting a bath, are you Snuggles." Victoria put her hand on his soft fur, rubbed he ears. Snuggles ran around her office in a circle, then out the door and barked once.

"Opps! Forgot your walk! Victoria bundled up and took Snuggles for a walk around the block. The cool crisp air was invigorating. The snowfall whitened their coats.

Back in her study, Victoria picked up the phone to call Gladys Bentley, her department chair, to ask her to cover her Friday class.

"Happy to cover for you. And I'm glad it is Friday not tomorrow," said Bentley. "I'm sorry to have to put more pressure on you just now, Victoria, but Dean Schenk asked to see you."

"What's it about?" Victoria's heart raced.

"He was vague, only that it is about a student complaint and that it is important. I told him I'd ask you to stop by tomorrow after class."

Victoria's heart pounded. She broke into a cold sweat "Oh shit, not more pressure from the disgruntled bigots," she thought. Then she wondered if it may be the wealthy student who plagarized his senior paper. She asked if there was any chance the college would be closed because of the snow and ice.

12

"No chance. Dean Schenck lives out in the country, but has his own tracter plow," said Bentley.

"Thanks for giving me the heads up, Gladys" said Victoria as she hung up.

With heavy eyelids, Victoria looked up at Mead's picture. He seemed to hear and understand. If only he could put his arms around me, she thought.

Victoria enjoyed the muffled sound of Tom's voice as he rendered a dramatic reading of *Beauty and the Beast* for the thousandth time. She had always loved the beast as a child, finding his cat/dog form more attractive than the prince he became. Tom's footsteps clumped down the long carpeted hallway towards her study. She wondered if his recent preference for Bluebeard was a kind of revelation, even a warning.

"Thought I'd say goodnight to you too. I can tell you are tired and may not be up late," he said, pecking her on the cheek, holding his brandy snifter filled to the brim.

"I'll be up working for a while," Victoria said. The corners of her mouth pulled up as she glared at her desk. She looked up at him. The light from her desk lamp shadowed his face.

"Working on your dissertation tonight?" she asked.

"Sure, darling, after I finish preparing tomorrow's lecture on third century Chinese philosophy and a report on guaranteed learning outcomes for the meeting with Sister Wilhelmena." Tom's acquired Oxbridge accent was resonant with satiric irony.

Victoria held her tongue. She had managed to complete her dissertation while teaching four courses as compared with his one, but why add fuel to the fire of his feelings of inadequacy.

"Will you come in when you're finished?" she asked. An ache clawed at her stomach.

"If I see your light on," his mouth pulled back in a grimace, "and if my leg isn't hurting like it is now."

"Hopefully it will feel better by morning for shoveling." She and Kathy could hardly do the driveway alone.

"Actually, the cold coming up the prosthesis from the snow numbs the pain."

As he turned toward the door Tom noticed the copy of Martin Heidegger's *Being and Time* on Victoria's desk and barked: "Don't waste your time reading Heidegger. He's dense and indecipherable!"

"He fascinates me, as does Mead. They both have important theories of how all levels of time intersect," said Victoria. "And Heidegger has a deep rich insight into human experience."

"Nonsense! Besides, you know that Heidegger was a Nazi, at least for a while, the opposite side of things from your beloved Mead," Tom glanced at the framed picture of Mead.

Victoria's back arched. Should she have to defend her affection for a dead philosopher? She felt her face flush, her palms moist.

"Who did you call?" said Tom.

She was about to say, "George Mead, of course," then caught herself. "Gladys Bentley, about my trip to the hospital. She told me the dean wants to see me tomorrow about a student."

"Oh, man, speaking of Nazi's! Schenk seems to expect you to click your heels," said Tom.

He slid a hand into his vest pocket, took out his watch and glanced at the time. He glanced lovingly at his brandy snifter, then clumped to his study and shut the door.

Victoria threw herself, stomach down, on her daybed. "I hate him. I hate him," she said as she pounded her pillow and sobbed. "Oh, my God, what am I saying? Of course I don't hate him. What's wrong with me?"

Snuggles walked into her study, wagging his tail and sat down at her feet. She ran her stockinged foot over his back, enjoying the soft warmth.

Chapter Three
Dr. Annabelle Carter Jackson

G uy Sartori, legal assistant, looked over the pile of proposals on his large walnut desk, when the deep voice of Dr. Annabelle Carter Jackson boomed into the reception area.

"Get in here, Guy, and bring my coffee. You know I've got that keynote address tonight."

Guy jumped up and put together a tray from the sideboard, yelling back, "coming madam," in a semi-humorous tone.

This job was a good step for an excop now in his third year of law school at Northwestern, he thought. Annabelle, as Dean of Black and Feminist studies at Chicago U. had lots of civil rights contacts in the area. In addition, as head of NIHL (National Institute of Human Learning) she had connections in D.C. government research circles.

"Those damn airlines cancel flights anytime they're not full," said Annabelle, referring to her early morning arrival from D.C. That Wisconsin blizzard was heading north, not south toward O'hare."

Guy loosened his tie with his left hand while balancing a silver tray with his right.

"Missing your days at Berghoff's?"

"It gave me exercise and paid my tuition. But the competition between waiters is twice as intense as among the law students."

"Good practice for the courtroom."

"Yes, otherwise you wouldn't get classic European service along with legal assistance."

"I'd get the service, you just may not be giving it to me. We've got to get these grant applications out for review. We're nearly a week behind task already." Guy loved the operatic intonations of her voice, which became more resonant when she was under pressure.

Annabelle swished her designer scarf over her padded shoulder reaching towards the ringing phone, stopping short of picking it up. A large gold pin in the image of Nefertiti held up the scarf.

"I've got your speech ready, using the notes you faxed me from Reagan last night," Guy said. I hope no one from the women's lawyer's caucus was at the WMLA last week," said Guy. He recalled the opening line Annabelle used in her last speech for the Women's Modern Language Association: "I drove my way out of my mother's womb kicking and screaming mad about being born into a white man's world. And that was before I had fifty years to watch'em."

"The lady language teachers loved it. If any of them are also attorneys they'll love it more. There's no more ruthless group than male lawyers."

"I don't know, Annabelle, some of the cops were pretty ruthless too, but those waiters are hard to beat. Walk in front of someone with seniority and you'd get a tray in your back."

"Yeah, all right, for guys the pecking order is what it is all about no matter what field they are in."

He floated the tray onto the side table as if it were a flying carpet landing on a featherbed.

Annabelle raised her eyebrows. Maybe you should have stayed with basketball. That tray toss you just performed reminded me of a Harlem Globe Trotter making a back hand shot."

"I'd only have had a chance with the scouts if there were affirmative action for whites in basketball." He winked and grinned to avert a lecture from her on whites not having been brought over on slave ships.

"Just don't have a near miss with the next tray. Now what about the proposals?"

"I pre-reviewed the three hundred some and pulled out the top thirty," said Guy.

Pour me some coffee, Guy, do your job."

"Beans are probably picked by brown slaves in Madagascar. Doesn't that bother you?" Guy sensed Annabelle's gaze as he poured coffee into her yellow mug.

"We'll tackle that one next week. Guy, you're one good looking piece of white meat. Good thing I'm not inclined towards men or we could have an office affair on our hands." A wink of one of her enormous eyes was a change in traffic lights, from yellow to green. She flashed her huge ivories. The gold from the bottoms caught the light from the large window.

"Hold your teeth in your head, Babe, with a look like that and my legal talent, I could slap you with sexual harassment, Title X," said Guy. He squeezed her shoulder, noticing how soft it was beneath the large pads.

"You know how far you would get, a WEM (White European Male) charging an AAL (African American Lesbian) who happens to be the government's top diversity trainer! Bring me the just the top ten proposals. The Nixon folks, who don't support thinkers, cut our budget again. You can't recognize what you don't have. No sense in going through thirty." She took a slug of coffee, her professionally manicured orange nails clicking against the mug. Her lips left a matching half moon on the rim.

Guy walked back into the reception area to get the proposals. His heart quickened. He had placed the proposal from his former professor, Dr. Victoria Von Dietz, on the top of the pile. He could picture her penetrating eyes and crested lips and again felt a surge of excitement. He believed so much in Victoria and her intellect, drive and authenticity. If she got a grant this would bring them into contact again. But he could not be too obvious about it. He needed to prep Annabelle. He pulled the second proposal out and slapped it on top.

Guy placed the files face down on her desk. Annabelle reached for the top one. In blue marking pen was the name, "Professor Helmut Wagner." The next line read: "Intellectual Biography of Alfred Schutz."

"My eyes are burning, honey, give me the Reader's Digest version," said Annabelle. She handed him the proposal, the large orange and gold bracelets clanking down her ample wrist.

Guy cleared his throat: "Listen, this is a good one." He looked back at the document. "Professor Helmut Wagner was a tool and dye maker in Germany who worked with Schutz in the anti-Nazi underground. Schutz was an international banker who finessed the funding for the escapes. He was also a renowed economist and philosopher. Both escaped to the U.S. where Wagner earned a doctorate under Schutz at the New School."

"That's quite a story, but we are looking for original ideas."

"Hold on Babe. Wagner wants to show how Schutz' research could revolutionize Western thinking. His studies of consciousness, reconnected scientific research to real human experiences and . . . ."

"That's enough," said Annabelle, holding out her hand for the proposal. Guy snapped it into her palm.

"You handle paper as if it were a blackjack. Echoes of your days as a cop."

"Or my Sicilian genes," he chuckled.

She shifted her big body in her maroon leather desk chair, causing it to squeak. She slapped the proposal down on her desk. "Another example of WEMs helping WEMs. These philosophers had their chance, and went right along with the tide of world war and colonialism."

Guy adjusted his weight and swallowed. He could understand Annabelle trying to counteract sexism and racism, but he felt that men, and especially white men, did not get a fair shake with her. He straightened his back and took a breath.

"Annabelle, I don't mind writing the WEMS concept into your speeches, but when you look at the proposals coming in, you've got to distinguish one white man from another. I suppose I am a WEM to you because I have white skin and penis and live in the U.S. that I must remind you is an ocean away from Europe. I have no sense of identification with white. I like being a male but don't think I would be all that deprived were I born female, except for being too tall." Guy walked towards the large window, overlooking university boulevard. He caught a glimpse of the sun through the shimmering snow as it struck a stained glass window on the gothic library.

"I would say we have a diversity of viewpoints and an open emotional climate in this office, would you not?" said Annabelle.

Guy turned, "Let's get back to the proposal. The new philosophy Schutz was expounding, phenomenology, was just getting started. They challenged the entire European academic establishment. You have a few philosophers and their students challenging an entire scientific tradition, a whole political economy, what can you expect? But at least they raised significant questions. I think we should give this Wagner some funds."

"All right, lawyer, I'll send it out for review," said Annabelle. Noted on the cover sheet: "Send to Gloria Burnem." Burnem was Chair of the Women's

Studies Program at Goleta Woman's College and editor of the *Journal of Lesbian Research*. She clipped a note to the proposal that said "Current Evaluative Criteria" at the top. She pulled out her gold marking pen and highlighted several phrases on the criteria list: "member of underrepresented group," "relevance to diversity ", and "sensitivity to social justice."

Guy looked at the check list. "Annabelle, please, give Wagner a chance, send it to someone who at least occasionally will support a man's research," he said.

Annabelle looked up at him. "These white male assholes think they can continue to get center stage for their high sounding undecipherable texts," she said. "But in this case, I'll think about it." She slapped the proposal down on her desk. "Now let me get on with the stack," she said.

Back in his office Guy paced back and forth, then sat at his desk. She would be reading Victoria's proposal now. His breath quickened at the thought that he could be working in a supportive capacity.

Cars slithered and slid in the sleet and the bantering of students coming out of classes echoed up from the street below. The clock tower sang five. Guy stepped back into Annabelle's office.

"Annabelle, have you looked at the Von Dietz proposal yet?" he asked.

"Yes, Guy, I'm just looking at it." She held up Victoria's proposal and read the title: "A New Theory of Time based on American Philosopher George Herbert Mead and German Philosopher Martin Heidegger." As she read the abstract the corners of her mouth turned down and her nose crinkled up. Annabelle slapped the proposal down on her desk. A large wooden sculpting of a naked pregnant woman with a large red stone for a belly button fell over with a clunk.

Guy wanted to make a pitch for Victoria's proposal, but Annabelle should be in a better mood. "How about an afternoon pick me up?" he said.

"Good idea. It'll be hours before I get fed at that lawyer ladies' dinner. Bring me some fresh coffee and a snifter of brandy. All this reading about high ideas has me weary," she said.

A few minutes later Guy returned, olives rolling around the plate of small egg sandwiches, pickles, and her favorite sweet dates. Guy tried to cover his anxiety. He recalled with delight being Victoria's student at Athens College. All his cop buddies in the Law Officers Training Program had the hots for her. Her mind stimulated him more than her body. Even more he enjoyed the conversations at the student center over coffee, where he'd wait for her to come in between classes. He respected her adeptness at thwarting his advances. Despite this, she helped him get into Northwestern Law School.

Annabelle looked at the tray with two coffee mugs and one brandy snifter. She said, "If that snifter is for you, you'd better get another one."

She picked up the snifter, took a sip and licked her rosy brown lips, her orange lipstick nearly worn off.

"Mine's already in my coffee," he noticed a scowl on Annabelle's face and Victoria's proposal lying on the top of the pile. "What's got you so perturbed?"

"The whole thing perpetuates itself. The guys have their female slaves, spending their careers adoringly at their feet. This brilliant woman is wasting her career as a Valkyrie for Mead and Heidegger. You know, Sartre could not have become famous were it not for Simone De Bouvoir, his perpetual audience, admiration society, and source of ideas, validation."

Blood rushed to his head. His neck tightened. He took a slug of coffee, cleared his throat. "Dr. Von Dietz may be writing on two well known male philosophers, but she is an original thinker in her own right." Remembering that Annabelle valued action, not just ideas. he added. "She is also a social activist in the civil rights and peace movements."

Annabelle stuffed a large olive in her mouth. Was she listening? She held it in her cheek when she asked:

"How do you know? I didn't read much about her life in the file, other than she teaches at the Athens College and wrote a book on time in women's lives." Annabelle chewed and swallowed, then picked up an egg sandwich and looking up at him took a bite.

Guy cleared his throat and grabbed Victoria's proposal. "She was my undergrad professor, and inspired me to leave my glorious life as a cop for Mayor Daly's mobsters. She is no white man's lackey or, if she is, it is only to the dead, great ones. She had us read *The Autobiography of Malcolm X*, the speeches of Martin Luther King. If anyone should get one of these grants, she should. She helped a number of young black women scholars get started as well." Guy took another slug of brandied coffee.

"Her proposal isn't about peace and civil rights. It's about time, something about past and future existing simultaneously. Far out stuff," said Annabelle, twirling her brandy around in the snifter. She stuffed a large date into her mouth. "Um, real sweet," she said, smacking her lips.

"Hrashpul dates, your favorite," he said, hoping they would sweeten her on Victoria's proposal.

Guy felt his stomach swirl. "If anyone can make something real out of this theory, Victoria Von Dietz can." he said. He stood by the window looking out at the cloud-streaked winter sunset. Street lights began to twinkle below. "Besides, don't you think it is sexist to think that all women have to write about is women's issues? That they can't advance science and philosophy except to document their own sour grapes?" He took out his handkerchief and patted his wet forehead.

Annabelle opened her eyes wide, "I get the feeling there is more to this than just a former professor. Is she attractive?

"Victoria Von Dietz looks like Marlene Dietrich, has the brains of Hannah Arendt and the political acumen of Eleanor Roosevelt."

"Sounds like a gal who would meet my standards, although there is nothing black about that list. All right, I'll send her out for review," said Annabelle.

"You won't regret it," Guy said. As he put the cups back on the tray, he noticed Annabelle put Victoria's proposal on top of the "to be reviewed" pile. He smiled and put up his thumb, noting that Annabelle did not attach a list of criteria.

Chapter Four
Snowstorm

Durations are a continual sliding of presents into each other.
— George Herbert Mead, *The Philosophy of the Present*

N ot yet able to open her eyes, Victoria reached over and turned off her alarm. Yes, it was already 5 A.M., and they would have to get up to shovel their way out of the driveway. Armwood Academy, Kathy's school, was always open as about half the students were boarding. At midnight, Victoria had barely finished her class preparations, then stayed up until after one getting another grant proposal ready to mail with a postmark deadline of today. She still had not heard from NIHL. What a surprise that Guy Santori, a handsome former student, had called from the NIHL office where he now worked as legal assistant to the director. While he encouraged her to remain hopeful, he did say there were several hundred applicants and their funds were again cut back. The thought of being able to travel to Germany to meet with Martin Heidegger, whose theory of time was so important to her work thrilled her. But she could not afford to do so on her Athens College salary, not with Kathy's tuition and Tom working part time.

She was about to call Tom, who had actually gone to bed before she did, when his own alarm went off. She heard a curse, scuffling sounds, then his study door opened.

"Are you awake? Time to go shovel," he shouted.

A squeal came from Kathy's room, which was between their studios. "Oh boy we can go out and make snow angels. It's all white out there." Snuggles raced around in circles.

"Be sure and put your long underwear on under your leggings," Victoria shouted back. Leaving her p.j.s on, she went downstairs into the cold front hall and slipped her sky pants and down jacket over them.

When she opened the front door her breath caught in her throat as a bluster of snow blew in her face. The fading moonlight reflected on the sparkling blanket of snow, lighting up Luther's image in the stained glass window. He seemed to say, "good little Lutheran girl, up early working hard."

Kathy looked like one of the even dwarfs, all bundled up, her small shovel in hand. Shimmering silver snowflakes floated on her cheeks, like a shower of stars. Plunk! a snow ball landed right on Victoria's back. The front door opened as Tom limped out. "Plunk! Plunk! both Kathy and Victoria snowballed him in the face and chest. After a few minutes of gleeful snow play, they knuckled down to shoveling. Snuggles, their golden retriever, barked and stepped high sinking down almost to her belly. One of the neighbors opened their front door, and yelled at them to hush up and go back to bed. After an hour of shoveling the driveway and walkway were clear. Kathy laid down on the front lawn and waved her legs and arms together making a snow angel.

"Come Dad and Mom, make angels with Snuggles and me."

With three angels and lots of dog tracks in the snow they brushed each other off at the front door and went inside. They hung their coats to dry in front of the radiator in the back hallway. Kathy asked if she could lie on the couch instead of going back up to bed.

"O.K., just don't let Snuggles get up there with you. And try and get some rest. You have a long day and Brownies after school," said Victoria.

Tom took Victoria's hand and pulled her into his study to climb in his large bed. "I need you to help warm me up. That leg gets my thigh extra cold." Victoria knew he meant his artificial leg. It was always "that" leg. He unbuckled his corduroy pants, unstrapped his left leg. He slapped his cold stump on her thigh. She massaged it as they cuddled. She knew what he wanted. A stump rub. Yet in the morning quiet, with his arms around her, she felt almost peaceful. Maybe her anger was due to externals, their jobs, money issues. Maybe things could be good between them after all. Noticing the disarray of papers on his desk she felt the burn of resentment in her belly. "Tom, when will you finish your dissertation? You'd have a chance at that tenure track opening at Forestside."

"God damn it, Victoria, you are such a frigging nag! My work means something real, not just a way to get a frigging job!" He jumped up and strapped his leg back on. Turning away from her, he went to his closet, opened the door and put on his pant and shirt.

Her whole body shook with rage. "Oh, as if my dissertation is less meaningful because I finished it!" She sat up, her shoulders and neck like iron, her stomach filled with moths.

"Castrating bitch! You don't have to work for a bunch of fascist nuns and commute 100 miles a day over icy roads." He picked a tie out of the closet and standing in front of the mirror began to tie it.

She felt frozen, like she had become the bitch he accused her of being. What a dilemma. She could either continue to be used and abused as a good little wife, all the while going on providing the bulk of the support for the family, or she could complain about it, making her into a constant bitchy mother figure. Or worse, another one of the castrating nuns from his college. In a no-win situation, she decided, best just be who you are.

"If I had something to castrate, it would certainly be long gone by now, what with you, Dean Schenck, and Dad's illness. Luckily, I'm not a male overladen with a penis driven ego to defend." She felt good about this response.

He topped off his shirt and tie with his vest, lodging the watch in the pocket, then put on his jacket. Ignoring her statement he said, "I may have to stay on campus tonight. Sister Karl is expecting us to finish the student evaluative summaries by the end of the week. Shit, she really loves to exploit the "lay teachers" as she calls us. I wonder if this isn't a bit of wishful thinking on her part, hoping one of the male faculty will lay her. We have to use her obtruse system, the ABC, Abilities Based Curriculum that she is using to gain fame and fortune for herself and St. Mary's."

Victoria's stomach churned and her heart sank. "I was hoping you could be here for Kathy when I go to see Dad in the hospital," she said. "Why can't you bring some of Sister Karl's grids home to work on? If you hate it so much there why do you stay there so late?" Really she wanted to ask him who he really was sleeping with. She could imagine the swooning coeds ogling him in class and waiting for him at his office hours.

Tom let out a growl. "Well, she can stay at the school until you or I get home. Or with her friend Karen, can't she? Phh, we now have to fill out certificates of guarantee to potential employers of our graduates that the are ABC, Able, Better, Competent and that if they don't do well on the job they will be replaced by another. Like they were washing machines." Tom emitted a loud sardonic laugh.

Realizing his intractability, Victoria chose to ignore her inward seething. Victoria mused that having a ball-crushing administrator at St. Mary's may exacerbate his feelings of inadequacy and contribute to their marital problems. She was proud of her ability in stressful times to be reasonable, try to mend things, hard as it was. "Tom, I think you project your resentment toward Sister Karl onto me. I'm not Sister Karl, and I'm not your mother. I'm concerned about our future including our finances."

"No time to deal with this now. I'm late." Tom flung his silk scarf around his neck and limped out the door and into his VW station wagon that her parents had purchased for him when his ancient car broke down. "That way the whole family and even Snuggles can get in," her Dad had said. But come to think of it they had never gone anywhere together as a family.

"See you tomorrow, I guess," said Victoria as Tom closed the door.

Chapter Five
Manifest Destiny

The Western man believed in the manifest destiny of his country. . .
The Indians had by this time been reduced to submission.
Henry Jackson Turner, *The Frontier in American History*

A fter a wearying morning of meetings and student conferences, Victoria lectured in her class, "racial and cultural minorities." Most of the students in the class were cops attending Athens College through Law Officers Training Program (LOTP) grants. They were a decade or more older than Victoria. Several of them had approached her for coffee or a date and persisted despite her wedding ring and her emphasizing that she did not date students.

Her neck and shoulders tightened dread of her meeting with Dean Schenck. Several of the cops leared at her as she put her notes in her briefcase. Bart Tutston, a tall burley guy, stood by the door, partially blocking her passage. "Not him again," she thought.

"Hey Victoria."

"Dr. Von Dietz, please. I'm in a hurry."

Bart placed his thick hand on her elbow. "You should come downtown with me some night. Then you'd see what really goes on with them so called 'minorities'."

She pulled her arm from his grip and shoved past him.

"I'm sorry, Bart. I have an appointment. If you need to discuss the material, my office hours are posted."

"Got to see the Dean, do you?"

Ignoring this comment but furious that he knew, she went to the ladies room to freshen up. Lewd laughter echoed down the hallway.

Schenck held a corner office with floor-to-ceiling windows overlooking Lake Michigan. Ice chunks shattered against the shore as the waves crashed on the craggy rocks. It sounded to Victoria like a giant calliope from a horror movie. The wind howled against the windows.

His navy blue suit hung loose over his slender shoulders, buldging at his belt. A red-stripped tie accented his protruding adams' apple. A plaque on his wall testified to his retirement as an army captain twenty years ago. An American flag hung from a pole on top of his bookcase.

He flicked his index finger at a stiff aluminum chair in front of his large desk.

"How is the snow shoveling for you? I don't suppose Tom can help much with it. Must be hard with a handicapped man like that," said Schenck. As he sat down at his desk, absently he scratched a thigh, brushed off his trousers.

"Thank you for your concern." Victoria tried to keep the outrage out of her voice. "Tom actually has more agility and strength than most so called able- bodied men. We all got up to shovel at 5 A.M." She sat primly forward to avoid slumping in the stiff backed chair.

Bitterly she remembered her car sliding on the icy streets as she took Kathy to school. "I'm glad Kathy goes to Armwood Academy, which stays open due to the boarding school."

Schenck raised his eyebrows and looked directly at her. "One of the problems of women's lib. Children become inconveniences," he said.

Victoria bit the inside of her cheek to hold back her tongue. It would not do to call him a male chauvinist pig. She swallowed and said calmly,

"Enlightened family and child care policies would benefit children much more, I think, than keeping women out of the work force. Not too many families can afford to live on one pay check anymore."

"If I can get here at 8 A.M. living thirty miles out in the country, so can my faculty." Victoria remembered a previous conversation in which Schenck described his huge tracter snowplow which he used to clear the driveway of his country estate. "Besides," he added, "we have to keep the kids on campus occupied. Idle hands, devil's workshop." Victoria couldn't imagine what the devil would have them do in a Lutheran college with sex segregated dorms, matronly dorm mothers and student counselors on each floor.

Trying to lighten the conversation, she said, "the devil must not be very busy if he looks here to increase the amount of sin."

Schenck mobilized his tight lips into a half smile. He sat back in his chair and brushed at the front of his jacket, then folded his hands over his stomach. He looked at Victoria, nose wrinkled nearly to his forehead: "I've been getting complaints from students about your racial and cultural minorities class."

The tension in Victoria's back and neck spread to her hands. She uncurled her fingers to avoid making fists. "I can imagine. The police students who got Cs on their exams don't like the reading assignments because they are obliged for the first time in their lives to try to take the perspective of most of their clients." She felt a rush of heat in her belly and lungs.

Schenck's face was red. He sat up straight in his desk. "They didn't say that, Victoria." He slapped his hand on a file on his desk. The tab on the side read "Von Dietz".

"The prick," Victoria thought. He's going to use this against me when he should support my efforts to educate these guys who come in with thick skulls and threatened cocks.

He leaned toward her. "They said you're prejudiced against Caucasians, that you support criminal characters like Malcolm X."

A wave crashed against the ice outside and splashed up on his window.

"I ask them to read Malcolm X's Autobiography," Victoria said. "You must have read it."

Schenck shook his head "no" twice. His cheeks sunk around his chin. Victoria continued: "It is an evocative document which covers his horrendous childhood, the reasons for his religious conversion and the factual basis for anti-white sentiment in the African-American community."

"He encourages violence against whites," said Schenck.

"Actually, in his essay, 'The Ballot or the Bullet,' he advocates voting as preferable to violence." She felt good about pushing back.

"Hmm, and if they don't get what they want start shooting, sounds like," said Schenck.

Victoria opened her mouth to respond, "television newshots distort"

He interrupted. "What else do you have them read?"

"*Occupied America: A History of the Southwest from the Mexican Perspective,*" replied Victoria.

Schenck licked his lips, cleared his throat. His left leg trembled as he stood. He walked to the window. With his back to her he shouted: "Faculty Members of Athens college have an obligation to teach the TRUTH about American culture, to edify and enlighten our students, not to indoctrinate them."

Schenck walked to his bookshelf, took a white and grey bound hardback book off the shelves, and threw it down in front of her on his desk. The smash startled Victoria. Her back stiffened. She picked up the book and read the cover: "*Manifest Destiny: The March of Civilization Across North America* by J. Jackson Turner."

She was proud of her ability to think fast, make a comeback under stress. The years of fighting it out in the bull ring of male dominated graduate seminars served her well. "It seems to me this is just the kind of viewpoint they already have internalized through their high school American history courses," she said. "That kind of thinking has justified violence against those of other cultures and races for centuries in the name of white European superiority."

"There are always forces for good and evil in the world," Schenck said, "for the advance of civilization and for its decline. Higher education has the obligation to promote the forces for its advance. Turner explains how America got to be the great country it is. He would balance the pernicious material you have assigned."

Oh hell, she thought, no way he will ever see another side. Better shift gears. "Dr. Schenck, back to the complaints. Please show me the letters."

"I can't do that. These letters were given to me in confidence. I must protect the anonymity of the students."

Redfaced, Victoria stood up. Her palms were moist and her face hot. "So, anonymous letters in my file can be used against me? Letters that I cannot answer because I cannot read them or know who wrote them!" She pictured again having to apply for an academic position with only one available for every 300 applicants, having to uproot Kathy again, having to move with her father ill with cancer.

"Dr. Von Dietz, I just gave you the chance to defend yourself. You know I respect your scholarly accomplishments. I want to help you straighten yourself out here at the college." He straightened his tie. His tone softened. "My daughter liked your classes very much."

I may still have a chance to save my job, Victoria thought. She recalled his shy and plump daughter, who visited her in her office, weeping about the rigid discipline at home. She had complained about a guess-the-new-word game they had to play each night at dinner. Shenck would pick an obscure word out of Oxford's Unabridged. If she, her mother or her sister knew the meaning they could get to pick a word. If they did not, they were obliged to clear table, do the dishes.

"My daughter gets my wife to read some provocative stuff she read for your class, like Betsy Friedem's 'The Female Mistake', no pun intended" he chortled.

Victoria put on a smile at his attempt at humor. "I understand you play a vocabulary game at home," she said.

"We're not a sexist household. Anytime I loose, I do the dishes. Haven't had to do them but once in twenty years," Schenk snickered.

"What was the word you missed?" asked Victoria.

"Clart. To spread with thick, sticky dirt. Clart, that was what they shot at me, my wife and daughters," he shouted. He brushed his jacket and pants though nothing could have dirtied them.

"Dr. Von Dietz, I have another appointment. You'd better let me see things turn around for the better in your class," he added.

The S.O.B. is really out to get me, she thought. She knew she could effect him if she apologized, in a poor little woman kind of way, but her sense of outrage got in her way. She stood up straight. "Dr. Schenck, I don't honestly think in this case it is me that needs straightening."

"That will be all for now" he said and turned his chair around to look out at the chunks of ice crashing against the shoreline.

Chapter Six
Cateclysm

Snow became sleet as Victoria drove home. As she needed to leave early the next morning for the hospital, Kathy would be staying overnight with a friend who lived near the school.

The woodwork in the living room and the antique furniture seemed morbidly dark. The ticking of the black mantel clock bounced off the high ceiling. Snuggles barked in anticipation of company and dinner. She opened the door, enjoying Snuggle's licks and the feel of her soft coat. Victoria picked up her dog food bowl, carried it to the pantry and filled it.

With no appetite for dinner or energy to cook for herself, she went upstairs and read student essays as a way to keep her mind off Dean Schenck. Unable to concentrate, she got up from her desk and looked out the window. The lights from the street below lit up the image of Martin Luther. He seemed to pop out of the window as the blues and reds from the stained glass shimmered through the prisms of falling snow.

The organist practiced a crashing version of "Onward Christian Soldiers." He seemed to be integrating John Coltrane's dissonant jazz style into his hymn improvisations. Her stomach felt tight, angry. She recognized the music now as a piece that was by the French composer Messian, while he was in a Nazi concentration camp.

She felt the dull ache in her back that usually came before her period. "Oh, that too! I should be thankful. At least I'm not pregnant." Her mind raced back to the abortion she had the previous year. Tom insisted it was not a good time for them to have a baby. She had reluctantly agreed, partly because of her angst about their relationship and also because she was afraid the baby might be born with Tom's "club foot". The Dr. had said, "You made a wise decision, Mrs. Blanchard. The fetus was severely malformed." She had felt distanced and patronized by his use of "Mrs." and Tom's last name, instead of as Dr. or Ms. Von Dietz.

Looking down the hallway toward Tom's empty study she realized that there was some comfort in his being there, even when they were each busy working. Tonight Tom would not be home. He had not phoned to see what the Dean had to say. She thought of calling the college, but there was no extension in his office. One of the sisters would answer and very sweetly make her feel like it was an enormous bother to try to find him, taking her time away from holier and more important tasks.

Should she have listened to the warnings about Tom? Her father was concerned about him before the marriage, saying that pain could make handicapped people mean. He revealed that he had been abused by his father who lost his arm in a factory accident. Victoria had written this off as overprotection. But now?

The heavy door to Tom's room was shut. She walked down the hallway, seeking the security and comfort she had once found with him. The door stuck. She pushed again and it popped open. In the dark room with the rising moonlight coming in his window, the aroma of his spicey new pipe tobacco hit her. She held her belly. Snuggles rubbed her head on Victoria's arm. "Truly my dearest friend," she thought.

Victoria's framed picture stood on top of his desk. "I'd like to have you with me in my office," he had said. She thought he meant his office at the college. Guess he doesn't want the coeds reminded that he's married. She was still in her twenties when that picture was taken. Glacing in the mirror on the closet door she looked old, stress lines around her eyes and her mouth.

She sat on his large bed, perpetually unmade. It smelled slightly musky. She leaned against the ornately carved back. "When have I last slept here? What is he always working on late these nights? As a rule, since he insisted on privacy, she did not look at what he was writing. But tonight she picked up the yellow pad on his desk and read some familiar sounding phrases about Bertrand Russell's theory of power, the topic of his dissertation. Two pieces of paper dropped to the rug. They had been torn out and stuffed in front of the cardboard backing. She picked them up, planning to leave without reading them. Putting the pages back into the tablet she noticed the words:

" . . . then I penetrated her for the first time."

She flipped to the first page, her hands quivering, her breath hard and shallow. Her eyes raced to the top of the page where the date, November 16, 1979 was next to the word "journal". She read:

"Christina sat in the front row, her beautiful blue eyes looking up at me with adoration. Everything I said was fascinating to her. She is petite and slender, like a frail little bird. She came to my office after every class. She frequently looked down at her knees, ostensibly to cover them with her short skirt, but never succeeding.

That day she came in and she sat on my lap and I kissed her, as I had before. And then we got excited and before I knew it she had removed her panties and I penetrated her for the first time."

The room swirled. She reached for her picture on his desk and threw it to the floor. She pounded on his bed, "I hate you, I hate you, you S.O.B." Her fists ached. Tears streamed down her cheeks. Snuggles ran under the bed. "He always used to say we would be like Bertrand Russell and Lady Edith, in love into old age. What a crashing phoney."

Her hands shook, rattling the pages she held. All that talk of ethics, undying loyalty and fidelity. He even taught ethics. She ran to the bathroom, bent over the toilet bowl and heaved. When the spasms stopped she splashed cold water on her face, washed her hands. She stormed back into the study. "I may have misread them, maybe it was just a story he was writing." She picked up the papers and read them again.

It was clearly a journal. She opened his desk drawer looking for more. She pulled the drawer all the way out and threw it to the floor. A package of the new tobacco fell out. She opened it to find it was from a store in North Chicago. On the label was written in flowering handwriting, "To Tom, Love, Christina."

Tears pouring down her cheeks, she threw the package on top of his desk its contents spilling over the journal pages. She ran down the stairs, Snuggles following closely behind.

She poured herself a large shot of brandy. She took a slug, petted Snuggles. "What am I to do?"

She called her friend and colleague, Shelley, in the history department.

"What's the matter, what happened? Is it your father?" Shelley asked.

"Oh, Shelley, I'm very worried about Dad, I'm going to the hospital tomorrow morning. But that isn't why I called. . . Tom is having an affair with one of his little students!" she realized she was shouting. "I'm sorry, Shelley, I don't know what I'm going to do." Victoria cried.

Shelley said she would have come right over if it weren't for the icy streets. "Are you sure, Victoria?"

Victoria recounted the way he had been staying away more, and then the journal entry.

"Most marriages have something like this. They can survive it if you want."

"You don't understand. Now I can never trust him again," said Victoria crying.

Victoria hung up the phone. She picked up George Herbert Mead's picture from her desk. She crawled under the covers on her daybed, held Mead to her heart and cried herself to sleep. Snuggles lay down next to the bed, her head up on Victoria's side.

Chapter Seven
George at Lutheran Hospital

Being towards death is grounded in care.
Martin Heidegger, *Being and Time*

"Will he be all right?" she whispered to the Deaconess/nurse who stood at her father's bedside adjusting the sheets. His closed eyelids were puffy, his face bluish grey. The florescent lighting cast a shadow of the IV unit on the wall behind the white iron bed. Victoria wondered what was in it that made the odor of body lotion in hospitals so unique. Not that she would ever want to have some at home.

The flowered curtains framing the large window blended with the lemon yellow walls. They looked hand sewn by the Lutheran Deaconesses living in the convent attached to the hospital. Victoria had considered this cloistered life of service, rejecting it in favor of marriage, career. Now it seemed appealing, secure.

The Deaconess/nurse ran her veined hand down her starched grey skirt. "Your father is doing well for someone just out of serious surgery," she said. Dad opened his eyelids, cleared his throat. Her large white hat tilted.

"That boat you have on your head isn't going to fall off on me, is it?" said George. Whiskers shadowed his still handsome face. A printed cotton hospital gown revealed pale arms.

"You should talk about fashion, Mr. Von Dietz. Your gown is really very, well just very." The nurse's erect posture and sense of calm was reassuring. The creases around her eyes told of much experience of suffering. "Not too many could joke after abdominal surgery. Your father is an amazing gentleman," she said.

Sounds of a gurgling respirator and gasping came from behind the curtain around the second bed.

"I'll let you visit, Dr. Von Dietz, but only for a short time," said the Deaconess. "He really needs his rest. Your mother just went home, having been here overnight."

"Call me Victoria, please, Sister." The Deaconess nodded and swished out the door.

"I told your ma to call and tell you not to drive here in the snow."

"Dad, you know I don't always take advice, not even yours," Victoria walked closer, touched his hand.

"I brought you some broth," she said, winking. She pulled a silver flask from her purse, put an accordion straw in and held it to his lips. He took a deep draw, smiling crookedly, much as he used to smile while smoking his favorite briar.

"Such nourishing broth," he swallowed, then grinned. "Ah my favorite claret." His shaking hand lifted his hospital shift revealing a mound of bandages. He explained his surgery in detail. "They had to cut in both directions, take out the tumor, sew my intestines back together."

Victoria's body was stiff with fear and pain at what was evident. The odds were slim, the Drs. had said. Should she have discouraged him from having the surgery? Just last Sunday Ma had taken him out for a ride. That seemed hopeful. Or was it just a last chance to go out in the sunshine, see home?

She was five years old, standing behind his desk in his basement workshop, trying to follow his explanations about how to fix watches, clocks, make metal fittings on a lathe, build cabinets. She would be prefer to be reading, even practicing the piano. "Bambi and Lamby are waiting for their dinner, Daddy," she'd say, referring to her stuffed animal friends.

"I wish as a child I'd paid more attention to your explanations of how to fix things, make things. I'd feel much more competent now." Talking about his projects and his workshop might cheer him.

"Kathy makes up for it," said Dad. "She can already fix just about any household item."

Kathy did not have to earn George's appreciation. Victoria always felt she had to do more, better, striving to become perfect, knowing she would fail. When George first saw his granddaughter, Kathy, it was unconditional love at first sight. Was it an accident that Mead and her father both were named "George", unattainable ideal men?

A doctor was paged to the emergency room. Two nurses stopped in the hall in front of the room, gossiped, laughed, moved on.

"You O.K.? You seem spacey," he asked.

She hesitated for a minute, looking down at the wedding band on her left hand, fingering it with her right hand. She didn't know whether to tell him what had happened in his condition. But she was no good at hiding her feelings.

"Can't keep anything from you, Dad, but really this is not the time for you to be concerned about me."

"Come on, Victoria, you know I'll just worry if you don't tell me."

She cleared her throat. "My marriage is in trouble."

He gasped; something stuck in his throat. Victoria held his water up to his lips. He shook his head "no". He pointed to her purse. "Have some yourself, Victoria, have one with me," he said. She walked over to the bathroom and pulled a paper cup out of the dispenser. She poured herself some claret, then gave him the flask. She held up her cup and he the flask and each drank. Victoria enjoyed the warmth as she swallowed.

"Now tell me," he said looking her in the eyes.

"Tom is having an affair with one of his students."

George's face puffed up. His eyebrows raised. "He's a conceited SOB and you'd be better off without him, his phony English accent, and three piece suits. Never trusted the man."

There was a long silence. Victoria felt tears swelling. She had not expected this reaction.

"Come here, Baby," he said. She walked up to him. He held her hand and squeezed. "You know, it's nothing on you. It's just the way men are." The light in his blue/green eyes shifted. "Divorce is a big thing," he said.

"I've tried so hard for so long, Dad. I just don't think I can any more," she put her hand on his. He feebly squeezed. Out the window snow fell against the grey sky.

"I'll have some of that water after all," he said. She held the water to his parched lips, bending the straw towards him.

"Dad, I wondered if you ever had an affair. I know you and Mom never were really happy. I could understand it if you did."

"I told you long ago, men always have sex in the back of their minds," said George.

"So do women. Or at least some of them. If they can break free of the influence of Martin Luther!"

"Or the Madonna," he said smiling. "Me have an affair, no never. But it wasn't easy. You know how Ma and I quarrel, but I have always been faithful." He coughed and sipped again.

He reached down to hold his belly. "Sweetie, will you bring me the tapes you made of the Mozart sonatas you play?"

"Sure, and one of Kathy playing her little violin as well."

He applied it with a shaky hand, then pushed his lips together.

"Phewey, don't like this stuff. I don't know how gals can stand wearing lipstick."

"It's not a matter of strength anymore. But the claret helped." He frowned and his hands trembled. "You can do better than Tom. Remember, no one will ever love you as much as your Dad," he said. His speech blurred, became faster, more singsong. Victoria rang the bell, feeling her insides shatter like an image in a broken mirror.

The nurse/deaconess brissled in. She put a strong arm behind his head and put a pill in his mouth. Then a sip of water. He went limp and fell asleep.

"Will he be all right?"

"He's a fighter, my dear." She reached her creased and veined hand to squeezeVictoria's arm, looking her in the eyes. "Victoria, sometimes we must let go . . ." she said.

Chapter Eight
Despair and Resolve

Tom called, saying he'd be late and not to wait dinner. Victoria held her breath. Her shoulders and neck, already tight, burst into flames. "More time with his little girlfriend," she thought. But she did not want to warn him that she knew. She must determine her next steps, be ready to act decisively. Besides, she it would be wasted energy to confront him on the phone. When he finally got around to asking how her day went she sensed his insincerity. "If I thought you gave a shit I'd tell you that my father is dying and my job is on the line," Victoria slammed down the phone. Lost her cool. Well, considering everything, I'm not doing too badly, she said to herself.

Actually, she was glad he wasn't coming right home. She had resolved that she had had enough of Tom, enough of this marriage. The conversation with Dad at the hospital confirmed that she needed to end the struggle.

After dinner Kathy was busy practicing her violin and her homework. Victoria had homework as well. Sitting at her desk, she again felt the gaze of Martin Luther from the stained glass window across the street. His famous words came to mind: "Here I stand, I can not do otherwise." These words came as he defied the Catholic church and nailed his 95 thesis to the door of Wittenberg chapel. She had some theses to write.

She pulled a yellow tablet out of her drawer, took up a sharpened pencil and divided the page into two columns. On the top she wrote "Marriage to Tom". She drew a line down the center of the page. The left column she called Pros, the right Cons.

I must really try to think of all the pros I can. I must be fair, she said to herself. Still, the pros list was short.

1. *He says "I love you" (yes but only in passing about twice a week, not like he means it).*

2. *He helps Kathy with her homework (she doesn't ask him much anymore)*

3. *He helped shovel snow the other morning (yes but he had to get to work).*

4. *He pays of the utility bills. (but I pay all of the mortgage).*

5. *His intellectual prowess can be entertaining (if only he could limit his outbursts to fifteen minutes).*

She thought about whether or not she could live without these things and said to herself. (Yes, I sure can.) Then she began on the con side of the page. She wrote:

1. *Leaves beer cans behind the sofa.*

2. *Drinks about a six pack every night plus wine and cognac*

3. *He is physically and emotionally cold.*

4. *He provides little financial support to me and Kathy.*

5. *He embarrassed me at the President's Christmas event by not showing up when he was supposed to perform a reading of Dickens.*

6. *No sex life.*

7. *Expects to be waited on.*

8. *Leaves messes everywhere in the house.*

9. *Is a liar and a cheat.*

10. *Is having an affair with a student.*

Looking at the list, she noticed all the positives had qualifications. She felt like an idiot having stayed with him for the past five years. She was ready for his arrival.

Kathy finished her homework. Victoria read her a story. When it was time for her to go to bed Victoria said, "Kathy, I'm going to have a serious conversation with your step-father when he gets home. Please don't be alarmed if you hear our voices raised."

Kathy washed down her cookie with a glass of milk. She licked the white moustache from around her mouth. "Mom, are you getting a divorce . . .?"

"Kathy, you are always a step ahead of me," she swallowed and poured herself a glass of wine. Kathy eyes looked like they would melt. Victoria opened her arms and hugged her. "I'm going to ask Tom to leave. Kathy, you and Tom can continue to have a relationship even if he is not living here anymore."

"Oh, like my friend Susie and her father." Kathy said, looking up.

"Yeah, like that, going places and things," said Victoria.

"Well if he wants," said Kathy. She looked up at Victoria. 'Mom, I'll tell you a secret."

Kathy's blue eyes were clear. She pushed her lips together, cleared her throat. "I like it better when Dad's not home. Things are calmer."

"I love you, Kathy."

Kathy was tucked in bed and asleep by the time Tom finally arrived. His car backed into the driveway, like a sliding scale in the tenor range, slipping on the packed snow, his tires whirling around several times on the ice. Victoria reread her list. She was waiting for him in the parlor, the half empty wine bottle and a pile of student papers on the coffee table in front of her.

The back door thumped shut. "Hello, Darling," he called.

Snuggles trotted to greet him. "Snuggles, show me some loyalty," she thought. But then Snuggles lives the here and now, ever forgiving of slights and neglects. Tom flustered through the kitchen, the dining area then to the parlor. His black cashmere overcoat hung open. He scrunched his face, as if to reset it from pleasure seeker to hard worker. He startled. "Surprised you're not in your office." Pecking at her cheek in passing, he took his coat to the front hall closet. His tie was loose and his vest open. Several papers twirled to the carpet.

Reminded of her attraction to him, Victoria felt her resolve slip away. The scent of his perfumy new tobacco jolted her back to sanity.

"You're still enjoying the gift from Christina."

"What are you talking about? What's gotten into you!" his eyes shifted contradicting his denial.

"The game's over. I know what's been going on." Her voice shook. Was she really doing this? Snuggles put his paw on her knee, tongue hanging out. "Sit Snuggles, I'm not mad at you," she said petting him on the neck. Snuggles sat at her feet, looked at Tom and woofed.

Tom raised his eyebrows and chin. "It must be that time of the month. This is another one of your distorted fits of jealousy." His chin tilted upward. He sat up straight in the antique chair with the carved lions on each arm in their living room. "Victoria, is there any more of that cognac, I've had a hell of a day."

"Get your own. I'm tired. Then sit down. We need to talk."

Tom limped to the liquor cabinet and groaned. Rubbing his thigh above the prothesis, he poured a snifter half full. "It'll have to be brief. I have a lot of work ahead of me tonight." He swirled the cognac around and took a deep slug.

"Damn it, Tom. I want you to move out. Tonight."

"Let's talk about this when you are feeling better, Victoria." He opened his vest, loosened his tie. "I know you are under stress. How's George, by the way?"

God, what an asshole, she thought and a low blow. How to honor her father but not give way to Tom's blatant manipulation of her feelings. She wanted so badly to be loved and comforted by Tom now that her father was dying. But she would not let her need destroy her better judgment as it did when she married him.

"Dad is fighting. The odds are against him. Don't change the subject. I found your journal, and your tobacco gift from 'Christina'. You can't lie to me any more."

Looking stunned, he recomposed himself. "It was only once and didn't mean anything. I love you".

"You don't understand, Tom. Now I can never trust you again." She stood up, her body on fire. Despite her intention to be reasonable, her outrage at the betrayal overcame her.

"Get out, Get out, Get the hell out of here and out of my life" she screamed and walked towards him. He stood as if to move out of her way. She held her fists up and shook them at him as if to hit him in the chest. He grabbed her wrists: "I love you Victoria. I don't love her."

"Get your hands off." The thought of Tom with another woman filled her with disgust. "I don't give a shit about love that means so little. Get the hell out of my life!" She twisted her wrist out of his hand.

She heard footsteps. "Mom, Is everything all right?" Kathy called down from the top of the stairs. Snuggles ran past them, up the stairs to join Kathy.

"Your mother and I are having a discussion," said Tom.

Victoria swallowed, speaking softly toward the stairs, "Go back to bed, Honey. Everything will be all right. Please close your door and go to sleep. Take Snuggles in with you."

Her voice an intense whisper, Victoria glared, "Your beard looks blue to me. Get out of here." Still standing, she turned her back to him.

"I told you not to question me," Tom snapped at Victoria in a whisper.

She mentally reviewed her list. Clearing her throat she stepped back and sat down. "Tom, its not just your affair. It's everything. Its been brewing for months, years. It's your drinking, our non-existent sex life, your lack of commitment to creating a viable career and financial future for us. Tom it's over." She looked him straight in the eye. "I want you out, tonight."

He walked to the other side of the room and reached into his pocket for his pipe. "But where will I go?"

"Being the mother figure bitch that you've always accused me of being, I've done one last thing for you. I've found you a place to stay for a while. Oscar Valentine is expecting you and will let you use his spare room until you can make other arrangements."

Victoria pictured Oscar, an aging bachelor in the biology department who was a notorius masher. He repeatedly took her aside at parties, and whispered in her ear, "Tom is not man enough for you."

"You never got it, Victoria, that I liked your motherliness." He blew perfumy smoke her way. "Hmmm, Oscar, good guy."

Victoria was tempted to say, "Two womanizers usually get along well, unless they are in competition." She instead said, "I packed a few things for you. Your bag is in your study. Please be out in a few minutes." She felt proud of herself for using her caring ability to do something for herself.

She turned and walked to the stairs. At the foot of the staircase she looked towards him.

"Good bye, Tom." She climbed to her study and closed the door. A while later she heard Tom come upstairs, packing things from his study. She heard his study door close, his footsteps stopped at Kathy's door. She didn't want him to disturb her. He didn't. His footsteps stopped at her door. She held her breath, feeling as if he was going to knock. He didn't. His footstep echoed down and out and his car slithered back over the icy driveway.

She slugged down another glass of wine to numb her thoughts so she could sleep. Nevertheless, she slept sporadically through the night. She felt like her world emptied. She opened her eyes and picked up the book on the side table. It was George Herbert Mead's *Philosophy of the Present* with his picture on the cover. Her trembling hand caressed the page. Warmth seemed to radiate from the book. She wrote in her journal:

"George Mead is my true love. He wants me. He needed (needs) a woman like me to worship and adore him—to be faithful. He needs a woman to think of everything in the world like he does. Is this the fate of women and men for all time, the desire for mastery and the desire for devotion and admiration, flowing back and forth? What would I do without Mead?"

Chapter Nine
Dreams and Nightmares

D espite her camel-hair jacket and turtle neck sweater, Victoria shivered as she walked down the marbled hallway to her dream-analysis class. With floor to ceiling windows it became the deck of a ship in a stormy sea, icy Lake Michigan waves crashing against the bow. Deep, clipped voices of the LOPT (police) students overpowered the banter of coeds and fraternity boys. Her back stiffened anticipating continued resistance from the student/cops to the hefty reading assignments of Freud and Jung. Not used to introspection, they grumbled about analyzing their own dreams. Being introspective herself, she wondered about taking an easier route, asking them to work with dreams in the literature. No, I want them to get the most out of the course. I know this is the best way, even if not the easy way. Martin Luther again.

Today they focused on Freud's *Tenth Lecture on Psychoanalysis*, on wish-fulfillment in dreams. Victoria explained that Freud's theory of dream symbolism was to be taken hypothetically and always in context. Jerry Barr, raising his bulky arm, volunteered to share his dream from the night before:

"Dispatch sent me to a DV (domestic violence) A raucous couple having a fight, a gun fired. A large woman was yelling and pointing a gun at a man. The guy was holding his shoulder, having taken a shot. It was bleeding down his arm and on his hand. Next thing I remember the guy and I were riding in the ambulance. We stopped at the Tasty Freeze on the way to the hospital and got two cones that we ate on the ride."

Bob Durand, a young, self-assured psychology major, waved his hand, barely waiting for Victoria's nod of acknowledgment. "Obviously homo-erotic with the ice cream cones as phallic symbols." He was a scholarship student who loved to demonstrate his intellectual prowess.

Jill Gorlick, a blond wearing a sorority pin on her pink sweater chimed in "Yea, and the big gal with the gun would certainly cause castration anxiety."

Snorts and titters rippled through the room. Victoria lifted her hands. She disliked the snobbery of some of the young students. Like Jill, most were from privileged backgrounds or their parents could not have afforded the tuition. Gorlick exuded the over-ripe confidence that came with popularity and wealth.

"You're calling me a queer," said Jerry his baritone voice raised, turning toward Bob. "Ask the babes on Rush Street."

"Whoa, nothing personal," said Bob, his palm raised.

Victoria pictured the hookers, pimps and red lights in the Rush Street area. She looked at her hands to clear her thoughts. Her naked ring finger felt like a slap in the face. What could she say to defuse Jerry's anger? She must forestall another complaint to Dean Schenck.

She cleared her throat. "Class, lets look at this a little deeper. According to Freud, all of us are born what he calls 'polymorphously perverse'. By age three or four our inherent attraction to the opposite or to the same sex emerges. Having such a dream does not necessarily indicate homoeroticism." Jerry's frown deepened.

She tried another angle. "From a another perspective, called 'Gestalt', all elements of the dream are part of the dreamer. That way Jerry is not only the cop but the gun shot, and the angry woman, looking for a more rewarding experience than calling on domestic dispute scenes—such as visiting an ice cream parlor."

Jerry sat back in his seat, "Yeah that's more like it." His face faded from crimson to pink. Victoria began to relax as the discussion continued, students reading dreams, applying both Freudian and Gestalt interpretations to them, and enjoying it.

"Its all about understanding ourselves," Victoria concluded. Her feeling of satisfaction came to a halt when she left the classroom. Jerry Barr stood just outside the door. He grabbed Victoria by her arm. The power of his six-foot stature and broad shoulders was contradicted by his pink baby face. She pulled away.

"Hey, Victoria. How about going out for a drink, or even a cup of coffee?" he said. "I want to discuss dreams some more, only in a more private place."

"God what an asshole," she wanted to say, feeling violated as he looked her up and down. But she must allay another complaint to Schenck.

"I'm sorry, Jerry, but I have an engagement. Besides, I told you I don't date students."

"I didn't ask to marry you, just go out for a drink. I want to convince you that Freud stuff about dreams is all wet."

She suppressed a chuckle at his unintended pun.

"Don't worry about the Rush street business. I'm clean as a whistle. Only go down there when the captain makes me back up the vice squad." His parka smelled like a stale pool hall.

She looked straight at him. "Jerry, I do have to go. I have another class to teach. However, if you come to my office hours we can discuss the material further should you wish to do so." Victoria regretted the condescending tone in her voice, but it was too late.

As she approached her office late that afternoon, Victoria noticed a note taped to the door. Her underarms moistened. Was it another note to see Schenck? Or worse, a call from the hospital? Saliva burned down her throat as she unfolded the note. Dr. Annabelle Carter Jackson from the National Institute of Human Learning would like her to call. Her mood of anxiety from the encounter with Jerry Barr dissolved. Was her grant going to be funded? She could travel to Germany and meet Heidegger. He was old, over eighty already. The prospect of meeting him was thrilling.

She recalled the warm rich sound of the German her mother and grandmother spoke at home when she was a child. At first it was a secret language she longed to learn. Her mother and grandmother used it to discuss things they didn't want "Die Kinder" to overhear. Seeing newsreels of goose-stepping soldiers and Hitler ranting to large cheering crowds, she felt ashamed of her German family background.

Her shame was mixed with pride. Her piano teachers rewarded her with small statues of Bach, Beethoven and Brahms when she played sections from their works. As a teenager, she was fascinated first with the titles of books by Schopenhauer, Hegel, Nietzsche. Later she poured over them line by line, loving the way they took her thinking to new heights and depths.

She startled as Gladys Bentley, her department chair, knocked on the doorsill and walked in. Bentley was wearing her usual suit with a frilly blouse, today is was the tweed, which she alternated with a navy.

"Victoria, are you all right? How is your father?" She was not called "Ma Bentley" for nothing. Her clear soft green eyes invited confidence.

Victoria flooded into tears. Gladys' walked over to her, placing her hand on her shoulder. After a moment of silence, she said, "I'm so sorry. If there is anything I can do . . ."

Victoria pulled a tissue from the box on her desktop and wiped her eyes. Relieved that Gladys did not also inquire after Tom, she thanked her for her concern. She realized Gladys must have seen the note on her door earlier and which may have prompted her stopping by. She told her of the note to call the NIHL office to follow up on her grant proposal. Gladys asked what the proposal was about.

Victora explained, "Heidegger in *Being and Time*, and George Herbert Mead, in *The Philosophy of the Present*, had powerful, but different, philosophies of the nature of time. Both believed that time was not simply linear. That our pasts and futures were contained in our present moments."

"Sounds like the 'eternal return' of Nietzsche the idea that everything that happens circles back upon itself, in a great cycle of creation and dissolution," said Bentley. Her naturally curly gray hair was tinged with red. She pushed an unruly lock back behind her ear.

"True," said Victoria, her voice brimming with excitement! "Physicists such as Neils Bohr posited overlapping universes, each of which exists within the cracks of the other, restimulating each other. If we could slip between those cracks, perhaps we could recreate the past, eliminating atrocities such as the holocaust."

Bentley patted Victoria's hand. "I can't say I understand what you are trying to do, but I can feel your energy. There are certainly many unfortunate events in the past I'd like to change if I could. Turning toward the door, Bentley smiled, "I'd better go and let you make your call."

Victoria's palms were moist as she dialed the NIHL office. Immediately she recognized Guy'd resonant baritone voice. "Guy? Guy Santori?"

"Dr. Von Dietz. Yes this is Guy, and this is Dr. Carter-Jackson's office. I'm a J.D. now, thanks to you."

Victoria recalled writing a letter of recommendation for Guy several years ago to Northwestern Law School.

"I'm assistant to Dr. Carter-Jackson, paying off my student loans, learning the ins and outs of affirmative action, scientific disputes, and human learning research grants. Getting ready to take the bar."

Guy's voice was resonant, assured. He'd been one of the nice, bright cops in her class. She recalled his swarthy good looks, and the twinge of loss when she declined his gentle request that they have coffee or perhaps a glass of wine together. Shaking away these thoughts she brought Guy up to date about her father's surgery and the stress of her tenure review. He asked about Tom, not surprised that they were separated. They arranged for her to meet Dr. Carter-Jackson for lunch the next day in Chicago at Sheo's on upper Michigan Avenue.

Victoria asked what Carter-Jackson expected, hoping to get some strategic insights from Guy without appearing to ask for a special favor.

"Dr. Von Dietz, or may I call you Victoria now that I am no longer your student?"

Not waiting for her to reply, he continued. "Victoria, what a beautiful name. Listen, Dr. Carter Jackson's fed up with white European males or their "lackeys", as she calls them, writing about each other and getting famous based on this. Annabelle feels that if ideas are worth anything they should be put into practice, to make the world a better place. If you show some real life applications, this will have a definite appeal for her."

"I always did like a challenge," said Victoria. "Seriously, Guy, if we could crack the time barrier, we could prevent cancer from metastasizing, we could have stopped the bombing of Pearl Harbor and Hiroshima, we could have prevented the Nazi's extermination of Jews."

"The Holocaust!" he replied. "How well,I remember reading Mead for your class where he said the future and the past exist in the present. It strikes me that you knew my future better than I did when I was your student."

"Surely not, Mr. Santori." She needed to deflect this intensity. I look forward to meeting Dr. Carter Jackson tomorrow. She's well-known in academic circles as a fiery African-American feminist," said Victoria.

"Annabelle's a formidable gal with intense values and desires. But she respects a strong argument, especially if it comes from the heart. And I know that's where your work comes from."

Victoria's breath quickened. Small beads of perspiration formed between her breasts. She wondered about his personal life, if he was married or engaged, amazed that she could think of this at such a time. Thanking him, she put down the phone. Guy Santori has no idea how much my heart is involved in my work. She looked at George Herbert Mead's framed picture on her desk. This photo was just his face unlike the full body picture she had at home. Mead seemed to smile back, share her excitement.

Her memory wafted back to their last encounter before Guy graduated, several years ago. He had stopped by her office and boldly confessed love for her. "I'm not your student anymore, Beautiful, and I'd do anything to be close to you."

"Guy, I'm married. Please don't." She had pushed his hand aside and walked away.

As she packed her brief case, heavy footsteps echoed in the hallway now nearly empty of students. Dean Schenck appeared at her office door, wearing a dark grey suit and a navy blue tie.

Victoria was startled to see him. Although his office was on the same floor, it was across the corridor, on the administrative side of the building. In her five years at Athens, she had never seen him on this side of the floor. Her heart pounded.

Schenck scratched his leg. The bright overhead lights in the hallway revealed spots on his glasses through which his cold blue eyes stared at her, then at Mead's picture on her desk.

"Picture of your father?" he asked.

"No, but another George, one I write about, George Herbert Mead. Schenck looked puzzled. "He's an American philosopher, associated with John Dewey," she said.

"Never heard of him," said Schenck.

"Pity few learn about the great American thinkers," she could not help but add especially as his doctorate was in American history. Schneck shrugged, raised one of his cheeks. He looked as if he would devour her.

" Dr. Von Dietz, I need to talk with you. Please come to my office."

"Is something wrong?" She feared the hospital had called with bad news about her father. "I need to pick my daughter up at school," she said.

"This won't take long," he turned away.

Their footsteps clicked on the tile floor of the waiting area between classrooms. Several chrome based leather benches stood in front of the floor-to-ceiling windows. The setting sun was barely visible through the dark clouds over Lake Michigan.

"I'll get through this", she said to herself, the image of Mead's smiling face flashed through her mind.

Schenck smelled of stale aftershave and cigarettes. Trying to relieve tension, she asked what the new word was from last night's dinner conversation. "Perfervid," said Schenck. "Wife thought she could catch me on that one— means intense feelings. But she did the dishes."

His office door stood open even though his secretary had left for the day. His leather chair behind the large walnut desk squeaked as he sat down. "You have a situation on your hands." He nodded towards a large leather chair.

"He's enjoying having this power," she thought. Victoria straightened her back, which ached from her shoulders to her hips. Her chair was low. Looking down at her, Schenck's double chin appeared.

"I received a complaint that you tell dirty jokes in the classroom and behave seductively towards the men." He looked her in the eyes, then passed them down over her white blouse and back up again.

Heat shimmered up her back. "I don't tell jokes of any kind. I can't remember them. Believe it or not, I have heard few dirty jokes in my life." Slow down, you're being defensive," she said to herself.

She cleared her throat. "I believe the accusation is based on a reaction to the Freudian theory we were studying." She thought of telling Schenck that two of them had been pushing her for a date. But no, he would blame this on her.

He squeezed his lips together. "The LOT program provides a good source of students and income to the college," said Schenck. "President Getz spent considerable time negotiating with the Chicago police training academy folks so they would grant Athens this program."

A deep thud came from the side window. A gull had smashed into it, seeing the reflection of the water and sky. Schenck looked over his shoulder and grinned.

Victoria ached for the bird. She imagined Schenck had a net under his window to catch the dead birds, taking the bird home for his wife to make soup.

"I suspect someone may have misinterpreted my light-hearted critique of Freud's concept of "penis envy," especially if he had not read the assignment or listened to my lectures. He may have interpreted my tone as joking." She stood as her voice rose: "if it was a joke, it was Freud's not mine."

"Dr. Von Dietz, I've warned you before that it is your obligation as an Athens Professor to teach what is good and right. If Freud is so ludicrous and prurient, why not just tell the students not to read him. Asking them to apply Freud to themselves is inappropriate." He took his desk pen from its marble holder and twirled it between his middle finger and his thumb, then stuck it in his mouth.

"Dr. Schenck, whether one agrees with Freud or not, an educated person is aware of his significance. Students learn best when they relate ideas and concepts to their own lives," she retorted before she could think the better of it.

Schenck gripped the arm of his chair.

As he opened his mouth, Victoria continued, "I'd like to see my file so I can answer in writing. I believe this one most likely came from Jerry Barr," said Victoria.

"You may put anything in writing you wish" he said curtly. "But only I have a right to say what goes in my files."

She told herself to remain calm, to control her outrage. But she could not. She stood up, shaking. "Employment records are legal documents not personal property, Dr. Schenck!"

His neck was red and he began to bite the edges of his thin mouth. I'm expecting a phone call," he said as he swiveled his chair around to face the lake.

"'Perfervid' certainly was the right word," Victoria thought, leaving his office.

Chapter Ten
Lunch with Annabelle Carter-Jackson

D riving South on I-94 to the Chicago Loop, Victoria was glad she could leave after morning rush hour. She was prepared to have several strikes against her, being white and even worse, blond, qualities that some black women resented. Guy's presence in Carter-Jackson's office explained why her proposal even had a chance. It was a theoretical work based on the ideas of two prominent white western male thinkers, more strikes against her. Guy had hinted that Carter-Jackson was a lesbian, which may mitigate against the envy factor but may make her topic less appealing.

Entering Sheo's French Bistro, Victoria checked her coat, then followed the Maitre-De to the dining room. "Dr. Carter-Jackson is expecting you," he grinned. Obviously she was a regular. Hmm, benefits of a high-level government position. Probably got reimbursed as well.

The white of Dr. Carter-Jackson's enormous smile matched the white linen tablecloth, both a stark contrast to her mahogany complexion. She did not get up as Victoria approached. Rather she showed her white palm, pointing to the seat opposite, making no attempt to conceal her perusal of Victoria.

Victoria had carefully selected a grey wool pantsuit, which stayed wrinkle free on the drive south to Chicago. Her light yellow blouse brought out her green eyes. Her blond hair was tied at the nape of her neck, with a few strands in front of her ears, showing that she was neat, but not compulsive. Victoria had learned to tone down her appearance by wearing glasses and dressing conservatively. That way she was more readily taken seriously.

Sheo's had all white male waiters, wearing black pants and bow ties with floor length aprons. Dr. Carter Jackson's gaze followed the waiters as they scuttled around, their aprons swishing at their shoes like Geisha robes.

"What goes around, comes around, at least sometimes," said Annabelle. "If they had to bind their feet or wear three inch heels the picture would be complete."

Startled that Carter Jackson was quipping on gender issues before even greeting her, Victoria decided to play it her way, while showing respect.

"Dr. Carter-Jackson, so pleased to meet you. And pleased to be waited on by syncophanous men."

"Likewise, Gal, I should say, Professor Von Dietz, but my satisfaction is intensified when the male waiters, as those around today, are white. And do sit down. I'm as hungry as a debutante trying to loose weight for a prom, except I'm not any of those things, obviously."

As Annabelle scanned the leather-clad menu, she spoke of her morning, facilitating a diversity workshop with the administrative officers of the U of Illinois personnel office. Victoria counted five rings and eight bracelets of platinum and gold on Carter-Jackson's thick fingers and bulging wrists.

"How'd it go?" Victoria asked directly, showing sincere interest.

"That one is going well. I got them so afraid of lawsuits they won't hire any white male unless there is absolutely no woman or non-white they can get to walk or wheel into the office. Got to start somewhere," said Annabelle.

"Be with you ladies in a minute," a slender, tall waiter glided to the next table. Turning his back on them to face the next table, his tenor voice rang out:

"Our specials for the day are crab-stuffed Ahi in an oyster and rigoulette sauce simmered in thickened cream and olive oil with cilantro and carmelized scallions."

Pushing this into the background Victoria asked, "What if the best brain surgery professor happens to be a white male and the others are mediocre or worse?" It was out of her mouth before the thought of how much she needed that grant. And here she was, challenging the chief grants officer. On the other hand ACJ is too brilliant to be impressed by simple agreement. Still she could have played it a better.

"I don't believe in all that surgery anyway. Most folks who set foot in a hospital would be better off staying home and watching General Hospital. I have the studies to prove it." Carter-Jackson sidestepped the question.

Victoria sighed. "All together true, I'm afraid," thinking of her father, her voice quivered.

"I didn't mean to offend you, honey. You have a Dr. in the family or something?"

"My father just had surgery for pancreatic cancer. A procedure that is almost never successful."

"I'm sorry," Annabelle closed her eyes slowly. It was as if someone had turned off the lights. Then she opened and beamed them at Victoria. "It riles me the way Western medicine makes Guinea pigs out of us."

The glossy haired waiter swung over. As he opened his mouth, Annabelle raised an imperious hand. "Keep it to yourself, Sonny." To Victoria, she said, "These days my stomach gets all jumbled from hearing about those sauces and herbs and exotic combinations. Besides, we already heard the specials from your performance at the next table."

Victoria found herself enjoying Carter-Jackson's banter. But she needed to bring the topic back to her proposal. "My mind is offended more than my stomach. More clutter in the mind, what Heidegger would call 'idle chatter'." My work is partly based on Heidegger, as you know, his philosophy of time.

Annabelle pointed to the sausages and pasta with cream sauce. Victoria ordered a shrimp salad. Both asked for iced tea. "Pick us a not too pricey California Chardonnay," Annabelle said. The waiter pivoted and floated to the bar. "A benefit to the restaurant from being on the same street as the Chicago School of Dance," said Annabelle, her eyes following his steps.

Victoria took a deep breath, trying to scope how to come back to her proposal. A bead of perspiration ran down her back. Too bad I didn't bring food into my research—slow food, fast food, food and time, overlapping meal zones. Here I am writing about white males, not this woman's favorite topic. And one of them is dead, the other almost dead, though Victoria was not sure whether the state of their mortality made them more or less favorable.

Before she could formulate her strategy Annabelle said, "I like your idea of a new concept of time based on Mead and Heidegger, but theories are worthless if they can't be put into practice, do some good. Philosophies too often are written to promote the careers of the good old white guys. They were "court appointed" to justify the doings of the rich and their elected officials. Damn convenient for Hitler that Nietzsche came up with his "Oberman" concept."

"Nietzsche's "overman" used the will to power to create, to reach for the sublime in the midst of the rubbish of life," said Victoria. She hoped she didn't seem to offer an excuse, or worse, a justification, for fascism.

"Most academics only know the popularized version of Nietzsche promoted by his sister when he was hospitalized with brain fever," said Annabelle. "You impress me, Dr. Von Dietz."

Carter Jackson's voice resonated through her formidable breast like a Diva's. Even her request for water carried significance, like a message from the gods. She recognized the scent Annabelle was wearing. "Gertrude" most likely named after Gertrude Stein, the early twentieth century Lesbian writer. The scent was an intense mix of musk, cinnamon, rose water and blue cheese.

Victoria wondered if she'd be able to eat at all, so much was at stake. Her work, her life depended upon her getting this grant.

Just as she was about to speak, the waiter slid to the table with the chilled wine in a white linen towel. He manipulated his chrome tool and twirled off the cork.

ACJ held out her hand. She eyed, then sniffed the cork. She sipped and nodded approval as she swallowed. The waiter poured as if he had a migraine, set the bottle in a hammered silver ice bucket and retreated two steps before again demonstrating the perfection of his pirouette.

Not able to hold back any longer, Victoria burst in. "Dr. Carter Jackson, I know I have something with potential. Both George Herbert Mead and Heidegger had profound insights into the nature of time. My instincts tell me bringing them together could unleash powers we can't yet imagine." She was already out on a limb, might as well go out to the end of it.

Carter Jackson scowled. "I'd like to see what your thinking would be like if you separated it from the ideas of these men," she said. Her lips spread to reveal a large mouth heavy with pink gums and hung with gold fillings. She played with the large ruby rings on her middle finger, sliding it up and down as she spoke.

"Colonization takes many forms. It's not just a matter of some country taking over another's governments, but of their ideas taking over our minds." Annabelle shifted, smoothing her silk slacks and leaning towards Victoria.

She thinks my mind is colonized by George and Martin. Well maybe it is but I've got to convince her otherwise, that I'm beyond their thinking. Victoria pulled her stomach back and up. "Dr. Carter Jackson, my research will reveal the extent to which we all are held hostage to oppressive notions of time."

Annabelle raised an eyebrow and made a low humming sound.

Another waiter intruded, presenting a platter of pasta thick with creamy mushroom sauce and several Italian sausages, topped with a sprig of fresh basil leaves.

Victoria breathed rapidly, trying to avert panic. I must address this from a position of strength, not defensiveness, she thought. Before Victoria could formulate a reply Annabelle continued:

"Let me offer an example of research that helped alleviate women's oppression. Why do men think that women enjoy being raped, when actually women's ideal sexual experiences have very little resemblance to fucking?"

Victoria was glad she hadn't yet taken a bite, because she might have spit it out, not from shock, but from surprise that another academic would be so candid. Which led her to risk:

"That reminds me of an article called "Fucking is Sexist," replied Victoria. Several shrimp sought escape off the side of Victoria's glass salad bowl, which bled red sauce. Victoria pushed the shrimp back under the lettuce with her fork.

"That's the work! By Professor Eleanor Miller Gorman," Annabelle said as if they were discussing political preferences in affluent suburbs. I funded her participant observation study of the Playboy Club. She did the research disguised as one of Hugh Hefner's bunnies." Her eyes glued to Victoria's neckline.

Wishing she had left only one button open on her blouse, Victoria at last thought of a strategy. She had to get that grant. "Dr. Carter Jackson, I know my work has far reaching potential. Sure it's at the theoretical stage, but I am on the verge of unlocking a secret of time with enormous possibilities.

ACJ raised her eyebrows and smiled. Victoria had her attention on her work and was determined to keep it there. "Both Mead and Heidegger's concepts of time fall short of practical application yet both find that the past and the future overlap with the present. This overlap is like a fold in time. If we can get it right we could jump into such a fold and co-exist at an earlier or later time.

ACJ's eyes beamed at Victoria. "Most folks would tell you your crazy and be out of here, but not me. For one thing the meal is too good. And besides I read your proposal, and it is a masterpiece of clarity. My heart jumps at the idea of being to go back in time, make things different, keep Martin Luther King out of Memphis, John Kennedy out of Dallas."

Now she felt like she had connected. Victoria smiled. "My work may not take us to that point, but I know I can push our understanding of time to a new level."

"Wondering whether she had jinxed her chances, Victoria pressed on. The image of Martin Luther once again hit her mind. "I propose to look with the eyes of an archeologist into the layers beneath my fields of knowledge. Incorporating their thoughts into my work was never just an intellectual game. As a woman, and the only woman at the time, sitting in graduate seminars, I fell in love with these men and their philosophies."

"In love?" said Annabelle, chewing slowly. ACJ took a large bite of sausage. She brought up her napkin to catch juice as it shimmered down her chin. "Anyway, the point is that you, one of the few published women social theorists in America, have been a handmaiden of white European and American male philosophers. Your proposal, as I read it, is to write your way out of this, to "deconstruct" your own scholarly history."

"I know more about how Mead looked at the world than I knew how my father looked at it," said Victoria. "I thought and felt about everything, from Mead's point of view and now Heidegger. These relationships to which male mentors drove me, determined who I fell in love with, who I married. These are not just "ideas" these are romances, deep loves, passions, which direct my entire life."

"No doubt your readers and students, too, my dear," said Annabelle. She had finished her sausages and pasta and glanced over her shoulder as she wiped her cheeks with the large linen napkin. "That slender fellow best notice we are ready for dessert."

Victoria's appetite was not focused on food. "The academic establishment does not like to think of these as "relationships" with flesh and blood thinkers, alive or dead, but simply as a battle of abstract ideas.

"Or a 'conflict over paradigms'," said ACJ.

"Spare me paradigm shifts and alternative epistemologies jargon," thought Victoria. Controlling herself, she said, "It is more like getting a divorce than changing theories."

"Ooh, I get you, such radical restriction of experience. Being told not to feel, only to think." said Annabelle. "That's the stuff of colonization, Sugar."

"I read Irigary, about the dilemmas of women writing which truly reflects their lives–using a language which evolved under patriarchy. The words and the structure of language available to us and our grammars are already gender determined and colonized." Victoria said, pouring herself the last of the wine since the waiter seemed allergic to feminists. ACJ bit into her cherry pie alamode, licking the whipped cream off her spoon. "Scholarly journals require this mode—the use of second person, objectified tones of voice. Even those who strove against this way of thinking, like Martin Heidegger, used these forms of expression," said Victoria. The wine was gone. She wanted more.

"You've got nerve and verve, Girl! I'm going to fund your work," said Annabelle, finishing her last bite of piecrust. "But I want you to write it in a form which overcomes the problem. Doing so would be ironic and contradictory. The form of the new theory would present itself as a demonstration of its power."

Victoria wondered if it were some sort of trap. It had come too easily. "Dr. Carter Jackson, I'm delighted with your confidence in me. But I must tell you that there is no such form!" said Victoria.

"We are talking about change, here. Real change. A time when words and theories and actions are all connected. Philosophies of time make an actual difference in the world. Feelings and ideas are connected with our bodies. Worth a shot," said Annabelle, leaning back, apparently satisfied that there were no more crumbs to capture.

She reached her hand across the table and grabbed Victoria's in her large sweaty palm and squeezed. To Victoria the pain was tolerable. She had her grant!

Chapter Eleven

Last Rites

my father moved through dooms of love
through sames of am through haves of give,
singing each morning out of each night
my father moved through depths of height
— e.e. cummings

The next afternoon as Victoria was leaving her office for the day, she got a call from Deaconess Hospital. Her father had taken a turn for the worse. She felt short of breath and then a rush of adrenaline. Oh my dear father, she thought, you always were there for me, my whole life. You can't leave me now. . .

He's so vital, so involved, so young. She reflected on how he had changed since his early retirement as a sergeant on the police force. Working in the neighborhood with the young priest from St. Andrew's parish in civil rights and peace discussion groups, running a tool loan center from which he coached low- income residents in the upkeep of their homes. He was enthused about this work and delighted in being Kathy's Grandpa. Her stomach churned.

He'll make it. He always does make it, she said to herself, getting into her Volvo. She swung by the house to feed Snuggles. Snuggles rubbed his head against her leg, looking sad. "Yes, he loved you too, Snuggles. She recalled the day her father had arrived in their driveway with a dog-house strapped to a trailer. The sign on the dog house he had made said "For Snuggling Only."

She had intended to leave Snuggles at home but he followed her to the door, pushed past her and ran over the snow packed from lawn to her car.

"You know when I really need you," she said.

Snuggles said, "Woof."

They picked Kathy up a school and headed north on I-94. The headlights on the cars reflected on the highway and the patches of ice and snow. "Is Grandpa dying?" asked Kathy.

Can Kathy stand this? Tom had in many ways been a good father to her, and now he was gone too. Dad can't die now, not when I'm loosing my marriage and possibly also my job. She pushed away these thoughts. She had to be strong for Kathy.

Victoria glanced at Kathy's face. Her eyes were pinched, her jaw tight. Victoria's mind raced. Kathy was aware of death. She had loved her great-grandmother, Ida, who she called "Mema." She learned from being with Mema through a long and painful decline from intestinal cancer, that death was part of life. Victoria was grateful that their family traditions included frequent visits to the cemetery to plant flowers for her grandfather and great aunts. Her mother and grandmother had turned these visits into picnics, bribing her with a visit to Leon's frozen custard on the way home.

Victoria took one hand off the wheel and squeezed Kathy's mittened hand. "Sweetheart, things don't look good," she said. She felt her nerve endings curl up inside her chest and couldn't breathe. All her years of training as an academic to repress her feelings helped. She could face this. In a male dominated academic environment for a woman to show feelings of any kind could be professional suicide.

Walking down the tiled corridor Victoria nodded to several deaconesses who seemed to sense her anguish. Steaming dinner carts oozed the smell of overcooked broccoli that clashed with the Lysol in the hallway.

"Dr. Von Dietz, excuse me, Victoria," said the same nurse-deaconess from her last visit. "Your mother just went down to the cafeteria with Pastor Kloph. She asked that her granddaughter, Kathy, come down when she arrives. This must be Kathy." She reached out for Kathys' hand.

Kathy pulled back. "I want to see my grandpa." Victoria looked at the nurse.

"She'll be alright." Victoria looked the nurse in the eyes.

"O.K. said the nurse. I'll take you in for just a minute."

Victoria's spine felt like it was stuck with pins. Her intestines swirled. The odds were slim, the Drs. had said. But we had to try. Just last week he went out for a ride with Ma. Things could still turn around. They had turned around before. A world without Dad was one without foundation, it could not stand. Her knees felt weak. Where were her feet?

George was sleeping in a seated position. Father Lindenbough stood at the foot of the bed. He greeted her with a bear hug. He felt strong and caring. She could have let go and cried but instead took a deep breath, letting a few teardrops melt down her face. George's association with Lindenbough at St. Andrews Catholic church had been the reason he had been excommunicated from the Lutheran church.

Lindenborgh looked at Kathy. He said hello and shook her hand. "Your grandpa talks about you a lot. So proud of your violin playing."

"Grandpa talks about you too," said Kathy. "You work for poor people and for peace." Lindenbough smiled. He was wearing a black leather jacket with a priest's collar, black jeans.

"Father Lindenbough, did you know that Kathy was in the march after Martin Luther King was assassinated? An African-American friend who was in graduate school with me carried her on his shoulders."

"We were in the same march, then. Oh my goodness what a family you have to be proud of Kathy. Your grandpa helps lots of folks in the neighborhood with his tool loan center," he said.

In her enthusiasm, Kathy finished his sentence. "And teaches them how to fix things too."

George stirred and twitched, emitting sounds as if he were having a bad dream. Victoria put her arm around Kathy's shoulder.

"Grandpa wants to tell us something," said Kathy.

The smell of pulverized meat on George's dinner tray nauseated Victoria as it blended with the smell of hospital body lotion. His handsome face had a grayish cast. His arms looked skinny sticking out from the cotton hospital gown. An IV monitor ticked as droplets of clear liquid moved down the tube into his arm. The other day he seemed so lively. This must just be a bad day," she said, looking at the nurse, wanting confirmation of what she knew was not true. She knew in her heart he was dying.

The nurse/deaconess looked at her with soft eyes. Gently she moved her head back and forth.

George made a rasping sound . ."Ppprrrincessss. . ."

The Nurse/deaconess led Kathy to the bedside. Kathy reached for her his hand.

"Grandpa, wake up!" Kathy said.

He opened his eyes. They were hazy, as if he was drunk.

"Grandpa, Grandpa."

As he reached for her, his hand shook. "Princ— cess"" prrracticce? He held up his hand and ran over it with a finger as if playing the violin.

"Grandpa when are you coming to visit us? I'll play my new piece for you. Its by Wolfgang Amadeus Mozart."

"Hummm," he said. He had difficulty holding up his head. He flashed her a half smile as she sang the melody.

"Kathy, Grandma is waiting for you downstairs and Grandpa needs his rest." Victoria was afraid Kathy would break down. Even though Kathy had been prepared, the stark reality may be too much for her.

"But he's been resting all day," said Kathy.

The nurse/deaconess stepped forward.

George held up one finger, his eyes raised to the nurse, one finger. He looked at Kathy and moved his finger slightly for her to come closer.

"Cccome, Prrrricesss,"

"Dad" Victoria said. She feared what he was going to say.

George held up his hand to stop her.

"For. . . both . . ," George's voice was scratchy, broken.

Tears streamed down Victoria's face.

"Allright, I'll go downstairs now," said Kathy.

George held up his index finger.

"Sit . . .Princess."

Kathy pulled herself up on the edge of the bed. George slowly reached for her hand.

He looked Kathy in the eyes. "G-g-g grandpa has to go. . . . You" he coughed "big girl". I'll be in h-h-heaven watching out for you. " His voice faded. Kathy looked at Victoria who was wiping her cheeks.

Victoria's heart pounded. She felt like screaming, "no, no don't go yet, please". She had to be strong. "Kathy, its time to kiss Grandpa goodbye."

Kathy leaned over and kissed George on the cheek.

"Grandpa loves . . .remember . . .violin . . ." George's head slumped over.

Victoria reached for Kathy and helped her down from the high bed.

"Time to go see Grandma now, she's waiting," said Victoria. Tears ran down Kathy's cheeks.

The nurse/deaconess came forward and held Kathy's hands.

"Let's go down to the cafeteria," she said, leading her out of the room.

Father Lindenbough motioned for Victoria to step out the door with him.

"He's been in and out of consciousness all afternoon. Do you want him to have last rites?"

She felt cold, goose bumps prickling up her wrists. "No, he is going to come back, he may get better again."

"The Drs. have only given him a few hours.'

Victoria started to shake. "Yes, I think he would want last rites," she said. I'm so grateful. You know he was raised Catholic, but officially is not a member.

"You know how official I am," said Lindenbough, with a gentle smile. He squeezed her hand as he moved away from her. "Your mother brought Reverend Kloph over to take his repentance so he could have Holy Communion," said Lindenbough.

Victoria felt a rush of heat up her spine. "She would get him when he is down! I ran into Kloph the other night here in the hospital doing rounds. He said the cancer was a blessing from God to bring George back to the fold. I think Ma would prefer him dead than excommunicated."

"Well, given her beliefs that would be the selfless perspective," said Lindenbough. His soft blue eyes reflected the indirect lighting. She wished she could dive inside of them.

"I'll give him his last rites now, Victoria." Lindenbough stepped into the room. His large body made a shadow over the bed as the door closed. His soft voice through the door was a Latin rhythmic chant.

After a long minute he came out. "George passed peacefully. He was a gracious and generous soul. I'll miss him. So will the whole community."

∾

Victoria, Kathy and Snuggles spent that night in the same house where Victoria grew up, along with her sister and her husband. George had asked for a plain pine box for his burial, however her mother and sister insisted on a nicely finished walnut. They returned home the next day.

"Where's Dad?" Kathy asked as they sat down to eat some chicken soup from a can.

"He went to stay with a friend, Dr. Valentine, for a while," said Victoria.

"Are you getting a divorce?"

Victoria told her they were talking about it but that she was not to worry, she could still see Tom.

"O.K., Mom, if you want," said Kathy. Victoria realized then that Tom's initially close relationship with Tom had deteriorated.

Victoria was exhausted. Kathy slumped at the dining counter, stirring her spoon in the soup, taking little sips.

"Where did Grandpa go?" said Kathy.

"He went to heaven," said Victoria.

"I want to go too," said Kathy.

"Me too," said Victoria. "But honey, we can't go now. We have too much to do." Kathy started to cry while Victoria held her close. "There is our work stopping the war, and helping poor people.

"and your writing, Mom?" asked Kathy.

"Yes, honey," said Victoria.

"Are you still writing about George Herbert Mead?" said Kathy.

"Yes, why do you ask?" said Victoria.

"Why don't you write about Grandpa instead? "You should write about your own daddy instead of some old sourpuss man."

Victoria's tears came so fast they dropped into her soup.

"I will some day. Or maybe in a way I already am," said Victoria.

She held Kathy close and her little girl seemed even wiser sitting quietly, not asking another question.

∾

The next week Victoria's hands shook as she picked up an envelope in her faculty mailbox from the Dean's office. There were five junior professors up for tenure that year. The other four were men. "Ma Bentley", her department chair, had given Victoria a strong recommendation, and she had several publications. Her student evaluations were mixed; the better students loved her while the poor students scored her as "disorganized" or too difficult. To them you were disorganized if you did not stick to three or four points in the textbook, which were guaranteed to be on the test. They had come to expect teaching out of the textbook. Victoria felt this was a lazy way to teach. Why have a professor tell you what you can read yourself?

Her friend Shelley's husband, Brian, had received tenure, as had Bob Bracker. She had a much stonger track record than them, so at first this made her feel confident. They had no publications, but Brian had completed his dissertation and had a manuscript being considered by a publisher. Bob was the football coach and had a successful season. But there was discussion about Athens College becoming "over tenured." That morning John Brunsworth had passed her in the hall, beaming. He had received tenure. She congratulated him all the while her heart was sinking.

It was likely that one or both of the two remaining would not get tenure. James Sneed, was standing by his mailbox. He ripped open his letter. He had not finished his dissertation but sat in the faculty coffee room each morning and schmoozed with the old timers. Victoria spent her early morning writing and preparing classes. She looked in the window at the schmoozers as she walked from the parking lot.

Snead squealed with delight when he opened his letter. "I got it. I got it. Mary will be so pleased. You know she's made friends with the Dean's wife and has worked hard on the events committee of the FWC."

Victoria reflected that FWC stood for faculty wives club but she and Tom referred to it as the WC. She recalled asking if there was a club for faculty husbands and getting a blank stare.

As an afterthought Sneed looked at the unopened letter in her hand. "Victoria, aren't you going to open it?"

"I recall discussions at the faculty meeting about the faculty being "tenured in" and an attempt to set up a quota. I know all four of you guys got it.

And, Dean Schenk has been on my case lately," she said, her hand shaking as she finished opening the letter.

"This is to inform you that you have not been granted tenure by the Athens faculty. Your terminal one year contract is enclosed." Victoria's stomach churned. Her back and neck felt like taught wires on an overtuned piano.

"Sorry, Victoria," said Snead. "But I know Tom never got on tenure track at Holy Rosary. Maybe it's best if you let him get the job this time."

"Perhaps I'll join a faculty that is more than a good old boys' club. By the way, is your wife still going to bake all those cookies for President Schrieber's wife's tea parties, or is she going to find something meaningful to do with her life." Victoria left Snead with his mouth hanging open. She had thought about saying that she didn't care what kind of track Tom was on as she wanted nothing to do with him anymore. But she didn't want to give Snead the satisfaction of being the one to spread the gossip.

Chapter Twelve
George Mead Emerges

Words are living fossils. The poet must piece
the skeleton together and make it sing.
— Lawrence Ferlinghetti, *Americus I*

Alone that evening after tucking Kathy into bed, Victoria felt empty and cold inside her chest. The large conch shell on the shelf in her study had been her grandmother's. She held it to her ear. Grandma had never seen an ocean but said she listened to the waves held inside the shell. I am like this shell, only less permanent. Victoria found this thought comforting.

She poured a glass of burgundy from the crystal decanter on her book-shelf. A light in the church window across the street brought Martin Luther into the room. He seemed to pointing a finger at her and saying, "Good Lutherans don't drink, especially the women." She pulled the blinds.

The warm rush of the wine revived her. Grief over her father's death, anger over Tom's betrayal, outrage and fear over the denial of tenure, all these emotions swirled in her belly. She'd have to again search for an academic position, at a time when universities were cutting their budgets. "What should I do?" She found herself saying this outloud.

"Come to me," a voice seemed to come from Mead's photograph on her desk.

Gazing at his visage, Victoria imagined him pulling a pipe out of his pocket, filling it and lighting it up. Gentle warm clouds of smoke embraced her. She breathed in the aroma of Mead's tobacco, so like her father's.

She got up and shook her head. It must be coming from Tom's study.

Half hoping he had come back, she walked down the hallway. "Tom?" she opened his door. No sign of him. His normally overstuffed bookcases were half empty. The room reeked of his new, sweet tobacco, selected by the little slut, Christina. He's probably with her now.

Shaking off those thoughts she walked out and closed the door. Maybe I should start smoking a pipe. Carl Jung said that women need to become the men they want to marry. Hmmm. . .

She picked up her black and white speckled notebook, noticing for the first time its brand name was "Mead." Her favorite corduroy tufted chair felt comfortable. Words flowed into the notebook:

"George Herbert Mead, I've devoted my life to you, explaining you, speaking for you. I see the world, people, events through your eyes."

Her hand caressed the page of the notebook, then continued to write: "I love you. You love and need me too; I see it from how you look at me. You said in *The Philosophy of the Present*, the past and future are contained in each moment. If only you had proved it."

She gazed at Mead's face in the picture. He smiled back at her.

A teardrop ran down his cheek, stopped by his moustache. She saw it happen. No, it was a bit of dust, a fantasy left over from the day's heartache. She took a deep draft of wine. All of the stress with Dad dying, my job, Tom's betrayal. "If only you could really be here," she wrote. Brushing his face with a fingertip, her knees shook. The corners of his mouth widened.

What was happening to her? She looked again. Still he smiled, not broadly but with compassion. Had she not noticed that smile after seeing so much else in the photo? She continued writing:

"George Herbert Mead, you are my true love. I long for you. You have lived with me every day since I read your first words. If only the fantasy I am having that you are coming alive were true. If only this weren't some exotic apparition, a vision, like others I have had that seem so real."

Victoria lifted his picture, pressed her lips over his mouth. She held her eyes closed, then pulled away, jolted by the feel of his lips responding to the kiss.

"I am losing my mind," she said to his eyes, which now had a sparkle.

Feeling foolish, she said: "I see you looking at me, speak up. I need your voice."

"What's happen–ing," Mead said. "Help–me–live again. Each word– makes me–real." Mead's words were barely distinct, though his baritone was rich and deep.

She shook her head. A Sanskrit chant came to mind: "Lead me from the unreal to the real, from the darkness to the light." Then she added, "but which is which?" Her stomach churned.

Mead's head turned as if he were eyeing her study. His voice was clear.

"I heard you speak of me to others, from here behind my picture, from within the pages of my books." He moved his shoulders more squarely towards her. He took his hand from his pocket and reached out to her.

Victoria glanced toward the wine glass. She'd had only a sip or two. She decided to succumb to the pleasure of this apparition. She cleared her throat:

"I came to understand my own identity, or 'self' as you call it, because of you. You are in truth my most "significant other," you coined this term, part of who I am."

His eyes penetrated her. He said nothing.

She continued: "I can't imagine how I could have thought about the world, life, my experiences, without you."

His mouth moved into a smile again. He said: "and I understand my thoughts better because of your work."

"How could you read my work?" She stopped short of saying, 'since you're dead.'

"As you write it, I know it," he said.

It felt to Victoria like a confession of love and emboldened her.

"Now I understand. Since I couldn't love you physically, I married Tom, because he reminded me of you. He was aware of your ideas. We talked about you at great length. He even reminded me of you in manner and appearance."

Mead's hand dug for his pocket watch, though time could mean nothing to him. "Yes, I noticed Tom also carried a pocket watch popular in my days," he said.

The sounds of a Bach fugue roared from the church organ. She looked up to see the glow of the Luther window shining through the drapes. "To a romantic like myself, especially one who was raised Lutheran, a sensuous bond should result in marriage. But you were always my true husband, the one who took care of my mind, my self, even my soul. I adore you and have always adored you since I first read your article "The Genesis of Self." You are the beginning of my life as author. For me this may be more basic than for you, because you believed in developing your ideas in conversation. As for me, "I write therefore I am."

"Don't be ridiculous. I've watched you write, but you also teach, raise a daughter, work for peace, cry yourself to sleep at night, play the piano, and think powerful new thoughts. You don't just switch verbs on Descartes' 'I think therefore I am' you multiply them," his smiled stretched across his face.

"You caught me being 'reductionistic', and about myself," she laughed.

Mead joined her. As he laughed puffs of dust came off his jacket. "Say no more, my dear, your professorial self is taking over. You know me, you understand me, like no one else." He reached out for her, but his arm could extend no more than its length in the picture. "I've always thought the past and the future were part of the present, making our intersection possible. His voice growing jagged, he said, "If only I could untangle it more precisely."

Still not believing what she was seeing, she continued: "You can do it, George! You have already done it! Havn't you demonstrated that coming together from different times and spaces is possible, even necessary? Give voice to it and it will happen. All things (bad and good), which we can articulate as possible, have an emotional reality. Strong emotions change our bodies, can slow down or quicken the passage of time." She had accepted these thoughts of Mead's but never imagined there would come a time to test it, or whether it was testable.

Mead cleared his throat. Though from an image no more than a foot high, the sound seemed to come from a full sized man. "Nature is the parent of an organism. Organisms exist because perspectives from different time systems intersect."

Victoria's heart pounded as she watched Mead's picture grow animated. As he continued to speak, the film became actual flesh.

Mead continued: "Slabs of nature exist in relativity, in different realms of space and time. When these intersect, new organisms emerge and reemerge."

"Whitehead" Her voice rose in excitement.

"And Minkowski, space/time," he replied.

She quivered with delight. Mead, a man whose mind she's plumbed only through his books, now she was speaking with him. But she wanted more.

"Your physical body, your "organism," has somehow come to intersect with mine. Come and hold me at last," she said, reaching out to him.

"Somehow, indeed," Mead replied. "Your love, like the kiss of the princess who turned the beast into a prince, pulls me forward." He moaned, as if from a deep well, a sound she couldn't decipher as pain or pleasure. Was he real or an image, a ghost, or simply a vision of her desire?

"Come," she said, reaching out to him, her fingers aching for touch, while her mind reveled in engagement with Mead. "Your theory of time, as intersecting perspectives, space and time are one, they fold back into each other. Einstein wrote the mathematics behind this, or did he write this part after you died?"

Flippantly, he replied: "I know Einstein is not the guy who used to deliver the milk. If I could have known you from this plane, I could also know of Einstein. His work followed on my thinking, after all."

She reached her hands towards his as he struggled to emerge from the picture. She half expected their hands to pass through each other but his were solid, strong and hot. She let go, then grabbed them again. "I expected your hands to be cold, come," she pulled on them.

"You heat me up," he said as he struggled forward and without her noticing the change, appeared full size, though with a long, low moan. "I anticipated the physical pain," he said, "but not the mental. I have seen so much already, the great war, the depression, so much suffering, so much avoidable," he said with growing rage. His groan sounded like labor pains of a giant beast. And there he was. The picture frame on her desk was empty.

Victoria reached up and touched his shoulders, her fingers brushing along the soft brown wool tweed. He smelled of her father's pipe tobacco. He touched her face and kissed her full on the mouth. She felt a deep ache in her belly.

They hugged and kissed. Her hands on his chest, she looked down at his vest. The bottom buttonhole seemed to be straining. "George, are you a few pounds heavier than you were in your picture?" He patted his tummy.

"I've been lying around for fifty years. Now that I have you I'll get back in shape very quickly."

"I adore you just as you are," she said pulling him towards her.

"I find you the most beautiful woman I have ever known," he smiled, "and that covers almost a century of time."

She replied, "I know that your wife Helen was a beauty, and there were many great beauties in your acquaintance in the 'roaring twenties' ".

"Your beauty is total because it includes the beauty of the soul and the mind."

"Your words thrill me and at the same time my sense of truth knows this to be something of an exaggeration."

His tongue pushed its way into her mouth as he began to unbutton her blouse. Was she dreaming? It was too delicious to question. He pulled her down on what was no longer the daybed in her study but a Victorian sofa. He reached under her blouse, moved his fingers up her spine. "What, no lacing?"

"Underwear styles have changed," she said.

"You have a remarkably lithe figure for a lady without a girdle. Ah, this is much easier." He fumbled with, then unclasped her bra. "I imagine the long ladies undergarment's of your era were more exciting to undo. All those hooks."

Victoria imagined Mead undoing such a garment on her, kissing her as he opened each one. In the present, having flown with him into his time, she unbuttoned his vest, opened his tie and shirt, noting the stay in his collar. She carefully folded his vest and put it on the end table, careful not to spill his watch out of the pocket. "You will have to invent a new kind of watch to account for time loops like the one we are in," she said.

"Please, darling, let's not talk theory now," he said putting his lips on her pink nipple which immediately became rigid and hot. She grabbed his erect member, squeezed it and guided it where she needed it to be.

Victoria woke up with the sun coming in the window, hitting her in the face as she lay on the sofa. She looked around, appreciating the high ceiling, the elegant antiques. Mead was sitting across the room in a wing-backed chair, gazing at her, wearing a dressing gown, reading Heidegger's *Being and Time*.

A sense of panic filled her as she realized she did not know whose life they inhabited. "Are we in your time frame or mine?" she said.

"Judging from this room this furniture we are in my house. But the calendar on the wall says 1936," said Mead. I grabbed this book from your study on the way.

But "what about Kathy? She just lost her grandfather, her stepfather who she had once loved and respected, and now her mother leaves her for another time?"

"You will be able to connect with Kathy. You can bring her along back. Children are very adaptable."

"No, I want to see how it is first. We are about to get involved in World War II. I'll arrange for her to board at her school. They will probably even take Snuggles as the headmaster and all the children love him," said Victoria. "Yet I cannot help but feel fear, regret."

Mead gazed at her and smiled. "Darling, do not worry. The temporal fold we are in, that allowed us to be together, can be crossed using a kind of telepathic radio device. It's sort of like a wireless telephone, but it can only be used by someone like you who knows how to direct her consciousness, through meditation." He reached into his pocket and pulled out a device that looked much like a silver pocket watch. He flipped open the cover and there was a mirror-like reflection of a watch.

"First you direct your consciousness, then you can enter the fold. The atmosphere has to be right, but it works. This one is for you."

Victoria's eyes were wide with amazement. "Oh, George, you are truly amazing." I can't wait to call Kathy."

Mead put his hand over hers. "I caution you to use it only when necessary. And remember, that time is passing much much slower in the future than it is here. So actually in their time you have only been gone," he looked at his watch, "about ten minutes."

She was amazed. "Ah, like we are in an accordion fold of time!"

Mead smiled as he closed the case of his unique watch and returned it to his pocket. "Yes, and others will be able to join us from the future and come and go in our life together."

She stood and walked unsteadily to him. "Life together?" she ran her hand through his hair. "Am I dreaming? Is this real? How could it be?"

"Yes, this is real. And, no, it isn't. How can we know what is real? Of course to the extent that it is real, we should be, we are married."

She laughed through her anxiety and doubt. "This is absurd, but it is also fun!" she said.

He pulled her against him. She laid her head against his cheek, felt his heart beat against her breasts.

"Well, what is your answer," he said. "Don't tell me you are going to turn me down after loving me for twenty years, raising children with me! Those brats!"

She laughed: "You mean the graduate students who wrote dissertations based on your "seminal" thoughts, your "penetrating" ideas?"

Mead's moustache, streaked with gray, twitched as he smiled. His hands caressed her shoulders.

"Darling, I've learned a lot in the past century, " he said. He took his pipe out of his jacket pocket and tapped it gently into a dish on the side table, where she had been reading his *Philosophy of the Present*. Then, reaching into his other pocket, he pulled out a soft brown leather tobacco pouch. He carefully unfolded it, the scent filling her nostrils, and began to fill his pipe.

He struck a match and sucked deeply on the pipe stem. His cheeks sunk in and then billowed out slightly. The smoke circled both of them with a veil of sweet burley fragrance. "Oh, it is wonderful to get a real smoke again," he smiled. "Incorporeal memory, while I'm grateful for it, provides scant satisfaction. The tobacco stayed pretty fresh in my pouch. I'm sure glad I got one with a plastic lining," he said.

"I'm amazed that your matches still light!" she said, sensing her own involuntary frown.

"What's wrong," said George, "I thought you adored pipes."

"My father's cancer began with a sore in his mouth opposite his usual place to draw in on his pipe."

"Oh, yes, my darling, you are still in shock and grief from his death."

"You were there with me, in my heart/mind," she said, "though I couldn't conceive that you'd know it, certainly not that you'd ever know me."

He smiled, enigmatically. "We are both learners, eternal and consummate. Perhaps as we perfect our practice of time transfer we can change things that we wish would not have happened, such as getting ill," said Mead. His cheeks sunk as he drew flame through the tobacco.

Victoria mused on how many delightful experiences are harmful, like smoking. She rose from his embrace and walked over to the window, appreciating the tall elms which graced the streets when she was a child, but which had been lost later to Dutch Elm disease. They had magically reappeared along with Mead.

"You made me and my work so much a part of your life I found myself drawn in, trying to influence things as I could," Mead said. But some of your adventures and the characters you had to deal with were quite a comedy. That Dean Schenck! Denying you tenure because you taught Freudian dream analysis and minorities to macho and racist police officers!" Mead's moustache jumped up as he laughed.

Victoria put her hands on her hips, "Laugh at my troubles, will you," then she too broke into vindictive laughter, recalling Schenck throwing Henry Jackson Turner's "Manifest Destiny" at her.

"There is nothing so upsetting to an old guard type of man as an uppity woman who is several times brighter then him," Mead said. My friend Jane Addams was denied a professorship at Chicago for similar reasons. She was a pacifist and a suffragette and started Hull House to help immigrants and minorities who suffered from the ravages of exploitative working conditions in factories, but you know this. All too much reality for the genteel students at the University of Chicago, many of whose parents owned or managed the sweat shops."

"Yes, of course I know of Jane Addams, I read many of her wonderful books. Didn't she just win the Nobel Peace prize?"

"Yes, but her pacifism was reviled here at home," said Mead.

"History is repeating itself," she said. She wondered, now that they were back in his time, whether he would be resuming his friendship with Jane. "I would love to meet Miss Addams, as she is called."

Mead looked away. "My friend John Dewey and I both lived in residence at Hull house for a while. Jane believed in democracy to the point of sharing her wealth with the poor and living in their neighborhood."

"There was more to it than that, I expect. I get a sense your relationship with her was more than Platonic," said Victoria.

Mead pulled his watch out of his vest pocket. "She was, is an incredible woman, much like you, and so courageous. She did not favor the idea of marriage. Didn't want to cede her right to control her own destiny, own her own property."

"Perhaps, like your former wife, Helen, I am also second fiddle to Jane," said Victoria. Her legs cramped and her stomach churned. Mead rose, walked to her, sliding his arms around her waist. "Shut up and don't be jealous," he said and kissed her firmly on the mouth.

She kissed him back, then spun away. Taking a deep breath, she said, "I'm parched. I'll set up some water for tea."

"I'll help you. But we do need to get some help, a butler, a maid," he said.

An image came to mind, Guy Santori. "I know someone who may work well as a butler and overall assistant. But can we afford it? I don't have a job here in your world."

"You are with me. You don't need to worry about such things. We are not wealthy. The children benefited most from Helen's estate, as they should have. But we are secure and can afford a helper. We'll need assistance, with all the guests who will come to call, some of them from the future."

"I am a professor and scholar, not a housewife. I must have a position," she said.

"Another Jane Addams," he said.

"I should be so blessed," she replied, thinking of Addams' amazing accomplishments of this founder of the settlement movement in Chicago at Hull House.

"Your work is so multidimensional that you could teach anything from social sciences to theoretical physics. I'll work on it," Mead said.

Victoria laughed: "Theoretical physics only if I can use musical notation instead of algebraic."

"The field of physics would greatly benefit if they focused more on the implications of harmony instead of on how to split atoms," said Mead.

"This help you say we'll need. Whom do you have in mind?" asked Mead.

She swallowed, then cleared her throat. "He's a former student of mine with wealthy parents who basically put him on his own after high school, believing so strongly in "survival of the fittest," ideology.

"Oh yes, that damned mistaken application of misguided evolutionary theory to economics, promulgated by Herbert Spencer in the nineteenth century. I'd love to bring Spencer forward for a healthy debate," said Mead frowning. "But back to the case in point, this Guy Santori."

"Guy is bitterly resentful of his parents. His anger comes out in startling brilliant repartee and writing with echoes of H. L. Mencken. He became a cop to support himself through college." Victoria felt she was going too much into Guy's background, not enough into what he was doing today and how having him around could help them.

"Oh, Mencken," Mead laughed. "A sardonic fellow. I knew him at Chicago where he came to teach a course now and then. He really could attract a crowd, but too pessimistic for my taste. One needs a positive vision to work towards."

"You, my dear, were so positive about the League of Nations. Look what happened then and is happening now!" said Victoria.

"At least the League held up a beacon for what could be—that there could be an international form of union, which upholds general principles of human rights, which works toward peace. Then came Hitler. Thank God, I was dead during all that."

"Your theories, they need revising, updating, given what occurred." Eternal students, the two of them, she thought.

"You've been working hard teaching me for a decade," Mead said. Perhaps this fellow can do double duty here as butler and research assistant, so we can get some of our work in print."

How deeply into her mind could he see? "A good idea," she said. "Guy works now assisting Dr. Annabelle Carter Jackson, who just gave me a research grant to develop my theories of time—based on your work and Heidegger's. I'm sure he'll be excited at the idea of testing the theory by entering a new time frame."

"He could explain it to Carter Jackson as needing a leave in order to help you with your research," said Mead.

"I don't know if she'll go for it, but its sure worth a try," said Victoria.

"Could be she'll want to come along later as things progress," added Mead.

"Hmm, we'll see. That would be most interesting indeed," she said.

PART II
1930s CHICAGO

Chapter Thirteen
Victoria and George

Love is itself unmoving,
Only the cause and end of movement,
Timeless and undesiring,
Except in the aspect of time,
Caught in the fear of limitation,
Between being and non-being.
— T.S. Elliot, "Burnt Norton", *Four Quartets*

Her hand slid along her silky inner thigh and felt moisture. Waking up naked next to a man felt strange. She and Tom had slept separately, at his insistence. Even more amazing that George Herbert Mead made love with her last night. Funny, even after several months together, she still thought of him by all three names. The full moon glowed through the curtain on the white eiderdown. She looked up at the embossed ceiling and the cast iron chandelier. She loved its graceful lines and pastel flowers and leaves.

A gray mustached mouth opened out of a mound of linens. "Helen", George said, "my dear Helen". The eiderdown billowed as he rolled, groping for her waist, laughing softly.

Victoria sat up and shoved him away. Mistaking her for his former wife again. "Helen, always Helen".

"Oh, Victoria. I'm sorry, I was not awake."

"Helen is dead. Helen is Dead! Remember?"

"It depends upon which time frame you are in, darling,' he pulled her breasts against his chest. He looked into her eyes. "I've never been happier than I am with you. Thank the time gods for revealing their secrets to us." His voice was resonant.

"I feel ridiculous, jealous of a dead woman." Aware of her disheveled appearance, she ran her hands through her tangled hair.

"Who is dead and who isn't is all relative in our world," he said. His erect member pushed against her belly.

"Your ability to transcend time certainly enhances our lovemaking," she stroked his chest.

"Around you my erection is reminiscent of Nietzshe's 'eternal return',," he said thrusting himself into her.

She looked into his eyes, they kissed. Victoria's intense desire for Mead blurred in her mind with his ideas. She pictured him lecturing as they made love, his lectures infused with the power of famous philosophers he discussed.

She threw her legs around his waste, locked her ankles together. "Don't come yet, please. I want to hold you . . . I feel our souls meet inside me," she whispered in his ear.

Mead cleared his throat. "The idea of the soul is hazy romanticism. But your "I" definitely calls out a response in my "me." As we respond nearly identically to each other, our "I's" and "me's" fuse. Our 'selves' are united.

She laughed as she squeezed her hips and thighs. "You talk just like your books. I remember reading those words in *Mind, Self and Society*. In the 70's my students grasped the idea by called it "Mead's explanation for a natural high."

He kissed her neck.

"Yet as I gave the lectures that became that book, I didn't imagine an exalted state like ours, a blend of mental and sexual intercourse, physical and philosophical orgasms." He thrust himself deeper inside her.

"This exemplifies your theory of the four stages of the act: impulse, perception, manipulation, consummation."

Victoria stroked his back gently.

"Oh yes it does." He started in a whisper, "Impulse, I think of you." He looked up in the distance, smiling. He sniffed ths air, "Ah, your perfume, Perception, I sense that you are near." He stroked her breasts gently. They both said together, "Manipulation!"

He thrust his hips forward. "Watch out her it comes," Consummation!'"

"Wait a minute, my dear, remember you wrote that consummation has to be put off or even imagined, much of the time, in the real world," she stopped moving, and rolled on top of him.

"This is one of those wonderful exceptions," he rolled her back underneath him increasing the speed of their dance.

He pulsated inside her until they both called out, "Consummmation!"

"I never imagined such a delightful way to test my hypotheses!"

Victoria glanced at the foggy window from their heavy breathing. The moon had moved down and the first rays of dawn sent a golden glow over the eiderdown. As they fell back asleep she lay on her side next to him with one leg over his, rubbing his feet with hers.

The clock on the mantel sang its rounds then chimed seven as Victoria woke. Guy would bring their breakfast soon. It has been a challenge to convince Annabelle Carter Jackson to let Guy join her back in time. However, Annabelle was keen to see if time travel could allow for strategic interventions in historical events. In the small adjoining bathroom, which had running water, though cold, she washed her face with a bar of Yardley's lavender, one of the few reminders of her former life. She shook some Brother's tooth powder in her palm, added water and put it on her brush. It tasted good, like baking soda mixed with peppermint.

She took the soft linen cloth from the hook, held it under the faucet, warmed the cold cloth in her hands before wiping the sticky film from her thighs. She pinned up her hair. It was wonderful to be with a man who engaged with her mind as well and her body. How different from the other men she had known who she had unwittingly allowed to dominate countless conversations. Now this seemed like mental gang rape. Men expect, need women to admire them, to listen. Mead was the first to hear her voice.

She returned from the bathroom, holding her bone handled hairbrush in one hand, fresh color on her lips. "I'm going out for a walk by the lake" she said. Would you like to join me?"

He sighed. "I've got to prepare my lecture notes and get to the university". He sat up in bed, stretched his legs and yawned.

"You seem to have lost your enthusiasm about teaching," she said, stepping into a light grey skirt. At times she wished she could have brought her

Nikis and ran along the beach in Lycra Spandex. Yet she appreciated the elegance of the other walkers, gentleman in tweed slacks and sweaters, ladies in flowing skirts or occasionally "risqué" slacks. She topped her skirt with a cotton blouse.

"Actually, I am newly energized about teaching," he said.

She sensed a building diatribe, but it was cut off by three short knocks on the paneled door. Guy opened the door without waiting for a response, pushing in a mahogany tea cart.

"Very good, Guy, but next time wait until we answer." Mead pinched his eyebrows together looking at Guy.

Mead cleared his throat. "As I was saying, dear, a new form of behaviorism is looming its ugly head based on research with rats. These guys think that all knowledge is centered in the brain cells. To them there is no such thing as understanding and meaning, only stimulus and response." He walked towards his Kleiderschrank.

Victoria's neck tightened, sensing that Guy must be barely repressing a witty critique. "I'm ever so famished, Guy," she said. Guy slid the embossed linen cloth from the tray on top of the caddy, revealing a white porcelain teapot, its handle and cover laced with gold. His eyes sparkled. He played this role with energy and aplumb. Since he arrived as their butler/research assistant a month ago, their lives had indeed run more smoothly.

Guy bent down to open the door to the cabinet. Victoria noticed he stayed in shape despite his years a law school. His biceps pressed against his white sleeve as he worked with the tea set. Just noticing his male attributes was not the same as being attracted to him, she told herself.

She recalled Guy's jokes about Mead made in her classroom. "Dear Old George Herbert and his overwrought magnum opus, *Mind, Self and Society*. Should be "The Unstoppable Rambling of the Unending Conversation." The class broke into laughter, forestalling any rejoinder from her. When Guy cut Mead's work in front of the class it was she who bled.

Shaking off this memory she smiled as Guy placed the silver bowl with fresh lemon slices, blueberries, freshly baked scones, scrambled eggs and sausages on the serving tray, she thought to herself: "Indeed, he meant what he said years ago—I'd do anything to be with you."

Guy's eyes flashed, a look she couldn't decipher. His deep voice felt like a cat's purr on her belly, "Research on rat behavior offers rigorous empirical evidence supportive of their hypotheses, Sir, very carefully researched."

George's eyebrows rose. "Bah! Their underlying assumption is that learning takes place due predominantly to the firing of electric circuits in the brain—completely ignoring higher processes of reflective understanding which evolve only as significant symbols shared in communicative acts."

"Assumptions and the processes of critical reflection are very difficult to ascertain, let alone measure," Guy retorted.

"Which supports my argument. You used critical reflective processes to critique my statement."

Victoria's stomach knotted, hoping Guy would let it drop. She had been excited about him coming. Yet often times over the past month she wished he would just serve the tea and leave them in peace. Guy would be thinking: 'But how could you know anything that you can't observe, measure, or even accurately define!' She looked at Guy piercingly. He tilted his chin.

"Very good, Sir, and good luck in your debates."

She hoped George would miss the sweetness in Guy's voice, which bordered on sarcasm.

"Sir, Madam, There's something I do need to bring up with you." Guy laid out their breakfast plates with care.

"Now is as good as later," said Mead, raising his eyebrows.

"Very good, sir, and in keeping with your philosophy," he said, his tongue pushed up against the inside of his cheek. All three chuckled.

"Annabelle, Dr. Carter-Jackson, has been calling, demanding to know what's going on here," he said darkening the tone.

"Please convey that we are most pleased with your work, and that my research is moving along as expected," said Victoria.

Guy stood up taller. "You don't understand. She is insisting that either both of us, Victoria and I, that is, come back to the 1970s or we bring her here to see for herself."

Mead dropped his fork full of scrambled eggs. "Victoria, you must bring Dr. Jackson-Carter, I mean Carter-Jackson, here. I need you with me, in the flesh."

Victoria frowned, sipped her tea, and said, "Guy, please tell her I'm working on the mechanism and can't risk bringing anyone else yet. I'm not even sure how I got here or how we got you here. Tell her I'll try to come for a visit back, I mean forward, as soon as I can break away from the work."

"With all due respect, I've been saying things like that to her the past two weeks. I think it's best if you tell her yourself," said Guy, emphatically.

Guy poured them more tea. He inquired how long George would be away that day, glancing at Victoria when George said he would be gone until afternoon tea. Victoria said, "Guy, I'll be needing your assistance with a manuscript. He turned towards the door. "Very good, my lady, I'll be ready for your pleasure." His smile revealed even, symmetrical teeth. He quietly closed the door behind him.

"Sometimes I wish we had an ordinary butler," said George. "I don't feel like refuting arguments over breakfast, especially when you and I are in the middle of something."

"I'll speak to him. But it's useful to have a strict and well-read thinker handy," she said.

"He does keep us on our toes. I do wonder if he is a bit too handy."

"Darling, surely you're not worried. As you know, I always kept a clear boundary with my students," said Victoria. She picked up a scone, smearing it with butter and jam.

'Yes dear and I recall, too, how you had to convince him to allow us to refer to him as "Guy" and not "Santori." Mead pinched his forehead together as he picked up his cup of tea.

"Yes, he must have learned the butler role from watching Masterpiece Theatre on the BBC." Mead pinched his nose.

"That's the British Broadcasting Company. Perhaps that's how he learned to make good scones, from a show called 'Upstairs-Downstairs'."

"You forget that television was beyond my time." Mead poured more fragrant Earl Grey tea into both cups, and smiled as he handed her one. He put two sugar cubes in his cup, picked up a spoon and stirred it gently. "You were wonderful last night, Darling," he said.

Victoria caressed the delicate cup with her long fingers. The tea was perfect, robust and steaming. She held the cup near her face inhaling its fragrance. The china seemed to sing as she placed the cup back in the saucer.

"My dear, you and beautiful things create a sense of blissful presence."

She took a forkful of scrambled eggs. "Thank you, my dear, but my experiences in teaching present evidence to the contrary. We had rousing debates about the viability of your theory of democracy in my classes," said Victoria.

"I try to make love to you and you start in on theory again." Mead took a sip of tea.

"I know where your heart lies." She took a bite of scone, chewed heartily, then licked the jam from her fingers.

"It lies with you, darling, however, the philosophy of democracy is mostly John's," said Mead.

"John?"

"Surely you've read John Dewey," said Mead. "Great scrambled eggs."

"Oh, I forgot. He was, is, a friend of yours! But your own explication of democracy goes well beyond Dewey's. The beauty of your philosophy is that it is at once about science, ethics, and social evolution."

She sensed his pleasure in her reply as he reached for a round of sausage. "I can't tell you how wonderful it is to live with a woman who knows my work better than I do. I had forgotten my piece on democracy as axiology," said Mead. He nibbled at the thin sliver of sausage, then folded it and consumed it.

Perceiving their minds running parallel, she decided to risk a little naughtiness. "Axiology. That word has always brought chopping wood to mind, rather than the study of values."

"Are you calling me a woodchuck? I have better things to bite," said Mead bending forward across the small table and nipped at her neck. She smelled the garlic on his breath just as she tasted it in her mouth.

"Your making me spill my tea," she said, looking down at the brown tea soaking into her white linen napkin.

Mead got up and took her hand, leading her back to the bed. "I'll lick it clean, " he said.

❧

A while later, Victoria woke up again, to the sound of Tommy Dorsey's mello trombone, playing "Embraceable You." Their neighbor was hard of hearing and liked also like fresh air. The morning sun had turned the tops of the trees golden. She grabbed her robe from the bedpost, enjoying its soft comfort, then looked out the window. On the street below several boys wearing knickers were playing marbles. The clip-clop of horse hooves and clatter of empty bottles a milk truck made an intricate rhythm. The percussion section was augmented by the ringing bells on the bicycles of two women, their baskets filled with vegetables, skirts billowing as they pushed the peddles. She had never seen a street quite like this before coming to this time frame, except, of course, in the movies. Hearing Mead stirring she turned around.

"Perhaps we will be able to get completely dressed this time," he said, "but we shall need some fresh tea. On second thought, coffee." He struggled into his briefs, bleery eyed. Victoria noted how trim his physique.

Mead opened the door, "Guy, bring fresh coffee please. Just leave it by the door."

"Yes, sir, anything else? Is everything all right?"

"Yes, Guy, just the coffee, please."

Victoria was glad, not wanting them to be interrupted.

"We are so exquisitely united," said Mead, pulling on his trousers.

"I'd call us 'soul-mates' except you disavow the soul."

Looking into the mirror, he straightened his suspenders, reaching for his vest. He was thinking about what to say. Perhaps she had him. He cleared his throat. "We, you and I, had no unity until we began to converse. You read my thoughts when you read my books." He selected a soft wool tie from his closet, another near eternity of perhaps ten seconds. It was as if he'd never before articulated these thoughts that shot a bolt of pleasure through her. "My identity was based on these significant others and how they perceived me." He pulled the tie through his hands, and turned away from her to face the mirror as he tossed the tick end around his collar. "You, my darling, not only read my works but discussed them in seminars, presenting them at professional meetings."

Mead opened the walnut wooden case on his dresser and lifted out a gold pocket watch. Another thoughtful delay, as if he were savoring their exchanges. He looped the fob through his vest buttonhole. "You in turn taught me to your students. I became part of your "lifeworld" as you would say after your affair with Schutz." He adjusted his watch fob and began buttoning his vest.

"Don't be ridiculous, darling. Schutz died years ago, before I had even heard of him. But I do love his essay on Multiple Realities."

This time his response was instantaneous. "Not so silly of me to be jealous of a corpse, I was one too."

She laughed, though it seemed an odd, embarrassing response.

Two light knocks on the door. "Coffee is here, Sir, Madam." She heard Guy's footsteps retreat down the stairs. She opened the door and brought in the coffee tray with two steaming cups. They both preferred it with cream and Guy had fixed them just right. She put George's down on his dresser. He took a large sip. "Ah, just what I need."

She continued. "Certainly Schutz is an admirable fellow. He used his connections as an international banker to finance the escape from Nazi Germany of scholars, musicians and artists. But these events have not yet happened from where we are right now."

Mead fussed with his tie knot, then ripped it open and began again. "Perhaps you should have put Schutz' picture on your desk," he said.

She hesitated, wanting to get it right. "Way before I knew about Schutz' work, you were my intellectual hero. No one else explained how one gets to have a mind, a self." Brushing a wisp of hair off her forehead, she added, "Darling, I needed you to hold me all night to make up a little bit, for all those nights, years, without you."

He ripped open the knot again and barked at the mirror, "I haven't done this in years!" then to her,

"You had Tom, who you said reminded you of me. . . and those others," he said, his voice bitter.

She took a sip of coffee, enjoying its warmth and rich aroma. Knowing she needed the proper tone here, she wasn't sure what that would be, only that it must not mock or challenge. Perhaps chiding would work.

"Sex with Tom, when it occurred was as fleeting as getting bit by a fly. As you know, Tom, insisted that we maintain separate bedrooms. Then he proceeded to work all night most nights and sleep through the mornings when I was up working."

"A good arrangement for two scholars," Mead said.

Victoria bounced back a bit too quickly, she realized, with, "Especially if one of them was really in love with a dead male philosopher, writing and teaching about him most of the time."

George finished his coffee, and returned his cup and saucer to the tray. He walked over to her and kissed her cheek. "I wish I could have been there in person. Tom was the surrogate I could locate at the time. Wore decent clothes, smoked a pipe, wore a pocket watch, spoke perfect French, and even more importantly, kept you away from that Martin Heidegger!"

A chill went through her, immediately followed by the flame of anger. "Do not tell me you have not only been guiding my thoughts these years, but have been stage managing my life. Am I to believe that you concocted my marriage to a cold man out of jealousy? From your grave? That is ridiculous?"

"Actually from that photo frame," said Mead, finally getting his tie right, which to her seemed wrong.

She stared at the frame, which had been either on her nightstand or on a bookshelf facing her bed since her graduate school days. Her mind was unable to handle rage and incredulity simultaneously. It felt, well, mushy, as in childhood she endured lectures on Luther's Catechism.

"Have I not emerged from the photo, made love to you, and discussed philosophy in the interstices?" If that is possible, why not my influence over your years with Tom . . . and more?"

To that she had no answer, except to proceed.

Victoria walked up to Mead, and adjusted his tie. "There is something else I hold against Tom. Discouraged me from reading Heidegger's work for so many years!"

"He tried to discourage you, but he was not strong enough for my Victoria's Prussian stubbornness," Mead stood up with a rush of red in his cheeks. He put his hands on her shoulders. "Why do you persist in engaging with Heidegger?" . . . The veins popped out of the back of his neck. There was a lengthy silence. He spun around and put his back to her. He took his watch from his pocket, breathed deeply and said "I can't deal with this all now, my dear, I will be late at the university."

"I won't have the same argument I had with Tom over my appreciation for Heidegger. Besides, we were talking about Tom, who you apparently saddled me with who was alcoholic, oppressive, unfaithful, always complaining . . ."

"And," Mead interrupted, "knew every major work of philosophy, Eastern as well as Western, backwards and forwards, could discuss them, loved Kathy."

She was shaking with fury and yelled, "until she caught on to him, realized that his lengthy discourses were disguises to keep him from real discussion, and lost respect for him seeing all the beer cans he left pile up. . ." She was spent, arguing with a ghost who had made love to her about a husband who did so rarely and poorly. "Now," she thought, "he knows he has the upper hand, because I lost my temper and he can lay this at the bound feet of female irrationality."

Mead breathed deeply and walked to the bay window. The sound of Tomey Dorsey was replaced by a loud speech in German followed by cheers and "Sig Heils." He turned, looking at her with understanding. He's really able to live his idea that ethics involves 'taking the role of the other towards the self', this is the Mead I'm in love with, she thought.

"Victoria, Darling," his voice was resonant. "You are overwrought. I suggest you lie back for a while. I'll ask Guy on the way up to bring you fresh tea in a half hour. Then I suggest you go out for a walk, or arrange some flowers from the garden. You'll be able to settle into your work in a better frame of mind."

She found his words soothing, but was not ready to concede. "George Herbert Mead, do not patronize me!" She turned away from him and sighed.

"Darling, I just want you to have a productive and happy day. But now, I do have to get to work." Mead was back to his normally calm and commanding self. "And my dear, I urge you to give up your interest in Heidegger. All those things you admire about my work on democracy are anathema to him."

More pressure, but now she could handle it. "Heidegger is correct about the dangers and limits of democracy. The many can be wrong, and are susceptible to being misled by greed and worse, by demagogues."

"And, none," he said pointing out the window, "more dangerous than that pompous little leader of the German Nazis, Herr Hitler." He bent and kissed her gently on the cheek and walked out the door. His polished brown shoes pulled the sound out of the oak floor as if it were a giant sounding board, as he walked firmly down the hall and the stairs.

None more dangerous? she reflected. Stalin murdered more, and more were napalmed and killed in the Vietnam. And what about the millions of Native Americans who were killed by the American Calvary for the "manifest destiny" of settlers from Northern Europe? Still, Hitler becomes the arch evil leader of the twentieth century. Now she lived during Hitler's time. Perhaps in this version he would be thwarted.

Chapter Fourteen
A Band of Amazons

(The poet) is the pickpocket of reality.
Lawrence Ferlinghetti,

Victoria sat at her writing desk by the window. The carved walnut frame now held yellow toned photo of the two of them. Mead looked the same as always, a three piece suit, pocket watch, vibrant eyes and subtle smile. Victoria barely recognized herself in puffed sleeved white blouse and long flared skirt. "Dr. Victoria Von Dietz Mead and Dr. George Herbert Mead. No, Mr. and Mrs. George Herbert Mead, No, Victoria Von Dietz and husband, George Mead." The Chicago Sun Times had called asking to interview her for a story following the announcement of their marriage. She would have to make an issue out of it if she wished to retain her name under the picture. Best not to make a fuss. Her name and professional identity could come out in the article. There would be questions about her parents, family, who were at that time actually younger than her. Time simultaneity does have its complications. She would answer close to the truth except skip a genera-tion. . ."Victoria Von Dietz is a cousin of Augusta and Friedrich Von Dietz of Milwaukee."

She felt protected with Mead, safe. Despite her feminist convictions, his paternalism was pleasing. She couldn't justify it, but it made her feel secure, loved, beautiful and sexy." She was indeed subdued. When such feelings washed over her, she realized that the discourses and challenges of feminism could be easily foregone when one enjoyed the privileges of a revered upper middle class wife. Feminist advocacy could lapse into coquetry, courting, charging into the gender fray for the sake of being overcome, not defeated, but treasured. As she sunk back into her chair, dozing, a familiar vision floated into her mind:

A band of women are ready for battle, each wearing shades of red, robust, strong. Horsewomen, archers, machine gunners, spear throwers, singers, followers and students of Bruhnhilde's courses in defense and aggression. They ride their horses without need of bit or saddle. Tired of being controlled and used by husbands, fathers, lovers, brothers, they forged a life by themselves in the forest. Training, working, hunting, cultivating fields of amaranth, soybeans, wheat and rye, husbanding the milk of Guernsey cows, celebrating the coming of fall by hunting venison, caped with buffalo skins dyed red from the leaves of desert paint brush and beet roots. Beautiful and hearty, this band of Amazons are convinced of their invincibility. Their Utopia is ruptured when they see signs of another onslaught of men from an outlying land, having gotten wind of them, coming to rape, take them as spoils. They are safe only so long as they remain anonymous. The battle is engaged, the women stave off the marauders with cunning and skill, winning in battle when they can, retreating and hiding when they feel outnumbered. They followed these dictates of Mao with success for fifteen years. However, one day dressed in their finest warrior garb, astride great steeds, ancestors of the Prussian horses which defeated Napoleon, they see their own sons atop similar horses on the opposite hillside. The sun rises behind these noble youths, sons schooled by the mothers in their arts and talents, now fully-grown young men.

The women did not think it possible that their darling little boys would ever rebel, not against this ideal matriarchy, which anticipated and met their every desire! The women's band fostered each child according to his or her talents and temperament. Only one desire of their sons could neither be met nor conquered— the desire for power, modeled so perfectly by their mothers. Travelers' rumors of their banished and abandoned fathers' accomplishments intrigued them. They resented being kept from the mysterious world of men, who they glimpsed as they rode in search parties, looking for the women. As they approach, the women see the sons clad in deep royal blue, dyed from the roots of beets mixed with the musky blue roots of English Mugwort. They carry trumpets of brass and, oddly, saxophones. Their herald has announced them with a wailing tenor saxophone solo, opening with Siegfried's theme, then becoming a fugue. They have shining brass shields and spears their own height. The women warriors, their own mothers and sisters, are stunned at the power and majesty of their young male beauty, the brilliance of their brass and saxophone chorus. At once they know the physical battle is all over before it has begun. Even were the youths not more physically powerful, the women could not ruthlessly attack and kill their own sons and brothers.

Horses whinney and snort, their instinct to turn tail, gallop away. The women hold reins, stand their ground. Spears and shields clatter, clash.

The High Mother first, then one by one all the mothers drop their weapons to the ground. They are hypnotized by the song of the sons, which is also the song of the Sun rising behind them on the hillside. One by one, the women dismount, their long hair gliding down the backs of their great mares and stallions. They begin to dance and sing to the music, spinning and turning in a chorus of release and joy, and yes, agony, despair. Their queendom, their separation, is all over.

Below a bleating claxon and a broken down mare pulling an ice cart whinnying startle Victoria awake. Goose bumps shimmer up her arms. Victoria felt shaken from the dream, whenever it occurred. And worse now that it had come in her shift to Mead's time world. . Women had just barely achieved the franchise. The struggle of women like Jane Addams and her friends, including Mead, had made it possible. But wages and opportunities for women still lag, and women and their children bear the brunt of the high rate of poverty in the nation.

She stood from her desk having written nothing and went to the window. Her hand stroked the maroon velvet drape as if it were a stallion's mane. The mixture of horses and cars was something that would soon vanish, the machines winning. Victoria could walk over to Hull House with Mead and he could introduce her to Jane Addams. What a tigress Addams must be, yet she was eloquent and soft spoken. Victoria wondered if George would stop by on his way home from the university to speak with Jane. Would he tell her about his new wife? Was he still in love with Addams? He used to live at Hull House and worked with her. A rush of agony filled her belly as she imagined Tom embracing his young student lover. But George was not Tom. Mead was a man of character who adored her. Why wait for George to introduce me? Her resolve formed so quickly, she spoke it. "I'll walk over to Hull House and introduce myself. I could use the fresh air and the exercise." Although if she was so certain, what need was there for a rationale?

She walked downstairs, put on her soft wool brown coat from the hall closet, noticing with regret its fur collar. This is pre-PETA days, she reminded herself, and the collar would be comforting if the winds shifted this warm fall afternoon. Guy came to the door.

"Going out?" he asked, raising his eyebrows.

"Just for a bit of air." She didn't wish to reveal her intent to meet Jane Addams.

"I'll go with you. Hyde Park is not safe for a woman alone," said Guy, his deep hazel eyes were warm, his voice resonant."

She almost accepted. But no, their relationship was already ripe with ambiguous boundaries.

She laughed. "This isn't the 1970s when the Blackstone Rangers competed with other gangs for turf beneath the high rise welfare warehouses." Victoria put her hand on the doorknob.

"But immigrants from countries at war with each other in Europe compete for knickle-a-week jobs in the steel mills and unemployed young men shoot crap in the streets," he retorted.

"I need you more here to complete editing the manuscript I gave you yesterday."

Guy placed his hand on top of hers and opened the door. "If you insist, Madam," he said.

Lake Michigan wind pushed against her as she walked down the cement steps of their home, one of several brick and limestone mansions between the lake and the University of Chicago. In Victoria's student days in the 1970s they had devolved into student apartments, rooming houses, and offices for non-profits and bail bonds officers. Today in 1935, it felt safe to walk around the neighborhood, especially in the daytime, or at least so she told herself.

Victoria greeted a lady who lived down the block and who walking her small white dog with its square black nose. A young woman with a tweed coat pushed a baby in a perambulator. The baby struggled to free himself from the mounds of covers.

The elegant homes designed by Frank Lloyd Wright had not yet been built. Instead, small frame homes with well cared for gardens, surrounded by low ornate wrought iron fences, burnt orange and fuzzy yellow daisy faces shown through the bars. A young woman with a full-length apron over her dress swept a brick walkway. Victoria turned a corner and there it was, Hull House, a three story brownstone mansion. It was already famous, yet announced itself only through an unimposing carved wood sign hung over the ornate mail slot.

Victoria stood in front of the walkway, as if the property, land and building were haunted. Her feelings were out of sync with the prosaic comings and goings. Small boys in knickers shot marbles on the wide front walkway, while several girls jumped rope. They seemed to understand each others' cries and commands, even though they occurred in Italian, Irish brogue, Spanish, and some Eastern European tongue.

Victoria gazed up at the tall windows fronting the house. Through lacey curtains, she saw a beautiful woman with auburn hair bend down, then rise with a boy in her arms with a stumped arm in a cast. The boy clung to her with his only hand. The woman looked familiar. It was Jane! She'd seen her picture in a book of her writings. She recalled Jane's powerful appeal for child labor laws and workman's compensation. Too late to help that little one, who may have lost his arm working on the line. Victoria took a step onto the walkway when she saw Mead approach Jane, smiling at the child in her arms, then at her. They stood close, signaling familiarity. Victoria turned and hustled home, chiding herself for lack of nerve. Mead would have been glad to see her, to introduce her, she was certain. Well, perhaps not so sure. Why did she feel like a spy, intruder? She felt like the other woman.

Chapter Fifteen
Mead Embraces Jane Addams

There are indications that the human consciousness is reaching the same stage of sensitiveness in regard to war as
that which has been attained in regard to human sacrifice.
In this moment of almost universal warfare there is envi-
sioned a widespread moral abhorrence against war.
Jane Addams, *Challenging War*

When Victoria arrived home she went immediately upstairs to the bedroom. She unlaced her soft leather walking shoes and rubbed her feet.
The sides of her big toes were red and swollen. Those summers while in college walking around on three-inch heels, working as department store model
were taking their toll. Guess the sins of the future stayed with my body here in
the past, she thought. Taking off her skirt and sweater, Victoria slipped into her
white soft wool robe. She lay down on the large four-poster bed.

Seeing Jane Addams even through a window thrilled her. Victoria had
allowed Addams' work to remain at the periphery for years. Why had she
been ignoring it? Only recently had she embraced Jane Addams' work. It was
as if she'd stubbed her toe on a gold nugget. Remarkable that Jane, a daughter of a successful miller in a small rural community would move to the inner
city to work with immigrants and laborers, for children and women's rights.

Her mind flashed to the image through the window, Mead putting his
arm around Jane, Jane welcoming him. She was bothered, edging toward
angry with him for visiting Jane and not taking her along. Certainly he would

not be tempted. Both Jane and George were old, although he didn't seem so last night in bed, or anytime for that matter. People connect from inside anyway, not with the eyes.

Her green envy toward Jane turned to red anger towards herself. Why had she spent all those years writing about Mead's thoughts, ignoring Jane's? In the past few months, living near Hull house, Victoria read Addams' work. Why hadn't it been assigned in seminars in her graduate training? Why hadn't she assigned it to her students? Was it because Addams' writing was clear and pertinent to immediate needs and problems? Academics make careers out of deciphering poorly written texts. Addams' work spoke for itself.

Three knocks at the door. Victoria stretched and got up. Guy came in with a tray of tea and small sandwiches, which he set on George's dresser. The tray held two cups and saucers and enough sandwiches for a small party, though Guy would know that George had academic senate on Thursday afternoons. "I thought I would join you," Guy said.

Not 'might', certainly not an inquiry to join her. Before she could object he poured the fragrant tea into both cups and popped a sandwich wedge into his mouth. He carried both cups to the window ledge where she stood. There was no room on the ledge for the sandwich plate and no other nearby surface for it to be placed. He was clearly hungry, as was she, but she would not move from the window. Let Guy figure out the logistics.

"So, how was your walk?" he said before gulping down the chewed remnants. He was crude and too familiar and wore a thin layer of insolence like a tight undershirt. Immediately she regretted her assessment, realizing that Jane Addams would have thought none of it. Instead, she'd likely have appreciated the efforts of a boy from South Dakota attempting to be a butler and research assistant to pay off his law school debts. When Guy was her student she had considered it quirky, even charming as it came with some interestingly fresh insights clearly not culled from academic mulling. Now she realized that what was enlivening a few hours a week in a classroom could be annoying or worse in one's home. At least he could also play the butler role perfectly.

Victoria paced a triangle from her bed to the window to the bookcase, lined now with Addams' works, grabbing and devouring a sandwich along the way.

"Mrs. Mead", he said as if it were a falsely formed substitute for her first name, "Although you didn't assign Addams, I read about her in an American history class, taught by Agnes Borphy, that feminist friend of yours. Jane Addams, in the book you have right there on your shelf, "Peace and Bread in a Time of War," advocated the nationalization of munitions factories. She felt that private companies were pushing for the election of war-oriented representatives. Did you know she was the first woman to receive the Nobel Peace Prize?" said Guy.

"Yes, of course, and from where we are today, just a few years ago," said Victoria, a bit defensively. She continued, "I love the way she wrote in the first person, direct, powerful, free of jargon and philosophical twists and turns. Does this make her less profound than the men, the academic philosophers, like John Dewey, like my husband?" Picking up his dirty socks from under the bed compromises the emotional impact, she found herself thinking. She felt hot in her wool robe.

"You are preaching to the choir," said Guy.

"I'm sorry, I can get on a horse about such things." She sipped from her tea, which already had lost much of its heat. "Jane is old now, but gloriously beautiful. Even seeing her through the window as I just did she radiates energy and light." Why was she telling Guy this rather than discussing Jane Addams' ideas, her work at Hull House? She sat down in her chintz-covered chair.

"She's a good horse to ride. People, nations, would be wise to pay her heed, especially about canceling the debts of the World War I. If only folks could know the debts would lead to a world wide depression and push the Germans to a 'savior' like Hitler," said Guy. He poured more tea for them both and even brought the sandwich plate to her, helping himself to a few more. He sat in the blue winged-back chair facing her. The tang of liverwurst on rye burst on her tongue.

"George spoke out about that danger," she said, taking a sip of tea.

"By the way, I heard Thorstein Veblen lecture at the university last night, on 'conspicuous consumption'. He portrayed the American wife as status display and consumer who enhances her husband's social standing. With the exception of a few serious students the audience held swarms of well dressed women, swooning even as he insulted them, falling over each other to speak with him afterwards." He took a wedge and drowned it in tea. He chewed and sipped as if it were hard-boiled eggs and beer at the corner tavern.

"Yes, but not for long. He gets in trouble with the university administration. An affair with the wrong wife." Victoria's eyebrows raised. Her mouth curved upward at the corners.

Guy chuckled."What a blast being from the future and seeing it unfold in real time before the players understand," said Guy. "The fact that he is popular with their wives gives the university drones a good excuse to ignore the way Veblen's work slams the sneaky hand of business interests interfering in the university." Taking a sip of tea, his eyes looked at Victoria as if he were sinking into quicksand.

"Are there no women in your life, Guy?" It would have been appropriate to add "to spoil or dominate" although she regretted opening that door in the first place. "Have you met anyone you care about, fell in love with?" she asked, unable to stop herself. She starred at the rose painted inside the teacup.

Guy put his hands on his knees, as if he were going to stand up. She hoped he would not stand, right there, directly in front of her. She got up, stood by the window, the glass radiating the sun's warmth.

Guy stood behind her, placing a hand on the back of her shoulder, reaching over what had seemed like an abyss between them. She noticed again the large black stone in the gold ring he wore on his right hand. The back of his hands were covered with dark brown fuzz. He dug his fingers into her shoulder, then dropped his hand. Her stomach fluttered uncomfortably. She was grateful she didn't have to ask him to step back.

"I've met lots of women. Some of them nice, often beautiful. But unlike you, none of them ever said anything I could remember the next week, or would want to remember." The sound of footsteps on the stairs startled her, whatever had made that moment, now unmade by the approaching steps.

His words thrilled, despite her better judgment. "Another woman lives just a few blocks away whose words you really remember, Jane Addams."

Mead walked in. He removed his jacket. "Warm afternoon." He kissed Victoria on the cheek. "Speaking of Jane, I saw you looking up at the window in front of Hull House this afternoon, Victoria. Why didn't you come in?"

"I'll get another cup, Sir," Guy said, slipping back into the formal role.

"A shot of brandy with mine, please," said Mead.

Guy left and Victoria turned towards Mead.

"I didn't want to push my way in like a jealous wife hunting down her man. Jane is quite beautiful. I wonder why she wrote about herself as plain and deformed. Her eyes are deep, her cheeks and chin strong, her bearing elegant. I would have wrung the bell and introduced myself, under ordinary circumstances. But then when I saw you beside her, I felt like an intruder."

Mead sighed deeply. "We didn't anticipate such confusions when we cracked into this time fold, he said. "I admit I wanted to get closer to Jane back in our former lives. But things are different now you are here."

"Does she know where I came from?" asked Victoria.

"No, I'll leave that up to you to explain when you meet," said Mead.

"Jane and I have lots to talk about," said Victoria, walking to the sandwich tray. She picked up another liverwurst and held it up to George's mouth.

After swallowing he said, "She is known as 'Miss Addams' to all but her closest friends."

"Good God, a leader of women's suffrage using that anachronism," said Victoria.

"Keep mind of this time frame and its protocols. For educated women of the these times, even a meager title is a badge of honor," said Mead."

"From what I hear around the neighborhood, Miss Addams is also called 'St. Jane'. At a time like this we need all the saints we can find," said Victoria.

"Hitler is already showing signs of putting Jews and anyone he doesn't like into the camps. Soon he will be expelling Jewish intellectuals from their jobs. We must see if our foreknowledge can provide some special powers to intervene," said Mead.

Chapter Sixteen
Letter from Martin Heidegger

Time is not to be found somewhere or other like
a thing among things, but in ourselves.
Martin Heidegger, *On Freedom*

Martin Heidegger, young and swarthy, too aware of his recent fame for his work, *Being and Time*, sits in his study by a fireplace in his cabin in the Bavarian highlands, with his childhood friend, Fetzer, a Bremen shipping magnate. Heidegger stands and reaches to the top of a bookshelf for two dimpled glass beer steins, their handles overlaid with stamped pewter. He picks up a large napkin from the tray on the walnut library table and wipes each to displace the dust that would have settled in them. He hands one to Fetzer. Heidegger fills them both from the pitcher pouring straight down to build a vigorous head. He sips, then rests his stein on one of the student term papers littering the table between Fetzer and himself. Pulling a large handkerchief from the pocket of his lederhosen, he wipes the foam from his think dark moustache. Fetzer cradles his beer stein as if it were a snoozing lap dog.

"Let me tell you, Mein Freund, about die schoene Frau Dr. Von Dietz Mead," said Heidegger holding his stein up to appreciate the golden beer.

"Ich seht Ihre zu Chicago last month. I spoke at a philosophy conference. Her husband ist Professor George H. Mead. I met this fellow when he was in Deutschland years back as a student of Herr Wundt. I was asked to present a critique on the so-called philosophy Americans have called "pragmatism.""

He slammed his stein on the table on that last word, slopping beer onto some of the student papers.

Fetzer raised an eyebrow and pursed one side of his lips.

"That is simply fancy talk about people doing what works!" continued Heidegger, again lifting his stein and taking a long drink. He swallowed and laughed, which Fetzer echoed. "Wouldn't it be wunderbar if that was really what people did," said Fetzer. "All this goose-stepping and parading these days does nothing to bring bread to the table. Germany cannot continue to pay war debts and survive. Our scientists and musicians and intellectuals are leaving the country. How can we maintain our unsurpassed culture? But now tell me more of your beautiful Frau Dr. Mead."

"Ah, if she were only mine instead of being wasted with Mead. She sat across from me at dinner that evening and spoke of her hometown, Milwaukee, to keep Herr Mead and I from spitting Bratwurst at each other. The wurst was surprisingly good, so I didn't think of it. She has been nourished by true Duetsche delicacies—the very best—since childhood, which explains the glow of her creamy skin, her bright blue eyes, her flaxen hair."

"My friend, even for a German romantic you embellish. Certainly it is her genes more than a diet of sauerbraten and red cabbage," said Fetzer.

"Nein, nein," said Heidegger, leaning forward. "These Nazis think too much of their gametes and zygotes when it is food and art that makes culture. These sustained her through significant periods of growth. She is, moreover, brighter than my best student, Hannah Arendt, and taller, more beautiful, the Aryan ideal, not stubby and bewhiskered, but fair with high cheekbones and sweet rosy lips. Her voice is gentle, high pitched and clear, her eyes blue-green, like the Rhein in summer. I imagine even her pubic hair is fine and light colored. Her legs and arms, also her underarms have only the lightest, dewy golden web. 'Komen Sie, meine liebschen, Ich schriebe. Komst Du hier un mit mir dormer und geschalften uber die longer kalten Nacht. Und sie auch einen beliebt mein arbeiter – das ist die Dasein unber alles Daseinen.' "

"Ach, aber Martin, Miene Freund, vas about Frau Heidegger, Elfride, Was willst Ihre Saght, vas gehts Ihr macht Nicht?" said Fetzer, taking a long slug of ale.

"Sie Mache Ihre way nur den Kinder, und Dei Schule und Kirche. My wife's always busy with the kids, fussing with the house, the maid, not much with me. We no longer sleep in the same bed. What about divorce? Elfriede is Einer Catholich Romanish. I would have to get a dispensation from Rome! Besides, Dr. Victoria is married now to one of my arch philosophical enemies, Professor George Herbert Mead." Heidegger said the name as if it forked his tongue.

"Don't tell me these excuses," said Fetzer, "like so many couples, you have fallen into a pattern of comfort. Comfort and practicality has little to do with Romance. They are, in fact, anathema. But meanwhile, you go on dreaming and your life's ultimate destiny and fulfillment eludes you. Isn't this what your existentialist philosophy is all about, accepting your mortality, go for the truths of the here and now," said Fetzer.

"That is the bastardized French version, promulgated by that young pretender, Sartre. Of course we must make choices. We must also accept our finitudes, the worldly limitations of the situation we are thrown into. Ah, but in the meantime let me tell you more of Frau Dr. Von Dietz Mead," said Heidegger, once more lifting his stein.

"When I saw this woman eat, how she ate, what she ate, what she would not touch, I realized she must be mine and return to Germany. This Queen of Prussia—stolen by forces of oppression and evil from a land saved from Napoleon by her great grandfather, a general under Kaiser Wilhelm. Wrested away to the American West, where her great grand parents built a wonderful village and there they replicated the life and cuisine of Prussia. The little place, 'Milwaukee", in the language of the Chippewa, the aboriginals, means the joining of three rivers. And the bakeries: Gastreich's, Heinneman's, Muerer's, all Duetsche bakeries, and the meat market, Vic and Al's, two Bavarian butchers, she grew up on their sausage and that of the great sausage maker, Usinger's. In these bakeries, and from her grandmother's own oven came Café Kucken, Gebrachen, Stollen, Fefernizzen, and served on lovely white linen table cloths, boiled and carefully hung in the morning sunshine."

"You'd best catch your breath, Martin, before you have a heart attack from your ecstatic imaginings of such food and of this goddess," said Fetzer.

"I nearly did have a heart attack with such food and that woman at one sitting. But I long to take such risks!"

Heidegger rose and laid his hands behind his back, walked up to the paned windows and looked out at the giant evergreens on the Bavarian mountainside. In the foreground several cows grazed, their bells clinking as they moved. The clouds overhead followed them across the meadow. Heidegger turned to face Fetzer.

"Now this once beautiful Prussia, the crown of Germany, is lost, lost to the homeland, taken over by Poland, part of the Versailles Treaty between the Western Allies and the Soviet Union. And what was lost was more than the land, but the lovely village way of life. Now it is all lost, this German star of the North, its brightest and purist sucked either to the Russians or to the distant America to be ground into Milwaukee sausage and the American advertising industry. She, my Queen, my Victoria, must return to her homeland, to live in my arms, enfolded in them on this hillside of the Rhine, me from the Suderland and Ihre von dem Nordlund! Die Zwie und Eternal Eins, muchten Sie Kom Gut Heim."

Fetzer adjusted his thick cable knit sweater over his brown woolen trousers tucked into mid-calf leather boots. He emptied his stein, sighed, then asked, "Was Dist Du Ihre Essen BeSehen?"

Heidegger's chest filled as he prepared to continue his tribute to food and to Victoria, "fresh fish baked in a bed of salt flown in from the Adriatic and filleted delicately, sprinkled lightly with Gewürztraminer, then pepper, a small amount only, freshly ground. This was her favorite luncheon dish."

"I am famished, ausgehungert," said Fetzer.

Heidegger stood in front of the window, ignored his friend, and continued: "I observed her also at lunch at the conference. She loves also sprouted mung beans sprinkled lightly over a radicchio salad. She insists it be finished with a sprinkling of emerald colored olive oil, and how she adores desert! Chocolate she holds in her closed mouth, moving her tongue over it slowly until it melts. She smiles, as she tastes each new delight. I imagine at home she eats always from joyful pottery painted by south Italians. Perhaps also she eats from China so delicate it sings when you touch it with fork or spoon.

"This wonderful Frau Dr. Professor Von Dietz, when does she arrive?" asked Fetzer.

"The conference is in two months, which will seems like years," said Martin.

"Herr Professor Mead will forbid her to come, if he has any sense," said Fetzer.

He may come with her, but he won't stop her," said Heidegger.

❧

After George left for the university Victoria sat at her desk, inlayed desk with lapis lazuli, the philosopher's stone, and orange and green jade. Mother of pearl in delicate floral patterns edged each drawer. Gold pen in hand she opened her notebook in which was her essay on the theory of emergent time, for which the editors *Philosophical Quarterly* awaited as the opening piece in the issue they were calling "21st Century Philosophy." But she couldn't concentrate. Her mind was fixed in this new life with Mead and why she had been fascinated with his ideas.

"I am fulfilled and happy as I never have been," she mused. I know now why Mead's ideas fascinated me. He liberated me by showing me how I came to be who I am. Why I felt such restlessness, being brought up in the Lutheran church, and with a mother who, lets face it, had her problems. George's theory helped me see how I had absorbed the teaching of my parents and older sister and taken in some things which helped me grow and others which blinded me.

Victoria rose and went to the window gazing down on the elms lining the rain-soaked street. "I made my place in a family filled with conflict as the one who exists in order to heal, to take care of, to make better, to soak up the anger of the larger ones, the ones who hollered so much with such loud voices."

Through memory, Victoria's shoulders stung. Hit, hit, hit, smash, her mother hitting her shoulders as she tried to escape around the dining table, then scuttled down to her place of safety behind the living room sofa wedged against the wall. She rubbed her neck. I must finish this project! The vision of Annabelle Carter Jackson came to Victoria, so much like her own mother—large, fearful, obsessed—albeit black. She wants the completed theory, though she might be appeased with a progress report. I have made progress, though to see it she would have to follow me back in time seventy years. She could not yet explain how she had come to be here, or how she was able to bring Guy backwards to join her. Victoria would need to visit the future soon or Annabelle may cut off her funds.

A familiar knock at the door.

"Come in, Guy", she said.

He came in softly, unsmiling, tense.

"Your mail, Madam." He placed a silver tray on the side of her desk. His hand quivered slightly. Through the light brown hair the back of his hands glistened with sweat. She could feel his tension.

"Special delivery, from Germany. Return address University of Freiberg, with Professor Heidegger's, handwritten signature above it.

"Heidegger!" she exclaimed, unable to curb her excitement. "A letter from Martin!"

"He will want you to come to Germany." Guy's lower jaw opened and shut twice though he held his lips tightly together. His countenance was muddy as he stood by the desk, waiting for her to open the letter.

She said to herself: "I will not open the letter until he leaves. I want to feel it fully myself." Her heart began to pound.

"You must talk to Annabelle about this. She will need to approve travel. Anyway, she is insisting you come to see her at once," said Guy.

His breath audible, Guy bent forward and brushed the letter with his palm, as if it needed dusting.

She pushed him aside, "Go to the library and call Annabelle. She expects a report. Tell her I'll deliver it in person. Also, check the references in my report draft." As he stood up she handed him a manuscript from the side of her desk.

"Let me open the envelope," he said, almost begging. He reached into his pants pocket and pulled out a swiss pocketknife which he pried open.

Victoria slapped her hand over the letter. "Guy, you know I appreciate how you always do this with bills, but not with letters. And you've already done the bills. Now I must get to work."

She turned her back to him and held the letter in both hands. She heard his knife snap shut. "And Guy, say nothing to Annabelle about the letter."

"Yes, Dr.," he said closing the door behind him.

Her hands quivered as she sliced the envelope's edge with George's opener, a miniature military sword complete with tassel. "Why am I so anxious?" she said aloud, then took a long, slow breath to affect a measure of calm.

The linen stationery reminded her of the finely woven shirts her father loved. Even more so, as she caressed the envelope, she glanced at the stamps—one an image of Kaiser Wilhelm the other a black four-armed cross with a wreath around it on a black background. She blew on the slit and the envelope's sides opened. With the tips of her pink pearl fingernails she pulled the letter free. For a moment it felt like a birthing. But she wasn't ready to be fixed by its words.

She caressed the letter with her thumbs. It felt like one of her father's folded handkerchiefs. Her first ironing lesson, as a girl of three with her little ironing board and tiny iron that really plugged in was with her father's handkerchiefs. They were of fine white cotton with embossed strips around the edges. She helped her mother sprinkle and roll them so they would carry just the right amount of moisture to be ironed. Then she would carefully folded until it as she ironed to be the correct size for Daddy's pocket.

Heidegger's letter smelled of pine and spruce, echoing the depths of the Black Forest from which it came. The paper made a lovely soft cracking sound as she unfolded it. What secrets may a man wipe on his handkerchief? She opened the letter.

She began to tremble, breathe faster. Her eyes went liquid, lingering on every word . . .

"My Dear Frau Dr. Professor Victoria Von Dietz:
Hello, my dear Friend."

Friend, she thought. This is not a word taken lightly in Germany. And based only on that one conversation across the table at dinner. She read on:

"I hope this letter finds you in good health, your work glowing with your inner flame, your surroundings reflecting your welcoming smile. Should your schedule permit, I would be honored if you come to Freiberg this October to present a lecture at a conference on current trends in the philosophy of time. Your contribution would be of great importance to our colleagues from all across Europe who will be attending.

Preceding and following the lecture, I would be pleased to escort you to nearby places, treasures of my homeland where the Spirit of Being surges through the valleys and moves directly to the core of my soul. Should your schedule permit you to stay for extended work on your manuscript, we could consult together as it progresses.

Yours, in truth and admiration,
Martin Heidegger"

He had begun the letter in impeccable formality, and ended it with statements that echoed those elements in his work that she found so captivating. He had plummeted down to primordial wellsprings, allusions to nature, to darkness, moist places, the deepest corners of the human heart and soul, to the forest. Still trembling, with cool perspiration on her upper lip, she felt like shouting for joy. She rose unsteadily and felt moisture between her thighs.

Chapter Seventeen
Victoria Meets Miss Addams

"We may either smother the divine fire of youth or we
may feed it. We may either stand stupidly staring as it sinks
into a murky fire of crime and flares into the intermittent
blaze of folly or we may tend it into a lambent flame with
power to make clean and bright our dingy city streets."
— Jane Addams, The Spirit of Youth and the City Streets

That afternoon on her walk Victoria saw the same woman with the baby
carriage–but today it was warm and sunny. The baby was howling, trying to kick off the voluminous covers. His mother tucked him in tighter, her
brown hair bisecting her face. Victoria tried to return the woman's smile.

"Roger, keep those covers on, you'll get a chill." She glanced at Victoria
again and said, "Ornery, just like his father."

"Likely to become a woman hater as well," Victoria wanted to say, but
instead said: "He is so handsome. He resembles you as a matter of fact. By
the way, I read in the *Ladies' Home Journal* that a doctor had done a study that
warned against keeping babies too constricted. He recommended light covers, allowing babies to kick their legs and wave their arms. It improves their
circulation and makes them stronger." Victoria hoped she didn't read the
journal as this research was actually done in the 1960s.

"Is that so? But I went to a babycare class over at Hull House, you know,
and the wonderful lady there instructed us on tucking in the blankets so the
babies wouldn't kick them off and catch a cold. She said a French woman, a

scientist, Madam Curie, had discovered invisible germs that carry sickness so not to cough on your hands and then hold your baby. Lots of babies around here don't make it to their second year."

"Was it Jane, I mean Miss Addams, who taught it?" asked Victoria.

"No, another lady who lives there, a Dr. Hamilton." said the woman. She reached down to tuck Roger in again who had struggled out of his covers. Victoria thought maybe the struggle out of the covers would strengthen him more that just kicking in the air.

"Oh, Alice Hamilton," said Victoria.

"You know Hull House ladies by their first names. You must be one of their friends."

"They are friends of my husband, Dr. Mead," said Victoria as the woman pushed the stroller down the curb.

Victoria had an urge to run, settling for a brisk walk, breaking into an occasional jog as the neat houses turned to tenements.

"Running away from someone?" said a man closing in behind her. Victoria cast a look over her shoulder. The man had cracked yellowish skin. He wore a thick wool jacket and a round hat with a visor.

"Excuse me," she turned quickly away. The man followed her and grabbed her by the elbow. He smelled of cigar smoke and bacon grease.

"I'll escort you, or drive you, Miss. I have a car parked in the next block. He squeezed her elbow and smirked. Victoria pulled away, walking fast.

"I'm quite all right if you please," she said.

"Sugar, you are more than all right. Scouting for the professional guys, huh? All the hookers try this, but there aren't many of us to go around. Best take me while you can. The running is a sure come-on. You know men, the sense of the chase. Your running makes me hot."

He walked so close behind her that she could smell his whiskey-tinged breath. He reached his arms around her waist and pulled her towards him.

"Get lost, or I'll scream for the police," growled Victoria. "My husband is a professor at the University of Chicago. You'll be put in jail if you don't let me go at once."

The man's upper lip curved down in a wide bow. "Yeah? What professor lets his wife go running the streets alone? Besides, it's no crime to use a whore, just to be one. If you scream, I'll tell the cops you solicited me. You'll be in the clinker before you know it." Her wrist burned as he squeezed and twisted it.

"I'll bet you make a lot of money with what's laced up in there." He brushed his free hand over her breast. Victoria looked for help. The woman with the pram was gone and no one else was in sight for over a block. She jerked around and gave him a karate chop to the back of his neck and a knee kick to his crotch. As he bent forward moaning she ran, turning the corner to Halstead breathless with rage. A few more blocks and her heart rate went down. "Thank god I took that women's self defense course," she said.

She thought of how the species had degenerated since women lost power, eons ago. Men freely indulge their base instincts and women become whores to survive, whether on fulltime lease as housewives, or by the hour on the streets. "What are you now but a kept woman, a housewife?" she asked herself. As was her tendency, she thought of additional failings, such as leaving Kathy in the future.

She tried to combat her self-criticism. But Kathy is better off there. Growing up is hard enough without trying to do it in two time zones. She recalled Kathy's tears when Victoria told her she'd be traveling on important work, and could only come to see her once in a while.

Kathy loved her school and had lots of friends and her grandmother nearby. In the meantime she had discovered a way to run a parallel emotional course with Kathy. She always knew how Kathy was doing, even from a distance. It had begun when Kathy was in her womb. Perhaps when Kathy was ready for high school she could come to Victoria in whatever year she was living and, if Kathy wanted, she might even stay. The Vietnam war raging, the protests growing; the Chicago Seven had recently burned draft records in front of the federal building streets. But would she want her child here, with Hitler and World War II on the horizon?

Only recently she had come to understand her own time travel. At first she'd seen it as turning a corner. But time was more like a page upon which events—human geologic, weather, knowledge—are written. The page is, or can be, folded in infinite ways. When it is folded just so, a person can step, leap, and slide from one time frame to another. A question remaining in Victoria's mind was: Who selects the precise fold? Was it the timekeeper or the Great Spirit? One day, should time fold travel become widespread, it could perhaps be thought an important part of a good education to visit a previous lifeworld. History classes could hold laboratories in the living past. This travel would alter the past, which would mean that when you returned to the present you would be a different person in a different world, changed by your having been there. Like Nietzsche's "eternal return" time would become infinitely recursive, just as Mead said in the *Philosophy of the Present*.

Another crucial question was whether one should be able to leap to the future. Was editing the past to arrive at a better present any different than editing a manuscript? The criterion, of course, would be the betterment of the earth and the totality of her inhabitants rather than individual or even one group's gain. The Great Spirit would have to monitor that. But future travel, that would be like Pandora's Gourd.

Still out of breath Victoria slowed down to a walk, a block away from Hull House. A group of girls were jumping rope on the front walk, "California Oranges Tap me on the Back, Hello Mrs." they sang in rhythm with the rope. "Hello, Ladies," she replied, sending them into a fit of giggles. She remembered this game from the schoolyard as a child, two girls turn the rope, the others line up and have to jump in and tap the one ahead on the back. Victoria walked up the cement, then the wood flight of steps and turned the bell handle, hearing its ring echo through the door. A little girl with braids pinned up on the side of her head, peasant style, with ears sticking out in front of them ran up to the base of the steps and said:

"Go on in, Mrs. You don't have to ring the bell, except at night."

Victoria opened the door and entered the large hall. A skinny young man, with grey trousers and a brown jacket over a sweater approached through a door to the right. Victoria handed him her card. He looked at it and looked at her and grinned, but only on one side of his face, like a stroke victim.

"Please tell Miss Addams I apologize for not calling ahead, but I was out for a walk. Should this be an inconvenient time I'll return again."

"Oh, you're a Dr. too. I know Dr. Mead. He taught me volleyball when I was a kid, and chess and gave me some books to read by a German guy, Fellow name of Emanuel Kant. Bet you know him. Couldn't decipher it much. Got something to do with only doing what you feel good about everyone else doing. Weren't a bad idea for making the world better, I thought. What say you?"

"I quite agree," said Victoria.

"Your husband, he kept me out of jail, He tell you? I suppose not, it being a little thing for him. Once I stole something out of a motor car. Sure like you better than his last wife the one what died. She didn't cotton to him coming here and hanging around with us "riff-raff. My name, Ma'am, I mean Dr., Dr. Von Ditz, is Kenney –Kenney Jorgans," he said.

'It's Von Dietz, pleased to meet you, Mr. Jorgans," she said.

He snickered. "We're not that fancy around Hull House, now, just Kenny'll do," he said, his smile hooking onto his ears. "I got me a night job, as a comedian in Jay's Bar. Once I kept 'em rolling at the Chicago Playhouse down in the loop, I did. Miss Addams, she helped me–saw me always joking around. That's my main talent. Seems to be paying off."

"That's very impressive," said Victoria.

"We got a theatre here upstairs, we do all kinds of shows, plays, vaudeville, music. He jiggled his head from side to side; she supposed to symbolize the music. His pants were suspended on his bony shoulders as if on a hanger, his small waist and hips floated between like he was wearing a hoola hoop.

"Wonderful. We'll come and see you perform. Now, Miss Addams is in, please ask if she will see me."

He tilted his head so far to the side on his long neck it seemed to be upside-down. His grin looked like a parenthesis, one side open. Then a different, high voice came from the sideways grin: "you're much too young and pretty to be with an old codger like Dr. Mead," it said. Kenny flipped his head to the other side, his grin closing the parentheses. "Oops, not supposed to say such things, sorry Ma'am," said Kenny in his normal voice.

"Your impertinence is funny on stage, but perhaps not so appropriate in the front hall," said Victoria.

"See, Ma'am, this front hall is where I gets to practice. Everybody comes through here, from the mayor to the local hookers."

Victoria wondered how far apart they were, the mayor and the hookers. Kenny extended his spindle-like arms out of sleeves six inches too short, opened both palms up, pulled his upper lip over his lower lip, held it there for a second then blew out of his lips vibrating them like a lawn mower. "Can't keep m'lips closed," he said. "But I don't play favorites. I tell everybody everything about everybody, fair and square, like I know Dr. Mead was here yesterday, and the day before, and lots more days before that. Miss Addams loves him, just dotes on him." Kenny stared at her as if the simple fact of his observation should have no emotional impact.

Victoria felt a flush of heat. George hadn't mentioned stopping at Hull House before yesterday, when she saw him through the window. Noticing her he added, "Miss Addams is devoted to us at Hull House and her special lady friend and other friends, you know. She loves everybody in the world, but especially us in the neighborhood."

Victoria heard muffled voices, footsteps. The double doors at the end of the hall opened. A lady wearing a deep blue suit and a white blouse with peaked collar stepped forward. The sun shone through a large window behind her. Her grey hair looked golden. She carried a book in one hand and a vase with a rose in the other. Victoria was breathless in awe and wonder.

"Whom do I love?" she said in a rich mellow voice that rang like a viola played with a fast vibrato. She looked Kenny straight in the eyes.

Kenny said, "Mrs. Mead, Miss Addams," then repeated both names four times in different voices, bobbing up and down extending his arms pointing from one to the other.

"Kenny, stop it. And stop your joking." Jane Addams looked Victoria up and down. "Mrs. Mead! Just because George was widowed and I continued to refuse him doesn't mean he should be allowed to cradle rob. You are far too young and lovely for a man of his years."

Victoria was at a loss for words, feeling both flattered and embarrassed at the same time. "And yet, through my studies of George's thought, I feel both the hopefulness of youth and the wisdom of age. If you balance the two it makes him middle aged, like me."

"Miss Addams, right. But the lady aren't just Mrs. Mead. She is Dr. Victoria Von Dietz Mead, to be exact," said Kenny moving his knees open and shut as he pointed to Victoria.

Jane Addams looked at Victoria with raised eyebrows. Kenny, you should say the lady 'isn't Mrs. Mead, not 'aren't. And you should have introduced her as Dr. as well.

Victoria smiled, "Kenny was most gracious, and entertaining! I'm honored and delighted to meet you, Miss Addams. You've been a heroine to me most of my life, but I've only recently come to read your works." Victoria wanted to stop there, but something, perhaps the full disclosure bent of Kenny, propelled her words. "I am the new Mrs. Mead. However, Mead is not a cradle robber, but rather I am a grave robber." But how to explain what might seem a slur? "I mean no disrespect to my dear George, but to the circumstances of our marriage," said Victoria, extending her hand.

Jane took it and squeezed gently. "Well then, Dr. Von Dietz, (and I presume you don't really wish to borrow a man's name, even a famous one), you must stay for tea and explain this all to me. I love to discuss ideas or ways of being that challenge my presuppositions."

They went into the parlor. Addams put the rose on the carved side table. It brought out the red in flowers in the still life oil painting on the wall. "Lovely, isn't it? Hull House's last rose of summer. One appreciates them more when you don't know if there will be a next summer for you. But then I don't wish to sadden you, Dr. Von Dietz. Lord knows there is enough to be afflicted with as the maddening wars flair up in Europe."

The two women each sat in matched Queen Mary chairs by a small fire. Jane handed Kenny a book from the side table, "Here's something for you to read, a new play by Mr. Shaw, you'd be perfect in the role of Butler. Now please run along and fetch us some tea."

"I'll ask Hilda to bring it, Miss Addams, because the girls' puppet league has arrived and they're waiting for me to teach them puppet make-up and costuming," Kenny said this while tugging on his trousers.

"If the girls' puppet league needs you, who am I to object. Now go and do your duty!"

Victoria glanced to a shelf lined with books by and about Jane Addams.

"Some of my critics say I am arrogant and self-aggrandizing. Believe me, I get little pleasure from fame. With each accolade comes more work, responsibilities. Still I need a formidable reputation for the sake of Hull House, the work."

"Your causes are noble and their success means greater happiness and success for all," said Victoria. She noticed a picture of a man standing with Abraham Lincoln in front of a large two-story home. She recognized it as Jane's childhood home in Cedarville, Illinois. The man must be Jane's father, a state legislator who worked closely with Lincoln.

Victoria noticed a framed photo with a caption in bronze which said "Twenty Years at Hull House." Jane stood in the center holding a copy of a book and next to her were John Dewey, H. Stanley Hall, and George. Jane's elegant dress had full sleeves and a skirt with long folds.

"I see my husband in the picture," said Victoria.

"George has been my dear friend for decades." A rosy color came to Jane's cheeks. Her broad face with simple, clear, yet warm features seemed like a cameo. Victoria could rest in that face. If Jane had had her way, if she had been heeded, the earth and all its creatures would be healthier, more blessed. Victoria felt like she did when in deep meditation. Bliss, deep understanding, sometimes with a sense of color, the smell of roses, light in her bones. Once or twice the image of a beautiful woman in a long gown appeared in these meditations. She knew why Jane was called "St. Addams".

Miss Addams sighed. "While I love George Mead, I could not marry him, or anyone else I can't devote myself to one person when I'm needed by many. One day relationships will not require such exclusive devotion from women," said Jane.

"George is devoted to me as I am to him," said Victoria. "Perhaps this is possible because he already has become a renowned philosopher and raised a family," said Victoria.

"My dear, far be it from me to burst your bubble. From what George tells me your work is an extension of his."

Victoria felt heat rising in her temples. She had to admit that while Jane was probably right, and so was Mead, there was much more to her work than they knew. Taking a deep breath, she replied: "True, in some ways, yet my work is taking both of us in unanticipated directions."

"I'm sure George did not mean anything derogatory about your work," said Jane. "To the contrary. There is also a way in which homemaking should be taken out to the neighborhoods, and communities. Some have called me "the world's housekeeper," said Jane.

"Perhaps men should also be trained in housekeeping and child care," said Victoria.

"I couldn't agree more. And at Hull House we do teach men as well as women in cooking, baking and sewing. Speaking of housekeeping, where is Hilda with that tea," said Jane. She rang a bell sitting on the table. A maid came in who was as short and round and sour of face as Kenny was tall and gangling and smiling. Hilda laid out the tea looking down at the table and not up at either of them.

"'Scuse the delay, Miss Addams. Kenney had us all in stitches in the kitchen telling about the beautiful young woman came to the door saying she was married to old Dr. Mead and we was all wondering about her and telling him he was free to tell us all he knew about what was actually going on in the house but don't make up such nonsense, not with his true wife Mrs. Helen not even in the ground a year." Then she looked up at Jane and Victoria. She turned beet red. "Goodness me, it is a young beautiful visitor you have just like Kenny said. But surely not old Dr. Mead's wife."

"Hilda, please do check on dinner preparations in the kitchen," Jane Adams said without a trace of embarrassment or reprimand. I'll explain everything to you and the others once I figure it all out myself."

Hilda left glancing once more at Victoria. Jane opened a door made of finely wrought iron set into a bookshelf. She put a key into a lock and removed a decanter and two small crystal glasses. "Sherry?" she said.

"Certainly, Miss Addams, but I thought you were a prohibitionist," said Victoria.

"I am, for those, especially men, who can't drink in moderation," Jane said, filling the two glasses, then catching the final drip with the side of the stopper and slipping it back into the decanter. A counter image of Tom came to Victoria, the husband of her former-future life, whether drinking solo or with her, pouring his damned Dramboui, catching the drip with a finger, licking it, then before putting the decanter down, tasting from his glass as if the stuff required tasting, then again wiping the drip and licking his finger, a drunk's ritual which she should have recognized the first time she'd seen it, rather than the thousandth.

"Drinking is worse among the Irish than the Italians, far as becoming alcoholics is concerned," Jane said. (Tom was, had been, Scotch, not Irish, but close enough.) "Not sure why, except that Italian men and women drink and eat good food together and talk a lot. Irish men get drunk in packs and they have lousy weather and a lousy cuisine, but don't quote me on this," said Jane.

"Or they drink solo hunched over their booze," said Victoria.

"Ah, you've been there,' said Jane, raising her glass. "To alcohol in moderation and great conversation in abundance," Jane said.

"I'll drink to that," said Victoria, and they did.

"However," said Victoria, "Isn't the idea of individual and cultural differences on such a matter an argument against prohibition? Why keep something from everyone which is only bad for some persons and even then only if they abuse it?"

"My dear, I'm more of a practical woman than a philosopher. Hollywood gangster movies aside, things have been a lot more peaceful and life has been in general better in our neighborhood since prohibition," said Jane.

"You care so much about your neighborhood that you walk around to pick up garbage cans that have spilled," said Victoria.

"Really I am checking up to see that the city doesn't neglect picking up garbage in this neighborhood. Some of the powers that be resent the immigrants. But how did you know about this? asked Jane.

"I read it in one of your books," said Victoria.

"I've only written about this in my journal which hasn't been published," said Jane. Victoria felt pinned by Jane Addams' odd stare.

She braced herself, "Miss Addams, Jane, what I must tell you is going to seem bazaar, even frightening. Or you may think me insane. Yet you are a woman who has resolutely faced the truth about the great pain and adversity in the world. You've traveled far and faced angry crowds because you wanted to feed starving children in Germany after the First— the Great War. You traveled by sea to Europe to ask the heads of state to call a truce in World War One."

"how could you . . . can you give that horror a number?"

"Please, hear me out, Jane. You believe that if each of us strives to become the best possible person we can be, that we can change the world. I was, and still am, a professor and philosopher working in part on the theory of time and the nature of the human self. My devotion to the thinking of George Herbert Mead, made it possible for me to transcend time, my time," said Victoria.

Jane Addams opened her eyes wide and said, "Bosh! I think you are in thrall to another George Herbert, except you've twisted the names. Of course, I speak of Mr. Wells and his time machine."

Victoria laughed, then got up and walked to the window and back. "You are familiar with my husband, and his fellow "pragmatists" as they are called, Dewey and James?"

Jane sat upright; squaring her shoulders, face suddenly a fortress. "I certainly do know about pragmatism. We at Hull House invented it. John, Bill and George wrote about it. We did it. But it was all in the ancient Greeks. Socrates did change minds in his open dialogue. Of course, his society was far from democratic, but in reality neither is ours. But I interrupted you." Jane looked pale and trembled as she spoke. She took a breath, sat back, clasped her hands in her lap. "I have dreamed of time travel but never claimed it as you do."

Victoria also was shaken, by recalling that Jane would develop cancer this winter and die this coming May. Perhaps such foreknowledge is beyond the human capacity to bear.

"Why do you look at me so oddly?" Jane said.

Victoria could not bring herself to answer honestly, so she ignored Jane's question and dove into the easier one of explaining her time travel.

"You know then of Mead's theory, in which the past and the future are components of the present. In my own work I became so intrigued with Mead's ideas and so in love with his powerful philosophy that I was able to communicate with him after he died and we have been able to realize our love in marriage. I came back into his time even though I lived my life in the late twentieth century. I know this sounds bizarre, but I've brought a picture of myself and my daughter, from the 1970s to show you." Victoria reached into her purse and pulled out a picture of her and Kathy standing in front of the new twin towers by the Chicago river, with the beautiful white Wrigley building in the background.

"The color, it's so realistic. I've never see . . .yes, this is indeed the Wrigley building in the background, but what are these monstrosities? Isn't one tower of Babel enough? This is certainly a trick, thought the people look real. And the strange cars," said Jane.

"I am trying to show you is that I was born years after both you and Mead died. I am obliged to tell you that your teachings about world peace have not been heeded," said Victoria.

"My dear, the latter is easier to believe than the former," said Jane.

Victoria continued, "There was a second world war and a continuous succession of wars since then with more and more efficient weapons. Often the United States was the aggressor or instigator. But the two world wars were both started by Germany. My great grandparents were immigrants from Prussia. Due to early deaths of both my great-grandfather and grandfather, we became a strong matriarchal family."

Jane sat back and sipped, and Victoria was encouraged to continue.

"My great-grandmother took orphans in her home, started the Lutheran Kinderheim in Milwaukee. I grew up ashamed of my German heritage and my grandmother and mother stopped speaking German at home. This was because all I saw of Germany were early movies of goose stepping Nazis and later of horrors of concentration camps when the allies went in to liberate them."

"And these 'allies' who were they?"

"The United States, the United Kingdom and the Soviet Union."

"America and the Soviets together? Dare I hope?"

"I don't want to misguide you along those lines," said Victoria.

"A moment of hope," Jane said and sipped. "Please continue. I'm enchanted."

"Bodies were piled up in pits, many of them elderly, women, children, babies. As you know, Adolph Hitler got elected at a time when people were desperate, due mostly to the German economy shattered by inflation due to the cost of reparations demanded of them by the allies," said Victoria.

"I spoke against the demands of that treaty," said Jane. "We at Hull House sent food to the orphans from the Great War. Little ragged girls picking through the streets looking for scraps of food. No coats. I've been watching this Hitler. He makes a few good points, but he's a dangerous anti-Semite war maker. So, how did you get here—what are you planning to do?" Jane's tone seemed to have lost its edge of disbelief. Was she accepting or merely inebriated?

"My work is in the philosophy of time and being. A German philosopher, Martin Heidegger, was . . . is also working on this theory, but only abstractly. I learned from the women in my family, and with you as a great example, that theories come from practice and that they can change the world. I can't explain why just yet, but that knowledge is what allowed Mead to come alive to me in the bodily sense in my time, then both of us to travel back to this place and time."

"Bodily, as you say, you remain as you were, are, will be . . . I am at a loss in selecting verb tense."

"George seems fixed by his age in the photograph on his book jacket. And I, apparently, am fixed at the time of his emergence. I don't think we should confuse matters any further by considering other possibilities."

"I have met my limit, dear. Today, at least, I can absorb no more."

Victoria's heart pounded. She recalled that Jane was to get ill and die in the next few years and wondered if her weariness was an early sign of the cancer that took her. Victoria took a deep breath, reassuring herself that Jane was known for her openness and tolerance of the points of view of everyone.

Jane rose and poured herself another glass of sherry. Victoria had yet to sip her own. "Another sip to steady my ears and settle our thoughts," said Jane.

"I've always found at least kernels of truth, important messages, even in the most bizarre stories," said Jane. "Until today I thought the story about the devil baby at Hull House, told and believed by numerous women in the neighborhood, was the strangest I had heard. That one was understandable as a myth, which allowed these uneducated women to feel that there was a god which sent just retributions for sinful acts. Perhaps you have been so hurt by the men in your life and their wars that you have gone, as they say, 'off your rocker'. I know what that is like as I fell into a depression and what was called 'hysteria' after graduating from college and seeing that there was no meaningful place for me or other intelligent women to use our talents for a better world. I decided after several years of reclusion to get together a couple of friends and do something ourselves. Luckily, we had the means to make a start."

Jane placed her glass on a crocheted doily on the side table." So, Dr. Von Dietz, you are welcome to work with us here. You are certainly beyond being able to stay sane with life as a housewife."

"I'm greatly honored. I'd be happy to learn what it is you think I may contribute, while here," said Victoria. She trembled, knowing that the perfection of the moment would be fully felt only later.

"And you should know that despite the doubts stirring in the more pragmatic part of my mind, I sense you are telling the truth about your time travel. George often muses about transcendent time zones. I tell him he'd be better off continuing to focus on what is happening now. If our intelligent men could learn to think of themselves more as husbands of the world and all its children instead of to their own egos, we could all live healthier and more peaceful lives."

Finally, Victoria needed the sherry and gulped half the glass. "Miss Addams, this is what I want. If we could put your knowledge of dialogue and change together with transcendent time zones perhaps we could prevent some awful things from happening."

Jane Addams' face seemed now to show her years of struggle against powerful people and institutions.

"I've read *Mein Kamph*," Jane said. "Some of the professors here laugh at Herr Hitler. I don't. I think he knows how to gain power and how to enlist the dedication of some and force the compliance of the rest. Perhaps since you know what is to follow, you can change his course." Jane started to cough and reached for a shawl which hung on the back of her chair.

Taking this as a sign that she must be taxing Jane's strength, Victoria thanked her and excused herself.

Kenny appeared, as if he were behind a curtain. "Going to change the world? From the future? Just think Miss Addams how much admission we could charge for folks to come and see the lady from next century who can tell us the future. Why we'd make a fortune. Best watch out though, she may be kidnapped by the bookies and the stock brokers."

"I'd be disappointing to them as I can only bring to the past what I've experienced and what I can remember. I never went to horse races or kept up with the stock market," said Victoria.

Chapter Eighteen
The Pillow Talk of George and Victoria

In a dream within a dream I dreamt a dream
of the reality of existence
inside the ultimate computer
which is the universe
in which the Arrow of Time
flies both ways
through bent space
Lawrence Ferlinghetti, *Rough Song of Animals Dying*

Victoria sat at her desk wearing a camisole, her shoulders and neck moist. Hot Indian summer breeze fluttered the lace window curtains over her face. The sky was white with mountainous thunderheads.

Muffled voices of George greeting Guy at the front door, then thumping as Mead mounted the steps, two at a time. Not at all like the geezer Kenney made him out to be. He was sixty-seven. At times he seemed thirty-seven. Yet, when in deep thought he seemed to be bearing the burden of a hundred years. He kissed the back of her neck, his lip lingering, then sliding across her shoulder. She felt his hand slithering on her back as he loosed his tie, then unbuttoned his vest.

Victoria turned to face him, put her hands on his waist. "You must disclaim your refutation of Pavlov, darling. Like his doggies, I salivate every time you remove your tie." Victoria felt heat rising to her forehead. George's eyes brightened.

"Come here." He sat on the sofa and held out his arms. She stood, glancing at the letter from Martin on her desk. A gust of wind teased the sheer curtains across her belly. She strode to him, even hard wood on her bare feet a pleasure after another day in heels.

"I never said Pavlov was wrong, just too simplistic. If he were right you'd already be undressed," Mead added.

"So, the problem is dogs don't wear clothes? If they did Pavlov would have got it right," she said.

"It's more of a problem that we do wear clothes. Take that lovely yet frustrating thing off." He removed his vest and unbuttoned his shirt.

She sat next to him, not ready to be naked while he was still dressed enough to walk on into the street. "Hot. My day was hot. Barbaric that there is yet no air-conditioning. No wonder that women carry fans. But what do the men do?" She slid her hand inside his shirt, feeling the soft hair on his chest.

He laughed. "We men are supposed to take everything in our stride." He tugged his shirt off his arms. "My students were in rare form today! Lots of discussion about war looming in Europe. They don't get it. World government, a League of Nations could become a United Nations."

He placed his hand on her belly, kissed her neck. She raised his hand to her lips, kissed his palm, and held it to her belly. "Your touch is soothing," she said.

"My students seem like your description of your own student years, split between pacifists and those who want to go to war to derail Hitler," said Mead.

"Yah. seems parallel to the Vietnam war era," said Victoria. She felt a wave of anxiety and anger, images of the war and the peace vigils, the campus closed down to avert the violence of the locals against the student and faculty protestors.

"But why are we discussing war and peace when all I want is a piece of you?" Mead moved his hand up under her camisole.

Disturbing thoughts had cooled her ardor. She held his roaming hand still. "Darling, I met Jane this afternoon. We had a wonderful talk. But as a pacifist she faces intense criticism, including threats and nasty names."

"Granted, but it would be much worse were she not an attractive woman of the upper classes." Mead pulled his undershirt off and threw it on the floor.

"You would bring up Jane's beauty at a time like this. Was Jane the real reason you pulled us into this time zone?" she said, unable to push down her feelings of jealousy. Mead put one hand over her mouth and the other on her breast. Victoria flung herself free. She jumped up and stood in front of him. He grabbed her wrists.

"I love you, you, you. We, you and I, have work to do, and yes, Jane Addams is an important part of the picture, period!" He released his grip and began to gently caress her back.

Stroking the top of his head, she said, "Your mustache tickles. We must trim it."

"I've had this mustache for forty years, so you'd better get used to it," he said, moving his face slowly from side to side.

"It's one thing to see your beard and mustache in a photo and quite another to be scratched by them," she said.

"A picture's worth many words, a good feel transcends them both," added Mead.

She sat up straight, and possessed his eyes.

"Back to our topic. Jane is eloquent in rebutting her presumed red leanings while defending freedom of speech for those who are communist. Looking ahead it's a shame her thoughts were not heeded." Victoria pressed herself softly against George's head and chest while thinking of the redbaiting of the 1950s and the colossal waste that was the cold war.

"What is unfortunate is that you still have this thing on." Mead plucked the ribbon of her camisole, pulled down the strap and kissed her shoulder.

She felt silly, torn between wanting George inside her and this chilling concern for the world's looming catastrophes. But she needed his mind to rekindle her. "Give me an answer George. Any answer from you will do."

"The League of Nations and the spread of democracy is the only answer to these extremes of attitude that shut down understanding and communication," he said. He kissed her other shoulder not the least bit paternally.

"No organization of world governments can challenge world corporations' and their wars and oil empires. Either you are a managerial slave or a minimum waged worker. This is reality, not idealistic notions of increasing democracy leading to universal peace," said Victoria as she twisted open the top button of his pants.

"You sound like that former lover of yours, that strange fellow who went to Cuba and started the Red Feather Institute, what is his name?" asked Mead.

"Young, you mean, T.R. Young. And he was not my lover, just a friend. He was one of the few social scientists with the balls to question not only the structural functional paradigm, but your cherished ""symbolic interaction- ism" as well, said Victoria." She slid between his legs to the floor, tugged on his shirt, and kissed his belly.

"Actually I like T.R. Young. An engaging critic, like you." He pulled her camisole up and over her head. She unbuttoned his shirt, and arranging, shifting and tumbling. She felt his hard thighs prying hers open, his belly to belly. Later he lay exhausted still holding her close.

The rays of the setting sun angled through the window. A glimmer of light flashed from the silver miniature sword in front of the letter on her desk. She felt Mead's body tense. His gaze was in the same direction hers had been, but would be fixed on the picture of Chancellor Hindenburg on one of the stamps, the swastika on the other.

"You have a letter from Germany. Herr Heidegger again, I presume," he said, his voice rising. She turned so they lay face to face.

"There's to be a conference on trends in social theory. Professor Heidegger invited me to give a talk."

George sat up, his back rigid.

He chanted in a whisper, "I won't be jealous, I won't be upset, take the role of the other towards the self, take the role of the other towards the self, use your reflective intelligence." He cleared his throat and swallowed.

"Its so pleasing to see you practicing what you preach, dear," she said. He could be such a dear.

"I try. What is your talk to be about?"

"Multiple realities and overlapping time, in relation to Mead's theory of self versus Heidegger's theory of 'being'," she said.

"We don't need a theory of 'being', who needs a theory to tell us we exist!" said Mead, his voice rising again.

She stroked his back as they sat up on the couch. She could give Mead her body because she cherished his mind. But that did not mean she had to yield her mind.

"You know Heidegger's concept of being human 'Dasein' is deeper and richer than your concept of self," she said as they dressed. Too late, she regretted putting it that way. "I should have said, 'more elaborate'" but it was too late.

Mead, now on the defensive, interrupted. "This purported depth in Herr Heidegger is a smoke screen for unsupportable conjecture. His thinking is so fuzzy it mystifies people into believing it is highly profound. They find it incomprehensible because it is, but blame themselves." Mead placed his right hand in his pants pocket.

"Your provocative gesture makes me want to pull you back down on the sofa. But I'll defer these urges to make a point," said Victoria.

"A guy can't even put his hand in his pocket without you wanting to jump on him. Making a point hasn't deferred your amorous advances before. Besides, you constantly bring me to a point," said Mead.

"To make a point is easy, but to have it stick is another," she said. "Like the poets, Heidegger transcends ordinary language. And please don't get your pipe out. It breaks my concentration as I bask in its erotic fragrance," said Victoria.

"Even though you've read Freud enough to trace such irrationalities to your childhood Electra complex and your father's pipe?" said Mead, pulling his pipe and tobacco pouch out of his pocket.

She laughed, "Knowing the secret formula for desire doesn't make it go away."

"Just as your digression from Heidegger to Freud doesn't refute my point. Philosophy is about clarification, about explanation, not mystification," Mead said. He probed his pipe from a pocket, looked at it, then slammed it into the leather corner of the side table. "Heidegger explains nothing, nothing about how we come into consciousness. We only can think at all because others spoke to us, because we learned language." Mead's face was red. Concern for him edged into a corner of her mind. He yanked up his pipe, sucked on it empty and cold.

Victoria felt it hard to focus on her argument because of the pipe. Just in time, she recalled relevant quote from Heidegger. "And language," says Martin, "is the house of Being."

"'Martin', now is it! First name basis? Your Marty has no explanation for the origins of language as I do, in the gesture, in the conversation of gestures!" shouted Mead, gripped his pipe tightly and waved it about.

"Then come with me to the conference," she shouted. "Address these issues with him directly."

He dismissed her suggestion with his pipe. "The man did not invite me, he invited you. In fact, did you ever stop to think about it? Why is this intellectual pup interested in you? To get back at me, to reverse the gains our American pragmatic philosophers have made."

"If that was his aim he could have invited your devoted former wife, Helen, to a conference," she shouted back.

"She was beyond such things," said Mead.

"Or beneath them, the cow," Victoria snarled. Suddenly feeling exposed in only her camisole, she slipped into a white dressing gown, ashamed for resorting to name-calling.

"She was a housewife and mother," said Mead, his ire abated, perhaps by thought of Helen.

"Just like Martin's Cow-wife, Frieda," Victoria said, her tongue now beyond her control. "Which reminds me that philosophers since Socrates have been trying to keep women out of philosophy, believing them incapable, too instinctual, too close to nature to be literate. Their concepts of women distorted by the types of women they married, women they could control, women who were content to peel the potatoes, stir the stew, not women of intellectual fire and passion."

"Actually," said Mead, "Heidegger's wife, Elfriede, was an economics student. She is also a teacher, of high school," said Mead.

Victoria stood, chagrined that she didn't know this but willing enough to tolerate an exception. Her robe flared at the hem as she paced the room.

"There is something wrong with the concept of philosophy which allows you to "profess" the ideas of Jane Addams, which you observed and supported during your stay at Hull House. She was only allowed to teach a couple of courses, with low pay, as an adjunct. You became a world renowned philosopher in part from discussing her ideas, refining them, of course, as a full professor," said Victoria, her rage grown to something she could only observe, not control.

"Look, my dear, I can't continue this with you. Jane is a brilliant woman, but she could never settle down enough to write a sustained scholarly argument."

"Sustained? Or strained and pedantic? Jane's writing is eloquent and clear, connecting ideas with real people's lives. Jane was busy doing philosophy in the streets and neighborhoods, working for women's suffrage." Her voice quivered. George raised his hand to stop her, but she would not be halted.

"Don't hide, I know you loved her, she is your soul mate! Was she too controversial for your career, not "respectable" enough? She might have jeopardized your professorship! And Jane used her wealth to help the poor, while Helen's wealth was accessible to you. What's more Helen's family wealth came from slave plantations in New Guinea! And you, the proponent of democracy," shouted Victoria.

"My dear there is nothing wrong with wealth. Indeed, you seem to enjoy living a comfortable life…" Mead grasped Victoria's hand and squeezed it, looking down at the large diamond wedding ring he gave her.

She let him put his hand around her waist and pull her to him. "Wives in this time and place don't travel without their husbands' permission, more than around the block to stroll the baby. I fought against such laws and customs, but you make me have second thoughts," he said, glaring at her.

"If you ever mention that to me again, I'll kidnap you and time travel us to the Amazon queens," she said.

"Try it! You've worked for women tyrants as well as men! But a stay with the Amazons may convince you once and for all that women are equally vulnerable to human foibles as men," Mead said evenly.

There was a quiet knock on the door.

"Another erotic interlude curtailed by roaring conflict. Your erection shrinks, as my statistically inclined friends would say, in inverse relationship to the intensity of our debates."

"You strengthen me just as you make me weak," Mead said, pulling her close as she braced elbows against his chest.

The knock at the door got louder and Guy said, "Sir, Madam, Excuse the interruption."

Mead released Victoria and wiped his brow with his handkerchief. He walked to the door and opened it. "Yes, Guy?"

"Sorry to interrupt, Sir. Dr. Carter Jackson is calling. She insists that you come to the phone at once.

"She's been calling for days. I'd best talk with her. She sent Guy with a special phone issued only to the state deparment."

"That woman is has far more going on that running an office of educational research," said Mead.

"Indeed," said Victoria. "But that is to our benefit."

When Victoria came back upstairs she found Mead dozed off in bed with a book in his hand. It was "Being and Time" by Martin Heidegger. I guess I got through to him, she said to herself.

Hearing her movements, he woke and asked her what Annabelle wanted.

"She warned me about going to Nazi Germany, feared I may never get back. Yet she also encouraged me. To see what I could do to avert the coming holocaust."

Mead sleepily said, "She doesn't expect much from you, does she."

"She insisted I come and talk with her before I go and I can't go without her support."

Chapter Nineteen
Back for a Visit

Modes of time are intra-temporality of that which is present.
Martin Heidegger, *On Freedom*

Victoria was back in 1976, driving north to her friend's country estate, where Kathy was staying over the weekend. How she missed her! Things had gone smoothly as she meditated and used the special watch Mead had given her. She was surprised that her Blue Volvo sedan started without difficulty, parked in the garage at their home in North Chicago. She couldn't yet explain what it was that made it work, but hopefully by bringing Mead's and Heidegger's philosophies of time together, she would find an answer.

Orange and red maple leaves glowed on the trees and hillside as she pulled into the long driveway. Even before she turned off the engine, Snuggles ran to the car full speed, climbing up on her when she opened the door, announcing her arrival with a joyous yelp. Up the hill, Kathy jumped off a large brown mare, and ran towards the car.

She and Kathy hugged. Tears came into both of their eyes. "I wish you could be with us here, with the horses," said Kathy. "Snuggles loves it, but I have to keep telling him you are coming.

"I'll be back as soon as I can, darling," said Victoria, giving Kathy a kiss. Pangs of guilt hit her about giving priority to her work, once again. Yet she seemed destined to move ahead with her life with Mead in that time zone as well. Perhaps soon she could explain fully.

"I know you are involved in really important work on your books, Mom," said Kathy. "Otherwise you'd tell me more about it."

Victoria felt torn. She was happily married now, to Mead, but in another time. How could she explain?

Kathy's friend Jane called from the house for Kathy to come to see something on television. Victoria followed to the house, had coffee with Jane's parents while the girls watched the show.

Tears ran down Victoria's cheeks, as she hugged Kathy and petted Snuggles and returned to her car. She needed to remember that for them she had only been away a short time, although she was not quite sure what the exact ratio ways.

Victoria got in her car and drove south to the Chicago loop to meet Annabelle Carter Jackson for lunch. Victoria wondered whether ACJ (as she privately referred to Annabelle) would want to time travel back to the 30s. And if so, could Victoria travel with her or help her devolve?

When she arrived at the Lavendar restaurant in North Chicago, Annabelle waved her over to the table, already replete with shrimp cocktails and wine. The scent of large pots of lavender near the windows followed her.

"What can you get from an old white ex-Nazi?" said Dr. Annabelle Carter Jackson as she dipped another jumbo shrimp into the blood red cocktail sauce.

The restaurant décor was stainless steel interposed with geometric arches painted lavendar. A bottle of California Chardonnay peaked out of silver cooler on a table between them. Beyond the large window two Lincolns and a Cadillac stood in line waiting to be valet parked.

"Heidegger was a Nazi for a only a short time, in the pre-war years. He thought he could move the party in a better direction. He believed in Hitler's early appeal to the land, the people, improving the economy from a deadly depression," said Victoria, sipping her fragrant white wine.

"They all find some excuse," said Annabelle.

Victoria's neck froze. She must have Annabelle's support. Everything depended upon it. She sat up straight. "Dr. Carter-Jackson, you urged me to go beyond developing a new theory of overlapping time, to putting it into practice. I need Heidegger to do this, to work with him in person, bring him into contact with persons in the anti-Nazi movement in Germany. I need an extension of my grant, all of which is going to pay for Kathy's boarding school while I'm away. I need travel funds. But most importantly, I need you to authorize my research visa," said Victoria. She swallowed a piece of sour dough bread that she had pulled through olive oil on the plate.

"Dr. Victoria, either you're nuts or I'm nuts buying this time travel stuff. I did think for a while that my former assistant, Guy, ran off with you and the story about your being with Professor Mead in the 30s was some kind of wild joke. But Guy is not that kind of guy (no pun intended) and the stuff you write is really solid. That being said, why in the blue-eyed world do you want to chance ending up in a prison camp where so many died? Don't expect any chilled Chardonnay, there. But come to think of it, an Aryan beauty like you will probably end up in one of the SS breeding camps. I'm afraid you don't realize the dangers." Annabelle blotted her mouth with the thick linen napkin. "This Heidegger guy must be more than just another philosopher to you."

Victoria tried to relax her shoulders where tension always found its home, but they remained rigid. "Yes, I feel passionate about men who think deeply, create ideas, and who care about the world. For me the flesh and the mind are inseparable. Such men are god men," she said.

"Don't forget there are goddesses too, and that gods and goddesses have clay feet," said Annabelle.

"Annabelle, interfering in the past was YOUR idea. You wanted not just a theory, but a practical application." Victoria was almost shouting. "I've devoted my career to developing theories that could be put into practice. The correct application of my theory of overlapping time can ameliorate the horrors humans inflict on each other."

"Relax, Dr. Von Dietz. I know your motives are righteous. At the same time, we are human, we do love, have attractions. And what's this with my former assistant, Guy, serving you tea. I thought he was to be your research assistant."

Annabelle's huge toothy smile helped ease Victoria. "Let me share with you some words, ideas from a recently translated book of Heidegger's, *History of the Concept of Time*." She reached into her bag and pulled out the book. "I'm only reading from the Table of Contents:"

"The Exposition of Time Itself;

Elaboration of the Question of Being Itself;

141

Interpretation of Death as a Phenomenon of Dasein (Heidegger's word for the human being);

The Phenomenon of Willing to Have a Conscience and of Being Guilty;

Time as the Being in which Dasein can be its Totality'."

Victoria closed the book and pressed it into her lap. "It's like a poem of being and time."

Annabelle rolled her eyes and held up her hand. "You'll find out that this god is a man, just like your George Mead. Or maybe you'll find out that you wish they were more like real men than they are—living in their lofty world of high ideas. I grant you his words take flight and that he will be a key figure in the political dramas about to unfold." Annabelle leaned forward and continued: "I bet he'd love getting his inky paws on your pure Aryan blond 'Design'." Annabelle looked at Victoria's breasts.

Victoria wished she had worn something other than a snug sweater. She had felt her nipples tighten.

"It's D-a-s-e-i-n, not design. Besides, he's attracted to Semitic types, like Hannah Arendt."

Annabelle fixed her enormous eyes on Victoria's long fingers holding the wine glass. "I read Fetzringer's book about that affair he had with Hannah Arendt when she was a student. Even though she later became a world famous scholar, with Heidegger she apparently was always only an adoring subject for his thoughts and urges. I bet that man didn't even read Arendt's *The Human Condition* or *The Origins of Totalitarianism*," Annabelle added.

"That comes later. Martin changes. The year we are going into, Heidegger is married to Elfriede, a housefrau who is in no way his equal," said Victoria.

"Well, darling, it didn't take you long to adopt an elitist attitude," said Annabelle. "I can't believe you putting down his Frau like that." Annabelle threw her napkin down on the table. "You of all people! She had a teaching job, kids to take care of, a household to run, Martin to cater to, put up with his affair. Let's not blame women for making the best choices available to them. Which set of male shackles are better, housewife or intellectual slave? Your work is supposed to be about overcoming that whole pile of shit."

"You're right," said Victoria. "It's so easy to get trapped in the mores of the times.

"What do you mean 'we,' white girl? Why would a fat black woman with a brain want to be messing around with Nazis? I'm not sure I really believe any of this time travel shit. Is it all a good excuse for you and my handsome assistant, Guy, to take off to the South Seas?"

"Please Annabelle," she said. "Just play along with me for awhile."

"Honey, playing along with you is the main reason I'm here. You know I gave up an afternoon reviewing grant proposals to be with you."

Victoria appreciated the sarcasm but not the leer, even though it might have been in jest, playing.

Please, Annabelle, but we have more to talk about, such as the book project. The point is, after *Being and Time* and the *Essay Concerning Technology*, no informed thinkers can free themselves from Heidegger."

"Well for God's sake, you don't have to fall in love with him, worship him, especially when your idol has clay feet," said Annabelle.

"What are the alternatives to Heidegger's vision? Blind, passionless bureaucratic management? A world where there are no gods, either human or immortal? A world where all of the forests are cut down for lumber?"

She managed to keep the rest of her thoughts to herself. If Mead, also, thrilled her mind, what was wrong with worshipping and loving him, too? Monogamy, Victoria thought, at least in this time-warped world, does not seem to work so well.

A waiter interrupted, wearing a white jacket. "Is everything all right, ladies? Coffee? A nice dessert? Our famous Chocolate lavender cake?"

Annabelle frowned at the interruption until his last word. "Chocolate Lavender cake! Yes. Will it be two?" she said, her eyes shining on Victoria as if she might as well substitute for the pastry.

Victoria did not like catering to Annabelle, but she needed to complete her work. She took a deep breath. It was too important to loose the support of NIHL now.

"Dr. Jackson," she began.

"As we seem to be drawing closer, you may call me Annabelle, dear." Her voice softened as she took the last bite of her lobster tail, dripping in butter.

"Dr. Carter-Jackson," Victoria said, her throat sticking, "You have proof already I am able to time travel. I even was able to bring your assistant, Guy to join us. Can't you see how I must go to Germany? If we can get Heidegger firmly on our side, how he may influence Hitler or if not reinforce the resistance?"

"What I have is a charming tale of your time travel which seems to me at this point to be as real as Gulliver's travels. Very entertaining. Perhaps even important in an intellectual way, but hardly proof of truth."

"How can I prove it to you?" said Victoria.

"Take me along! When are you going again?"

Were her problems solved so easily? Too easily, Victoria thought. "Soon," she said. "A day or two." But could she do it again, and with another woman? "I thought you were afraid to go."

"I'd prefer southern Spain in the time of the Moors, but I suppose that's not my choice, you being the pilot or whatever. Besides, if I can stop that little bastard with the stringy moustache, I'll die happy." Carter Jackson drained her wine glass and said, "I can't believe I'm even entertaining the validity of this fantasy."

"My grant?" said Victoria.

Just as the cake arrived, Annabelle said: "I'll extend your grant and help you get your visa. But we need results, real results, not just a book. You have an opportunity of a lifetime—of two lifetimes. What can you do to prevent atrocities that will otherwise happen? You can't fight a war without death. And the death of one cultural hero, such as a leading philosopher of the nation, knocked out of commission in his time, is worth the lives of thousands of ordinary soldiers."

Annabelle continued in a whisper: "You are one of the few Americans who can get close to him. Research visas are not going these days, to any work that cannot be justified to the State Department."

Victoria's stomach churned and it wasn't from the food. "This is beyond the realm of my work. I'm a scholar, not a spy. I applied for a human learning research visa, not to work for the U.S. intelligence service or the department of war," said Victoria.

"Now that you, George and Martin have put us into split time, the circumstances for all of us is political! You've lived through enough of the capitalist patriarchy to realize that everything men do with a few breaks for gang rape is linked to war. Men are programmed for aggression. As it is, I must practically put my job on the line with the NIHL to justify your work." Annabelle reached out and put a warm palm on top of Victoria's hand.

Victoria slipped her hand away, stood to leave. She said, "you won't regret it, Annabelle," but wondered if she herself would. She was, after all, a child of this war that was about to come. Her Momma and Grandma both spoke Deutsch at home when she was a small girl. As a child she learned to despise the German language, because it was that of the awful Nazi's with their high goosesteps, clicking heels, hands thrust in the air, which she saw in the Hollywood films and newsreels shown at the Liberty theatre. Now as an adult when she heard the warmth of the language, especially spoken by women, she cried.

The two men of her heart stood on each side of the Atlantic, ready to do battle. Pragmatists and existentialists. On the one hand, you had George's thoughtful and optimistic humanism, which ordered and explained individual human and social life as communication processes, best achieved in democratic societies. Across the Atlantic, Martin saw this as appeasement, which covered up injustice and pain but also drove Being and Nature into hiding, grinding everything beneath the wheels of technology and bureaucracy.

"I know you must return soon," said Annabelle. I can't come with you yet, I have things to clear up here, arrangements to make for us all there. I'll let you know when I can come over."

Annabelle reached into her purse, pulled out two palm sized yellow egg-shaped items. She handed one to Victoria. "Keep this with you at all times. It's a transmitter signal, like a walky talky or cellular phone, but uses a different means of transmission. It's hard to detect as the vehicle for sending the signal changes at random. You can reach me on mine twenty-four hours a day, anywhere on the planet or between here and the moon. It hasn't been tested beyond that. I want you to be safe above all. And I will make plans to join you as the work progresses. You're going to need me. And before you leave for Germany I want some coaching in stepping through the overlap."

"So that's how Guy calls you." Victoria held the egg in her hand, squeezed it, put it into her purse.

"Yeah, Guy screwed one of those into your telephone line as well."

"And don't expect me to loose weight before I come. I don't believe in dieting. So make my time hole extra large," said Annabelle, taking another bit of cake.

A waiter approached saying there was a call for Dr Von Dietz. Victoria thanked Annabelle and left to take the call on her way out.

Annabelle waved as Victoria left, "Victoria, keep in touch," I'll expect regular calls." Annabelle held up her yellow egg, then slipped it into her bosom.

"How much drool did you catch?" said Guy, his voice richer on the phone then in actual life. "Shall I call Dr. Carter Jackson with an emergency to get her sweaty hands off you?"

"Your timing was perfect," said Victoria. "And my grant is renewed with travel funds, and a visa to Germany."

Guy shouted, "I'm coming with you."

"Guy, its best if you and George join me later. I'll ask Annabelle to get visas for you also," said Victoria and hung up.

In the ladies' room Victoria exchanged her black slacks for a calf-length skirt and pinned her hair into a bun at the nape of her neck. She put on her hat with a bow and a feather as she walked out. She pulled her black speckled notebook out of her bag and wrote in it, focusing deeply, as she wrote. " I wish to be with George Herbert Mead." Then she took out her special watch and meditated on being with him.

The front door of the restaurant, opened into a large atrium with glass walls and ceilings extending the five-story height of the building. She took a deep breath, and thought of her new home, in Mead's time, where the air was not so polluted. The freeway noise dissolved into the background, the buildings lower as she walked. A horse-drawn milk wagon intermingled with the fewer smaller cars. She put her hand out for a cab. A small yellow Buick with fender lamps pulled up to her. She stepped on the running board and through the open door. The driver had dark hair and an Italian accent. "2518 Brownell St." she said. "Near Halsted?" he asked.

PART III
GERMANY 1930s-1940s

Chapter Twenty
Heidegger and Fetzer

Can we live in this world where historical occur-
rence is nothing but an unending concatenation of illu-
sory progress and bitter disappointment?
Edmund Husserl, *The Crisis of the European Sciences*

The sun was just beginning to set over the Rhine, throwing soft light into Martin Heidegger's library window. His long time friend Fetzer, head of his family's ship building firm, had stopped by on his way home for beer and conversation.

Pacing back and forth, Fetzer shouted, "Double the production of sub-marines, orders from the Reich. Double! Can you imagine? So I asked Verpel, this little beedy-eyed Nazi bureaucrat, where am I to get the iron, the skilled labor, the factory space at shoreline to increase at all, let alone double". Drops of beer fell on the ancient Persian rug as he waived his stein in the air.

Weary from a day of lecturing and writing Heidegger nevertheless attempted to cheer up his usually jovial friend. "Yah, but Fetzer Ships will make millions of mark!" Instantly he realized this was the wrong thing to have said as his friend's breath became deeper.

Fetzer slammed down his stein on the table as he sat down, looking straight at Martin. "More submarines when people are hungry! Besides, the Brits will know find out and they will increase their surveillance." he shouted.

Martin put his hands inside his suspender straps. The springs in his chair creaked as he leaned back. He could counter Emil Fetzer's position. "Hitler says we have the Bolshevik wolves at our back door and the French in front of us. We must have strength at sea to ward off the British colonialist robbers. And there is some truth to what he says. The taxes for the reparations and the inflation are making slaves of all Germans," said Heidegger. His dark eyes were moist, and his brow furrowed. Recently installed as the rector of Freiburg University, he had to join the party and be supportive at least on the surface. Leaving the party would have dire consequences for his family and the university, which would be put in the hands of a party hack.

"So you admit he is preparing for war, a war which we cannot afford," said Fetzer. He bottomed out his stein, then reached over for the pitcher and poured another.

"None of us wants war, but we have to be prepared to defend ourselves. The British have an enormous navy. But Mein Freund, lets not talk politics. I have news for you. I heard from Frau Dr. Von Dietz, Sie Komst hier." He tipped his stein towards Emil and took a drink. His face flushed.

Fetzer's faced changed from grimace to grin. "Javol, Martin. Zo Sie ist Verkommen, die Frau Dr. Von Dietz Mead, to vork mit du?"

"Yahvol, she will stay a few months." Emil raised his eyebrows. Martin jumped in to justify. "We must work on completion of a manuscript."

Fetzer removed his jacket, revealing an elegant sweater vest of forest green. Considering all the beer Fetzer drank his physique remained toned. "Of course this will require long days together and morning walks in the forest," Emil said.

Martin felt happy, unusual, for him. "You know, Herr Hesse (under direct orders from our new leader, Adoph Hitler) is interested in seeing our work together published and widely distributed. This may be a way for my work to reach an English speaking audience."

Fetzer rolled his eyes. "Yavol, my friend, of course there is no time allowed for pleasure unless ordered by the Fuhrer. When Adolph's portrait gets on beer bottles we'll know what German national socialism really means."

Martin hooked his thumbs under the suspenders and walked to the window looking out at the snow-capped mountains.

"The party wishes to show the world that German scholarship is fair-minded, is not anti-American and shows acceptance for women scholars," Martin said. Predicting Fetzer's critical response he added, "the party is doing this for propaganda, but at least some women, such as Dr. Von Dietz, will be given a chance."

But Fetzer jumped right in. "Another meaningless display of pseudo-open-mindedness. But Frau Victoria is not just any American scholar. She's the wife of your philosophical opponent, George Herbert Mead!" He slapped Martin on his back and walked to the opposite side of the room. He looked at the deep valley below. Rows of vineyards wound down the side of the valley, the sun setting in gold and amber over the Rhine.

Heidegger turned toward Fetzer with a broad grin. "That's just a coincidence. Her work is on the nature of time. She has depth of understanding for my work, more than any other American scholar."

"Depth, depth, certainly you wish to penetrate her very deeply," laughed Fetzer.

"Don't mock her at least until you have read her," said Martin. He was glad things had turned over towards their more typical way of friendly sparing.

"Martin, I vonder how much of Frau Von Dietz' work YOU have actually read," said Fetzer. He thrust his right hand into his jacket pocket and pointed it towards Martin.

"Johann, lets not be boyish about this with vulgar gestures," said Martin, frowning at his friend.

"You are defending her honor like a fine knight. I must know more about this Gwenaviere," said Fetzer.

"Frau Dr. Von Dietz' work goes beyond thinking to action. She learned from Hegel how humans may take control of their own history. She is a musician, and contends that the timing of existence can be composed, time can over lap just as in music, two different rhythms can be played simultaneously." Heidegger's voice rose with excitement, he walked back to his desk and sat to regain his composure.

"Martin, You are way over my head, and your heels seem to be over yours. To borrow an expression from you, she has . . . 'opened a clearing for new beings to appear'." Fetzer refilled his stein from the pitcher, then took a long draw then sat on a bench under the window. "But what about your Elfriede? Vill she tolerate this extended visit from a beautiful colleague?" he asked.

"Meine Frau is ready to make friends with her, they already exchanged letters," said Martin. "They both have great grandparents from the same part of Prussia, and have family backgrounds which include Prussian Calvary officers and clergy."

"You must watch these women, Martin. Females may act like sisters, but they are really, after all, in competition for your affections and attentions," said Fetzer. "Women are more naturally the sexual predators, not men, who are far too busy with more important things, like riding horses and making wars."

"Elfriede will explain how I throw my socks under the bed and don't listen when she talks," said Martin. Victoria will want to know what sweet names I call Elfriede. She'll tell Elfriede how significant my work is. Elfriede will agree, but then add that none of it bears any relationship to actual life. Besides, the Frau Professor's husband, Professor George Mead, follows six weeks after. Elfriede is happy about this. She is, as you know, a very solid, everyday realist. Even my theories of Being and Time thwart the limits of her imagination. Despite teaching at the Hochschule, mein Frau is a KKK woman, Kinder, Kirche, Kuchen (children, church, kitchen)."

"Elfriede is good counterfoil for life with a deep thinking philosopher" said Fetzer.

It will be fun to see you and Herr Professor Mead engage each other. I've heard you rant regularly about those shallow University of Chicago pragmatists." A breeze coming in brought an aroma of the tall rustling juniper. The Horst Wesel song echoed in the valley as a troup of Hitler Youth hiked past. A mockingbird sang from a high tree just below the window.

"This I know, Fetzer. American intellectuals can be so disgustingly optimistic only because they have not experienced war or invasion of their own soil," said Martin. Their civil war so traumatized them that Americans don't discuss politics! They freed the slaves, but only to roam the streets in the northern cities, unemployed, ending up in prison. They put their Native Americans, "Indians' as they call them as if the Pacific still was not discovered, into rural concentration camps. So much for democracy and tolerance."

Martin turned and picked his long-stemmed meerschaum pipe up from his desk and lifted the silver top off the glass jar of tobacco: "Professor Mead had tried, in his way, to explain the nature of time. He packed tobacco into the bowl with his thumb and forefinger. He held the bowl of the pipe up to his nose."

"You know, Fetzer, this fine tobacco from the American south smells just as good before it is lit. Professor George Mead sent it to me as a sign of good will." He walked over to the fireplace, opened a metal container and took out a match. The container had a filigree design with images of knights on it. "He said it is Frau Mead's favorite."

The aroma of rum soaked tobacco filled the air. Fetzer took a sniff and raised his eyebrows. "The man is either naïve or is willing to tempt fate, that aroma is intoxicating!"

"It must be the former. Herr Mead also has the belief that truth, democracy and ethics develop together. He sees no greater truths than the will of the masses." He looked at his image in the bookshelf glass and adjusted his expression to a slight smile.

"The rule of Das Man," said Martin slapping his hand on his knee.

Fetzer laughed, "and you give them modern technology, which is their version of science und alles ist Kaput!"

"Finished!" said Martin, with fervor.

Chapter Twenty-One
Victoria and Martin

(The poet) must be the gadfly mating with a firefly.
Lawrence Ferlinghetti, *Americus*

She recognized Heidegger from the train, standing on the station platform in Freiburg. A reddish light of the beginning sunset cascaded through the glass, making a rainbow on her skirt. His image caught in her throat. She gasped for air. The porter groaned from the weight of her bag, muttering about Die Frauen and the chemistry sets they carry. "Nein, Das ist mein work. Mein book," she asserted. No need to fess up to the few jars of facial cleansers and creams she brought along for her sensitive skin.

Off the train, she lost sight of Heidegger as a carload of uniformed men filled the platform, shovels hanging over their shoulders like rifles. Hmm, these were most likely the "worker corps", a way of keeping military buildup hidden. A cold damp wind chilled her.

A hand reached through the crowd—it was Heidegger! Looking into his amber eyes, she felt as if she had dived into a deep warm pool. She recalled what her mother used to say whenever "Komst Du Gut Heim, Come Good Home." Tears melted down her cheeks. Why should this strange place and time feel like home?

Heidegger said softly, "Is something wrong?" A rosy color came to his cheeks as he looked at her. His left hand reached forward and held her elbow, as if he were almost to lead her in a waltz across a ballroom floor. The rhythm of the music was in his voice and in the pulsating current from his body. She placed her hand on his forearm, feeling the soft wool of his dark grey jacket. "Ich liebe dich, I love you," she thought. She cast out the thought, replacing it with "It is just admiration for his work."

"Nothing wrong. I am fine, Herr Dr. Heidegger, just a sweet thought of my mother."

"You think of your mother when you see me?" The gentle humor in his eyes made her smile.

"She had never seen Germany, nor did my Grandmother, yet both spoke German perfectly."

"Your work is about transcending distance and time, perhaps we could conspire to also bring her," said Heidegger.

"That would be lovely, but she was such a big talker we couldn't get anything done," Victoria said, still bewildered by the time travel lag, and how prescient Heidegger's comment, given that he didn't realize yet that she originated from a future time.

He deposited her bag with a porter. "Let's take a walk, he said nodding to a path into a forest behind the station. The pine fragrance from the giant trees surrounded them. "Lovely," she said, the trees remind me of our family's lake home in Northern Wisconsin."

They walked through the forest, their feet sinking down into the soft pine needle and moss path. Martin's shoes had thick soles, perhaps he didn't feel the unevenness of the path as much as she. She felt vibrant, though her sore feet burned. Above crows flapped their wings, busy in the dusk, filling their bellies against the dark night coming.

As they turned back toward the station, she saw the shadows of soldiers, these with rifles, not shovels. A war was in progress. "I've heard that universities and some professors are threatened under Hitler. I worried that you, your work, may be effected."

He pulled back his shoulders, cleared his throat. "There is much to be desired in any real political situation. I fear the manipulation of all aspects of life by technological forces." He plunged his hands into his pockets and his stride shortened. "There is a driven logic to Western science which is to control, to dominate both nature and man. It leads us even deeper into an abyss, to what theologians called the 'death of god'." She recalled that he began his academic life as a theology student just after World War I, when the "god is dead" concept emerged.

As the dusk descended, the pine scent befell her like a soft blanket. It was hard to breathe. The boughs and brush were manicured around the walkway. Suddenly Martin took a turn to the left under a bow, to a narrow pathway. She hesitated. His look penetrated her. "Come, only the deer and elves come this way," he winked. She stayed close behind Martin. His shadow engulfed hers so it became a two-headed beast of the forest. His footsteps were slow and relentless even as his arms spread, clearing the branches. Her shoulder bag slapped against her left hip on each step, like a downbeat, with the right step swishing as an after beat. Her heart beat faster as her body felt the rhythm. She imagined him behind instead of in front, close behind, touching, his hips against her quivering buttocks. Her nipples stood erect beneath her blouse. She felt intimidated, powerless. She pictured herself naked, lying in bed, burning beneath him, even as they entered a small clearing, where the sunset glimmed like a rainbow through the millions of pine needles. He led her to a tree stump in the clearing. He knelt beside her, looking up at the light. She recalled his writing that the gods who men had driven away may appear if we made a clearing for them, in time and space. She could think of no words to capture her feelings and also did not want to engage in what he derogatively called "Gerade" or "idle chatter".

His silent presence in the forest was intoxicating. He stood in front of her, bowed and kissed her hand and led her back to the path. She shook her head to free herself of erotic thoughts. "I wonder, Dr. Heidegger, since you speak of god and the gods, why you left your studies of theology?"

"My dear Frau Dr. Mead," he sighed. "I'm often asked that question. It is one question that has many answers." He continued to walk as he spoke. She quickened her pace to stay close and hear, close enough to catch his intoxicating over-heated scent. This was Heidegger offering explanation! She needed to suppress her phantasies.

"Western theologians, like metaphysicians, try to limit, explain what is beyond human capacity. They end up with crippled notions. The Hindus don't limit god to one form, and they know him or her (yes they include the goddesses, as we did in ancient times) in many ways." he said.

Heidegger slowed suddenly at a rise in the path, and Victoria bumped into him. Gently, with her hands on his back, she steadied herself "Enschultegen Sie Mir, Bitte." Now composed, she added, "Yes, I know the yogis practices include karma (good works), hatha (postures), prana (breath), kriya (worship) and raja (philosophy)." She felt like a schoolgirl, reciting her lesson.

"You are quite the scholar of what is wrongly called "Hinduism" but is really a complex array of philosophies and religious practices based on the ancient Vedantic texts. But the purpose of all the yogas, as I understand from my conversations with a Japanese Zen master, is in order to become one with the universe through clearing the mind," said Martin.

He apparently had not noticed, was absorbed in their walk, perhaps the conversation, the momentary touch of her body against his back.

But no, he had noticed. He stopped and turned, pulled her close. "I've often imagined bringing you to my forest," he said and kissed her deeply.

This was where and when she wanted to be more than anywhere and anytime else.

Later, as they walked to his Mercedes, the lowering sun disappeared behind some clouds and it began to drizzle. She flashed to a time soon to come, a long line of fighter planes, taking off on an icy runway in North Hesse, flying Northwest, one after another, each engine pulling forward, pilots starring out the windshield, as the rain drops rushed into rivers of tears sliding down their mothers' cheeks, which became blood pooled on their fathers', uncles,' brothers' bullet-laden chests.

Could anything ever be done to stop wars which seemed so inevitable? Even if millions stood up all over the world and said no to war, would that stop the war makers?

Six Weeks Later

"Liebschen, kommst Du here by me" Martin said, and opened his arms. His dark eyes melted into her. Their warmth was echoed in his brown tweed jacket. Though also warming dressed in a black wool skirt and beige sweater, Victoria trembled. Hanging on a chain around her neck were two pearls, her white pearl and now also a black pearl. "You are wearing the pearl I gave you, but you still also are wearing the white pearl," said Heidegger.

"I wear the white one as it is a connection with my daughter, back in Chicago," she said, touching the white pearl. She looked down at the black pearl, rolling it between her thumb and forefinger. "Six weeks of bliss. It's lovely, I treasure it!"

"I got it when I was in southern France last year from Van Der Hyde, a childhood friend. Now he raises them in French Polynesia." He pulled her close to him, smiled and looked into her eyes. "Your eyes are as deep as the ocean the black pearl came from." He kissed her mouth. Then he stopped to say, "they sparkle like the diamonds he nests in between." He kissed her lips again then down her neck until his head rested between her breasts.

Fast, breathless and dark. Dreadful and dark, down digging, panting, running away and coming back, and coming and coming, tearing and dredging up her father's face, his smell, but he was tall and blond, not Jewish. Oh my God, Martin, of course is not Jewish either, but south German, swarthy, dark, pounding and sweating, he seems now in heat like a Nebelung, the deepest plunge, deeper even than their first. Beating and hot, nothing matters except that he keep on her until they fall, fall fall into a sea underneath the ocean. Oh, Oh Gut in Himmel, sweet Krishna, Hare, Hare, roulette gambling wheel.

As they fell asleep Martin hummed a melody from Brahm's 4th symphony. When his baritone cut off she continued the movement in mezzo-soprano.

"I hope I'm pregnant," she shouted, waking up, an hour later. "Oh my god, what did I say."

"Darling, you are. There is life growing here, and you've had no cycle since you arrived six weeks ago. " He pressed his hand gently on her belly. "Herr must be Deutschland gebornen, Gebunsright"

"Sie may be en Madschen," she said, putting her hand on his.

"Nein, Ich habe herren auch (only)," he said.

"When I read your idea of "the nothing that underlies all being" I thought of how I felt many times when my menstrual period arrived. Like the reassertion of "Das Nichts".

"Blood running down your legs is hardly like Nothing." Martin's voice was resonant. "The Nothing is more like the vast black hole the physicists speak of, which is somehow beyond space and time."

She thought that this may be the secret for her time travel. Should she reveal herself to him? "We must explore this further in our work," she said.

He arose and dressed in his lederhosen and high socks. "Listen to me, Mein Leibschen. We don't have much time. You must tell me what is going on in America. People there do not much care about European border disputes, do they? They are too busy making cars and refrigerators and highways, no? They must know Germany had to recover the lost homeland from the war, restore the self-respect of her people. Your Prussia, our Prussia must be saved from the Pollack barbarians. The Russians as well have designs on us."

"Martin, how can such a brilliant man be so politically naïve? You don't see the realities of Hitler and the National Socialist Party. You think he is for the people, and against the large corporations and the rampant mechanization of the world. But really he is only after his own power and won't stop until millions have died," said Victoria.

"Of course Hitler is after power." He was dissatisfied with his tie and stripped it off. "Germans were starving, could not afford bread, due to the great costs imposed on us by the Versailles Treaty. Germany must have power if our culture is to survive." Martin redid his tie and threaded it under his short collar. "Whatever you think of his manner, Herr Hitler loves the Germany. And how do you know millions will die? They need protection from the ravages of their own governments, look how Austria welcomed us!" said Heidegger.

Victoria threw off the down quilt and walked naked across the floor; her feet felt the cold when she reached the edge of the rug. She had to explain who she really was or he'd never understand what she was about, wouldn't be able to trust her. She picked her sweater up from the chair and pulled it over her head.

Sensing a change in her mood, he said, "What's wrong, my dear. What troubles you?"

She pulled her black hosiery up and stepped into her slip without answering. Silently she pulled her skirt on. He waited patiently, watching her. "I must tell you, Martin, there's more to my work than just a theory. Overlapping time is also a practice. I know things from the future that you can't know from this time. "You must do all you can to resist Hitler and the Nazis. My friend, who

I knew, or will know, in the future, Helmut Wagner, is in the resistance. He is on his way to meet you," said Victoria.

"You told me of your vision of what will happen. But this is just your vision. I am in my position here to help the Third Reich resist the strangulation of the being and culture by forces of technology and the mass mind," said Heidegger.

Victoria put her hands on Heidegger's shoulders, shaking him gently as she spoke, "Darling, you must see that Hitler's rhetoric about a better world is shrouded in robes of death and unreason. Anyone who blames problems on a scapegoat people, like the Jews, is not going to address the real problems. He is only after more power," she said, not knowing how to explain to him that she was from the future.

"I refuse to believe this. Hitler's policies have already helped the economy. He has pulled us out of starvation, raised our spirits as well as our standard of living, given us hope for the first time in eighteen years. Let's not argue about whose predictions are true. If we are going to discuss anything, it should be about your husband's near arrival here. What are we going to do about this? I can't bear being away from you." Martin reached for his suspenders and buttoned them on his trousers, slipped them over his shoulder, his mind shut like a vault door to the mayhem building on the horizon.

She loved the smell of his woolen clothing mixed with the pine and his pipe tobacco. She felt her breast swelling. Yet she also missed George. George was much less dramatic, but somehow more real. She'd noticed that people like the Germans who grew up with war around them were inwardly wounded, even those who escaped physical injury.

"I know it will be difficult. But he must come. George spends hours a day with his work, and has lots of old friends from his student days to visit here. He also plans to engage academic and political colleagues, pushing forward on his League of Nations efforts."

"Ach yah, and he must leave us alone together each day when he works. Speaking of spouses, my dear, I must run. Elfriede was expecting me an hour ago. We'll talk about this all later." Martin kissed her again. He walked across the wood floor of her room, put on his jacket, then out the door and down the stairs of the Black Eagle Gasthaus.

"More heavy thinking today Professor Heidegger?" said the housekeeper as he walked past the kitchen. "Yah, Frau Professor Dr. Von Dietz and I are making great progress on the manuscript." He reached in his pocket and pulled out a ten-mark note and pushed it in her hand.

"Take Frau Von Dietz some fresh fruit and some whole goats milk in a little while, and some of that nice plum cake I smell coming from your wonderful kitchen," he said. He pinched her on the cheek, and patted her on the buttocks.

"You're such a sweet plum cake yourself," she said, turning toward the kitchen.

Chapter Twenty-Two
George and Guy Arrive in Germany

The university was to renew itself on its own, thus establish-
ing a firm position against the politicization of knowledge.
Martin Heidegger, *Only a God Can Save Us Now*

"The editor wants to know whether 'Dasein" should be 'decent' or 'descent', said Victoria, laughing as she held a page proof in her hand. If anything it is 'indecent'," said Martin, looking over her shoulders at a thick pile of typed paper with lots of red ink.

"But descended from a long line of deep thinkers," said Victoria. She grabbed his hand and squeezed it. He pulled her to him, kissing her palm.

As the sun was setting through the paned window, an x-shaped shadow crossed Martin's desk.

Three sharp knocks on the door. Elfriede stormed in without waiting for a reply. Victoria pulled away. Did Elfriede suspect! Never before had she slept with a married man. Her face felt as if Elfreide had slapped her. She genuinely liked Elfriede and adored George. Yet, intersecting time zones made each situation a different incarnation. Victoria's belly tightened as she remembered the pain of Tom's betrayal. The body holds emotions, whether from the past or the future.

"Victoria, Herr Mead ist heir und ein anderen, Mr. Guy. My what a fine looking gentlemen." The corners of her mouth and her eyebrows rose as she glanced at Martin, as if to say, 'you're not the only man around, honey.' Instead she did say,

"Martin, do you want them to come up?" ruffling her skirt and smoothing her hair.

"Nein, mein Liebchen," said Martin. We'll come down and have coffee in the library."

Victoria felt weak with a wave of morning sickness. She wished for mashed potatoes and gravy, just as she had with Kathy. Martin assumed the baby is his, but it could be George's, from the night before she left. Hopefully this is what George would assume. She forced herself to stand, masking the deep breath needed to steady herself.

"Victoria, are you feeling alright? You look pale. Perhaps it is a shock to see your husband after such a time away," said Elfriede.

"She's been working hard, that's all," said Martin. "I'll pour her a little brandy first, then we'll come down."

"Don't be long." Elfriede left. Martin poured a double shot of brandy. Victoria took a sip, then another and handed it to Martin to finish. "Ah, now I can face Herr Mead," he said.

The setting sun cascaded red and orange on the thickly carpeted stairs.

Martin squeezed Victoria's shoulder, opened the library door. The burgundy rug seemed to wave toward her. George rushed up and held her, guiding her to a high-backed chair covered with a heraldic pattern.

George's blue eyes glimmered as if he were about to make love with her. His moustache twitched as he smiled. He hugged and kissed her and said, "You look beautiful my dear, if a bit pale. Are you well?

She wished to rub her belly to sooth it, but resisted, not wishing to bring attention. "I'm fine dear, it's just the excitement of seeing you here.

Guy cleared his throat.

"And Guy, so good to see you, as well."

Mead stepped back, as if sensing her inner conflict. He looked at Martin who stood regally erect. Elfriede stepped forward, gesturing towards George.

"No introductions are necessary, my dear," said Martin to Elfriede. "Welcome, Herr Dr. Mead. I've anticipated with pleasure your arrival." He put his hand out to Mead, and in shaking his hand, pulled Mead away from Victoria. "Und Gustaf, here, welcome, welcome."

Towering over him Guy said, "It's "Guy", Herr Dr. Heidegger, Bitte," and pulled his hand away just a little bit too soon.

Victoria watched the men's gentile sparring, her heart pounding. I love both of them, and appreciate Guy's devotion. She didn't know if she was the luckiest woman alive or the most confused.

"Und you've met Mein Frau, Elfriede," said Martin. He nodded towards her and smiled. Elfriede slid against him. He squeezed her waist.

"I've already met both charming gentleman. I hope your trip was not so difficult,' said Elfriede.

"The plane stopped in Newfoundland, and again in England to fuel. Then in England there with lots of security clearances, delays."

"Too bad your flight had to be in this time of international tension," said Victoria, barely catching herself from saying "pre-jet".

Elfriede raised her eyebrows, looking at Martin. "I thought all flights were cancelled since the crash of the Hinderberg last year."

"We came via a special U. S. Air Force plane," said Mead, "thanks to Victoria's research grant officer, Annabelle Carter Jackson, who pulled some strings."

"Ah zehr gut. This is much preferable to travel by ship, with the British navy out with heavy guns."

"Ships are slow. I could not have born any more time away from my dear," said Mead. "But the flight was grueling, for a man of my age."

"My dear you seem younger all the time," said Victoria. In seeing Heidegger and Mead together at this time, however, Heidegger was twenty-some years younger. Maybe she could do something about this as she worked out the mathematics of the time travel.

Guy reached in his satchel and pulled out a bottle of wine wrapped in tissue. He handed it Victoria. "Complements of Dr. Annabelle Carter Jackson."

"Oh, my favorite, a Napa Valley chardonnay. Lets all have some," said Victoria. She handed it back to Guy.

"Napa valley? Chardonnay? Was ist das? Elfriede's eyebrows were raised.

"Its like your Liebfraumilch only it is not sweet." said Guy.

"I made some fresh plum cake this morning and will bring you some to go with the wine. This is our maid's day off. It always comes on the wrong day." Elfriede moved to the door.

"I'll help you gladly, Frau Heidegger," said Guy, following.

Guy looked back at them over a shoulder, his neck red. He held up the bottle and pointed to the 1974 date on the label. Victoria pondered. How did Annabelle get the wine to Guy? Would Elfriede notice?

"I'm happy to have the company of such a young handsome assistant," said Elfriede as they left.

Suddenly the room became tense, with Victoria sitting between the two men.

Mead broke in, "The book, my darling. How goes it?" Mead asked.

"Victoria has made remarkable strides in attempting to reconcile your theory of time with mine," said Martin.

"Victoria had been living my thoughts and ideas, my books, so fully and intentionally, that she brought me again into being, and together with her." His eyes rested on Victoria.

"A wonderfully romantic notion, for a behaviorist," said Heidegger.

Guy returned pushing a caddie with the bottle of wine and five glasses, saucers and napkins.

"One can come upon oneself most fully when one makes a clearing–an opening for Being and beings to come out of concealment," said Victoria. This thought of yours, Martin, has brought us all together here today.

Since Elfriede was not aware of them as time travelers, Victoria wanted to conversation to shift before she returned, but the men were energetic in continuing the point.

"Ach, this is a misinterpretation of what I was saying," Martin said. "I emphasized the particular history of each of us, saying we are "thrown" into the world at a particular time and place, have no choice in the matter, must deal with it as it comes." Martin ended at a tight, high pitch.

Guy stepped forward, folded his arms in front of his chest, cleared his throat. "Surely the most interesting question before us is not the fine points between your philosophies. Rather it is how Victoria drew upon these con- tradictions and made it possible for us to come together into Heidegger's' world. Mead from the past of this frame and Victoria and I from the future. Victoria, not either one of you, brought your philosophies to life, and here you are arguing about it!" Guy stopped short, smiled. He poured the wine into the five glasses. "We shall see how well wine travels in space as well as time," he said.

Victoria admired both his instantaneous defense of her and his ability to take a quick breath and restore the calm and joy. And just in time, as Elfriede entered with a tray of warm plum cake. She set it down on the table in front of them.

"Please, help yourselves," said Elfriede.

Martin said, "Before any more explanations, lets taste this California wine." Guy passed the glasses around.

"Prosit" said Elfriede.

Victoria took a sip hoping it had not somehow turned to vinegar. She smiled, "it has held up very well to travel."

Frieda sipped and puckered her lips. "Too tart for me. I'm sorry, Victoria, but I prefer my Liebfraumilch. She looked at the bottle on the tray. "Hmm, must be something wrong with the label printers in California, it says 1974!"

Victoria hoped she would not have to reveal her origins to Elfriede. She is too tight with the party. She may report Victoria as crazy or dangerous.

Guy jumped in. "Frau Heidegger, that is the date the Vintner projects as the last date at which the wine will be good to drink."

"Ah, such as system," Elfried said, " we should live so long."

"Perhaps if we drank enough of the wine then we would," Mead chortled. "However, I'm not going to ignore the sweet plum cakes whose aroma fills the room."

Victoria rose and reached for a large slice, placing it on a rose tinted glass plate. "If the rest of you get caught up in words, you may find the cake all gone," she said. Victoria cut another slice and handed it to George.

"It says a lot for what my life was like when, before we met in person, I felt closer to George from reading his books than to people I knew," said Victoria.

"All this talk of words makes me dizzy," said Elfriede. "But I understand what Victoria said. I had only seen the Fuhrer's picture and was already enthralled. Then when I heard his voice on the radio, I felt like I used to as a little girl with my father. Here was someone who cares about me so deeply he would make war with the world to protect our home."

Four sets of eyes raised.

"Meine Frau, like most women," said Heidegger, "is in love with Herr Hitler. But we men don't concern ourselves with it. Only if he lived next door." Then, deflecting the tension, he smiled at her, taking a bite of cake. "This is your best yet, my dear."

"Victoria is correct to dig down to the roots of an idea. She shows us the power of authentic willing. With this weapon of knowledge we will channel the energies aroused by our new Fuhrer," Martin said.

Mead frowned," I wouldn't be so sure."

Guy took a deep breath, as Victoria looked him in the eye.

"Now we live at the times of the world's night, though a new dawn is coming. Don't you see how, with your help, we could influence the Fuhrer, to bring forward the best of culture, not only in Germany, but in the world?" said Martin.

Guy, now red in the face said: "Herr Professor Heidegger, you speak as remarkably as you write. But please, sir, that's not what's happening. You don't get the same news here as we get in the rest of the world. Your Nazi party screens it out. Already Hitler is pushing Jewish scholars and scientists out of the country, and the future will be worse, herding them and their families into work camps, gassing them by thousands. How can you work as university Chancellor in such a system?"

Martin looked at Victoria and Mead, who were nodding at what Guy said. "So what would you have me to do? If I resign like some of the others, the Reich will appoint a party functionary to administer the university. This will mean more losses. Whereas if I stay on, we all can have a chance to access and influence Hitler."

Victoria thought of how especially unfair it was that this man, her love, her Martin, was to be condemned after the war for holding this position for the short time he did. Americans were so self-righteous, condemning other cultures when they have gone around the world committing mass murder as in Vietnam and assisting vicious dictators in other countries if it served their economic and political interests.

"Oh, my, what ridiculous rumors are spread in America about our Fuhrer. You will soon learn the truth of what a wonderful gift he is to Germans and to the world," said Elfriede.

Noticing that Guy was about to offer a rebuttal, Mead looked him in the eye and shook his head slightly.

"Frau Heidegger, I apologize, we have all gotten too quickly into discussions of theories and politics," said Mead.

"Indeed, Dr. Mead," said Elfriede. "Please Guy, pour more tea and coffee. Dr. Mead, Victoria tells me of her daughter Kathy, back in Chicago. How is she?"

"Thank you for asking. She is well and in school in Chicago."

Elfriede smiled but her eyes remained with an intense focus. "Very good." She looked towards Victoria's belly and continued. "Now of course with a little one on the way, she will have a little brother or sister soon," smiled Elfriede, looking at Victoria's belly.

Victoria flushed red. How did she know? And how dare she?

Mead looked flushed, his mouth opened. "Darling, you didn't tell me. I thought it must be the good German food," he said, looking at Victoria.

"Oh, I'm so sorry if I made a slipup. I assumed you were expecting and perhaps it is just Ilse's cooking. But no, I am usually right about such things," said Elfriede.

Victoria blushed. "Your intuitions are correct, Elfriede, but I have not told George yet. George, I was waiting to tell you in person," she said looking at George.

Guy took a step back, looked away.

"It's wonderful, my darling," said Mead.

"Then we all have something to celebrate," said Elfriede. Martin, get a bottle of Liebsfraumilch out of the wine cellar. No two bottles."

Guy coughed, covering his confused feelings. "Yes, lets drink to the new parents," he said.

"And to the child to come," said Martin.

Chapter Twenty-Three
Elfriede's Wooden Spoon

Elfriede Heidegger fussed and doted over her husband at his breakfast, moving the salt and pepper shakers, adjusting the spoon in the sugar bowl, sniffing at the pot of cream. Her hands grasped the points of his collar, her fingers reaching around his neck.

Martin knew it was best to remain calm, though he wondered: Does she want to choke me? I wouldn't blame her. Of course she's suspicious of my relationship with Victoria, all the time we spend together.

As much as he cared for Victoria, he had no intention of leaving Elfriede and his boys.

"Vielen Danken Mein Liebshen. Come sit and have coffee with me." He gave her his best smile.

"I've had mine much earlier, with the boys." Her eyes were pinched. Glaring at him from across the table, her knuckles white as she gripped the top of the chair. She's a tall and handsome woman, he observed, bright and righteous.

"Martin, who is it you said is coming this afternoon? And don't bother to tell me Dr. Von Dietz. No matter what else is going on Dr. Von Dietz comes. It could be Herr Braun come to discus his cows today. Dr. Von Dietz would be asked to give counsel on how he should treat his lame heifer. And just call her Victoria, as you do when I'm not around. Don't hide behind her formal names and titles. After all, I use her Christian name. We are friendly, you know."

He must not react. This would only inflame things. He picked up a fresh baked roll from the basket and sniffed it.

"Still warm. Gastreich's must have delivered late this morning." He enjoyed the crunchy sound when he broke it open to spread the thick plum preserves. He bit and chewed, humming his pleasure.

"No, dear. I warmed them up for you. I always warm them up, but often these days you are getting up later." She took the coffee pot off the stove, poured herself a cup. She swished her skirt. Not a usual gesture for her, looks like its new, better say something.

"The skirt is very becoming, mein Liebchin. Is it new?" He held his cup up, "Bitte?" She poured. "Yes a sale downtown. I liked the colors."

"Very good colors for you, dear," he said looking down at the "Freiburg Zietung". The headlines read: "German Troops Welcomed in Austria". There was a picture of two women, one young and one old, and two children waving out of a second story window.

"Martin, I asked you a question earlier."

"Ach Ya about Dr. Von Dietz' knowledge of cows. Yes she does know something about cows. They raise Guernsey's in Wisconsin, her home state," said Martin.

"French cows in Wisconsin?" said Elfriede.

"Yes, Liebchen, French cows, and with the milk they make Swiss cheese. They have so-called German breweries as well in Wisconsin. Meine Gute Frau, I thought now that Professor Mead has arrived you'd no longer be so jealous. Victoria and I have much work to do on the manuscripts, as you know," he said, stretching and snapping his suspenders.

Finally, she sat flaring her skirt over the side of the chair. "Professor Mead is a delight. So charming," said Elfriede. "But a little bit old for her, no? And he doesn't seem to spend much time with her. But I do like their assistant, Guy, So helpful he is."

"I have to hold you back from mauling him," said Martin.

"Now look who's jealous!"

He stood up and went behind her, put his hands on her shoulders. "My dear, we are so much more than husband and wife. We are also guten Freunden. This means whatever comes up we can work it out. Now I must go to the university."

"Don't you leave until you answer my real question. Is anyone coming over this afternoon?"

"Ach, that question. Yes, Helmut Wagner, a tool and dye maker from Bremen. But not to the house. We are meeting at Brauhauser. Come over. Schutz will also be there," said Heidegger.

"Tool and dye maker? I know you write about a man and his tools at great length in *Being and Time*. I had retyped the thing so many times. Does this mean you are revising it yet again?"

Heidegger sighed. "You know my work is always in revision. But this was just my point. The man working becomes most aware of the nature of what he is doing when his tools break."

Elfriede brushed his hands from her shoulder and stood. She picked a wooden spoon off the counter and held it up over his head. "So, I vood know a lot more about you if I broke this spoon over your head." Heidegger ran around the table and she followed, beating him on the hinder. He turned around and grabbed her wrist and pulled her to him with his other arm.

"You know that your spoon arouses me, you temptress, you," he said.

"I do, love, but I've no time for shenanigans. I'm substitute teaching today at the hochschule. She hung up her apron and took a deep breath. "I can't go tonight to Braumeister's to meet your tool and dye maker. I have a Third Reich Woman's Auxiliary Meeting. Say Hello to Dr. Schutz, as well as Dr. Mead. Give Guy a kiss for me."

"What, nothing for Victoria?" he asked as she walked toward the door. He regretted instantly raising the image. Yet their joking and jousting was a way of both revealing and concealing.

"Ach, don't take things too far."

Martin put the remaining rolls back in the white cotton baker's bag on the counter. The boys would finish them off after school.

As he left the kitchen and went up to his study Martin thought of the utter uniqueness of the situation. Victoria had already met Helmut Wagner in the future when Wagner was much older. Now she is coming back to a time when he is younger and the same age as her. As it is, she will know the future, he will not. She must have special help from the gods, or be a kind of goddess herself to do these things. My philosophy of the finitude of human existence bounded by death does not fit this situation. Perhaps time is more like music, things coming back and referring to themselves. Hmm, I'll talk this over with Victoria when she arrives.

Chapter Twenty-Four
Singing for Dietrich

Underneath the lamplight
By the garden gate
Darling I remember
The way you used to wait . . .Song, Lily Marlene

"We will see some of the Freiburg night life," said Martin looking first at George, then Guy. Victoria hugged herself in her long loden coat as a cold wind swept through the cobblestone street. She walked next to George, following behind Martin and Guy. Guy's stride was jaunty, revealing his excitement at not only being in Germany in the 1930s but also out for a beer with their most famous philosopher. She was pleased that Martin and Guy got along so well, as this diffused the tension between the two philosophical rivals.

"Victoria, of course, has been here before." They turned the corner on the cobblestone street and saw the large hanging sign "Braumeister's Greywolf Hall". A nearly life sized image of Marlene Dietrich hung on the sandwich board next to the heavy wooden door.

"Is this where you've sung?" asked Guy.

"Only when she can't make it," said Victoria glancing up at Marlene.

Walking into the dark bar, they found their way to a large wooden table in the back. The room was packed with locals, ready for an evening of beer and fellowship. A dozen or so wore uniforms.

The waiter filled their steins from a large pitcher of dark beer. "Prosit! To our friendship and our work together, across oceans," said Mead, raising his stein.

"And across time," said Martin, looking at Victoria.

"And to the best beer in the world," said Guy. He tilted his stein toward the mural that depicted little elves, grinding grain into mash, crawling up ladders to stir huge barrels of beer, tasting the results, rolling around in haystacks.

A thick pall of pipe and cigarette smoke mixed with the aromas of steaming sauerkraut and knackwurst. A group of students at one of the front tables raised their steins singing a fasching song. In another corner, two-deep around a large table, young men in crisp brown shirts half sang, half shouted.

"The place is more and more filled with the fanatic idiots," Martin said. "The Nazi party gives the school failures and illiterates a way to feel good about their stupidity." Martin waved at Karl Keinhoph behind the bar. He pointed to the empty pitcher on the table. Keinhoph nodded.

"Schutz and Wagner should be here soon," said Martin. "Schutz wrote to me while he was still a student. Quite a bright fellow, became a member of the Vienna circle. Also he's a prominent international banker."

"Yah and Wagner goes on to study under Schutz after they emigrate to the U.S., later writing Schutz intellectual biography," said Guy.

Victoria sat in the chair she was accustomed to, next to Martin. Guy was about to sit on her other side, then stepped back to let Mead take this place.

Keinhoph arrived with a fresh pitcher of beer on a tray with a platter of sausage, brown bread, sauerkraut and mustard. Mead's eyes lit up. Victoria swallowed hard to restrain her nausea.

"My dear are you all right? You look pale," said Mead.

"Morning sickness is misnamed. It can come also in the evening. I'll feel better after eating." She swallowed the cold beer, looking forward to the tension release it was to bring. Martin filled a plate for her with bread and sausage.

"No kraut, tonight," she said. Trying to change the focus she said, "I'm enormously excited about meeting Schutz face to face. But it will be tricky with Wagner. Please help me with this as Wagner and I were friends, in the future, which at this time, of course he has not yet experienced."

"Should our associations with Wagner and Schutz continue they will eventually have to know." Mead piled his bread with sauerkraut and sausage, took a bite.

"Ach, this temporal fold may become a quagmire. But we must see what we can do," said Heidegger. "There is too much at stake to let things continue on the path that Victoria tells me is ahead."

Two men entered the club. A cool wind wafted behind them, bringing a fresh supply of oxygen. One wore a long tweed overcoat, a beige wool scarf and fedora. The other, taller, younger, with broad shoulders and a ruddy complexion wore a loden jacket and a knit ski cap.

"That must be Schutz and Wagner," said Victoria. But now Wagner has no idea he will ever be anything other than a skilled laborer."

"Victoria, remember not to let on about your future knowledge. Guy, you neither. They must be prepared for this," said Mead.

"Even if I hadn't seen pictures of Schutz or met Wagner when he was a visiting professor at Athens College, I would have guessed who they are," said Guy. They seem at least 25% more intelligent than everyone else here, present company excepted. Funny how intelligence shows."

"Sounds like an undemocratic idea to me," said Martin, with a wry grin.

"Democracy does not require us to pretend we are equally intelligent," said Mead.

"All of this debate on equality makes us forget who we really are," said Martin.

Victoria smiled inwardly. These three brilliant men provide everything I need, she thought. Then caught herself. I still look for fulfillment outside, from men. When will I grow up?

"You're laughing at us, Victoria," said Martin.

"No, at myself for enjoying the three of you during your struggles," she said.

The singing brownshirts got louder and less articulate. Victoria felt dizzy from the boom of feet stomping on the wood floor, glasses clinking and intermittent laughter.

The band struck up Deutschland Uber Alles, the German national anthem. The rowdy crowd became silent. They stood bellowed with their hands over hearts.

Guy walked up to get Schutz and Wagner.

Victoria and Martin stood, then Mead, raising his eyes and his chin. "We must show respect for our host country. They don't know what lies ahead." Victoria looked toward the band. Before Guy reached the front, Schutz approached the musicians. He turned his back to them and stood silently hands at his side.

"What's he doing?" asked Mead.

"He's Viennese. Most Austrians, did not welcome Hitler's invasion and occupation. Hitler was careful to photograph a street where he had personally seen to it that he would be cheered," said Martin.

Two mug-faced men in brown shirts walked up to Schutz, shoved him around to face the band. "All stand with respect here!" He pushed Schutz' arm in front of his chest and placed it on his heart, holding it there for a moment.

Guy pulled the brownshirt's hands off Schutz. Schutz grabbed Guy's arms in turn, just as two other brownshirts edged closer, angry looks on their ruddy faces. Schutz said, "I've made my point." Guy relented, the brownshirt stepped aside, warily. Schutz turned and faced the band for the remainder of the song.

"We can't work from prison," said Schutz as the song ended. Guy introduced himself and pointed back to the table. They shook hands. Schutz told them to go ahead to the table. He walked up to the accordion player on the platform, the bandleader. He pointed to the piano, gesturing with his hands like playing on a keyboard. The piano player got up from the bench and invited Schutz to play. He played a series of folksongs in the South German and North Austrian tradition. The accordion player joined in, said something to the others— a violinist, and a guy who moved between drums and trombone. The pianist led everyone singing together. After a few songs Schutz got up to cheers and whistles. Victoria recalled Schutz' famous essay, which he had not yet written, on the closeness required for making music together.

Schutz walked over to the table. The brownshirts' watched, still standing. Martin shook Schutz' hand. "Here's the gentleman who looked like he was ready to save my life," Schutz said, shaking Guy's hand.

"Honored to meet you," said Guy. "I've read your essays on phenomenology of the lifeworld. I want to be sure you're around to write the next volume soon. A selfish motive."

"You must read German. I didn't know my work had reached the attention of Americans." Schutz had a warm voice and an energetic look.

"We discussed your work in my seminars, based, I'm embarrassed to say, on my flawed translations," said Victoria, trying to cover Guy's slip as Schutz was not translated into English until the 60s.

Keinhoff came over with more beer, food. "My apologies, sir. Those young guys go overboard. The beer and food are on the house, and thanks to you for stepping in," he looked at Guy.

"Dr. Schutz, wonderful way to calm them down, with the songs," he added.

"All Germans, south and north of the border love music," said Schutz. "Herr Wagner has been working with me the past few months, he is one of us, Herr Keinhoff."

Wagner and Keinhoof shook hands. Victoria surmised that Keinhoff was working with Schutz in the underground.

"There will be no more trouble from them tonight, sir, but for your safety sake, I would keep dissenting viewpoints to yourself," said Keinhoff in a low voice. He turned and went back to the bar.

Victoria and Guy shared a quick glance. Wagner had still been handsome in his seventies, with startling white hair. Now he was like a German Adonis. His blond hair combed in the same style, straight back from his youthful forehead.

"How is it you are not in uniform?" said Martin, looking at Wagner.

"I'm a master tool and dye maker, supervising a whole factory floor. We are deemed an essential industry to the nation." He could not seem to take his eyes off Victoria.

"Excuse me, Frau Dr. Von Dietz Mead, but I know you from somewhere," he said.

"Surely, not, Sir. This is my first time out of the United States," said Victoria.

"Ah, nothing like German rye bread," said Guy, reaching for a slice and passing the platter. Victoria appreciated the distraction.

"Perhaps, Herr Wagner, it is your mutual love for philosophy that brings a sense of familiarity," said Mead.

"Indeed, I've become interested in the work of American thinkers, especially those working in the frontier regions, like Chicago. You fellows connect your work to the needs of the community," said Wagner.

"Its not just the males from Chicago," said Victoria. "Perhaps you heard of Jane Addams, who came to Berlin in 1916 to plead to the Kaiser to end the war. She and George worked to establish a League of Nations."

"If Addams had been heeded after the war," said Martin, "we wouldn't be having another one now. She raised money for food for the starving children in Germany and stood up against the harsh war reparations which crushed our economy."

"I must learn more about this Jane Addams and the others in Chicago," said Wagner, looking at Victoria.

"And I would like to learn how to ski. Perhaps we could make an exchange," said Victoria, heavy with the sense that she knew more of Schutz' future than he did.

"Why not meet me up at the ski cabin outside of Arzburg?" said Wagner. "I must ski down from there next Thursday. I will arrange for you to ride up on my donkey."

"Oh, what fun," she said, overenthusiastically. Then sat back and looked at Martin and George. "That is if Martin and George can spare me."

"I have much university business to attend to," said Martin. "I get so wrapped up in our work that I let things pile up."

"And I could catch up on my sleep," said George.

"Then I'm left to escort you up," said Guy.

"Hertzhog, like all Alpine donkeys, knows the way. He will be her escort," said Helmut.

"Surely we can find another jackass," said Mead, looking up at the brown-shirts by the bandstand.

The bandleader put down his accordion and stood up at the mike. He announced that Fraulein Dietrich would not be appearing that night. She had taken ill, sent her apologies. The room roared with booing, stomping boots on the plank floor, moans of disappointment. A group of men in uniform stood up at a table, held up their steins and said: "Marlene, Marlene, we need Marlene." The band leader started to play her famous song, "Lili Marlene," on the accordion and many sang: 'Under the lantern, by the garden gate,

Darling you remember, the way we used to wait," a song of a soldier on leave meeting his sweetheart in a few stolen minutes before going off to battle once again. One of the violinists slithered around the stage as if he were Marlene leaning on the lamppost. The students whistled.

When the mirth subsided, Schutz stood up. "Excuse me, there's something I must do," he said. He walked up to the band platform. The accordion player stood and motioned for Schutz to sit at the piano. Schutz played the Viennese waltz, then a series of other Waltzes by Strauss, the violinist and accordionist joining. The drummer used a brush on his snare.

A number of couples waltzed, whirled. Mead took Victoria's hand, guiding her to the dance floor. "I didn't know you danced," said Victoria.

Mead led her with the kind of subtle firmness and grace which makes any woman look like a lovely dancer, holding her in pauses with a bent back, swooping her up into swirls and spins. "The brownshirts don't seem to notice that Schutz' music was a political statement on behalf of Austria," he said.

"Perhaps they feel a closer tie to their comrades and friends here at Braumeister's than they do to the Fuhrer," said Victoria.

"Insofar as this is true we have hope," said Mead, his arm around her waist as they spun on the floor. A student couple brushed against Victoria, oblivious to the direction of the waltz.

The tall girl looked back, "Enshultegen Sie Bitte," she said to Victoria.

Heidegger walked up to the dance floor and tapped Mead's shoulder, cutting in. He held her closer and twirled faster. As the waltz ended they were near the steps to the stage and without releasing her left hand took the first step up. She tried to pull away, but he grasped her hand tightly and put his other arm around her waist. She sensed the crowd watching and so as not to embarrass him, relented. He spoke easily into the microphone, introducing himself and Victoria, pointing out also Guy and George, friends from America. The crowd clapped and cheered. Heidegger said looking at Mead, "It is the custom here for visiting dignitaries to say a few words." Victoria thought of how different German culture is from American, when persons in a bar respect a local philosopher and want one from abroad to speak.

Guy tapped Helmut on the shoulder, "Amazing that our philosophers, especially in the heartland of America, write about human concerns and political issues, and at best the people ignore them, at worse never know of their existence. In Germany, philosophers write of high level obscurities, and people love and revere them."

"It's not so simple," said Helmut. "Here people are so nosy about everything and talk about everything. Professors are like gods and people even in bars talk about them. But they don't go far enough in criticizing the many works of junk philosophy pouring forward, like *Mein Kamph*."

Schutz chuckled, "We can't take the works of every would be thinker seriously. Aren't there lots of crack pot junk writers in America, too?"

"Yeah," said Guy, "but so far none of them have become President."

Mead took the mike and said a few words about the importance of democracy and for taking the scientific attitude towards problems which in the social sphere would mean taking the perspective of other people, not just those in one's own country. Much of the audience stamped their feet, shouted "hier, hier." The young men at the brownshirt table laughed about something one of them had said. Another lifted a stein toward the stage and turned it, spilling the beer onto the floor.

Heidegger took the mike: "A nation must stand up for itself, for its inherent integrity." The crowd cheered louder. "And even more important is to hear the songs of the sirens, like the Lorelei on the Rhein. Frau Dr. Von Dietz is descendent from General Von Dietz of the Prussian Calvary. Let's listen to her song."

The crowd whistled and cheered. Victoria raised her hand for them to be silent. She said, "I can't replace Miss Dietrich, but I am honored to be here, a return to my grandmother's homeland." (She was careful to say grandmother rather than great-grandmother, the dates coming out better.) "This song was to remind her and teach me of grandmother in Prussia. But first I need a little beer to moisten my throat."

The crowd cheered. A man at the foot of the stage handed up a full stein, eliciting another cheer. She sipped and handed it to Martin, whose gazed at her sweetly. She cleared her throat and hummed a few notes of the long-remembered melody, then filled her lungs and sang, even to the brownshirts in the far corner.

"My man is on his horse
His tall white steed
He carries a sword

The cavalry leads
He rode through the woods
Our land to defend
I'm calling him back
He's only on lend.
I'm calling him back
To hold to my heart
Please come to me dear,
Never to part."
Victoria had them all join in the refrain
"Please come to me dear, never to part."

The audience shouted, whistled and cheered, asking for more songs. The accordion player began "Edelweiss" and they all joined in.

Victoria left the stage to more applause, cheers and lifted steins.

At the table, Wagner asked Martin if he could stop by. He needed to speak with him. Shortly they got up to leave. Mead, Heidegger, Guy and Victoria walked home down the cobblestone streets to the Inn. At Heidegger's street, he turned. Victoria felt a pang at his not coming with her. But I have my husband, dear George. What is wrong with me? she mused.

"Tomorrow, then, Victoria, said Heidegger. To work on the manuscript again, yah?" He turned in the direction of his house.

Chapter Twenty-Five
Helmut and Victoria on the Slopes

The wind whistled in Helmut Wagner's ears as he swerved down the slopes outside Freiburg. 'I'm late, I'm late, my dear Dr. Victoria' he said to himself. The crisp sound of his skis on the snowy mountain accompanied his thoughts. (Swish, swish) Good thing I'm in shape from so much running through the forest, checking remote cabins for our supplies and weapons.

How things had changed in the past few months! Germany had annexed Austria, effortlessly, then invaded France and Sudentenland. The resistance urgently needed Victoria's help and that of George Mead, to help get innocents out.

He'd been skiing since dawn and he could feel it. His thighs tightened at each turn, a deep bend in his knees. Ice crystals caught the sun, blinding him for an instant. I'll get my mind on something to ease the pain, the cold.

He pictured Victoria's sweetness, her gentle smile at the bar last night. He imagined pushing her fair hair aside and kissing the back of her neck. Flash, his wife's angry mouth appeared before him, corners slanted downward as she spit curse words at him—"you Swinehund," her eyes on fire. Janesha's image pushed Victoria from his mind. He caught an edge of his left ski, fought off the imminent tumble and regained his smooth descent. How she disparages me for being a tool and dye maker. To her, from an entrepreneurial family and a few clergy–when God and money get together there is no relief–I am a come down, a low life. (Swish Swish.) Hope she doesn't go off in one of her rages. She can't help it, she was not wanted as a child. . . Got in Himmel Helfen Sie Mich.

Ouch! A boulder covered in snow rose seemed to jump out at him. Just in time he swooped away from it, but it scaped his left ski. He widened his pattern to regain his form.

Ah, around the next turn, what a relief to see the log cabin. He slid gently down to the cabin. With fingers nearly numb, he unbound his boots from the skis and stabbed his ski poles upright into the snow. He pushed his goggles up to his knit cap.

The cabin's windows were steamy. He knocked then pulled the heavy plank door handle. A gust of howling wind came up behind him and tore it from his gloved hand. "It's not a fit night out for man nor beast," he muttered, quoting W.C. Fields, in that funny American film. They often showed foreign films in town, usually American cowboy movies. It amused him that the culture ministry was so busy routing out Jewish and Bolshevik books and films that they let Charlie Chaplain in "The Little Dictator" slip by. It ran in all the major cities before Herr Goebbels banned it. He pulled the door open firmly this time, braced it with a boot and stepped inside. There was no one in the room. The delicious aroma of venison stew on the wood stove awoke his voracious appetite.

Again Janesha's image crowded out a pleasure. Her fanatic disavowal of hunting meant that such delicacies were never served in their home. Inwardly he screamed to destroy her intrusion. The scream etched on his face.

"I didn't know our stew was so bad that you can't stand the smell of it!" Victoria said coming down the stairs.

He sensed Victoria, then saw her, coming through the small arched doorway to the left of the entrance to the kitchen.

"Ah, Dr. Von Dietz, Victoria, if I may. My frown was of something far away. The fragrance of the stew is wunderbar!"

"Victoria, is fine, Herr Wagner." She showed her pearly teeth. "I heard you yodel from the mountaintop. Did you hear me sing back?"

She took his breath away, more than the cold damp air. "Helmut, please. Such a lovely soprano. It was you or the phantom goddess yodeler of the valley." His nose burned as it released the icy chill from his descent. His hands burned too, though he had worn both gloves and mittens. "Your yodel is very different from your sultry night club voice."

He ached for her. Sweat ran under his long johns. He felt the heat spread across his face. They kissed each other on both cheeks, European friendly, standing apart.

Her face registered his complement with a slight nod. She deflected attention back to him. "I'm so glad you're all right. Such a strenuous trip to be skiing alone. Please, come and warm yourself." He removed his jacket, hat, and gloves and hung them on a hook behind the stove.

"It took longer than usual, as the winds got strong. But I've been doing this since I was a boy. Now I feel it in my knees and hips more." He wanted her to offer a massage, miffed at himself for not having the nerve to ask. Merely her touch would do quite well, if he were honest.

Her silent gaze bore a faint smile. She was not crossing the bridge he'd built.

"Climbing the hills between the downhill runs is the most difficult part. My father scorned the hanging trolleys put up for tourists. He always said if you can't climb up a mountain you have no right to ski down."

Was that a soft light in her gaze? Probably mistaken. "I was concerned about you getting a fire started, or having to shovel snow in front of the door."

"Guy came up with me. We rode up, didn't climb. He found another donkey in town. It's just as well. I know nothing of building fires," said Victoria.

He tried not to show his disappointment by smiling slightly. "Your assistant is very devoted to you. Yet I was hoping we'd have some time to talk, just the two of us."

"Guy left after we got the fire going. My donkey is in the shed in back and knows the way. But you could have said anything in front of Guy. I trust him with everything. And he prepared a hot bath for you upstairs."

It's not what I would have SAID that required privacy. But I must put these yearnings aside, he thought. "Vunderbar," he said. "A hot bath and a sumptuous stew. When I come down I'll tell you what I was grimacing about when I opened the door.

He started towards the stairs, then hesitated. "You know, somehow I feel like I have always known you, and I may share even some of my private pains and joys with you." He took her shoulders in his hands and squeezed them. "We are friends, I feel I can tell you things."

"Yes, certainly, " she said. "What is it, Helmut? Please sit down." She took one wooden chair at the table, pulled one out for him. He sank into it. She looked at him, waiting, folded her hands on the table.

He rubbed his hands together, warming them as he spoke. "I usually can ski, swooshing off my tensions, fears. Or, if I can't ski, I run. But yesterday my wife had one of her troublesome episodes. She is Jewish but has converted to Catholicism. She must get out soon. She is extremely disturbed. Not just from the situation now. You see, as a child she saw her parents and brother and sister die as their house burned down in a French bombardment. She was never sure if the Americans or German soldiers in retreat torched the house. It was an American soldier who tried to get them out. He came out staggering and black with a scorched shoulder, but with none of her family." Helmut pulled a leather envelope from his satchel. "This is what happened to her when she was a child." He removed several pages and handed them to Victoria.

As he walked up the stairs Victoria recalled the time they first met, ahead in the 1970s. He was a renowned social theorist by then, having received his doctorate at the New School for Social Research under Alfred Schutz, who became a professor there after the war.

She held him in awe. Ahead in the 70s he was in a heated discussion at a philosophy conference when she approached him to lecture at her university. She felt good about his reception there, and how many students came to have lunch and dinner with him and even breakfast his last day. She had arranged a special party for him at her home.

A week after he left she received a letter that changed and deepened the course of their relationship. It was a scrupulously cordial letter, expressing appreciation for the lecture, reception, and other activities. But Wagner revealed the main purpose of the letter in a powerful sentence:

"During my entire stay there was no opportunity for just the two of us to talk. I came there, you remember, because of you."

His letter had shaken her. She looked up to him as she had her father. A man to be admired, stern, with excruciatingly high standards. She had written back, confessing to this, as well as expressing her awe of him.

Wagner would bring her back, again and again, to her true nature—for she had the mind of a philosopher, and he had recognized her gift for writing it. Like her father, Helmut Wagner's standards were high. Yet, he was always pleased with her work—but like in the letter, he often said to her: "Yes, that is good, so why not get on with it!" In other words, this is just a beginning to what the real work is about.

Taking a deep breath, she looked at the pages he had given her to read. The writing was neat and precise. As she read her brow wrinkled and her eyes teared:

"I was seven and the oldest. Momma sent me out to look for bread or anything to eat in the deserted houses. The houses across the street were rubble. An awful odor came from piles of garbage and what I later came to recognize as dead people.

Wounded people lay in the streets, some of them pinned under the rubble. Shot rang out from building to building. Dogs pulled out body parts, bones. My father was on sentinel duty with the army in France. I loved my father, a hero trying to protect me. He called me Kleine Sargeant, as he was a captain. When he left he saluted me. "I'm leaving you in charge of the post. Remember to take care of everyone." My mother was very feminine, very dependent, crying and going into fits.

A little grey cat found something in the garbage, so I dug around where she was. I found a half open can of sardines. I gave some of it to the cat and put the rest in my knapsack.

I found the end of a loaf of bread and some carrot tops. This was a meal and I happily ran home with the treasures. Just as I turned the corner I heard machine guns firing on my block. It seemed to come from everywhere and hurt my ears. I heard a screeching sound and then a loud crash. I saw the front stairs, porch and walls of my house explode all over the street. I ran to get in but a soldier stopped me. He made me promise to wait. He ran into the fire himself, came out all black, his hand wrapped in his jacket, shaking his head, no, no. I tried to go in, but he held me back and said I would not want to remember my family as they looked now."

Victoria's stomach churned with pity and rage. Her hands holding the pages were still shaking when Helmut came down the stairs.

"I'm so sorry, Helmut. How awful for her as such a small girl. Of course Janesha must get to America, where she will be safe and can get help."

Come, have some wine. She had opened a bottle of red wine and poured some into two pewter mugs. They clinked mugs, "prosit" and drank. She took a long sip of wine.

Wagner picked up the papers she had placed in front of him and put them back in his valise.

"I admire your deep empathy for your wife," she said, looking up at him.

"I admire you for saying so, as this shows you have even greater empathy for me," said Wagner.

He wore a clean pair of woolen slacks and a grey ski sweater, wool socks and sheepskin slippers. Amazing what kind of wardrobe he carries in a small backpack, she thought. She filled both glasses again, stood up. She took two bowls from the sideboard shelves, filled them with stew, and brought a loaf of bread and some cheese to the table.

They devoured the stew in silence; neither wanting words to adulterate the savory meal. They wiped the last bits of gravy out of their bowls with pieces of bread.

"So tell me now, what is going on with Martin? He could be of great help to us, in the underground." Helmut helped himself to a second glass of wine. He offered to refill Victoria's glass. She held her glass up and sighed, still shaken by Janeshka's story.

"He is closely watched by Fragenzimmer, a Nazi assigned as Chancellor's secretary. Martin's name was on a document removing Hullerst and other Jewish scholars from their academic positions. Fragenzimmer brings the documents from the central party. Martin resists when he can," said Victoria.

"What brings you to know him so well?" asked Helmut. He took a sip of wine, held it in his mouth, then swallowed slowly. "A nice rich burgundy," he said. "Yes, we can obtain French wine easier than we can talk with a French person," said Helmut.

"Commerce must go on. Guy also used it in the stew." Victoria almost mentioned Julia Child and her television show, that Guy watched to get his recipes, but then caught herself. This was something way in the future.

"Martin and I work on a manuscript on the theory of time, nearly every day." She got up and served Helmut more stew and removed a loaf of bread from the shelf above the stove. Taking a knife from behind the counter, she sliced several pieces and put them on the table. She reached into her valise under the counter and pulled out a small vial of an amber green liquid. "Olive oil," she said. "I always bring some with me. It helps counteract the effects of all the animal fat I eat here." Victoria swished a piece of bread in the oil, took a bite. "I learned this from an Italian friend," she said. His puzzled look changed to a smile. He imitated her, enjoying the oil soaked bread.

"Ach, we were happy to have goat cheese or even lard to spread on our bread. We are close to Italy but our cuisine is much less healthy." After swallowing he looked at her with his forehead pinched together. "Herr Heidegger puts himself in extreme jeopardy. His speech when he took the rectorship could easily be seen as a critique of the direction Hitler and the SS are moving." He cleaned the bottom of his bowl with a piece of bread, took a bite. "Delicious," he said.

"Martin told me he hopes to influence the party in a positive direction." Victoria wondered how much to tell Helmut about the future, where she was really from.

"Of course he hopes to do this," said Helmut. "Don't we all. But I don't think that in his real mission. He really wants to help save what remains of the German university for true scholars. This is why von Moldendorf begged him to take the position. He knew that if he did not accept, Hitler would put in a vulgar bureaucrat. Do you realize what could be lost in one generation? The books, the archives? The ongoing research of the brightest minds in Germany?"

"But can we stop it anyway, from one side or another? Mediocrity and bureaucracy are rampant and increasing", she said. "Martin told me of two Jewish deans he kept from being deposed. He also wrote of his preventing the dissemination of anti-Semitic tracts," Victoria said.

"There have been book burnings on some campuses, of works deemed to be Bolshevik, decadent, or "Jewish," said Helmut.

"They wanted to have one in Freiburg as well, in front of the library, but Martin would not allow it," said Victoria.

"This is the kind of thing which will put him in jeopardy," said Helmut.

"If it weren't for his friend, Fetzer, a wealthy shipping magnate with lots of connections, he may have been unable to prevent the book burning," said Victoria.

The look in Helmut's eyes deepened. He looked above and past her, then back to her face. His lips were moist. "We must act quickly," he said. "Schutz has arranged for money in his bank, transferring it to Switzerland, so their passage can be bought. But this brings another problem. The Nazis need money fast to build their war machine. It is not so important to eliminate Jews if they can bring in large sums of money. The Nazis sell the lives of Jews to purchase weapons."

"The horror of it," said Victoria "The money used to rescue scholars results in the Nazis being able to amass the resources to kill thousands of others. What good is such a rescue mission?"

"We cannot think that way," said Helmut. We must try to save those we can." He wiped his mouth with the linen napkin she had placed next to his bowl. "And you must help."

They heard the donkey brae out in the stable, followed by another call. Shortly the door opened and Guy stepped inside, snowflakes falling off his long brown coat.

"I couldn't let you face the return alone," he said, smiling at Victoria.

"I wouldn't have been alone, I had my donkey," she said.

"Herr Wagner! How was my stew?" Guy asked.

"Delicious, but not so delicious as the hot bath. Vielen Danken, Herr Santori," said Wagner.

"Victoria, I see you have finished eating. We should head back before sunset," said Guy. He looked at Wagner.

"I'm glad you came back, Herr Santori. I couldn't have let Dr. Von Dietz ride down alone. I would have skied down with her, but this would have kept me from my work."

Helmut stood up. "Und zo, lets get on vit it," he said.

Chapter Twenty-Six
Helmut Asks Martin for Help

Thinking begins only when we have come to know that reason,
glorified for centuries, is the most stiff-necked adversary
of thought.–Heidegger, *Essay Concerning Technology*

The fire in Martin Heidegger's study began to dry Helmut Wagner's corduroy trousers, damp from walking up the hillside that dark, sleety afternoon in late November. Helmut's temple's throbbed. Victoria had assured him that Heidegger would help him and Alfred Schutz in the anti-Nazi underground. Heidegger sat behind his large desk, clear of all but a writing pad, fountain pen and a typed manuscript neatly stacked under a paperweight. This evening he was stiff, remote, unlike his friendly persona in the pub.

Helmut pressed the tips of his fingers into his moist palms. Might as well jump in and raise the issue.

He cleared his throat. "Herr Heidegger, I'll get right to the point. I, we, need your help." His sentence was cut short by three sharp knocks at the study door. Ach Scheisse! Frau Elfriede. Helmut had hoped she would stay away, as Victoria warned she's an active party member. "Hello, Herr Wagner, Wie Geht es Ihnen." She carried a large wooden tray of coffee, schnapps, kuchen, cold cuts, cheese, and black bread. She glanced at his threadbare sweater that had a snowflake pattern.

"Meine Frau knit this for me years ago, it's worn, but still my favorite," he said.

Her smile did not echoe in her eyes. "Yah, don't take a look at Martin's socks, he won't part with them even though they are unraveling," she said grinning.

"They were from my Mudder, how could I," Martin said.

She put the tray down on the side table and smoothed her floral skirt. A bottle of schnapps and three small glasses sparkled on the tray.

Heck. She was joining them. Well, he'd use the time to his advantage, to get in her good graces. He wondered if she would be amenable to complements from a nearly strange man. He decided not to risk this as even if she liked such attention, it may turn Heidegger against him.

The green schnapps turned aqua as she poured it into the blue glasses. Helmut considered his glass in the light. It brought to mind a curvaceous woman, like Victoria. Frau Heidegger watched as he caressed the glass between his thumb and forefinger.

Elfriede poured coffee, leaning over him. Her boiled wool jacket fit snuggly around her ample breasts. Was she flirting with him? "Wielen Dank, Frau Heidegger." Schutz took bread and summer sausage, a piece of cheese from the tray. If only she hadn't brought all this food. Would he ever get back to the request.

Elfriede arranged a plate of bread, cheese and summer sausage, and placed it in front of Martin. Martin held a pleased expression. He was used to being waited on. She took a plate for herself and sat down.

Hell, thought Wagner, she sure is taking her time. Best try to relax and win her over.

She asked polite questions about Helmut's family.

"My wife is in Frankfurt, seeing her family. We have no children," he said.

"Herr Wagner is a friend of Professor Schutz," said Martin.

"What brings you here this afternoon, Herr Wagner," Elfriede asked.

Martin answered the question, "Herr Wagner has come to ask me for some assistance, but he hasn't yet told me in what he needs help."

Wishing the nosey Votze would get out of there, Wagner would have to think of something other than helping with the underground. "Schutz got me into that phenomenology stuff, told me your husband worked with the founder, Dr. Hullerst, " Wagner said.

Martin rolled his eyes to the ceiling and took a sip of coffee. "I owe Hullerst a great debt, and still I have been critical of him. Despite our intellectual disagreements, he supported me to move into his Chair when he retired."

Wagner nearly bit his tongue. He wanted to ask how they could sit by and let Hullerst loose his emeritus position, forced to move out of his house. How could he brooch the topic? He took a sip of schnapps, rolling it around with his tongue.

Heidegger's forehead wrinkled, his mouth curved downward. Elfriede fussed with the food, brushing her hip against Helmut's arm as she passed his chair, then sat back down with her schnapps in hand.

Wagner tipped his glass towards her. "The mint fragrance is delightful, Frau Heidegger."

"Do you mean hers or the schnapps," said Heidegger, the corners of his lips slightly raised.

"Really, Martin, none of my perfumes smell like schnapps." Elfriede sent him a piercing look, raised her glass and took a sip, then cleared her throat. "To get to Herr Wagner's reason for being here, I'm impressed that a factory worker such as yourself would be so interested in philosophy," said Elfriede.

The slut! Helmut resented being called a factory worker when he was actually a skilled tool and dye maker and a foreman over an entire factory floor. He stuffed his anger like a hot potatoe down his throat.

Heidegger broke the silence. "Those who work with tools, making things, are aware of the fundamental nature, the being of things. I couldn't have written the first part of *Being and Time* without my long talks with my friend Klubber, the shoemaker."

"Martin could just as easily have watched me cook. I use lots of tools," said Elfriede.

Regaining his cool, Helmut tried to appease her. "Perhaps Frau Dr. Von Dietz will put a woman's perspective into Herr Heidegger's work." He bit into the liverwurst sandwich, chewed, swallowed and patted his lips with a napkin.

Elfriede grimaced. Too late, Helmut realized his tactical error. Victoria was not a happy subject for Frau Heidegger. Who would want her husband to work closely with such a luscious woman as Victoria.

Martin cleared his throat, sat up in his chair. "Frau Dr. Von Dietz has been working with me on a new theory of time, a kind of 'Ur-Time' I was only beginning to explore. The universe has vast cycles, which if we can tap into them, explain time warps, dejavois, premonitions." Martin put a thick slice of summer sausage on his dark bread.

"Ah, like Nietzsche's 'eternal return'." Wagner felt excited about the idea, forgetting for a minute why he had come.

"In a sense. Ur-time may infuse everyday experience, causing ruptures, lapses," said Heidegger. He continued to chew on his sandwich.

Helmut found his heart beating with excitement. These ideas may even help the resistance. "Sort of like an earthquake that up-ends layers from the past, so we can see the strata, walk on them, cut into them," said Wagner. He took a sip of schnapps. "Shmecks gut," he said, licking his lips.

Frau Heidegger acknowledged with "Bitte Schoen," lifting her schnapps glass to him in a toast. She took a dainty sip.

"That's one way. Another is through cosmic speed up, or slowing down, due to changes in magnetic force fields," said Martin. As if to accent his words the wind howled against the window.

"Imagine if you could see the future well enough to change its course," said Wagner. Perhaps this line of thinking would warm him up for helping with the underground.

"Ach humans are humans, we'd still be caught up in the political debates and intrigues. We'd get into war over who gets to reshape the past," said Martin.

"We have enough trouble already with one time span." Elfriede's high cheekbones lifted as she smiled. Herr Himler is watching Martin's work very carefully. It seems he thinks it is good for the Fatherland."

"Hitler and his chronies pay more attention to Hiesenberg's work on atomic energy. Still, they are becoming inquisitive. It seems philosophy has suddenly become important to them." Martin bottomed out his schnapps. He got up and picked up the bottle, offering refills.

Helmut held up his glass. He had to keep Heidegger engaged but some-how get Elfriede out of the room. Perhaps he could get her out by making her uncomfortable.

"Frau Heidegger, there is much to be concerned about the SS and the well-being of persons of Jewish background, such as Professor Hullerst."

Her cheek turned red, as if she had been slapped. "Yah, such upheaval for them, and their families" she frowned. "Change does not come easy.

Over the years ever increasing numbers of Jewish professors are in the universities. Perhaps too many. Still, they shouldn't take outstanding scholars out of their positions to be filled by persons of less knowledge and ability. This would not be good for German culture," she said, picking up the tray.

"I couldn't agree more, Frau Heidegger," said Helmut. "Furthermore, it is not only those in positions who are in danger, but, like Hullerst, those already retired."

"I'd like to talk philosophy with you gentlemen the rest of the evening," said Elfriede. "But I must see after the children and dinner. The Mary and Martha story in the Bible would more appropriately have been Martin and Martha, since it is usually men who get to sit around and discuss ideas."

"Elfe, you know you much prefer the children's discourse to mine," said Martin.

"Yeah, mien Man, but I also enjoy giving you the hard time." She smiled closing the door behind her.

Wagner breathed deeply. Now he'd finally be able to get to his reason for coming. Yet Heidegger seemed preoccupied with his coffee and schnapps.

"This is the way," said Martin, "to observe Plato's 'golden mean'," holding up his schnapps in one hand and coffee mug in the other. He drank from each, and put them down. "Now, Herr Wagner, tell me really why you have come." Martin's eyes were focused intensely.

Wagner settled both feet on the floor, leaned forward, pressing his elbows on the arm rests. "We Germans are so far from a Platonic ideal and that brings me to the reason for this visit. Herr Heidegger, Professor Schutz and I need your help. We need information about Hullerst, his wife and children, and the other Jewish professors who are threatened. It won't be long until they too are taken away to work camps," said Helmut.

Martin's cheeks turned red. He squirmed in his lederhosen and adjusted one of his hand knit knee socks. "I could do nothing to prevent this," he said. The SS ordered the 'de-Judification' of the university. The form and letters all came directly from Himmler's office in Berlin." He tugged his green turtle neck sweater away from his neck. "My signature as Rector was already typed on the letters." He snapped his suspenders against his chest:

"Herr Fragenzimmer, my designated assistant, is official liaison to Berlin, and watches every move I make." His voice had fallen to a whisper. "He brings my letters and documents to be signed each morning, as he puts it: 'by direct request'. Every day I wonder, is this the day a letter will come, telling me I'm 'demoted' or 'transferred'?" Heidegger's face was red, his cheeks puffed out.

Helmut's right fist tightened around his mug. "You gone and Herr Fragenzimmer, or another Arschloch like him, would get the job." Wagner slapped his mug down on the armrest.

Snap! Snap! went Martin's suspenders, one than the other. "And you know what Fraggy would do then? He immediately would command that books be removed from the library that he deems were not written with the best interests of the party, the Fuhrer and therefore the German people and the Homeland. Fragenzimmer has already asked me several times to order the Germanification of the library. All 'questionable' books are to be put under government reserve for investigation. Investigation by such boneheads that anything with a term above the grammar school level is deemed pernicious. Those which don't pass his muster would be burned! I still smell the smoke from the Marburg books! So many, in such a gross bonfire, people stopped by to warm themselves. A group of brown shirts were leading the show, and students participated with glee and laughter. It is up to me and a few others to keep arguing that the works of the great German philosophers and historians guard the heart and soul of German culture."

"Sickening to smell burning books, but near Auswitsch, there are ovens for burning humans" said Helmut.

"Surely not!" said Martin.

Helmut stood, opened his worn briefcase. He pulled out some notes, waved them at Martin. "A list of the fired professors. Get me their addresses and phone numbers, and the names of their nearest family or friends. Also, I need the names and ages of wives, children and dependents current photographs are helpful to prevent fraud."

Martin poured himself and Wagner another schnapps. Wagner put the list in front of him. "You exaggerate from fear and hysteria," he said looking at the list. "These lost academic positions, but each was offered a position in the Bundestate or the military, commensurate with their abilities."

"Nonesense! To the Nazis, Jews, dissidents, artists are all assigned to slave labor in these so called Arbeit camps," said Wagner.

Martin took a drink of coffee. He stood up, looking out the window. The back of his neck bristled red. "It is a tremendous promise, the Fuhrer has made, that no one will be out of work," said Martin.

"We've been to Auswitch, and Dachau," said Helmut. These "work centers" are in fact prisons. Once you enter, you die of disease, hunger, exposure or work. They have gas chambers. They have ovens the size to take humans."

Heidegger turned around and gestured toward the window. "Gerade, idle chatter! These rumors are much exaggerated," he said. "Of course in any densely populated area people will get sick and die. Diseased bodies must be decontaminated, the healthy protected. It suits the enemy to twist the truth about this, of course."

"All we are asking for is a list of names and addresses, photos if you can get them," said Helmut. "Let us check up on friends and colleagues, help those who may prefer to emigrate. Please Dr. Heidegger. It could be you and your family, if Catholics were considered anti-German."

"I'm no longer a Catholic. We are all Lutherans now," said Heidegger.

"By Nazi logic all it would take is that you were once Catholic. Don't you see the insidious nature of this form of thinking?"

"Of course I see it. I'm living it." Martin's voice was high and loud. He got up, stomped to the window, the sleet sliding fast behind the glass. "All it will take for me to be put to work digging ditches would be for one of the students in my Nietzche class to pass it on to the party that the underlying message in my interpretation is anti-Nazi.

"I thought Nietzsche's 'Oberman' would seem friendly to the Nazi ideologists who feel they are destined to rule the world," said Wagner.

'Ah, that is Nietzsche's sister's interpretation. The real message is strongly against the mass parading of armies in blind conformity. The Nazis are Nietzsche's "Pueriles" who seek to bring down the "Nobles". The Nobles are the artists, intellectuals, poets, creators of the human world." Heidegger pulled a handkerchief from his lederhosen pocket and wiped his brow. He sat back down behind his desk, exhaling deeply.

"You'll help us then?" said Wagner, inhaling.

Heidegger looked down at his hands. He looked old and sad. "I will find what you want. Wait until after the university closes tomorrow evening. I will work late in my office. You must come and copy the material from the files. If a lamp is lit in my window, come up. If not stay away as it means Fragenzimmer is still here. Heidegger tossed down his schnapps in a single gulp. "Should the lamp not be in the window, come back the next night."

"Thank you, friend," Helmut stood.

"Will you bring a camera?" Heidegger asked.

"I will just use pencil and paper. I have a small camera, but it requires development chemicals that are hard to obtain these days. A government permit is required," said Wagner.

"Bring the camera. Elfriede can get the chemicals from the Gymnasium where she teaches. Aufwiedersehen, Herr Wagner. I hope to see you tomorrow evening," said Martin without rising.

Vielen Dank, Herr Heidegger," said Wagner. He put out his hand for Heidegger to shake. Martin hesitated, then lifted his hand to Helmut's.

Chapter Twenty-Seven

Fragenzimmer

Here is the testament of a man who swung a great people into his wake. Let us watch it carefully. . . that we may know, with greater accuracy, exactly what to guard against, if we are to forestall the concocting of similar medicine in America. — "The Rhetoric of Hitler's Battle" — *The Philosophy of Literary Form*— Kenneth Burke

Heidegger sat at his desk in his office at the top floor of the castle that had become part of the university. He enjoyed the warmth of the large fireplace as he had just returned from a chilly walk from the lecture hall across the courtyard. What a contrast between Fragenzimmer, the pale and fussy weasel the party had sent to "assist" him, and the images of the dukes and knights painted on the tiles that framed the fireplace. Fragenzimmer stood at a large table at the far end of the large and ornately decorated Rector's office, fidgeting through papers and files. Would that raty ferret ever leave him alone? The list of names with the information Wagner wanted was locked in his bottom desk drawer. He must get Fragenzimmer out before dark when Wagner was coming to pick up the information.

Below, students sang and laughed as they traversed the walkways, on their way to the library or dinner, to work in the laboratories or practice halls, then perhaps a late night excursion to the beer halls. How long would it be before they all were in uniform? Some wore the brown shirts of the Hitler youth or hats with swastikas. The mediocre students always gravitated to such things. They carry little resistance to the lure of "Das Man" the "They", the Masses.

And yet am I not also taking the coward's way out, having accepted the rectorship? I should resign in protest—but then what? Emigrate? But this is my home and Elfriede would never leave. And what of Victoria and our child to come . . .

Fragenzimmer's strident voice cut off Heidegger's musings: "These accounts and departmental budgets must be rectified. The party says we must cut costs in every department by 30%. The Reichsminister demands the revised budgets by tomorrow."

Heidegger spun around in his chair facing the vermin. "I'll be working late," said Heidegger. Leave them for me and I'll go over them tonight." How unappealing Fragenzimmer looked with his pasty white skin, his hair gray and oily, his body thin but flabby. He stood about 5'5". How did someone so far from the tall blond strong Aryan ideal get so high up in the party?

"There are many directives about making the cuts that you must follow," said Fragenzimmer. "I've phoned my wife that I'll be working late. I'll have our dinner delivered."

"Nein, that is not necessary," said Martin. "Leave the directives for me. There is other work I must complete first." He stood tall at his desk and glared at Fragenzimmer.

"That's all right, Herr Dr. Heidegger. I will wait until you are ready." Fragenzimmer lifted the phone. His fingers were boney with blue veins. His long nose twitched.

Heidegger slammed his hand on the phone switch. "Nein! I must not be disturbed during my work. Tell me what I need to know. I'll work on the budget later. You can check on it tomorrow." His stomach tightened. He had to get the slimy weasel out. He did not want him seeing Wagner. And he dare not risk him finding the locked drawer and asking to see its contents. Fragenzimmer had already read an edict to him about everyone working for the Reich and there were to be no secrets from the party.

Fragenzimmer grimaced and moved his hand towards Heidegger's, then pulled back and snorted. He turned, walked to the table. He picked a piece of paper out of a folder, slapped the paper down in his left palm as if swatting a fly.

"As you wish, Rector Heidegger. Here are the new budget directives, as ordered by Herr Himmler. Bitte, look them over in case you have any questions before I leave." He walked to Heidegger's desk and handed him a document.

Heidegger read, trying to keep his pounding heart from exploding:

Urgent Memorandum
Der Fuhrer's Directives for Budget Management

1. All professor positions must be justified in relation to German interests. Course outlines, lectures and publications are subject to approval by the Reichsminister of Culture.

2. No salaries or retirement annuities are to be paid to Jews or other non-Aryans.

Subpoint A. "Jew" is a legal designation assigned based on criteria of blood or marriage. It may also be a chosen designation through religious affiliation.

Subpoint B. Association with Jews requires legal recategorization as Jewish.

Subpoint C. Writing Jewish publications requires designation of authors as Jewish.

3. All staff positions will be reviewed and non-essential positions eliminated.

4. All Jews or other non-Germans on the staff will be issued permits to work at designated Reichscontrolled work facilities."

"We already relocated all Jewish professors and staff," said Heidegger. "They must be crazy!"

"There must be some designated Jews teaching and on the staff. Supporters of Jews or non-German ideas are by definition Jewish," said Fragenzimmer.

"Preposterous," said Heidegger. "We can't look for a Jew under every library table! Nor can I run a university with such outrageous cutbacks.

"The Fuhrer himself makes sacrifices," said Fragenzimmer. "He eats only a simple breakfast of bread and coffee. He has dinner, but no lunch."

"Herr Fragenzimmer, such stories of the Fuhrer's nobility are inspiring. I wonder if he also puts his dogs on a diet." Martin stood and walked around his desk; reaching under his cardigan sweater he grabbed his suspenders. "Snap, SNAP!"

One corner of Fragenzimmer's thin mouth crept up the side of his face. "Professor Heidegger makes light of a dire situation."

Heidegger turned and looked directly at him. Fragenzimmer always wears grey, thought Heidegger, as he is certainly one of the Masses, Das Man. And always a navy or dark tweed necktie with his swastika tie pin. Why is it that some people love to get swallowed up? How he loathed such toads.

But he must not let his disgust for Fragenzimmer cause him to slip up. Better to swallow his ire and appeal to his vanity and self interest. He cleared his throat, mellowed his tone of voice.

"As much as I rely upon your daily assistance and organization talents, I must set a good example and forego secretarial help in such times. I will henceforth do my own administrative work."

Fragenzimmer puffed. The veins stood out on the front of his neck and on his hands. "My position cannot count as part of the university's 30%. I work for the NDSP directly. I have no direct reporting responsibility to you or the university. It is not your prerogative to reassign me!"

What a Swinehund. But I must play along, for now. "Oh, but if I am willing to sacrifice for the sake of the Fuhrer, you could expend your enormous talents where they are better needed. Perhaps a promotion would be in order. Someone to read books recommended as potentially dangerous to the Reich. It would indeed take someone with brains to comprehend some of the masters on the expanding list of dangerous philosophy," said Martin, smiling with closed lips.

Fragenzimmer's eyebrows rose.

"As always, you put new thoughts into my head, Professor Heidegger. Perhaps such a suggestion coming from someone of your stature . . . but no, all of the directives and orders that need to be processed . . ." said Fragenzimmer.

"My Frau will help me," said Heidegger.

Fragenzimmer uncurled his rounded back and straightened his shoulders. The normally drooping corners of his mouth approached a straight line. His voice became fast and choppy. "Yes, a good idea, as she is well connected in the party. We shall see. I leave you to work tonight, Herr Doktor Professor Heidegger." Fragenzimmer walked to the door and left without saying goodnight.

Once he heard Fragenzimmer's Mercedes drive off, Heidegger put the lamp to the window to signal Wagner. After two hours and no Wagner, he left for home.

Chapter Twenty-Eight
Heidegger's List

For this reason the sons of the broad masses are required. They alone
are determined enough to carry through the fight to its bloody end.
— Adolph Hitler, *Mein Kamph*

Looking in his mirror the next morning while shaving, Heidegger con-
templated the list he compiled for Wagner. His shoulders slumped. The
skin of his face felt loose, sagging. Perhaps old age was visiting him prematurely. He ached for Victoria. With Mead here and Guy, their guard dog, it
was hard to find a way for them to be together.

Speaking through the bathroom door, Elfriede told him Helmut Wagner
called, apologized for not seeing him yesterday evening. Schutz would be at
the university late this afternoon to pick up the documents.

"Looks like it'll be another late night for you," she said, with a tone of
resignation.

"Hell, if I can get rid of Fragenzimmer it won't take long." He was grateful that Elfriede has helped him pull the information together. He came out
of the bathroom and gave her a hug.

"Du bist meine beste Freundin." he said.

"Just be careful Liebschen," Elfriede said, leaving for a day of teaching.

Heidegger gazed out the window at the shifting clouds over his beloved
hillside below. I am caught between two worlds, two women, two lives. I
want Germany to become great again, assert its cultural superiority. No other
culture could have produced Bach, Beethoven, Richard Wagner. I want the

earth, the peasants, the pine trees, the forests, the simple folk to prevail. This is what the Nazi party has meant to me—to bring forward the good, the wholeness of the earth, sky, mortals, immortals. I wanted that so much I couldn't see what Schutz and Helmut Wagner see. I stood aside even as my great mentor, Hullerst, was brought down for being Jewish.

All this I could have continued to do and more, were it not for Victoria. She's an angel coming from the future, to tell me not to let my romantic and patriotic emotions overcome my better self.

He moved away from the window. He continued to muse as he dressed in trousers, over a white shirt and tie topped by a tweed jacket. Others see the signs of evil. I've wished to ignore them. To recognize them is to betray my homeland. I'd become a traitor and this I cannot do. But I stand in between and let myself surreptitiously help Victoria and Schutz. I stand on Bavarian soil that is sacred to me and yet I betray this soil for what Victoria tells me lies ahead. I pray for the gods to return so that the undercurrents of time can wash us free.

When Schutz and Wagner arrived that afternoon, Heidegger sent Fragenzimmer out for refreshments. Quickly he unlocked his bottom desk drawer, pulled out an envelop. "I have the information you requested. Jewish, or 'officially declared Jewish' professors and graduate assistants who lost their jobs. Elfriede also checked the records for family members. We found some photographs as well."

"Zehr gut, vielen dank," said Helmut Wagner.

Heidegger handed the envelope to Schutz. Wagner took a small camera out of his pocket.

Heidegger held up his hand. "No need. Mein Frau copied the photos. "

"Elfriede helped?" queried Wagner.

"Don't worry". Heidegger wrinkled his chin. "She is a party member, however she also cares about these folks many of whom were long time friends. She thinks you are helping them relocate, find new jobs."

"Which is true," said Schutz.

Standing behind his desk, Heidegger glanced out the window. The setting sun glowed on the statue of Goethe below, turning his marble robes bright orange. "Faust's choices were so much clearer than ours," he said.

Schutz raised his eyebrows. "Or so Goethe made them. But his Satin was easy to recognize."

Heidegger motioned for Schutz and Wagner to sit down. They settled into leather-covered chairs. Schutz opened the envelope.

"The Reich is in dire need of funds," said Martin. "We are required to cut back our staff 30% more, including those on pension. The definition of "Jew" has expanded to include anyone who is married to a Jew, or an associate, or is deemed to 'think Jewish'." He drew his forehead together in sharp creases.

"So this explains why they are willing to trade some of the older ones who have money. They ask ten thousand Marks per family. But the money must be in foreign currency, or it would already have been confiscated. I have money for ten, in Zurich," said Schutz as he opened the envelope, skimming through several pages.

Schutz sure has connections, thought Heidegger. He noted the depth of expression in his face, the strength yet delicacy in his fingers.

"The older ones can't work very hard," said Wagner, "it will kill them."

"But some of those older ones, mostly the scientists, they want to keep," said Schutz. "Perhaps you could help us get Von Heisenburg out by writing a private memo stating that his physics work is outdated."

"The physicists in the party would not agree," said Heidegger. "But check with Grestein at Cologne.By the way, Herr Dr. Schutz, how is it you are a pianist as well as a banker. You played so well at the pub!"

"Ach, I mostly prefer to play Mozart, not bar songs, but I wanted to appease the brown shirts, and make a point on behalf of Austria."

"He's also adept with a surgical knife," said Wagner. "On the front as a physician's assistant."

Schutz held a wry smile. "And in our work these days, I never know when I'll need it."

Two sharp knocks at the door interrupted them. "Heil Hitler" said Fragenzimmer as he burst in, carrying a tray with three large decorative steins and a glass pitcher with a pewter top, filled with frothy brown beer.

Schutz quietly slipped the envelop into his briefcase.

Martin felt his back and neck strain. This weasel suspected something.

"To quench your thirst, gentlemen." He filled their steins slowly, waiting for the foam to settle.

"Herr Dr. Schutz, Herr Wagner, would like some bread and sausages as well?" asked Fragenzimmer.

Schutz and Wagner declined. Heidegger had no appetite. "You may go ahead home." Heidegger directed his chin up and towards the door.

Vielen Dank, Herr Professor, but I must stay on to finish your correspondence," said Fragenzimmer, looking over Schutz' shoulder.

"Don't bother. You may complete it in the morning," said Martin.

"But the steins, sir." Fragenzimmer's beady eyes glared directly at Schutz. "Are you not Dr. Schutz, the famous economist from Vienna?"

"My name is indeed Schutz and I lived in Vienna. However my excursions into economic theory have brought me neither fame nor fortune."

"You are humble, Herr Dr. Schutz, for your name is also spoken of in as a high level financier," said Fragenzimmer.

Heidegger's mind raced. How to get rid of this Arschlach who has more power than he has as professor and rector.

"There are many exaggerations that float around," said Schutz.

"Bitte, Herr, Fragenzimmer, Wir haben arbeiten," said Martin. He reached under his jacket as if to snap his suspenders, and finding none, tapped his chest.

"Yahwohl, Herr Dr. Heidegger," he said, turning sharply, a flush of red on his neck. Having reached the door he turned again. "I will come back for the steins in a little while."

"That is not necessary," said Martin. "You may go on home. I am sure Frau Fragenzimmer will be glad to have you home on time for dinner for a change."

"Thank you sir, but she is away this afternoon at a women's Third Reich auxiliary meeting. They are reading the third chapter of *Mein Kampf* out loud." Fragenzimmer looked directly at Schutz, pinching his eyebrows. "In our new Reich even full professors offer to clear their own steins."

"Soon we professors will be serving as well," said Martin.

Schutz added, "so that men like you, Herr Fragenzimmer, may make better use of your talent."

"Ah, my work for Professor Heidegger and the university is most rewarding. Allow me to suggest that I may also be of help to you, Dr. Schutz, in negotiations with the party. I am a direct laisson to the Bundespeilen Minister for New Labor," said Fragenzimmer, squaring his shoulders.

Wagner glanced at Heidegger.

Heidegger's eyebrows rose, this little snake is creeping upward. "A new role for you, Herr Fragenzimmer?" he asked.

"Ach, our necessary functions keep expanding," said Fragenzimmer, "but all for the good of the Fatherland."

"Most kind of you," said Schutz. "We will most likely discuss these matters with you at a later date."

Heidegger was relieved that Schutz handled Fragenzimmer so adroitly. He'd a good ally, he thought.

Fragenzimmer turned toward Wagner, as if the meeting was in his office, rather than Heidegger's. "Herr Wagner is away from his work in the factory. What brings you up to the university?"

"As a floor director at the plant, I've been asked to oversee some special projects." Wagner matched Fragenzimmer's gaze.

Fragenzimmer walked toward the door, stopped in front of Wagner. "And special projects with Frau Dr. Von Dietz Mead as well? What does a factory manager have to discuss with a lady philosopher up in the mountains?" He licked his thin lips.

Martin Heidegger's mind raced. The asshole must have spies everywhere. His stomach churned with jealousy. Could he trust this Wagner fellow? He's obviously attracted to Victoria, and Elfriede as well. But then Victoria knew Wagner in the future and openly arranged the meeting at the ski cabin that night at the bar.

Heidegger stood, managing to keep steady despite his burning rage. He felt as if he was having a nightmare. "Herr Fragenzimmer, I insist you end your impertinent inquiries and leave us this moment."

Fragenzimmer glared back. "A simple question, Sir, in regards to foreigners." He turned towards Wagner.

Wagner shrugged in a nonchalant manner.

Heidegger spoke rapidly and in a high pitched voice, his jaw tight. "Professor Von Dietz wanted the opportunity to practice skiing. You never know these days when it may become a necessary form of travel, with the government expropriating the railroads to the point where sometimes citizens can't get tickets."

Heidegger appreciated Wagner's cool. Still standing, he spoke rapidly. "Have you any more questions? Or perhaps you have not enough work to occupy you." Heidegger raised his arm straight up, "Heil Hitler Herr Fragenzimmer," he said dismissing him.

Fragenzimmer Heil-Hitlered back and moved toward the door. "Should you change your mind and want the sausages, gentleman, I will be at my desk outside yet for a while." He opened the door, then turned and looked back with a half smile. With a sharp click he closed the door behind him.

"Got in Himmel!" expelled Heidegger. "I hope to get that weasel promoted out of my hair soon." He sat at his desk, took a slug of beer.

"The petty bureaucrat, given a little power, stretches it to the limit," said Schutz, taking out a cigarette case. He offered one to Heidegger, then Wagner. Both declined. Wagner reached in his jacket for matches, gave Schutz a light.

Schutz walked to the bay window, took a long draw on his cigarette. He sat at the window seat, adjacent to Martin's desk. The sun was setting down the hillside, making the dark evergreens simmer with gold. A large hawk circled above. "When things were more settled, I usually played the piano at this time of day," said Schutz. "Ilse used to love this, and it helped me get all of the banking stuff out of my head so that I could write in the evenings."

"Ilse and your children are settling in Paris alright?" asked Martin.

"So far O.K., although she misses Vienna very much," said Alfred.

"This negotiation for Jewish persons of note is the direct result of the eidos of technological thinking," said Martin, filling his pipe. "All beings are stockpiled for use, from chickens, to trees, to humans. And Hitler came in on an agrarian, Romantic platform."

"Goes to show, you can never believe a crazy man, or a politician, and Hitler is both," said Wagner.

"This is why Von Mise in Vienna and his circle are positivists," said Schutz. "They see the flaws in Romantic thinking which does not look logically and clearly at what is actually the case."

"But in doing so, as Hullerst pointed out, they lose track of the beings, the "things in themselves" of actual lived experience," said Martin.

"I'm impressed with Professor Hullerst's work. He predicted that this war was swelling up while most academics battled over their narrowly defined turf, neglecting the questions of overall values and life of the people," said Schutz.

"I've read your articles on this," said Martin, drawing a deep breath of smoke and blowing it out. "Large scale forces of technology and politics are destroying lifeworlds with impunity."

"We bomb buildings and kill soldiers, and these we read about in the papers. But lifeworlds, communities, webs of relationships are also destroyed," said Schutz. He pinched his forehead together.

Helmut Wagner took a slug of beer. He breathed deeply, filling his lungs with Schutz' smoke. "You gents talk as if Hullerst had not already been taken. This is beyond debating over theory."

"Oppression, slavery, and genocide are not new with Western technology," said Schutz. "We are rather more aware of them. They stand out more starkly against the background of the Magna Carta and the American revolution." He put his cigarette out in a large pewter ashtray that looked like a small table. He lifted his stein from the windowsill and took a long drink. Putting it down, he looked at the image on it. "Ah, Hans Sachs, poet and shoemaker," he said.

"The hero of Richard Wagner's opera, *Die Meistersinger's Von Nurenberg*," said Martin.

"If only Nurenberg were still the seat of singing contests, instead of marching troops," said Schutz.

"Ah would we could return to those days. But back to our work. What will you do with the lists?" asked Martin. "Can you help these people?"

"We do what we can," said Schutz. "For those who still have money, property, we can make deals."

"Whoever we help, we ask for 30% or more extra, if they can afford it, to help the others," said Wagner.

"You two are true socialists," said Martin. "Do the Professors Mead and Von Dietz Mead play a role in your plans?"

"George Mead's fame and connections in America opens many possibilities for us. And Dr. Von Dietz is tireless," said Schutz.

Behind Schutz and Wagner, the door opened silently. Fragenzimmer entered. Martin wanted to signal Wagner and Schutz, but this would have been too obvious.

"But she must return home soon, while she still can, before the child is born and is claimed by the Fuhrer," said Wagner.

Fragenzimmer's raspy voice startled Schutz and Wagner who turned in their seats. "I could not help but overhear. It is Professor Von Dietz, you are talking about gentleman. Allow me to interject. It is too late. Hitler already lays a claim to all unborn babies on German soil. According to law number 6217 she would have to apply to the Fuhrer himself for a dispensation to leave Germany while pregnant."

His voice raised in ire, Heidegger said. "Bitte, Herr Fragenzimmer. You must not enter unannounced!"

While he said this Schutz raised his voice. "Surely this law 6217 would not apply to Dr. Von Dietz, an American, invited here as a guest? The Fuhrer would not want to risk making Americans more angry, perhaps enter the conflict."

Fragenzimmer laughed. "Dr. Von Dietz' work is of great interest to the Fuhrer, but her becoming a mother is even more significant."

"Surely you can help Frau Dr. Von Dietz return home," said Schutz, looking first at Fragenzimmer, than at Heidegger. Wagner was alert, ready to move.

Heidegger stood. "Get us more beer, Fragenzimmer, since you are still around after all." He felt as if he were being drawn and quartered, torn in different irreconcilable directions by equally powerful forces of nature. He walked to the window, looked down the hillside, turned back. His cheeks were flushed. "A German is a German. Dr. Von Dietz is more primordially German, than most of us. She is 100% aristocratic Prussian blood. The child also must stay."

"You must know what kind of danger that puts her in," said Wagner.

"These are hard times. A return to America is for her to lose her soul," said Heidegger.

"The only way out is for her to appeal to Hitler himself," said Fragenzimmer.

"Should he see her, she is lost," said Wagner.

"Was den Deutsch ist always Deutsch," said Fragenzimmer.

Chapter Twenty-nine
The Standing Reserve

When destiny reigns in the mode of Enframing, it is the
supreme danger. . . man comes to the point where he himself will have to be taken as standing-reserve
–Martin Heidegger, *Essay Concerning Technology*

The jeep's tires crunched the icy gravel as Guy drove under the arched sign, 'Arbeit Macht Frei'. "Work Makes Free," said Victoria. "Dr. Goebbels must have written it. He loves irony." Victoria bumped against Guy. Wagner reached from behind and put his hands on her shoulders to steady her over the potholes.

Schutz, sitting behind Guy said, "Goebbels is clever, brilliant, and violently anti-semitic. He could well have written it."

Victoria insisted on going along with Schutz and Wagner to see if they could spot Professor Hullerst and others from Martin's list. Schutz' Mercedes got barely a mile from the camp. There a rocky unpaved road required a tougher vehicle that Guy arranged to meet them in.

She had seen films of Nazi concentration camps, but this was beyond what she had imagined. She could not place the smell, both damp and smoky, like outhouse and slaughterhouse mixed together. And what they would see would not be the worst of it, which had not yet occurred, which she hoped they could prevent.

They passed rows of long grey barracks, with no one in sight. A faded red swastika, like the one on the door of the jeep was the only color. When they turned a corner Victoria gasped. A long shadowy line of men, sodden with sleet, as far as she could see.

An SS guard held up his hand. "Halten-Sie! Stop!" Guy stepped on the brakes. The tall guard approached, held out his hand for papers. Guy reached into his pocket, held out their passes. The guard looked at them for what seemed like a long time. What if they were not allowed to leave, thought Victoria. Finally the guard waved them along a narrow path barely four yards from the line of men. The jeep bounced and wavered along.

"Slow," said Schutz.

The line extended a half-kilometer. Water dripped off their hats down their cheeks like tears. A few wore glasses, fogged and smeared. Frosted fingertips poked through holes in gloves.

"Why are they kept in line, in this rain," asked Victoria. She glanced back at Wagner, his face red with rage.

"Who knows. To keep them under control, give them a bit of exercise," said Schutz, his voice a forced calm.

"It reminds me of what Martin calls the 'Standing Reserve', where everything, including humans, are stockpiled for use in the productive apparatus."

"Yeah, in the war machine," said Guy.

Victoria was cold to the bone, as the jeep had no sides, and no heater. The sleet continued to fall and wind blew it across their laps.

Guards paced along the line. A guard with broad shoulders had an elegant German shepherd walking at his heel. Stench of human waste and mold rose from the slush.

"Slow down," said Schutz. "That's Hullerst, there by the dog." The bearded man looked at the dog as if she were his only friend. Perhaps he imagines the dog could empathize with his plight, come to rescue him at night, chew off the ankle chain, lead him to freedom, thought Victoria.

As if sensing this possibility, the guard stopped in front of Hullerst. "She is a beautiful creature, nicht va? From the best breeder, a cousin of Der Fuhrer's dog, Blondie. Beautiful, yes, but did I not control her, she would tear you to shreds, eat you, and bring what remains to her pups."

Hullerst's eyebrows lifted.

"He recognized me. Does not want it known," whispered Schutz.

The guard's mouth turned up at the corners. He glanced at the jeep, then looked back at Hullerst. "The other day a man walked too far from the barracks after work hour, she ran after him and before I could stop her . . ." The guard opened his jaw and snapped it shut. "Gone, one bite to the throat. That day she was not hungry." He bent and scratched the black streak between the dog's ears.

The eyes of the men scanned the jeep. There had been too many tears not cried, screams of outrage unheard, even unthought. They were eyes of loss, whether hazel or brown. Eyes of worry about wives, children, pets, homes.

Victoria wanted to curse at the guard, run up to Hullerst, drag him up onto the jeep. Schutz had warned them to show no signs of recognition, no gestures, no smiles.

A man in a crumpled tweed jacket, about a foot shorter than most swung his head from side to side in a perpetual "no." Who is that man? Victoria had seen him before, or seen his picture. Ah she remembered. "Is he not Professor Cassirer? I recognize him from a book cover."

"Yeah, he's an ardent critic of the Nazis," said Schutz. "I'm surprised he's still alive. We have his family in sanctuary, waiting to cross the border when we obtain his release. I couldn't convince his wife to go ahead without him."

As they turned back toward the entrance Hullerst again raised his eyes toward them, almost imperceptibly. A guard shouted. Hullerst followed after the other soaked men, filing back into the leaky barracks.

Way down the line a man stepped forward, started to run. A shot rang out, the man fell.

A guard yelled toward the jeep, "Rouse Mit Dich, Macht Schnell. Turn Around, Get Going, Time to Get Out!" Guy spun the car around towards the gate.

Shivering with cold, Victoria could barely breathe. The cramps in her belly told her the baby felt the stress also. Perhaps a miscarriage would be the best thing, not to bring new life into such a dark time and place. The air was thick with the stench of unwashed bodied, urine and mold.

Sensing her stress, Guy put his hand on hers. "We'll get you out of here," he whispered.

∾

That afternoon Wagner and Schutz left Victoria off at the Old Vienna Inn. She was nauseated. This troubled her as her morning sickness had ended weeks ago. She took off her coat and opened the closet. It was stuffed with Mead's clothes as well as her own. She dropped the coat on the bench. She must air it out. It reeked from the odors of the camp that seemed to cling to her skin. She looked in the large closet mirror, placing her hands under her belly. "Little one, you are going to be large," she said, massaging her stomach. Thoughts of what she had seen made her dizzy. Those men. People just didn't know, or didn't want to know.

Her lower back throbbed and her ankles were swollen. She undressed, then filled the bath tub, sprinkling in Epson salts and cologne. Soaking in the warm water she was able to relax.

In deep meditation, she got mentally in touch with Kathy, who she pictured smiling, at school. Tears went down her cheeks as she imagined her sending back the message "I miss you too, Mom." Victoria had not yet worked out what would happen when she returned to Kathy and was again forward in time. Ouch, the complications of overlapping time zones. She had followed her path, with diligence and an open heart, and it brought her here. When her mentor and kundalini yoga teacher, Amritaprana, told her most changes can come in a moment, when she is truly open, she hardly imagined the magnitude of these possibilities.

Voices in the hall, the familiar footsteps of Martin brought her back. He knocked, came in without waiting for her to answer.

She got out of the tub, quickly getting into her soft bathrobe.

He held a bouquet of yellow and orange crysanthemums.

"For you, my lovely." He kissed her on the cheek, placed the flowers on the dresser. He hung his coat on the back of the door. Victoria admired the flowers, placing them in a vase.

Taking her in his arms he led her to the bed, kissed her, rubbed her back.

"I love, you, Victoria, how are you? How is my little one?"

"Martin, I've just been meditating, and then I am always peaceful," she said, kissing him back. She kissed him lightly. He untied her robe, pulled her close to him. She stiffened.

"What is it, my love? You know how much I've longed for you. Do you not?"

Thoughts of her trip to the work camp filled her. She looked directly into his eyes. "Martin, I must tell you. The "work camp" we visited this morning was horrendous. A long line of men, professors, doctors, none of them used to hard labor. In the cold rain, very thin, many of them ill. Hullerst was in the line, so was Cassirrer. Herded like cattle. Threatened by dogs. One of them panicked and started to run. He was shot down!"

"Germany is at war. What do you expect? Those running such places get tense and make mistakes," said Martin, sitting up.

Victoria got up, retied her robe. "Martin, you are blind. Your love for Germany, your university position, and your philosophic dreams distort your perceptions. You are attracted by the sense of mission, destiny, the heraldic imagery, the music. Look at what's actually happening! Men of the stature of Hullerst and Cassirer, reduced to degrading treatment and conditions, the expanding war. You must help," said Victoria.

Heidegger looked sorrowful, then resolute. He snapped his suspenders in place, slipped into his tweed jacket. "Can't you see I'm doing that already? I got the information for Schutz and Wagner. There were high risks. Of course the party has much wrong with it. But once I quit the party, my career is finished. My family is in jeopardy. You are in jeopardy."

Victoria felt trapped. She stroked her lover's face. His eyes were moist.

"Martin, you must go. George will return soon."

Martin got up. "It makes it so much more difficult for us with him here. I hate to leave you. And tomorrow I promised Elfriede I would stay home with the boys so that she could attend the Hitler Women's Auxilliary meeting. If she is missing, questions will be asked."

Victoria's stomach churned. Martin was used to thinking of his world, his thoughts as primary, as ultimate. She choose not to respond.

Martin continued, his face flushed. "Germany's alternatives now are non-existent. We must go forward or we will loose our land," said Martin. He put on his coat and walked to the door.

She realized that he may be right. The allies were eager to take over Germany, and of course she knew that was what would happen, unless . . .

He put on his coat and walked to the door. She put her arms around his neck and kissed him. "Aufwedersehen, my dear Martin," said Victoria and shut the door.

On his way downstairs, Martin felt his head was in a maze. He felt trapped, confused. He was used to women acquiescing to him, worshipping him because of his superior intellect, his earnest intensity, his vision. Victoria challenged him to the core. Should he relinquish everything? His position, his family? His hopes for a better Germany? Abandon it all and try to escape with the Jews?

Frau Bunge saw him coming and waved him toward the bar. "Professor Heidegger, come and have a stein!" a barmaid said. He jovially refused, saying he had to get home.

Guy and George entered the Inn just as Heidegger reached the doorway.

"Oh Herr Heidegger, you and my wife working late again? Mead stood tall in front of the door. "I have much to talk with you about. Please stay and dine with us."

"I'm sorry Dr. Mead. My wife und Kinder wait for me."

Mead stepped aside, keeping his hand on the door. "Herr Heidegger, this will only take a minute. I need you to push with Fragenzimmer and the authorities for our visas and tickets home. Victoria is getting on in her pregnancy and needs to be near her home, her doctor," said Mead.

"Ah, Nein, this is impossible. We are having the best doctors in the world right here in Deutschland. The doctors come from all over the world to hear the lectures of Dr. Lindenstromph, Victoria's physician."

"However good your doctors are here, must have our baby at home in Chicago." said Mead, standing taller.

Guy stepped forward, looming over Martin. "Herr Heidegger, you have not heard Professor Mead. Victoria must go home."

Martin took a step back, cleared his throat. "Nevertheless, it is not possible for pregnant women to leave Germany. To even be considered she would have to go to Berlin for special permission from the Fuhrer's office of external affairs," said Martin. He put his hand on Mead's shoulder, reached around him for the door. Guy placed his foot in front of the door.

"That's absurd. She only came here to do her work, as a visiting scholar. She's already been here much longer than expected," said Guy.

"The nature of our work on the theory of time has come to the attention of the authorities lately. Now they cannot let Dr. Victoria leave. So much has changed in six months," said Martin. "Now I really must go!" He pushed past them.

Chapter Thirty
Payment

In the summer of 1944 I was ordered to work on the fortifications on
the Rhine. . . I was included in the category of 'completely dispensable'.
Martin Heidegger, *Only a God Can Save Us Now*

S chutz felt the acid burn rising up from his belly. Lucky he wasn't prone
to ulcers or he'd be sure to get them now. Lora, his wife and his daughter
and sons were safe in London now. Lora wanted him to join them at once.
But this was not to be. Each of us must make the most of our situation in the
lifeworld, in history. "The participating citizen" is what I called it in my essay.
If he didn't act now using his resources in the international banking community, the scholars and their families would have little chance to get out alive.

"You should let me handle these negotiations with Fragenzimmer," said
Wagner as they got out of the Mercedes.

From the driver's seat, Guy said. "I'll be waiting for you across the street
in the parking lot." Students were walking by jostling each other, on their
way to classes. It was a sunny fall day, with colored leaves dropping from the
maple trees.

"I'm worried about you being Jewish and working so directly with them,"
continued Wagner, his forehead wrinkled into a frown.

"Helmut, you could just as easily be taken because you are working with
me. Just now I am not worried as they need us—I should say, our money."

They walked across the cobble stone lane and up into the brick administration building.

"They could confiscate your assests as well," said Wagner. "They need me to keep the munitions plant running."

"My assests are safe in a Swiss bank," said Schutz.

An attractive young woman at a desk in a reception area, seemed to be expecting them and immediately announced them to Fragenzimmer.

Schutz smiled and whispered to Wagner. "She's a real honey who could make more money downtown," and winked. Despite his love and devotion to his family, he was susceptible to attractive women.

"Perhaps that's where Fragenzimmer got her from," said Wagner.

"Vielen Danken, Fraulein," said Schutz to the girl, smiling.

Fragenzimmer' spacious office was furnished in mahogany. Crossed swords hung behind him above a large framed photograph of Die Fuhrer.

"Won't you sit down, Dr. Schutz, Herr Wagner," said Fragenzimmer, who sat at a large desk. He did not stand. A brass sign on his desk read, H. Fragenzimmer. A silver cardholder displayed his name embossed next to a swastika with the title, "Vice Chancellor for Reichsministry Ober Education."

"Congratulations on your promotion, Herr Fragenzimmer." The small-boned man with a weasel like face sat up straighter in his leather chair.

Ah, thought Schutz, he is subject to flattery. Schutz sat directly in front of Fragenzimmer. He needed to project confidence, a sense of class superiority, but not too much. Fragenzimmer had spent most of his career keeping books for a shoemaker, way below the stature of Schutz, a banker and well-known economist from the Vienna circle. This puny minded guy will resent me. Schutz made small talk about the university soccer team as a leveling device.

Fragenzimmer brought the conversation back to his promotion. "It was Professor Heidegger's idea, as there is much to be done to update the education system throughout Deutschland. Just last week we removed two hundred traitorous and morally depraved titles from our libraries. With copies this made 10,000 books." The corners of Fragenzimmer's mouth angled upward to a thin horizontal line across his pallid face.

"A shame to see them go up in smoke. They may bring money elsewhere," said Schutz. He knew this weasel was about money, not ideas or knowledge.

"At least going up in smoke the air will clear the way for German youth to know the truth," said Fragenzimmer. "And about selling the books, we have thought about this already. Some workers are being sent from the camps to package them for shipping. We will burn a pile or two for the newspapers, sell the rest."

"Aren't you afraid of corrupting minds abroad?" said Wagner, who was seated to the side. He looked directly at Fragenzimmer.

Schutz thought of the radical difference between Fragenzimmer's point of view and Wagner's. Each person's conception of a situation depends upon what their 'stock of knowledge', what they read, studied, grew up with, came to find out by chance and by choice. He made a mental note to write about this in his next article.

"What do we care? They will be impressed with German writers, that will confuse them," said Fragenzimmer. Wagner shrugged his shoulders.

Fragenzimmer opened a large humidor on his desk and offered Guy and Schutz cigars. "Cuban specials. Only available through the party."

Schutz did not normally smoke cigars, but in this situation thought it best to accept. Wagner followed suit, also picking the lighter off Fragenzimmer's desk. He held the flame first to Fraggy, then Schutz, then his own cigar.

Fragenzimmer spoke though several circles of smoke blown over his long tongue. "As you know, the Fuhrer is not interested in sending intellectual resources abroad, but in retraining them, helping them to realize the truth and destiny of the Third Reich and of Germany and the coming world empire," said Fragenzimmer. He flicked his tongue around his lips as he pushed his cigar butt down in the pewter tray.

Schutz kept his disgust at this lizardly gesture at bay.

"Delightful smoke, Herr Fragenzimmer," he said, smiling. "Surely middle aged and retired professors, their wives and families, can be of little use to such a grand endeavor. Stronger, younger, fresher minds, such as yours are needed, Herr Fragenzimmer," said Schutz.

"You flatter me, sir. But I do agree about the need for resources for reeducation," said Fragenzimmer.

"Of course you've reviewed the books carefully," said Schutz.

"So much as I can, I look them over. I've gotten so I can smell the trash in the first two pages," said Fragenzimmer, blowing a thick cloud of smoke above his desk. "Don't worry, Professor Schutz, your books have not been selected for extinction, yet. Except for Hullerst's *Collapse of the European Sciences* the philosophers write at a very abstract level, harmless because no-one can understand them," he added.

Helmut Wagner's body tightened. He began to stand. Schutz caught his eye, moved his head from side to side slightly. Wagner sat back in the chair.

"I'm alarmed to hear that Hullerst's "The Collapse" that warned us ten years ago of a coming war is on your list. Much worse is that a person of his stature has been sent to a work camp. What we saw there at the camp yesterday has put my friend Wagner and I in an anxious state of mind," said Schutz.

"My dear Dr. Schutz," said Fragenzimmer with ironic condescension. "It seems you have not read the most important philosophy book for Germany and, yes, even the world, for this century, *Mein Kamph*, where the Fuhrer says:

'The loss of blood purity alone destroys inner happiness forever, plunges man into the abyss for all time.'

Wagner's fist tightened on the armrest. He stood up. "We're not here to debate philosophy, if you can call it that. Let's get on with it," he said. "When can we arrange pick up and transportation? We need emigration papers, visas, for those on the list and their families."

"Ah zo, this is what Dr. Heidegger tells me," said Fragenzimmer.

Schutz sat forward in his chair and said, "Vice Chancellor Fragenzimmer, when can you release them?"

As the sun left the horizon a chill entered the room. Schutz pulled his leather gloves from his pocket, put them on.

"We have all ten of them ready to go, five tomorrow, the others next week. I must have the money immediately," said Herr Fragenzimmer.

"I can give you 25,000DM tomorrow morning, upon their arrival, the other half when they reach Geneva, as we agreed," said Schutz. He reached his hand inside his vest pocket and pulled out a gold watch. With his thumb he flipped open the lid.

Fragenzimmer jumped up from his desk, stomping his foot. His grey uniform hung on his scrawny frame like a wet washcloth. There were perspiration stains under his arms, despite the chill in the room.

Fragenzimmer cleared his throat: "Did you not want their families also? The five each have a wife and with the children this makes seventeen additional, plus their elderly makes twenty-five. This means I must have 65,000 Marks by tonight." His voice got higher and louder as he spoke.

"That is impossible! We can't pay that much. Then we would have nothing left for their transportation, food, lodging!" said Schutz.

"Nein! The price was for each one and his family! Not just the man alone!" said Helmut.

"What I say now is the price. As you said yourself, you are removing a great resource from our homeland." With the three men standing Fragenzimmer looked small and withered.

"I'm sorry it has come to this. Good day, Herr Fragenzimmer," said Schutz. He and Wagner walked to the door.

Fragenzimmer stood up and shouted.

"Halten Sie! I will do what I can for you." His voice had turned more guttural, betraying a south German village background. Schutz mused that his weak physique and low German accent must be detriments in the party.

"I make this special arrangement for Herr Professor Hullerst. Only because of his relationship to Heidegger and to you. $50,000 marks total. 25 now 25 later. It is the best I can do."

Schutz hesitated, Wagner moved slightly more towards the door.

"$40,000 marks 20 now 20 later, and a letter with your signature giving all on the list safe passage, with passports and visas," said Schutz.

"Sit down, please, gentleman. I will order coffee and schnapps while I write the letter and we discuss arrangements," said Fragenzimmer.

The little smirk at one corner of Fragenzimmer's mouth bothered Schutz. Perhaps the little man was just pleased with his newfound 40,000 Marks. Or, there may be more to his conniving.

Chapter Thirty-One
Tapping the Akashic Record

Love is itself unmoving
Only the cause and end of movement,
Timeless and undesiring
Except in the aspect of time,
Caught in the form of limitation,
Between being and non-being
— T. S. Elliot, "Burnt Norton," *Four Quartets*

Martin placed his hand gently on the soft sweater over Victoria's large belly. They sat on the small sofa in the rooms she and George occupied at the Old Vienna Inn. She was pleased to have an afternoon alone with him.

Here at the Inn Martin and Victoria were safe from the eyes and ears at the university, or the interruptions of Elfriede at Martin's home. Mead was frequently away, lecturing at various universities or to work with Wagner and Schutz, in the underground. Mead's popularity as a visiting lecturer made him less jealous of Victoria's time with Martin. This could not last, as George was facing increased danger from Nazi protestors at his talks. Guy, in his role as butler and general assistant, occupied rooms downstairs. He was often away as well, acting as chauffeur and bodyguard to Schutz and Wagner.

For now, the warmth and energy between Martin and Victoria was all she wanted to focus on. She had been teaching him Kundalini yoga, as she felt the need to intensify her practice during her pregnancy. They explored the link between this and her ability to execute time travel.

"Oph! Did you feel that?" Victoria's belly rose up under Martin's hand.

Martin smiled. "Two kicks. I think the little one is impatient to come out, see his Papa," he said. Victoria avoided his eyes. How could she tell him her pregnancy may just as well have been the result of her farewell night with George before departing for Germany?

She covered Martin's hand with hers. "Not so impatient as I am for HER to arrive. I feel like I'm carrying an elephant around. Yet I'm just not ready for HER, in this situation. I was practicing pranayama, especially breath of fire, to raise the energy levels up my Chakras. Considering how much I practice during this pregnancy, perhaps she will be born enlightened." Victoria knew it would take extra spiritual practice for her to remain calm and strong with the trials they were facing.

Martin stood and held out his arms. She stood, first reaching high up with both hands over her head as if to do a sun salute. Martin followed suit then bent forward putting his hands on the floor next to his feet. "I can't do much of a forward bend in this condition." She placed her hands on her belly. He stood up, put his hands over hers. After several long full breaths, they began to rapidly inhale and exhale, forcing the air out their nostrils by pushing up on their diaphragms. After about a minute they held their breaths. A response from her belly poked up under her right hand, Martin's left hand over it.

"I think when I do breath of fire I tickle his feet! I think he loves the stimulation," said Victoria.

"You see, when you don't think about it you intuitively know our child is a boy," said Martin. His brown eyes pierced her heart.

She put her forehead against his, stroked his hair. "Yes, that is my sense, but Mother Nature sometimes likes to prove even intuition wrong."

Ping! Victoria's left hand covered by Martin's right got kicked from down under. Martin gasped. "Victoria, really, he didn't turn all the way around in there!

Ping!Ping! Her belly rose at both sides at once. Victoria's heart rate went up. "I've been wondering for a while, Martin, there's got to be two in there."

"Hallelujah," said Martin. They sat down on the soft carpet, moving through yoga postures and breath flows to support and massage each other.

As they took a rest break, Martin spoke.

"Victoria, I've been thinking about your time travel and your yoga." He cleared his throat. "You tapped into Akashic Energies (what the Hindus and Buddhist call the records of past lives) without being fully aware of what you were doing. You were already practicing yoga when you meditated on Mead's picture and crossed over into his time—this time?" he asked.

"Yes, George had been long dead in my time, but we somehow came together," said Victoria. "At first I was practicing only Hatha yoga, physical postures to deal with severe lower back pain. I had lots of stress from writing a dissertation, being a mother and dealing with an unfaithful husband and an oppressive dean. I did not put this together with the increased intensity of my relationship with Mead, from what was then the past."

Victoria and Martin resumed their breath work and postures. Since they had begun practicing yoga together, they grew blissful on deeper levels. At first Martin had agreed to it as a way of helping her endure the pregnancy. Now he really enjoyed it. Clothing was irrelevant, even though fully dressed they felt no barrier to their energetic interpenetration of each other. They needed nothing more, as they reached the higher levels of bliss of which the act of sex is an illusion, a crude metaphor, a way of bringing enough of the Akashic energy forward for another incarnation.

Victoria could not keep her focus on the experience. She felt pounding in her temples. She must broach the subject of the babies' paternity. Would Martin pull away? She could not bear it if he abandoned her. They were soul mates as well as intellectual partners. She felt a tear running down her cheek. She must face this. She pulled away from him, suddenly feeling cold.

"Tell me, what is it?' he whispered.

"Martin, please understand." She stood up. He followed suit.

"What's wrong, darling?" He put his hands on her shoulders. Out the window a siren blared its dissonant tritones. He held her close, which in her condition meant more side to side.

She stepped back, looked at him, panicky. She must tell him now.

"Please, Martin, the baby, or babies, may be George's." Was this going to change everything? She filled the gulf with words, fearing it would only make things worse but compelled to speak. "And legally George is the father regardless."

Martin turned away, walked to the window.

She trembled as she walked up behind him. "Martin, please understand."

He turned, his face a blank, his eyes looking into the distance. He put his hands on her shoulders. Tears melted down her cheeks. The energy shifted. He held her gaze, his eyes warm, his face softened.

"Ah, Victoria, Victoria. What is between us is beyond physical or legal. It is eternal." He kissed her with abandon. She forgot her concern.

He guided her gently back down to the Persian carpet. They extended their legs, feet touching feet, while pulling on each other's arms, like a seasaw. They worked together, noting images and visions as they occurred. Their breaths were varied, echoing each other musically, sometimes rapid, sometimes deep and long. Their sense of time faded away. They floated in the vastness of ananda—the bliss state. "In this position we realize time on the ethereal plane," whispered Martin. After one last intense breath of fire they lay down in the corps pose, Savasanna, in deep relaxation.

Robust footsteps sounded in the hallway. Victoria jumped up. Halfway through Guy's five knock sequence, Martin yelled:

"Guy, we're in Savasanna, Come back in ten. With coffee!"

They stretched. Martin got up, held out his hand to Victoria.

"I feel so refreshed," she said "But we need to explore time expansion."

"That will be our next theoretical work," said Martin with a twinkle in his eye.

Guy returned with a tray of coffee and streusel cake balanced in one hand, his briefcase under his other arm. "Let me know next time you practice Kundalini. I'd like to join you. You know I started to study yoga back at Athens, as I saw how much it helped my dear professor, here. I was a cop at the time as well as in school. Lots of stress." He set the tray down, put his brief case on the side table.

"I brought an extra mug, as Professor Mead will arrive soon. He lectured in Tubingen today and is returning by car with Schutz and Wagner" he said.

"George always keeps Guy informed of his whereabouts, rather than me," said Victoria. "He doesn't want me to worry when he's on the road."

"Herr Mead does have an extraordinary sense of ethics," said Martin.

"Perhaps he just doesn't want to be nagged or inhibited." Guy grinned.

"Be cautious about your assumptions," said Victoria, smiling.

Guy poured each of them a mug of coffee, putting lots of cream in Victoria's, cut each a slice of cake. He sat in a stuffed chair by the fire, mug in hand.

Victoria felt happy, there between these two brilliant men, who cared for her.

"You become more and more German by the day," Martin, said, looking at Guy's blue ski sweater with a snowflake pattern.

"I may be able to fool a few Germans if I don't say more than "Bitte, Danke, Viedersehen or especially "Heil Hitler", but my complexion and brown eyes would still cause them to wonder," said Guy.

"Even the Fuhrer's eyes are brown," said Martin.

"And yours as well, Martin," said Victoria. "This race thing is ridiculous."

Guy gulped his coffee. His tone of voice was strong yet warm. "Yes, Hitler had his cranium measured by a phrenologist and it was found, much to his dismay, to be quite normal. I think he was hoping it would prove to be like Alexander the Great."

"Speaking of Hitler, any progress on the manuscript?" asked Victoria. "I know you've been very busy helping Wagner and Schutz." Victoria and Martin had asked Guy to write a distorted but convincing version of their theory of time to satisfy the Nazis.

"Don't worry. I'm used to working nights, working myself through Athens, then law school."

He put his coffee mug on the tray, reached for his brief case, pulled out some papers. "Here's my latest installment, ready for your edits and additions," said Guy. He held the document out to her.

"Fragenzimmer is getting impatient for this," said Martin, taking a sip of coffee. "Yesterday he came to my office saying that Herr Himmler had brought it to the attention of the Fuhrer who got excited about the idea. Himmler explained it as a way to win in battle by being able to see ahead what your enemy will do."

Victoria paged through the draft, writing notes in the margin. Guy poured her coffee, added cream. "It's crucial that this is close to what we are doing, but leads them off the track. That way Martin and I can keep our manuscript out of their hands."

"Or any political hands. It's painful to have to write two versions," said Martin. "I feel like one of those Chicago gangsters in the movies who keep two sets of books."

Guy cleared his throat. "I hate to think what those bastards would do with time travel capacity. Human inventions can be used for evil as well as good. Look at what happened to Einstein's theory—or what will happen."

"Einstein, yah, the fellow who is working on atomic energy, e=mc2," said Martin.

Victoria interrupted. "I wonder if it would matter if they got the real manuscript? They wouldn't understand it anyway. And if they could come to truly understand it wouldn't that change them? I believe it's inherent in the nature of tapping the Akashic energy that it can only be done by those who are highly evolved, who would not be capable of using it except for deepening enlightenment."

"Victoria, it sounds like you only believe in good gods, no Terrible Mother, no daemons," said Martin.

Victoria's heart raced. With a burst of energy she stood up. "Martin, Guy, I've got it! I've finally got it!"

Martin and Guy looked up at her in eager anticipation. "Our theory is just an explanation for how time travel is possible. But what makes it happen is intense Kundalini yoga practice!"

"Oh, Shaw, Victoria, surely not." said Guy. "But then I could never understand how you brought me back to Mead's time." He turned color. "Yes, that's it. It could be it. I'd been practicing pranayama yoga that you taught me the whole time, it's all in the breath!"

"The secret vas right in front of us. Our minds just had to catch up with our breath." said Martin, his voice resonant with pleasure. "And of course, the ancient Yogis, as described in the Vedas, were able to transcend time and space."

Guy added, "That means we could give the Nazis the actual theory. Unless they practice advanced Kundalini they could never make it work," said Guy.

"Ah, but we'd better not take the chance. Who knows if there's a closet yogi in the Nazi party," said Victoria.

"If there is he'd be in the underground," said Guy.

"Hmm, maybe, but technologies, like religions, are used for good or evil. Just to be on the safe side, lets give them the altered version and hide ours," said Victoria. "Martin, put it in the safest place you can find."

"I'll send Wagner to bury it by my Alpine hut," said Martin.

"In the meantime," said Victoria, "lets get to work editing Guy's copy."

ℭ

The sunset out the second story window of the Vienna Inn. Shades of auburn, brown and tan of the tiles rooftops on the shops and homes shown bronze and gold. A late afternoon crescendo of clinking glasses and steins came from the pub below, along with muffled voices raised in greetings and jests.

Victoria, Martin and Guy had completed editing the two versions of time travel theory, now safely lodged in Martin's brief case. They did some yoga stretches and deep breaths to both rest and restore their energy. Guy joked with Victoria. "Watch what you envision now, Victoria, we don't want to end up in China."

"Hmm, that may not be a bad idea," clipped Martin. He began to hmmm in Chinese style.

"Martin, stop it, its not funny," said Victoria.

A thunder of footsteps and and rich alto/tenor laughter sounded in the hallway. Victoria raised her eyebrows with surprise.

"Sounds familiar," Guy said. His eyebrows peaked in unison with Martin's. "Could this be Annabelle?"

"The footsteps as well as the resonant laugh are those of a formidable person," said Martin.

"Like Dr. Annabelle Carter Jackson!" Victoria felt warm, excited. "We were working on her transport, but there were many obstacles." She put her hands over her belly. Annabelle will be surprised to see her pregnant.

"Ach, I remember. Annabelle's the gal who funded your research, so you could be here," said Martin.

"Yes, and my boss until Victoria brought me over here!" said Guy. He stood up, walked to the door.

"That was Annabelle's doing," said Victoria. She wondered just how much was really Annabelle's doing and how much came from Guy. . .

"Don't underestimate Annabelle. She's from an ancient African royal family, been practicing tribal rituals all her life." He opened the door.

Mead stepped in, then stood aside, his arm open wide toward the opening. "My dear, I brought Professor Schutz and Herr Wagner with me, and a special surprise" he said.

Schutz and Wagner entered, greeted all. Guy took their coats, hung them on the coat rack near the door. The stairs creaked and the stomping sound got louder, along with puffing and panting. Was it an apparition appearing the doorway? There was stunned silence, then gasps. Annabelle emerged at the doorway, wearing a huge Zebra coat and colorful turban. Her face shone like a black pearl with her white teeth glowing.

"Girl, I thought you were coming back with the book months ago and now here you are, stuck in this Nazi Burg." Her operatic voice filled the small room. She squeezed through the doorway, her large eyes circling around the room.

"Annabelle! I didn't know if my instructions were refined enough to actually bring you here," said Victoria. "And I'm only now realizing what made it work."

"They got me about half way. Got stuck somewhere in Africa, actually much earlier in time. Almost got caught in a slave camel train, got help from an ancestor with the same real family name as mine, Ogubiko. Ogu conjured a way for me to come back here. By boat. Whew, what a ride! And don't say anything about my coat. It was given to me by my Tribal Mother who said she skinned the zebra herself, after it died of natural causes. I imagine political correctness has a different slant here and now, but Annabelle Carter Jackson carries hers wherever she goes. And whenever." She shed the coat, handed it to Guy.

Seeing the puzzled expression on Schutz and Wagner's faces, Victoria explained about the animal rights advocacy movement in the U.S.

"What an amazing and formidable patron you have, Dr. Von Dietz," said Schutz.

"Victoria stole my best assistant, as well, so I figured I'd come over, be sure you'll get back." She squeezed Guy's shoulder. Her eyes bulged out of their sockets at Victoria's belly. "Oh my Gawd, Victoria, you not only got yourself trapped here you got yourself in trouble as well,"

Her use of "in trouble" made Victoria laugh, as the phrase was used back in her high school to refer to pregnancy. Victoria embraced her, at arms length because of the size of both their bellies.

"Annabelle, with that African garb, you are triply conspicuous. I'm surprised you weren't arrested," said Guy.

"To the contrary. I'm royalty. Queen, 'Lagrete Ogubiko'." Her stately bearing and resonant voice confirmed her assertion. "Hitler needs allies in Africa. Believe me, I'm safer this way, especially since most folks know nothing about the place."

Schutz nodded, "Ah yeah, this is true."

" And to my friends from home, I'm here doing research, having deepened my ancestral roots," said Annabelle.

Martin could not conceal his fascination. Victoria realized he may not have ever seen an African woman.

He walked towards her, bowed and lifted her ringed hand to his lips. "Delighted to meet you, Dr. Carter-Jackson, Queen Ogubiko'. To you I owe Victoria having come." Victoria lifted her hands to her face to hide the the blush of affection she felt for her lover.

Ever attentive to Victoria's needs, Guy stepped forward. "Time travel is not so different from any kind of travel, once you get used to it," he said. "Just problems with language, and politics."

Mead suggested they all be seated with a sweep of his arm towards the sofa and several chairs. Annabelle sunk deeply into the sofa, taking up a chunk of it.

"I'll bring coffee and refreshments for all," Guy said, picking up the tray. He winked at Annabelle.

"You are still honey on the spot, Guy," said Annabelle. "Make mine brandy." Annabelle's huge eyes settled again on Victoria, first to her belly, then her eyes.

"You didn't tell me, girl, you got yourself knocked up," said Annabelle. Looking up at Schutz and Wagner's puzzled look, she added, "That's Chicago street talk for pregnant." She looked back at Victoria, now sitting opposite her on a sofa between Mead and Martin.

"Hmmm Hmm. Vicky, I hope you know there's more than one cooking in there. You gonna have twins," said Annabelle. She winked at Mead who had his eyebrows raised. "I used to be a midwife before I got my Ph.D. I know."

Victoria took a deep breath. "I just realized this myself today, as I got kicked on both sides at once," she said.

Mead put his arm behind her and gently rubbed her neck. "Two will be splendid, my dear," he said.

Martin leaned forward, reached inside his jacket, snapped his suspenders.

Victoria suddenly felt cold. Where did she belong? With whom? She loved two men, both in another time zone and was pregnant with twins. Her daughter, Kathy, was ahead in the 1970s. 'Focus on the here and now', she told herself, 'be in the present.' But which present? She forced herself to move the conversation.

"How are the plans for the men in the camps going?" she looked at Schutz.

"Fragenzimmer is stalling, the need for more paper work, trying to weasel more money." Schutz looked grey, weary.

Guy returned with fresh coffee, mugs, brandy and sandwiches. He poured brandy into shot glasses for all, passed them around.

"Wunderbar, Guy," said Victoria, holding the brandy up to her nostrils.

Wagner, contemplative since arriving, said, "We have a plan to get them on a train to Geneva. But we'll need all of your help."

They raised their glasses and all took a sip. "Prozit!"

Chapter Thirty-Two
Breakfast with Queen Annabelle Ogubiko

It was and it is the Jews who bring the Negroes into the Rhineland, always with the same secret thought and clear aim of ruining the hated white race by the necessarily resulting bastardization, throwing it down from its cultural and political height, and himself rising to be its master.
— Adolph Hitler, *Mein Kamph*

"Your detour through Africa is amazing." Victoria glanced out the paned window in the cafe at the Inn. Children and matrons bussled by on bicycles on their way to school or shopping. Red and orange maple leaves swirled on the streets.

"I'll have to revise my theory," Victoria continued. 'You can get the time warp just a little bit off, it seems, and travel to an unexpected space/time location. Now that you're here, lets go shopping for some nice conservative suits and coats for you to wear, make you less conspicuous."

"Victoria, there's no way a large black babe in Germany is not conspicuous so there's no point in trying to turn me into a blond in a grey flannel suit. This queen thing gives me some clout. We're going to need it in Berlin."

"Berlin? I'm challenged enough with the local environment here," said Victoria. Annabelle's presence would attract attention like a siren. Would this endanger their work? On the other hand, Annabelle had connections in high places with the U.S. Embassy.

"No way round it, girl. We've got to go," said Annabelle. She lifted a bronze arm revealing a wide banded silver bracelet. An orange and red patterned dress with a wide orange shawl matched her elaborate turban. A bronze and silver chain with a dancing goddess lay suspended across her enormous breasts.

"Annabelle, if you were the subject of a painting the storm troopers would set it aflame along with the books they'd never read nor had the brains to understand. You'll be a moving target on the streets of Berlin," said Victoria. "Besides, you heard what Schutz said yesterday. He needs our help with the Geneva escape plan."

Frau Bunge approached their booth, looking tired though it was only 8 A.M. "Guten Morgen, Frauen. Was wollen Sie?" She smiled and placed a small vase with a white rose on the wood plank table. Her eyes opened wide as she appraised Annabelle. "Your Highness, please tell me what suits your dietary needs," she said, bowing her head.

"Frau Bunge, darlin, thank you for the courtesy," said Annabelle. "German sausage and grated potato dumplings are very much like home cooking in Africa. I'll have a plate of those and tapioca pudding and coffee."

"It's an honor to have an African Queen here in Hochheim," said Bunge. Lowering her voice she added, "It's probably in your best interest to be seen as a Queen. People can be pretty rough with those who are different." Frau Bunge looked over at some uniformed men at a nearby table, she smiled their way. By now the word was around this little suburban town that an African Queen was visiting.

Victoria nodded agreement. She ordered scrambled eggs, brochen, and cocoa. As Frau Bunge turned towards the kitchen Victoria added, "and please bring some of your wonderful plum jam."

"Glad the plum tree bore well this summer, as it seems you Americans can't get enough of my plum cakes and jam." Bunge walked to the kitchen. Several local heads turned towards her on the way, their eyebrows lifted. An echo of whispers, faces turned to look at Annabelle, "Queen, Congo, doctorate from America," Annabelle called in her low contralto, pointing to herself. They nodded, said "Guten Tag," They seemed delighted. Annabelle was indeed a source of magnetic energy.

"Your presence challenges their racist notions."

"Like a Ming Vase in a Bull Pen, to reverse a popular metaphor," said Annabelle. "And Victoria, Honey, it's more than a disguise. My time travel detour through my Congolese ancestral home turned out to be quite informative. I met my great-great grandmother. According to tradition, her soul was passed to me. Back then, the tribes were matriarchal. She Ruled!"

"How did you explain who you are to Great-Grandma?" Victoria was delighted with this development in their lives.

Annabelle grinned from ear to ear. "Ah, that was easy. She didn't need an explanation. She knew in her bones I am a part of her. In Okubi mythology the times of the soul's journey are all overlapping. They knew about time travel way back."

Frau Bunge arrived with a tray. She placed a plate of steaming sausages on the table, a bowl of scrambled eggs, a basket of hot rolls, and a platter of potato pancakes. "The tapioca I will bring later. I'm glad you ladies are hearty eaters. Shall I set a plate for Dr. Mead and Mr. Guy?"

"Nein, Danke, Frau Bunge," said Victoria. "They left early for Leipzig on business. They'll be back tonight. I'm sure they'll want a late dinner."

"Yavohl, I will put some stew aside for them." Frau Bunge fussed with this arrangment of dishes. Her facial features were chiseled, expressive. "They are so busy since they arrived. I hoped you'd have more company. Of course Professor Heidegger is here often with you."

Victoria felt herself blushing. Frau Bunge must suspect they may be lovers. How could she play this down?

"Yah, Dr. Heidegger comes as often as he can. And now Dr. Okuburi is also here to work with me," said Victoria, looking at Annabelle.

"You are a physician?" asked Frau Bunge.

"No, but I'm a mid-wife, nurse and psychologist, in Maloko, where my tribe lives, Queens have lots of responsibilities," said Annabelle.

"All that as well as Queen, Ach, ve haf some midwives practicing in Bavaria, and also some lady doctors. I am happy Professor Von Dietz is in such good hands with the little one on the way. A midwife is better than specialist doctors who are more interested in their research than in you and the baby," said Bunge. She straightened the pancake platter and left.

"Talkative, isn't she?" said Annabelle.

"You can't be sure if it is friendly or politically motivated spying. I do hate being so mistrustful, but this is a world of intrigue," said Victoria. She helped herself to eggs and potato pancakes. She put plum jam on the pancakes, then took a large forkful. The two women chewed slowly, savoring their food. "I love the oniony taste of these pancakes. Annabelle, what if the Nazi authorities find out you are not really the Queen of the Umoru tribe? I'm sure they have envoys in Africa."

Annabelle cut a sausage in half and put it in her mouth. Some of the juice escaped down the side of her lips. She picked up her napkin, wiped her chin. "Frau Bunge is an excellent cook. But you know, even German sausage can't hold a candle to Louisiana andrille," she said. She finished the rest of the sausage, cut into another. Victoria looked straight at Annabelle, hoping she'd get off of the food topic. They had plans to make.

"I really am that Queen, Darlin," said Annabelle. "For African tribal culture, the transmigration of souls, time travel, out of body experiences are part of everyday life. These things are communicated to us every night in our dreams which are still in control of the underworld," said Annabelle.

"But what about the Queen your great grandma who is still living in Africa? How will we explain her being here and there at the same time if a German official should travel and meet her?" asked Victoria.

"The chance of that happening is slim. Germans are mostly in North Africa. And if someone should have met her, she has lots of names. I look just like her, but to Germans, as with Americans, we black folk all look alike anyways," said Annabelle, attacking a stack of pancakes on her plate. "Now, Victoria, back to the issue at hand. Berlin. Guy told me this Nazi dude, Fragenzimmer, said you can't leave Germany without special dispensation from the Fuhrer! What a great opportunity get to the devil!" The pancakes gone, she looked at her plate of eggs. "Don't they have Tabasco sauce here? How do they expect a gal to eat scrambled eggs?" Annabelle waved at Frau Bunge.

"Annabelle, they don't have hot sauce or even red pepper. Would sauerkraut do?" said Victoria.

"Blat. You know I like things hot and sweet. Not sour," said Annabelle. She put her hands palms up and shook her head "no" as Frau Bunge started towards the table. "Never mind. It's O.K.," she said.

Frau Bunge smiled back, "O.K., I know, Gut, Gut," and walked to a table where six soldiers sat. They glanced at Annabelle and Victoria, nodding and smiling. Annabelle gave them a queenly wave and a smile.

"Just so they don't mistake me for the wrong kind of queen," Annabelle said.

"I didn't think of that. It could make for interesting developments. Seriously, I have no desire to go to Berlin, but if it's the only way to get back to Chicago, I'll do it. The thought of having a baby in the middle of what will become a major bombing target terrifies me," said Victoria. "But what about Schutz and Wagner needing help with the Geneva plan?"

"We can help them as much, maybe more from Berlin," said Annabelle. "I have lots more connections there, special intelligence support. Along with bringing myself in from the 70s I brought some high tech communications equipment. My African brain's been at work!"

Chapter Thirty-Three
Escape Before Dawn

Schutz spent his nights writing innumerable letters, inquiries, peti-
tions, and applications in desperate efforts to extricate a number of his friends from Austria, where they were trapped.
— Helmut Wagner, *Alfred Schutz: An Intellectual Biography*

G uy glanced at his Elgin. 3 A.M. He pulled himself out of his sleeping
bag, which he had only been in for about two hours. He slept in his
wool trousers and sweater as he needed to be ready. He went into the bathroom up the hall and splashed cold water on his face. His back ached from
hoisting his human cargo and all the worldly possessions they could cram
into a few bags on and off vans.

"Time to get up. Rouse mit Dich" said Guy, walking down the narrow
hallway. The Langsdorfs were generous and courageous to share their home
to those trying to escape Germany, he thought. Wagner's and Schutz' underground connections were impressive. The Langsdorf's house was a two-story
stucco. It was like most of the other family homes in Hagenheim, this small
once farming town now a suburban community.

Guy was apprehensive. His task of escorting them over a snowy slope to
the train station before dawn was wrought with hazards. All of them, young
and old, had to share these two large bedrooms and one bathroom. They
were on their way to catch a train to Geneva, meeting up with their fathers,
husbands and sons who had been in workcamps.

Frau Hullerst was already dressed, in a white blouse and navy wool skirt. Her skin looked sallow as she had been ill with flu. She was helping her aging mother and father get dressed. She pulled a greenish-blue paisley wool dress over her mother's white curly hair. The old man struggled to pull his trousers up his muscular legs. The old man reminded Guy of his own aging father safe in a retirement community outside Chicago.

Threads of light crept in under the drapes. Guy noticed several lumps in the double bed. Five, he counted out of the corner of his eye as he opened the drapes a crack. The moon was full, doubling itself in the mirror on the opposite wall. He reached down to pick up the three large canvas travel bags. He braced his lower back with his left hand. Hopefully these items, one per family, with prepaid shipment clearance of 2500 Marks, will actually arrive in New York.

"Is everything packed?" he whispered. Frau Hullerst looked up at him with luminous eyes. Even with all the stress and little sleep she was beautiful. For a second the fourteen others disappeared. He imagined laying her down on the bed. Hell it would be satisfying for a moment but then he'd only wish she was Victoria.

The beauty's low smoker's voice shook away his reverie. "Yah, but Frau Langsdorf has some bread und sausage to send along with us, I'll carry them in my satchel."

"Kinder (children), time to get up," whispered Frau Eckstein, Frau Hullerst's mother. The old woman tapped each child on the shoulder. The lumps became faces as little arms reached out and pulled back the top of the eiderdown. Their nervous giggling was strained, thin. The Frau Mutter shussed them, holding her fingers to her lips.

Frau Hullerst pulled the covers back and kissed her eleven year old son, Dieter and her daughter, six.

"Guten Morgen Kinder," said old Dr. Karl Eckstein. He began to cough. He pulled a thick mottled sweater over his balding head. "Come, get dressed," he said, ruffling the hair of a little boy.

"Is there cocoa?" This voice was attached to two long brown pigtails.

"Downstairs, Inge, " said her mother, Frau Elise Schwartz, a short and squat woman, with graying hair. She seemed subdued this morning, whereas over the past week she had constantly complained of discomforts, demanding news of her husband, a professor of literature, who had been in a workcamp for several months.

"Mama, Mama" whined another high-pitched voice.

"I'm here, darling," said Frau Crannach, a large-boned woman who slipped her slacks up under her robe as she dressed in the hallway. "Macht Schnell, Get up quickly. We have to go for a long walk before the sun comes up. We're going to meet Daddy."

Guy frowned. He discouraged telling the children they were to meet their fathers. Helmut Wagner had gone to the work camp to escort them via skiis to the Banhoff (train station) where they were all to embark coming from the south. There was too much that could go wrong, including that the men may not survive the journey in their weakened condition. "Hurry" said Guy. They could just make it before sunlight.

There was rustling under the eiderdown. "Stop pulling on my toes" said Dieter, a boy of nine or ten. "I'm not," said Klaus, age six, pointing to the little girl with the long braids.

"Why must we be so cautious? said old Dr. Eckstein. "Did Schutz not pay for our visas?"

"Yes, but it's not like buying a sure thing. There's opposition from Nazi purists. They stopped the group last week. Seized their belongings and sent them back to the camps," said Guy.

"Did Fragenzimmer return the money?" asked Frau Hullerst as the eleven of them, now all bundled in sweaters, boots and parkas headed down the stairs behind Guy, looking like a giant Quasimodo, loaded with the canvas bags.

"Not yet," snorted Guy. "But we are demanding credit. Ten more passengers. And we are asking their return. That means stepping on high placed toes."

"When will we see Daddy?" asked Inge, blowing her nose in a large man's handkerchief she pulled out of her coat pocket.

"We're going for a walk to meet him now. In the woods," said Frau Elise Schwartz.

"No, Inge, we will not try to meet them in the woods. We must all be very quiet until we get on the train." Guy thought of warning them of sharp shooters on the hills, but thought the better of it. "Once we are all on the train you can greet them there. Now lets get out of here." Guy turned and headed downstairs.

∾

Coming from Schwaggenvold, five men skied down a mountain slope, the sky gray with a blanket of thick clouds. The first two men fell several times. Helmut Wagner swooped down from behind them each time to assist. Herr Dr. Schwartz, a short, large-boned man whined repeatedly; "I can't keep going. We must stop."

Wagner wanted to say, "Anyone living near the mountains during these times ought to have learned to ski." But then like most Germans they probably didn't believe things could get this bad, or if they did somehow they would be an exception.

The first skier, Dr. Crannach, a math professor from Mainz, slight in build and stature, fell several times. Crannach got near Schwartz and said, "Schwartz, you will keep going, even if I have to tie you to your skis." The third man was muscular. "The money got you out and gave you and your families' visas. There is no guarantee of making it, as the SS and others in the army oppose such efforts," said Hullerst.

Herr Dr. Bloomberg, an ophthalmologist, with a puffy round face, a graying beard, and penetrating eyes. "We must not think about not making it."

Hullerst, though the oldest and most frail, skied smoothly and without complaining. "That is the best way to think of it, Bloomberg, that we will make it," he affirmed.

"Scheis, we gave the Swine 10,000 Mark for each of you and they only get the rest when you are safe in Switzerland. Don't worry, we'll make it!" said Wagner. He chose not to mention the recapture of the previous group. They were fearful enough.

Wagner cut some smaller loops in the deep powder between their large ones. His face was bright red. He said what he could to each one as he passed them. "We don't have far to go, but you must keep quiet. We are very near the border. Heavily patrolled. We are lucky for the cloud cover. No shadows to attract the eye, but that can shift with the wind."

Wagner sited the lights from the station below. The hill became steeper and icy. "Shhhh. We are near Hagenheim station, see the lights?" The five skiers sliding over the icy snow sounded like muted screech owls.

❧

"I must have the rest of the money now, so I can signal clear passage," said Fragenzimmer. He paced back and forth in ForstKeller, Hagenheim's only bar just next to the train station. It was officially closed at this early hour, but the proprietor gave special favors to Fraggy as a party higher up. The smells of stale beer, coffee, cigarette smoke and fried sausage from the small kitchen hung in the air. A framed picture of Marlene Dietrich was on the wall behind the bar. Schutz noticed the signature:

"To Friedrich, my brave soldier, with all my love, Marlene." As he drank a large sip of steaming coffee her voice echoed through his mind singing "Lily Marlene." "Vom der Caserne, under the lantern, through the garden gate. Darling I remember, the way you used to wait . . . Wie Einz, Lily Marlene. My own, Lily Marlene."

Schutz thought with longing of his own wife, son and daughter, now waiting for him in Paris. He had urged them to go on to New York as soon as possible, in case Paris fell. But his wife, optimistic that things would change, that Hitler would be turned around by the allies, was stubborn, waiting for him to join them before crossing the ocean.

"When they are here, and the women and children, then you will have the money," said Schutz. He sat at a small table, unbuttoned his coat. Playing at nonchalance was his strategy. Fraggy's ego would be served by looking down at Schutz.

Fragenzimmer said, "You are true to your profession, and your race. You Jew bankers are always precise when it is in your interests. Give me the money." He spun around, went behind the bar and poured himself a whiskey. After drinking a shot in one gulp he poured another. He glared at Schutz, breathing odorous whiskey and garlic.

"You must trust me. If I wanted I could kill you, take the money and let all of them try to run their way to freedom on their own, with sharp-shooters on the hillside, ready to earn medals from the Fuhrer for defending and protecting the homeland." Fragy downed his second whiskey, then poured a third. He took another glass off the shelf "Pour you one?"

"I'd prefer schnapps," said Schutz. "To run with the money as you threaten to do would be like killing the golden goose." Schutz focused on the garden gnome replicas on the shelves behind the bar. Each gnome wore a little red cap. One of them was playing a tiny piano. How long had it been since he'd had a chance to sit at the keyboard? Ilse and the children loved hearing his renditions of Mozart each night when he got home from the bank. In Paris, Ilse was just as busy as he, sorting out the arriving persons and their trunks and helping them make arrangements on to New York. How he missed her. Letters were infrequent, phone calls superficial, as the operators were engaged by the Nazis to listen and report.

Fragenzimmer's face turned red. "The Jewish Bourgeoisie is so particular."

"You sound like a Marxist," said Schutz. Perhaps a little goading will put him off balance. He inherently could intimidate, a professor and banker with a Hoch Deutsch accent vs. this little bureaucrat.

Zimmer took a schnapps off the shelf and plunked it down on the table along with a heavy glass. Schutz nodded and poured himself a full one. "Over some things Marx was correct. Respect for workers and peasants is a cornerstone of the Fuhrer's efforts for Germany. If you Jews would honestly work for your keep, you wouldn't be in this predicament."

Schutz took a deep breath, feeling his soft grey wool coat rise and fall in his chest. He wanted to slug the swine but he must do what he had to to make this work out. He swirled the scotch around in the glass, took a drag. He could not resist a retort.

"Extortion for lives is a far cry from productive labor," he said. Fragenzimmer glared at him, a tic under his left eye.

Schutz stood, buttoned his coat, now towering over the man. "Without funds the Reich can do nothing. We are not here to discuss Nazi ideology but to complete a task. Signal the passage. We are running out of time before the border security changes hands."

A shot rang out on the hillside, followed by another. Then another.

◆

Guy's breath made a fog in front of his face. It was chilly on the hillside opposite the station. The snow glistened in the moonlight as he led them through it. Looking back, he waved his arm, urging them on.

Guy's charges slugged on through the powder. The old Eckstein couple were in the middle with Frau Schwartz and Frau Hullerst and their children up front, Frau Crannach and Bloomberg, children in tow, behind the elderly couple. They craned their necks looking eagerly through the haze for their fathers, husbands. Would they make it in time?

A train pulled to a halt in the station. As planned, it was a passenger train with only three cars and some freight cars. Not as planned, it was coming from the wrong direction, heading into Germany instead of toward Geneva. Things were changing fast. But Guy could not deal with this now. Their only hope was to get on the train.

With a sigh of relief Guy sited the men skiing down the other side of the gulley!

Guy turned around holding his fingers to his lips, "Shh!" But it was too late.

Inge cried "Daddy!" and ran to meet Schwartz. Her braids stuck out stiff with frost.

Schwartz yelled: "Inge, stay there, Daddy's coming. The little girl ran towards him anyway, falling several times in the deep crusty snow. Schwartz continued clumsily down the hill towards her. Her voice frozen with fear, Frau Schwartz screamed. "Inge!" Guy threw down the bags and ran after the little girl. The women picked up the bags. A shot rang out from the hills behind them and another from above the station.

Dieter, Hullerst's oldest boy of twelve ran up the icy slope behind Guy, toward his father.

Guy caught Inge by the leg and pulled her down, shielding her with his body. Another shot rang out from behind. Guy felt a searing heat in his arm and chest. Inge screamed.

Schwartz said, "No, no, mein Kind!"

A second shot. Then another. Schwartz fell, the snow around him turning red, then pink. The boy Dieter fell. Screams echoed in the valley like a distorted yodel.

"Halt! Halt! Guy shouted, said "Don't panic," said Guy. "Do not come here. Go immediately down to the station." Old Herr Eckstein took the lead, urging them all to continue to the station.

One more shot. A cry echoed off the hills. Then silence.

The only sound was the swish of Helmut Wagner's skis as he sped down to help Schwartz. Wagner shook his head "no". It was too late. Schwartz' head bobbed unnaturally against his shoulders. The bullet must have broken his neck. Guy was certain that the boy, Deiter had been killed instantly, as the bullet hit him square in the forehead. Wagner skied past the boy, again moving his head side to side. "No".

Searing pain ran down Guy's shoulder. He took his neck scarf and wrapped it tightly around his shoulder. Good thing it was so cold out, it would help stop the bleeding. No one moved. It seemed like the hill's heart pounded as Helmut rose and skied over to Guy and Inge.

A few feet behind, Hullerst lay face down in the snow, an expanding halo of red around him. Guy said, "It's no use, he's gone, the boy too. Get the others to the train." Guy held Inge to his breast with his good arm. He rocked her gently as she sobbed. "Sh, sh, your mama's coming."

Guy put his hand over Inge's mouth muffling her sobs. He whispered in her ear to be brave, keep silent. He got up motioning the others to continue down towards the station.

Frau Hullerst looked towards her son Dieter, then Edmund, her husband, fallen in the snow. She held on to her daughter's hand. Her parents, stood behind her. "Momma and Papa, we can do nothing for them now." Their heads fallen, they trudged towards the station.

Frau Schwartz continued on towards her husband. The wind pulled and bit on her face. Helmut raised his left hand with his palm facing her and his ski pole dangling from his wrist. She stopped. As snowflakes fell on her tears she resembled Lot's wife, turned into a stumbling pillar of salt.

"Give the signal, damn it!" said Schutz back in the station-bar.

"First the money," said Fragenzimmer. "They must get on the train. The train will not open its doors unless I give the order."

"No, Fragenzimmer," said Schutz. "This is not what we agreed. The train they were to get on was to go directly into Switzerland. You must order it to reverse direction. They must hide here in the station until the train comes back to go the other way. When it returns and all are safely on it, you will get half the money. The other half will be delivered in Geneva."

"I give the signal or all will be killed. Give me the money." Fragenzimmer held out his open palm. Schutz reached down for his stainless steel case lodged in his vest pocket. He handed it to Fragenzimmer. "Here. If they do not reach Geneva there can be no more payments."

The case had a small dial requiring a combination to open. "The combination!" Fragenzimmer shouted.

"Beethoven's birthday," said Schutz. "I wanted to remind you of the music of world peace and liberation."

"Schwein, what is it?"

"12-16-1770" said Schutz. This was no time to quibble about the debates among musicologists about the exact date.

Fragenzimmer turned the dial. The case snapped open. As he fingered the DM, a stream of saliva oozed down his chin.

Two more shots rang out.

Fragenzimmer closed the case and took it over to the bar. He opened the large glass jar and pulled out a pickled pigs foot. He took a bite out of it and licked his lips. "Financial dealings always make me hungry," he said. Another shot rang out. He took out his walkie-talkie and said, "Yavol. Es ist alles gut. Hold your fire."

Schutz wanted to strangle the man, but this would have to wait.

Schutz and Fragenzimmer left the bar and hurried along the street towards the train. "This is not what we planned. The train was supposed to be coming from the other direction," Schutz said.

"Machts nicht. Don't worry. We had to disguise things," said Fragenzimmer. "It will go forward to the next station. There the engine will be removed and replaced by one pulling it back. That was the only way we could accommodate the irregular stops. There is no time to waste. We must not quibble over details now." He began issuing orders to station attendants in low German.

Rays of the rising sun came up from behind the mountain. "There they are" said Fragenzimmer. "Yes, they must get on the train quickly. It is already light."

Schutz counted shadows, moving down the slope. They were so covered with snow they looked like a flock of white birds. Schutz counted three missing. Fragenzimmer ordered the conductor to open the door. Schutz got on the train, and opened the door on the mountainside with a clunk. "Get on, hurry," he yelled.

Guy ran ahead. "The train's going the wrong way," he yelled back.

Schutz told him they would turn around next stop. No time to quibble now. He had held back half the money pending their safe arrival. Guy motioned the others to follow while holding his wounded shoulder with his one good arm.

Fragenzimmer yelled: "You must get on at once! Macht schnell!"

Their feet made crunching sounds on the icy embankment. With Guy injured, the three Frau's each carried a satchel. Frau Marina Hullerst and her daughter arrived first followed by the old Echsteins. The others followed, almost as if in a dream. Schutz held out his hand, helping them up the stairs as the steam engine puffed and billowed.

Guy and Schutz exchanged a look and a nod. "Hullerst and Schwartz are dead. And the Hullerst boy. Shot in the head." Schutz turned white, then cleared his throat. "Wagner will dispose of the bodies. They must not be found."

Fragenzimmer jumped off the train, station side. "Schutz, get off! The train is departing." The train started to slowly move.

Schutz yelled back. "I will go along. Guy is injured. I have to remove the bullet."

"Ach do as you want, machts nichts," said Fragy with a wave of his hand and a smile revealing a gold capped fang.

The train slowly moved back into Germany towards Zeltoph.

From the windy mountainside, Wagner waved silently to the train, knowing no one could see him, through the snowfall. He looked around 360 degrees for snipers. From behind he heard a slushing sound, a twig snap. Like that of a black bear, sulking, angry at being awakened in the middle of its winter's rest, required to hunt at a time when prey were scarce. But his bear dropped a hard object on the ice and gasped for air. Helmut reached for his small automatic under his jacket, then again restrained himself. Any retaliation or defensive reaction on his part would lead to them all being killed.

The two men and the boy's bodies were nearly frozen barely visible through a blanket of sleet. They looked strangely beautiful, like an impressionist painting in the morning sunlight. He dug two trenches in the snow with his hands and shifted the bodies in, placing the boy next to his father he was so eager to join. Then Wagner covered them. No words came to him, except goodbye. He felt as if on the side of a deep abyss. He tied his skis together and slung them over his shoulder as he trudged up a knoll. It will be a long climb back. A knot in his stomach signaled hunger, as he had not eaten for at least twelve hours. He felt weak as the adrenaline rush from the trip subsided. He reached into his inner jacket pocket and pulled out a flask, pulled the cork, and took a slug of brandy. A piece of cheese and a hunk of bread completed the funeral meal. "May your souls be in peace."

Anger rolled through him. What has become of a country that destroys its philosophers, sells off its brightest thinkers? Oh Great Spirit, what will become of us?" He cried soulfully as he climbed back up the slope.

Chapter Thirty-Four
Mayhem at Mead's Berlin Lecture

War makes the good of the community the supreme good of the individual. What has the pacifist who would abolish war to put in its place?
— George Herbert Mead, National Mindedness
and International-Mindedness

S nowflakes fell on Victoria and Annabelle's coats. They linked arms for
support up the icy staircase of Berlin University auditorium. Victoria
gazed at the statue of Goethe at the landing, in awe of this monumental
structure. The stairs were high and deep.

"I wish I had listened to your objections to coming to Berlin," said
Annabelle as her boot crunched on the ice. Annabelle guided Victoria toward
the railing in the center where she could get a grip. "Hold on, Vicky. It won't
do for you to fall, darling, weeks from delivery." Annabelle, breathed clouds
of vapor.

Through the sleet, the statues on the sides of the staircase statues looked
like hovering satyrs, waiting to pounce on anyone who lost her footing. A
mixture of salt and ash on the stairs melted some of the ice, but made walking sloppy and difficult. Victoria felt awkward, out of balance with so much
weight at her belly. Comforted by Annabelle's care and strength, she realized
how much she missed female companionship since her arrival in Germany.

Ahead, students and Berliners in loden coats and fur parkas, about half
women, jostled up the stairs and through the giant front doors. As the young
men were drafted or enlisted, more women were admitted.

Two old men with bent backs shoveled a pathway.

"Guten Morgen, Frauen," one of the men tipped his hat. He wore a coat of fine wool. Too fine for a laborer, thought Victoria. His eyes widened at Annabelle's chocolate face and turban.

"Guten Morgan Herren," returned Annabelle. Her German was perfect and accent free. "They should get some of the young students to do this work."

The face of the man looked familiar. Was it Dr. Koenig, the well known mathematician made to labor? Martin spoke of this practice. Victoria thought it best not to inquire.

The man replied. "Young men are all drafted. We were taken from retirement as Professor Emeriti. I used to teach mathematics. Elgar here is a prominent biologist."

"We're so sorry," said Victoria taking Annabelle's arm and continuing up the stairs. "We'd best not call attention to them. This job keeps them out of the camps. And unless the future can be altered, Martin will end up ousted and made to build roads in a few years."

They were puffing with exertion by the time they reached the top. Victoria was thrilled to see the placard by the huge doorway:

"Minkowski Lecture Series in Modern Physics
Presents
Herr Dr. Professor George Herbert Mead
from University of Chicago
"The Interpenetration of Past and Future in the Present"

The lobby floor was wet from melted snow as students removed their jackets. Many of them were in uniform, puffing on cigarettes, crushing them out in large astrays at the entrance. Older women and men removed elegant cashmere and fur coats.

"Older students? I didn't think they had them," said Annabelle.

"Local intelligentsia frequent university lectures," said Victoria.

"Sure beats sitting in front of a TV watching 'Leave it to Beaver'." said Annabelle. "No wonder so many Americans get Alzheimers."

They took off their coats and brushed off the sleat. Stares and whispers accompanied them as they walked towards the stage to their reserved front row seats: "Americanishe Frau und Africanishe Negroe. Queen. Jew Lovers."

"They don't want us here, nor do they want to hear George. They're here to make trouble," said Victoria. Though still cold she felt a chill sweep through her bones.

"I'm glad I planted some help in the audience," whispered Annabelle. Annabelle kept the details of much of her work to herself, however Victoria knew she had connections with American and British intelligence.

They spread their coats on the seats, draped them around their shoulders.

The vast stage was empty except for a podium, two hard-backed chairs, and a small table with a pitcher of water and two glasses. Victoria felt excited and yet a sense of foreboding.

An old man stood at the side of the stage. He wore a baggy uniform and a badge saying Goethe Universitat Berlin Officer. A gun hung in a holster around his large belly. He wore a police cap and thick glasses.

"Doesn't look like he can see well enough to tell the balcony from the front row," said Victoria.

"That's the idea, girl. He's actually twenty-five and a terrific marksman," said Annabelle. "Don't worry, we have our security network well stationed."

A small man in a tweed suit also wearing glasses walked on stage followed by Mead. Students slapped their hands on their chair arms. Victoria felt the floor vibrating from stamping feet. Minkowski raised his arms high. She was excited to see the famed physicist in person, and with her husband! The buzz in the audience fell to silence and everyone stood up. When Minkowski reached the podium he said "Heil Hitler!" All followed suit and sat down.

Victoria's heart raced as Minkowski introduced George to roaring applause and pounding on tables, arm rests or fold out writing tables attached to the walnut chairs. Was she dreaming of Mead lecturing, or was she really here, and as his wife? She shook her head.

"Are they trying to drown him out before he begins?" asked Annabelle.

Victoria smiled, "No, German students show approval by pounding on their tables. It makes for good psychological release," she said.

"Much more fun than our classrooms which don't even allow for applause," said Annabelle, trying to squeeze herself and her coat more comfortably in the narrow seat.

"Shh, he's beginning," whispered Victoria.

Mead flashed a warm smile her way. He cleared his throat and looked at his notes under the podium light. He spoke in a clear and elegant Deutsch, with occasional questions to Minkowski about a term or phrase.

"Space and time are not separable. There is only spacetime. Objects in the universe, such as stars, the sun, planets, are always in motion in spacetime. Some of the stars we are seeing no longer exist, but were so far away from the earth that their light is just now reaching us. As we see them they exist in the temporal dimension only here and have no actual space. Or, their space as we experience it is a moving time/space. We experience objects in our space/time sector which are not yet manifest in others. We are the future of some space/time segments just as we are the past of others," said Mead.

Stamping, pounding and cheering rose. Sitting in the front row, Victoria felt a thrill of admiration for this man, who had led her to explore the nature of time, into a new life, even though perilous.

The lecture hall was cold and drafty. Several steam heaters hissed and squealed in the background, but to little effect. Victoria could still see her breath. She pulled her fur coat around her legs. She was glad she had worn woolen stockings under her high top laced boots. Germans were notoriously stingy about heat. Growing up in a German American community she often stood in front of the radiator. Their ground floor flat received only glimpses of the reticent winter sunlight.

The room buzzed with excitement. "I can't imagine filling a public lecture hall in Chicago to hear some old professor talk about the theory of time," Annabelle whispered to Victoria.

"Yes, here philosophy is another kind of music," said Victoria. She was as enraptured hearing George lecture today as when she had first read his works. "And what a thrill to see the famous Minkowski."

Minkowski stood, raising his hands for the crowd to quiet down. Mead continued on for some time, then concluding:

"Manifestations, echoes of our past as well as our future, are with us here, in this present moment. This has vast implications for how we understand human existence, but my time/space here is over so I cannot entertain them in this lecture."

The room swelled once again with applause and pounding on the desks. Again Minkowski stood, raised his hands. "We have only a few minutes for questions or comments from the audience."

Annabelle tapped her elbow against Victoria's. "Who is that Minkowski guy, anyway? I know I've heard of him."

Victoria explained. "He's known for his theory of the 'specious present'. Mead studied with him as a graduate student. It means that the present is infinity—the smallest amount of time can again be divided, into infinity."

Annabelle wrinkled her brow. "O.K., but please don't try to divide us up any more," she whispered.

Victoria watched Mead on the stage with admiration, as he calmly looked over the crowd and lit his pipe. This ritual put him above the fray, in complete control, as if chatting with Oxford fellows over sherry.

Annabelle fidgeted in her seat, throwing her fur off her shoulders, revealing her orange and purple scarf. "Oh, hell, Victoria, everyone knows that for us, the ordinary mortals with normal sized brains, that minute or second is going to pass, just like we all are going to pass. These brilliant men have so much time on their hands they don't know what to think or write about, is the way I see it."

"Einstein was influenced by Minkowski. He radically changed the world," said Victoria.

"Yeah, he sure did, putting all of us in fear of annihilation," said Annabelle.

Hands sprouted out all over the hall, voices shouting "Question, Question."

A young woman stood in front. She wore a long full wool skirt and jacket, and a fur shawl. "Professor Mead, I understand your wife, Frau Dr. Von Dietz, is also working on a theory of time which extends both yours and Professor Heidegger's theory. When will she be invited to lecture?" There were cheers mostly from the women in the audience.

"A good idea, perhaps. I will look into it," Minkowski said, taking out his pocket watch.

Mead cleared his throat. "Professor Von Dietz is here with us today, along with Her Royal Highness, Queen Ogubiko from Africa," he said, pointing to them in the audience. He motioned for Victoria and Annabelle to stand. Nodding to enthusiastic applause, Annabelle whispered to Victoria, "I bet he couldn't remember the name of my tribe."

The young woman who asked the question said, "Thank you, we of the women's academic society will be sure to follow up."

Throughout the hall, hands raised. "Question, Question., Herr Mead, Professor Minkowski" they shouted. A number of young men with brown shirts stood up. Minkowski pointed to one of them.

"Heil Hitler" the student said. Echoes of "Heil Hitlers" filled the hall. Minkowski also raised his hand and said "Heil Hitler," then raised both arms to shush the crowd. "Your question, please," he said.

'Herr Dr. Mead, isn't it the case that the theory you are promulgating is Jewish in its origins, as that Heisenberg also works on its mathematical ramifications. A radical design to disorient the truth and destiny of Germany. I denounce this theory as part of the Bolshevik/Jewish conspiracy" his voice rising in intensity, with his fist.

A wave of young men stood and shouted in unison, "Defeat Commie Jews, Defeat Commie Jews . . . ." stamping their boots. Others stood up, shouting back. There was a push toward the doors as fist fighting broke out. Guards with clubs smashed into the crowd increasing the chaos. Student opposing the brown shirts or resentful of the guards joined in.

"Go down!" said Annabelle, nudging Victoria down and leaning over to shield her.

Minkowski raised his hands. "Silence! This is a university, not a beer hall! I demand quiet at once. . .Silence!" He looked to the side of the stage, for the security guards, who seemed to have disappeared. Students raised their fists against the brown shirts setting off more fights in the seats and the aisles.

The old security guard jumped down from the stage and pulled Annabelle and Victoria in front of him. He guided them toward the door at the foot of the stage. Guards at the back of the room came forward, attempting to break up the fighting. Minkowski took the mike, tried to calm the crowd, "This is a university, a place for the exchange of ideas. I insist on quiet and order, please quiet and order."

On the stage a splotch of red ran down Minkowski's chest. "Commie Pole," someone yelled. Looking up and back, Victoria screamed, seeing red running down Mead's face.

"It's O.K. Vicky, it's just a tomato," said Annabelle, taking her by the arm as they went through the exit door. Fights continued to break out around the room. Three students jumped onto the stage acting as a shield between Mead and Minkowski and the audience as they left the stage.

The buffer group (were they students or more of Annabelle's 'helpers'?) escorted Mead and Minkowski out the back door, into the black Mercedes limousine with Victoria and Annabelle. Minkowski was about to turn back to the hall. "I must help restore order. Students will be hurt." Mead pulled him into the car. "Order will come quicker with us gone." The car pulled away fast, with police escort.

Victoria's heart pounded as the car raced away from the campus, around several Berlin streets, sirens blaring from the escort vehicles. Once the car was out of the fray, driving at a moderate pace down a broad Charlottenberg boulevard, Minkowski broke their stunned silence. "Frau Dr. Von Dietz, Honorable Queen, my apologies for meeting you in such dire circumstances," he nodded.

"Dr Minkowski, I must say I'm thrilled to be here, in more ways than I can tell you," said Annabelle.

"We're lucky that the Chancellor and the Lord Mayor of Berlin remain somewhat independent of the Third Reich still. Otherwise the police would not answer the call. How long this will last, I don't know."

"Unfortunately, I'm used to such outbursts as my tribal homeland is constantly faced with attempted coups, mostly staged by the colonizers. Sometimes it is even my own brothers who don't support our matriarchal lineage," said Annabelle.

Annabelle and Victoria spread their coats over Mead and Minkowski's knees, as they had left their overcoats.

"We'd be better off if Europe and America were still matriarchal," said Mead. Women make caring for people the primary aim of government. Men seem to think the purpose of government is to make war or to make money," said Annabelle.

Victoria reached into her bag for a handkerchief, wiped tomato from Mead's face. Professor Minkowski, may I," she said, then reaching to wipe the tomato from his suit jacket.

"Vielen Danke. Frau Professor Von Dietz, You do me an honor I hope never to be required to return, " said Minkowski. "I would love to have you lecture, but I do not wish to expose you to any more such dangers."

"As you can see, my wife is pregnant. We're in Berlin seeking visas to go home to have our child," said Mead.

"Ach yah. Act 6317. And so late she cannot hide her pregnancy. Many women go over the border to have their babies in Switzerland or France. Perhaps being Americans, you can get the proper audience for your request," said Minkowski.

"Herr Fetzer, you know, of Fetzer Shipbuilding, is helping us gain audience with Herr Goerring for a special permit," said Mead.

"Fetzer—why he is a Nazi supporter. Of course wars ist wunderbar for the shipping industry," said Minkowski.

"There are many sides to Fetzer," said Victoria. "He is a friend of Professor Heidegger, and I have been working with Heidegger on a manuscript."

"Well, this Fetzer is an important person to the Reich. He is 4th generation in the business. You know, he used to be a student of mine. He is intelligent, and doesn't fit the mold. His father was also a student of mine and not nearly so bright," said Minkowski.

"However, he certainly is no Engels," said Mead, in reference to Engels support for Marx.

"If he were, he'd be in a work camp and the shipping industry would belong to the Reich," said Minkowski. "The Reich is only against socialism when it comes to other states. They are otherwise adept at confiscation of private property, especially if it belongs to Jews or dissidents."

The car turned a corner and pulled into the driveway of their hotel. Victoria's stomach churned. The babies kicked her belly vigorously and rhythmically, as if dancing to release stress. They would definitely want to come out soon. But where would they be born?

Chapter Thirty-Five
At Berlin Kirche

The German girl is a subject and only becomes a citizen
when she marries . . . but the right of citizenship can also be
granted a female German subject active in economic life.
— Adolph Hitler, *Mein Kamph*

Victoria stood beside George at Krissel Kirche in Berlin. Her neck cramped as she looked up at its lofty gothic spires, the sun reflecting high off the giant rosette windows. "I visited here as a student in 1963. Then it will have been nearly destroyed by American bombs. Berliners did not repair its shattered towers to remind them of the vast destructiveness of war," she said. "It is so beautiful. If only we could save it." A cold wind blew Victoria's long coat open. She felt the ground shake beneath her at the sound of the powerful organ rendering Bach's fugue in c minor.

"The music I heard then was also Bach, but a different fugue. But why bomb the cathedral?" Victoria felt burning anger. Jane Addams was right. No war is justified.

Mead nodded, took her hand. "Come, darling, lets go in," he said, holding her arm. "You're chilled."

The pulse in Mead's hand was in sync with the organ. Church had not been a part of their lives. The images in the statues and windows of Christ and the saints had long lost their power for Victoria, or so she thought. But here somehow, she could feel their presence.

The fugue came to a climax. The entire sanctuary settled into a sense of heavenly justice, finality. A man in uniform sat at the organ counsel up in the loft. He pushed a number of stops above the rows of keyboards. Whole registers of pipes closed. A soft, gentle prelude flowed from his fingertips. Victoria ached to think this lovely organ would be blown to bits, unless . . .

The sun streamed through the stained glass window showing three figures. Christ was in the middle, wearing a white robe, his palms turned upward. A dove hovered over his left shoulder and a bolt of lightning over his right. St. Peter, holding a plate of fish, stood next to Christ. On his left was Dr. Martin Luther, holding a scroll, presumably the ninety-five thesis.

Victoria gasped. "It's the same image of Luther as on Our Savior's church across the street from my study back in North Chicago. I can't get away from him. And in a way, I'm still acting under his influence—do my darnest to make the world a better place."

Mead squeezed her hand. "My father was a minister, as you know, and though I could not follow in his footsteps, I turned to philosophy, using reason to reach for answers to great questions. But here in this sacred place, I too feel the power."

They walked towards the front of the cathedral hand in hand, then went into a pew a few rows from the front, knelt and crossed themselves, then sat holding hands. They fell into deep meditation. Later, Mead got out his pocket watch, and stood, supporting Victoria by the elbow.

"Time to go to meet Herr Fetzer," he whispered.

Walking out down the aisle, Victoria said softly, "Darling, at last we are walking down the aisle together."

Mead had a wide smile. "Hmm, since you entered my time zone already married to me, what was I to do?"

"That's o.k. dear, I was never one for ritual," said Victoria.

Their footsteps echoed through the lofty atrium. The tower bells struck 11 times, reminding Victoria they had but an hour to make their appointment with Fetzer. A double decker bus swooped to the curb, even when no one got on or off. German efficiency. "The drivers pay heed to their schedules more than whether passengers embark safely," said Victoria.

Victoria buttoned her coat and tied her scarf around her head as they stepped out into the cold wind. Mead waved for a taxi. One beeped its horn, pulled over.

"Nice of Martin to ask his influential friend to help us navigate the Third Reich's bureaucracy," said Mead, holding the taxi door.

"I'm not so sure where Fetzer really stands," said Victoria.

"Yeah, he's Martin's close friend and I know Martin wants you to stay in Germany," said George. The back of his neck blushed red.

Victoria did not respond. Best to let this sleeping dog lie. She did wish to go home, but knew she would miss Martin terribly.

"In any case, Fetzer is a step closer to the Fuhrer, and hopefully our visas, said George.

The taxi bullied its way through Berlin traffic. A police siren squealed, imposing its pain down the streets and alleys.

Mead asked the driver about why a shipbuilder was located in Berlin.

"The main yards are in Bremen, but here Fetzer and Braun shipping is on the canal that leads to the river. The ships are started here, then they go out the canal to the river. The Fetzer family had the canal built for that purpose, way back." Victoria hated the drivers' tone, snobbish and arrogant. But he may have recognized their Amerian accent.

They pulled up in front of a stone building. A large brass sign over the double front doors said, "Fetzer and Braun Shipping, 1823." Underneath this sign was a smaller one saying the entrance was in the back.

The driver complained at how little he could purchase with the marks Mead gave him, despite the large tip. "Dollars are better," he said. The driver had discerned an American accent in Mead's German. Mead explained that he had only marks. The driver grabbed the money and screeched away from the icy curb.

A crowd swarmed around a newsstand. They held out ten-pfennig coins, reaching for copies of the *Berliner Zeitung*. The newsboy handed them papers with one hand, catching their coins in a lunch pail with the other. He yelled, "Die Englisher hat Der War Becomen! Extra, Extra"

Mead held up his hand for a paper. Victoria felt her feet disappear beneath her weight. She leaned against Mead who put his arm around her waist, holding her up.

"Breathe, my dear, breathe. We knew this was coming," he said. Victoria pulled her scarf around her face as a cold wind gusted.

They walked along the side of the building to the back that faced the canal. Ship frames hung from enormous scaffolds along the docks like dinosaur carcasses.

"They're building the submarines and navy ships for the war. Enormous profits," said Mead. "Jane Addams' idea that all war industries should be nationalized is good. There is so much war lobbying from munitions companies."

Victoria felt a surge of jealousy over George and Jane's relationship. She imagined Jane 40 years younger and beautiful, addressing the Kaiser to end WWI. Taking a breath, Victoria quickly pushed these feelings aside. She had no cause, especially in the face of her affair with Martin.

Victoria swallowed and said, "I admire you both so much." Mead put his arm around her, pulled her close.

"Now if I can only get us safely home," said Mead.

Victoria looked down at her huge abdomen.

"If Fetzer can help us, I'll even ride back with you in a Nazi submarine," said Mead.

"I'd rather try to move us forward or backward in time than through that channel now," said Victoria, thinking of the German submarines and the British navy. She reached up and pinched his cheek.

"Best not to mess with time travel while pregnant," said Mead. "Don't know what this could mean for the little ones."

Fetzer's office was on the top floor. Men on scaffolds pounded metal, providing a rough tempo to the crackle and hiss of the arc welders. A hundred different fragments sparked from the hulk. A mammoth skeleton of a ship in progress loomed like a dying dragon spitting fire.

"Seems more like Jonah in the belly of the whale," said Mead.

An open birdcage elevator took them up the twelve stories to Fetzer's penthouse. A grey haired man was waiting for them. The man was bent over, and walked with bowed legs. His hands were gnarled with protruding knuckles. "I built ships for Herr Fetzer's father thirty years ago," he said.

The old man smiled, wrinkling his nose and showing two gold front teeth. He looked at Victoria deeply, almost as if he knew her, then looked away.

"We are close to the forest from which we build the shells and transport them by river to be completed," said the man. "You are from America, No? There you have much more sea than we do. You can build ships all over," the man added.

"Yes, so we do, and also the Great Lakes," said Mead.

The old man raised his eyebrows. "You are not German, then Frau Von Dietz?" he said. "Excuse me, but you look so familiar."

"Many Germans left for America in the past century," she answered, "as did my great-grandparents."

He led them through a room with women working at desks and filing cabinets to a large carved doorway. Noticing a buldge under his jacket, Victoria counted him also as a bodyguard. He opened the door, announcing them, then sat on a nearby chair.

Fetzer stood as they entered. He wore a pinstriped suit, instead of the Bavarian clothes Victoria had seen in his pictures with Martin. He was tall, in good shape, with graying temples adding depth to his blond hair. His large walnut desk was stacked with papers, drawings.

Victoria was impressed by the panorama out the windows behind him. The shipyards were in the foreground, then the bridge decorated with huge marble statues, behind that lovely mansions and castles along the river.

"Frau Dr. Victoria is liking the view? Please to sit down," he said. He walked to the front of his desk and pulled out a chair for Victoria.

"The view is stunning," she said, sitting deeply in the soft cushion.

"Mine is also beautiful," said Fetzer. He bowed and kissed her hand. He smelled of rum aftershave. Victoria flushed.

"Herr Fetzer, I'm sure you want very much to see this view of Berlin remain unspoiled. We are both shocked and saddened with today's news with Britain declaring war. It is awful what the devastations of war can bring," said Mead.

"Of course. We've been preparing for such an unfortunate possibility." He waved his arm down towards the ships in progress below. "Berlin is most secure," said Fetzer.

Victoria cringed at such complacency. Knowing that if she spoke at all she was likely to show her deep outrage, she held back.

"Unfortunately, Herr Fetzer, no place is secure in such a war. Mead pulled his pipe out of his jacket pocket.

"Herr Mead. Perhaps you'd prefer a cigar." Fetzer reached for a large carved box on a side table, opened it and offered it to Mead. Mead thanked Fetzer, returned his pipe to his pocket and reached for one.

"Havanna, I see," said Mead, looking at the label. He held the cigar to his nose. Victoria knew that importing them at this time had to be expensive. She thought about raising an objection, on the grounds of her pregnancy, but things may go smoother if these men had their customary rituals.

The old gentleman returned with a tray, placed it on the side table, picked up a large brass lighter and lit first Mead's cigar, than Fetzer's.

"Thank you, Gerhard," said Fetzer. "Gerhard has been with our family since I was a small child," said Fetzer as Gerhard served the coffee and brandy, then returned to take a seat by the door.

"As you know, the Fuhrer was hoping for British neutrality in this conflict," he said, leaning back in his leather-backed chair, blowing smoke rings towards his walnut bookshelves.

"And we so much hope for peace," said Victoria.

"It is most painful for me, as I have many friends in England, as I do in America," said Fetzer, gazing into Victoria's eyes. She looked away as he blew a smoke rings up towards the bookshelves at his right. They carried leather bound copies of philosophers in chronological order—Plato, Aristotle, Aquinus, Kant, Hegel, Marx, Schopenhauer, culminating with Heidegger's *Being and Time*.

A picture of Heidegger and Fetzer both in lederhosen, knee-highs, and feathered caps, each with their arm around a woman with a dirndl and several small children, dressed as miniature copies. Noticing her focus, Fetzer said, "A Yah. That one with Die Frauen was up at Martin's mountain hut, at Todnauberg. So lovely there, is it not, Frau Dr. Mead?"

Mead raised his eyebrows and looked at Victoria.

Victoria swallowed so as not to blush. "Professor Heidegger often spoke of it as where he does his best writing," she said. "However, I have not been there." She had wished to go, but Martin could not see how to arrange this with Elfriede.

Mead seemed to relax as he took a puff of the cigar. "A smooth smoke," he said, nodding at Fetzer.

A second picture, also in a walnut frame, was Fetzer, two other men, and Adolph Hitler at a mountain lodge.

"Perhaps Martin can arrange for the two of you to visit their sometime. But beware, it is a challenging climb."

Victoria struggled to sit still through this polite talk. She looked at Mead who read her thoughts.

Mead cleared his throat. "Herr Fetzer, we have come here for a reason. We would like your assistance. Surely Herr Heidegger has spoken with you regarding my wife's pregnancy," he said. Mead took a puff of his cigar and blew the smoke after Fetzer's.

Victoria swallowed, surely Mead meant told by Heidegger, not caused by him. "If not, Herr Fetzer would certainly know it now, seeing my size," said Victoria, smiling and sipping coffee.

"Frau Dr. Victoria, I certainly did notice your robustness. However, that could be attributed to several causes, for example, a sense of wellbeing from back in your true homeland. Or perhaps simply to the succulence of Frau Bunge's meals at the Inn."

"Herr Fetzer, you're right about the later, but it is my lack of comfort about the former that brings us here. To put it simply, I would very much like to return to what is now my home, Chicago, to have my child," said Victoria.

"My wife and I must return home to Chicago for so that she may give birth at home," said Mead. "A visa is required and a guarantee of safe passage. Can you help us gain audience with the Reichsminister for this purpose?" said Mead.

Fetzer's eyes rolled toward the ceiling following his cigar smoke. He folded his hands on his desk, looking directly at Victoria. "I understand your predicament. But even if we were not at war, what you are asking is not a simple matter. The Fuhrer has explicitly stated that law 6317 will be upheld without exception. No pregnant women are allowed to emigrate and all Aryan fetuses are invested with German citizenship. The Reichsminister will not grant audiences in such cases. I'm very sorry," said Fetzer. He pushed the lit end of his cigar down into the ashtray on his desk, leaned back and took a sip of brandy.

Mead raised his voice sharply in protest: "This is absurd. We are American citizens and have rights that our ambassador will enforce. Our child carries our citizenship," said Mead.

"My dear sir, bitte do not worry. I realize I may be touching on something rather delicate now, Dr. Victoria. However, it must be said that even should audience be granted, it would be necessary for you to undergo an examination so as to establish that you were most likely pregnant prior to coming to Germany."

Mead stood. "Herr Fetzer! You are impugning my wife's character! Of course she was pregnant before she came here. As you well know, I did not come with her immediately," said Mead.

Victoria's heart pounded. She knew Mead suspected and feared her attachment to Martin. She admired the elegance with which he handled the situation.

Gerhard stood up and walked behind Fetzer. He placed his hand inside his jacket.

"Herr Dr. Mead, I have personally the deepest reverence for Frau Dr. Von Dietz Mead. However, even if your wife were not pregnant, as a person of Prussian heritage she herself is legally a German subject and as an economically productive woman, a German citizen as well. As a citizen or subject it is considered treasonous to leave Germany at time of war."

Victoria looked at Fetzer, who had seen her many times at Martin's home. "Really, Herr Fetzer, surely Germany could not benefit from the presence of one who does not wish to stay." Her voice revealed her inner trembling.

"Victoria, of course were it up to me, and were only you involved, it could be arranged. But the best interests of the child and of the Fatherland are also important," said Fetzer. He waived his had dismissively at Gerhard.

"Gerhard, please clear these dishes away," said Fetzer.

Victoria raised her arm, tapped on Mead's arm until he sat back down. "Dear, it is best to remain calm," she said.

"Herr Fetzer, is there no recourse? Please, I'll speak with the Fuhrer in person if I am allowed," said Victoria. She put one hand on Mead's and the other in her lap.

Fetzer stared at his desk, drumming his fingers.

"For you I will try. I know Herr Strogoff, science minister, is interested in your work on time and of course its military potential. Perhaps a word from him, and an informal request from me . . . but I will not promise anything.

Victoria wondered if Strogoff would be astute enough to realize the manuscript alone would not explain time travel.

"Please, please do try, Herr Fetzer." Victoria stood. She wavered slightly from side to side. Mead stood beside her, grabbed her arm.

"In the meantime, you move into a manor, within Charlottenberg castle. The best doctors in the world are practicing there now in the castle, for any wounded officers. You will be able to use their services. Gerhard will arrange for your move." Fetzer signaled the interview was almost over by putting out his cigar in a giant brass ashtray on his desk. He slid it forward towards Mead who stood to crush his cigar next to Fetzer's.

"Vielen Danken, Herr Fetzer, but we are fine in the hotel," said Mead.

"Believe me, Herr Professor, you will be safer and better served in the Charlottenberg manor. Of course we will also prepare accommodations there for your colleagues, Dr. Carter-Jackson, Queen Nokoba, or something like that, and your assistant, Mr. Guy."

He stood at his desk, pulled at the knot on his tie. The interview was over. "Bavarian clothes are more comfortable. I'll call a driver for you. Frau Victoria must not tax herself ." He pushed a button on his desk, issued some orders. They were being dismissed.

He kissed Victoria's hand. Gerhard came forward and showed them to the door. He again looked at Victoria deeply, strangely.

"Did you notice the way he looked at me, George," she said. "Kind of odd."

"My dear, he was simply struck by your Aryan beauty, as most men are. This doesn't stop with age," said Mead.

❧

Immediately, Gerhard returned to Fetzer's office.

"What is it, Gerhard," said Fetzer, looking up from his desk.

"I know what it is about Frau Von Dietz Mead. She looks just like Geli, Herr Hitler's neice!"

"Ah yeah, of course. Now I know what struck me about Frau Victoria. And this neice is the one who Hitler was so enamored of and so mysteriously found shot when she attempted to leave his household," said Fetzer.

"Yes, tragic, that one so beautiful died so young," said Gerhard.
Fetzer looked out the window. Thinking. He would like to help Victoria.
Maybe there was a way.

Chapter Thirty-Six
Noble Bandages

Everyday reality seems to us to be the natural one, and we are not ready
to abandon our attitude toward it without having experienced a spe-
cific shock which compels us to break through the limits of the 'finite
province of meaning' and to shift the accent of reality to another one.
— Alfred Schutz, *Transcendences and Multiple Realities*

The train smelled of oil and coal and iron mixed with cigarette smoke
and schnapps. It rocked and squealed as if it were too old and too wise
to be carrying this cargo, too worn and tired to make any more trips. "No
more, I'm tired, no more, no more, I'm tired," it cried.

Schutz was deeply shaken. The three deaths on the hillside, Hullerst,
reknown philosopher, Schwartz, acclaimed mathematician, cut off at the
height of their powers. If he hadn't tried to get them out they'd still be alive.
Now they were lost, not only to their families but to the world. Yet his deepest anguish was the boy, Deiter Hullerst. Twelve years old, the same as his
own son.

Schutz took off his black overcoat. Instead of offering it to the freshly
widowed Frau Schwartz, which was his initial impulse, he put it over the
back of his seat. There were documents, ammunition, gold coins and other
essentials sequestered in the pockets and lining.

Guy slumped over in the seat in front of him, leaned against the window
on his right arm, his left arm hung in front of him in a makeshift sling. The
bloodstain on his sleeve was slowly getting larger. His face looked gray.

"Why did the snippers get trigger happy, the train came from the wrong direction. Something else is going on." Guy's voice was shaky.

"Fragenzimmer was trying to extort more money. Squirrelly fellow. He may be trying to engineer his own exit, playing both sides," said Schutz.

As the train picked up speed, blowing its whistle, Schutz reached into the inner pocket of his loden colored suit, same as his WWI army uniform. He had survived that war against all odds. As a paramedic, he had done surgeon's work among rows of wounded in agony—removing bullets, sewing up wounds, sometimes ending the pain with a handkerchief held gently over the nose of a soldier in agony with no hope of survivial. Schutz pulled a long pocketknife with a bone handle out of his pocket. This may be quite serious, he mused. I'd better do it right.

Schutz mentally thanked his wife, Ilse, for reminding him via her last letter to be sure to keep his knife sharp. He smiled to himself realizing that Ilse may have meant this metaphorically, perhaps even sexually.

"The Nazi bastards nearly killed me. If I hadn't turned when I did it would have been square in my heart." Guy's voice quivered with rage. The tightness around his eyes, the grip of his jaw the only signs of what must be agonizing pain.

"You're a hero. If you hadn't tackled little Inge she would have been killed!" said Frau Hullerst. She looked pale, her voice shaky. Despite loosing both her son and her husband, her delicate features and soft eyes were lovely. A strand of auburn hair fell over her face as she looked adoringly at Guy.

Schutz' heart ached from his sense of failure for not securing safety. "I can't express how sorry I am, Frau Hullerst." He flashed back to his visits to their home in Freiburg to discuss philosophy with Edmund. That she had lived up to her reputation as a vamp even with him was all now irrelevant against the deep loss. He half expected her to scream at him.

Instead, she took a deep breath. "Now what can I do, Dr. Schutz." She stood erect. "I understand you are the surgeon on duty."

"Bring hot water and clean cloth. Quickly," said Schutz.

She stumbled down the aisle, like a drunk, from the rocking of the train.

"Best to keep her busy now," said Schutz.

The corner of Guy's mouth turned up. "She'd like to keep me exhausted."

"Be careful," said Schutz, winking.

Schutz recognized beneath Guy's bravado that he was failing. He couldn't imagine continuing their efforts without him. To help Guy take his mind off his pain he said, "Amazing what the attentions of a beautiful woman can do for a man in dire straights." He put his hand inside his vest and pulled out a thin metal canister, pulled it open. It contained tiny blue pills and white capsules.

"Here take these," said Schutz as he held three capsules up to Guy's mouth. He handed him a flask of brandy to wash them down.

"I guess there's still hope. Otherwise I'd be getting the blue ones," said Guy. He put the pills in his mouth, slugged down some brandy.

"No you wouldn't. I know you carry your own cyanide. I must keep mine in case I am put in prison in circumstances that I can't endure," said Schutz.

"Underground pharmacies are getting rich on cyanide these days," said Guy.

Schutz took off his jacket and rolled up his sleeves. He loosened the makeshift sling around Guy's arm. He clicked open the knife and cut through Guy's coat, sweater and woolen undershirt. He tied the sling band tightly around Guy's shoulder, above the wound. Kolya came back with a steamy kettle and a large bowl. She put them down on the seat across the aisle.

"There are no clean rags or soap. All of the soldiers have used them up or packed them in their cases. I'll get something from my bag," said Kolya.

She went down the aisle and pulled a suitcase from a rack. Rummaging in it she pulled out a white linen tablecloth, thickly woven with a crest embroidered on the edge. She pulled out a bottle of alcohol and a bar of soap, handed them to Schutz.

"It was a hard choice to make, between clothing, or books or linens. I could bring only one table cloth, so I brought my grandmother's, been in my family since they lived in Herxborg castle, 1632." She caressed the cloth with her long fingers.

"I'm sorry to have to use such a lovely cloth. But the German porters say there are no towels or sheets," Schutz washed his hands.

"This is a worthy end for the cloth. Guy is a hero," said Kolya. She took a scissors out of her handbag, and cut small notches into the side of the cloth. The sharp sound as she tore the tablecloth into strips seemed like screams and cries.

"Now, Guy, my good man, you must survive or I'll have to find Kolya another castle heirloom," said Schutz, washing his hands.

"With such noble bandages I should heal fast," said Guy.

He dried his hands. "Are you ready?" He dabbed alcohol around the wound and sterilized his knife. Guy's pale face troubled Schutz. Had he lost too much blood? They had no facilities for a transfusion on the train.

"Another spot of brandy, please. I've been through this before, in Vietnam," said Guy.

"Vietnam, where is that?" asked Kolya.

"French Indochina," said Schutz. He flashed a look at Guy hoping he would say no more from the future that would confuse Kolya. He recalled that Guy had spoken of a long awful war there to come that he had been drafted into and then came to protest against.

"My husband warned that this war of Hitler's was in the making twenty years ago. He was then writing *The Malaise of the European Sciences*," said Kolya. "Now he lies dead because he was not heeded."

Kolya's looked faint.

"My dear, take a shot of brandy. You've been through a terrible shock." Schutz handed her the flask. "We don't, of course, have proper glasses," he added, trying to take the edge off the scene with a bit of wit.

A corner of her mouth turned upward. She opened the flask and wiped the rim with a handkerchief, then took a slug.

"I feel numb and stiff with fear, mostly for the others. I hear Edmund's voice in my head saying the flow of time is internal," said Kolya as she washed her hands.

"Philosophy is a great way to escape from the horrors of the real world," he said. Looking at Kolya, Schutz said, "You may be aware of the work on the theory of time that Dr. Von Dietz is working on with Professor Heidegger."

Her eyes lighter, she said, "Yah, my husband, as you may know, was Heidegger's teacher." She placed a hand on Guy's left arm, the other on his right knee.

"Edmund's work on bodily experience contended that we carry sensations of touch in our bodies after the actual touch is gone."

"Re-mem-ber . . when you . . .to cut me," said Guy, his speech weak and his eyes closing.

Guy's breath was fast and deep. Schutz was concerned, would he have lost too much blood already?

Schutz was anxious as he waited for signs that the pills and brandy were taking effect.

"Women who speak philosophy are especially fascinating when they retain their sense of warmth and grace," said Schutz, looking at Kolya. "You have that quality, and Victoria Von Dietz also comes to mind," said Schutz. "She relates to philosophy with total love and devotion."

"It is rumoured her devotion goes beyond the intellectual realm into love for the real men, such as Mead and Heidegger. I'm glad she didn't get to meet my husband," said Kolya.

The brandy, pills and rocking motion of the train had Guy almost sleeping when Schutz dug into his shoulder with the sleek blade of the knife.

Guy looked at Kolya's hands as she wrung out the cloth into the bowl of hot water, the plain gold band on her left hand. "You . . . are . . .beau-ti-ful," he said.

"No one has said that to me in a long time," a bit of color rose in her face, accenting her high cheekbones. "Edmund was very affectionate, but not with words," said Kolya. She put her hand on Guy's left shoulder.

"Put pressure on his shoulder, below the wound," said Schutz. "All the weight you can. We must slow down the blood flow."

Schutz pierced deeper into Guy's arm. Guy's face pinched, but he did not back away from the knife. Despite the jiggling of the train, Schutz' gaze and knife remained steady, the sweat on his brow, the only sign of his intense focus.

Guy moaned as Schutz dug in. He pulled out the bullet and held it up. "Got the bugger!" Kolya took it out of Schutz' hand, kissed it and put it in the pocket of her dress. A drop of blood stuck to her lower lip. She licked it off. Guy's head tousled from side to side as the train moved forward.

"Another eighth of an inch and the bullet would have pierced the artery," said Schutz. "Kolya, thread that embroidery needle I layed out with dental floss. Then dip both in alcohol. Hurry!"

As Kolya threaded the needle she said, "you are very skilled. Where did you get your medical training?" asked Kolya.

"On the Italian front in WWI and from Hollywood movies," said Schutz. "This is a piece of cake compared with many I cut." The horror of the thousands he saw who died in agony flashed through his mind. He took a deep breath.

As he stiched and wrapped the wound he said. "Guy will make it. Best he rests now.

Guy's head dropped back on the pillow. Kolya covered Guy with her coat, then picked up the bowl and scraps of cloth and left.

Schutz' mind floated back to Berlin. Once the others are safely over the border, his plan was to fly immediately to Berlin with Guy, to see how Victoria was faring. He had assisted in numerous births. You could never tell in the middle of war if she would get adequate attention, being from a declared enemy country. Victoria is unfathomable, he thought. Now what will she do? Stay in Hitler's Germany with Martin? She could not do this unless she disclaimed her American citizenship. Schutz continued to muse as he worked on Guy. The Reich laid claim by edict–luckily as a banker he received copies of all the governmental edicts–to all Aryan babies born within the German territory. Would they force Victoria to either stay or leave her child?

Chapter Thirty-Seven
Pictures by Leni

Meanwhile back in Berlin
Hitler was painting himself into a corner
And his ovens were heating
as a Tin Drum began beating.
Lawrence Ferlinghetti, *Expressionist History of German Expressionism*

Exhausted from what the journey across Berlin and the encounter with Fetzer, Victoria sunk into the ornate four-poster bed. Out the window of their 4th floor Suite at Charlottenburg Manor, she saw what was once the Palace of the King of Prussia, now the Headquarters for Hitler's administration.

"Such luxury. I wonder why the Reischminister set us up here? Mind, you, I'm not complaining. She smoothed her hand over the silky quilt," she said.

"My dear, professors in Germany are revered, not poorly paid slaves as they are in the U.S.", said Mead, taking off his coat.

She put her hands on her large belly. "It's strange not being able to see your own feet." she said.

Victoria and George were assigned the full fourth floor of rooms and the services of the manor's staff. A suite on the third floor was reserved for Annabelle, which was appropriate to her status as Queen Okubigo. Guy was assigned a spacious servant's room on the second floor. Victoria missed him intensely, especially now hearing that he had been wounded, nearly killed.

With both George and Martin pre-occupied as they were with their battle of ideas, she had come to rely more and more on Guy as a companion and helpmate.

"When he returns from helping escapees, let's offer Guy a couple of rooms on our floor," said Victoria. "That way he'll be more accessible to us."

Mead unbuttoned his vest and stretched out beside her. "It could be most useful for him to hear what the servants say downstairs," he said. "Hear the scuttlebutt about the officials and military officers who also stay in this Manor."

Was he trying to keep Guy away from her? Victoria moved closer to Mead, lying her head on his shoulder. "I feel so bad that he was wounded, almost killed. He wouldn't be here in this midst of this hell if it weren't for me."

"You do see my point, darling, about Guy's usefulness downstairs?" said Mead, turning to look at her.

She had to accede, yet she hesitated. "Yes, it makes sense. Such information may be useful. I just miss his assistance."

"I'm sure Guy will come as soon as Schutz and Wagner get the folks on the train on their way," Mead squeezed Victoria's shoulder. His face crinkled. "Useless tragedy, the bastards killed Hullerst, Swartz and the Hullerst boy. Tragic and senseless."

A cold shiver ran up Victoria's spine. What would she do if she lost Guy?

There was a sharp knock on the outer door. Mead got up to answer. A young woman's voice, Mead invited her in. Victoria rose, straightened her skirts and walked as gracefully as she could into the parlor.

"Victoria, dear, this is Miss Reifenstahl," said Mead. He was beaming as he looked at the tall and rosy-cheeked young woman, loaded down with camera equipment. Her light brown hair was tied up behind her head with a silk scarf. Her long grey cashmere coat hung open.

"Leni, please," said the young woman, reaching out her hand. "Everyone calls me Leni." Her voice was low and melodious.

"Leni! I'm delighted to meet you," said Victoria, beaming. She quickly pulled back her enthusiasm. Leni was not yet a world famous photographer, known most of all for her masterly filming of the coming Olympics and Nazi rallies.

"May I take some pictures, please, of you and Professor Mead? I'm photographer for the Herr Goebbels, Reichsminister of culture," she said, pulling an ID from her bag.

"I regret to disappoint you, Fraulein Reifenstahl, however in my condition I'm not at all suitable for pictures," said Victoria. Yet she wondered. Did Fetzer have anything to do with this?

Reifenstahl already had her light attachment set up on a stand and was placing fresh film into the large, square camera.

"Bitte, don't worry, Dr. Von Dietz. I'll be quick and you'll look lovely. The Reichsminister said it was most important to supplement your visa and safe transport request which he must justify to the Fuhrer." Reifenstahl clicked the camera, the light flashing frequently, and continued to slide new film panels into the camera. She took a few pictures of George and Victoria together, then asked Victoria to sit on the loveseat, by a vase of flowers, capturing her full body and her face from many angles.

"The Fuhrer especially loves pictures of pregnant females." Reifenstahl smiled as she snapped some full body shots of Victoria.

"Oh, does that include pregnant animals as well?" asked Victoria, smiling. "I noticed you said 'females', not 'women'."

"Excuse please my poor English," said Leni, snapping several shots rapidly. "Hold your chin up. That's it."

"I understand Herr Hitler has no children," said Victoria.

"That's right, and no signs of marrying. Perhaps he thinks he will loose his sex appeal if he marries. However, he breeds his favorite dog, Blondi, every year. And I must take hundreds of pictures of her growing belly." The scarf fell out of her hair. Each time she pushed the flash her hair showered with light.

"I'm sure he'll want to meet you after he sees your picture," Riefenstahl said.

"This is most intriguing," said Mead.

"Surely he is extremely busy and overtaxed," said Victoria.

"Yah, that is why Herr Fetzer's idea about the pictures was such a good one," said Reifenstahl. Hmm, Victoria's intuition was correct.

"Well, he's right about something. You look like his niece, Geli, beautiful, tall, blond, and something about your eyes, their intelligence, wistful, knowing, like hers," said Reifenstahl.

"Why would he want to meet me just because I may look like his niece?" asked Victoria.

"Oh, you haven't heard? It was in the papers, almost a year ago now," said Reifenstahl.

"I wasn't here at that time," said Victoria.

"I've found that American papers are very sparse in reporting on foreign news. I try to keep up with the German and French papers at least, but have heard nothing about Hitler's niece," said Mead.

"Well, she was shot. Hitler's special guards, elite members of the Gestapo found her with a gun." Reifenstahl's voice shook slightly. She pushed her hair back behind her ears, tied it back in the scarf. She packed up her equipment. "They said she shot herself, but, well, she was so full of life. We had become, well, friends. I encouraged her to go. She was to leave for Italy to study voice with Madam Vallangia. And Hitler, the Fuhrer, had forbidden it, you see. He was like a madman when she left his lodge."

George said, "This sounds quite tragic. Quite tragic."

"It certainly was. She was lovely and a talented singer," said Reifenstahl as she walked to the door. She turned and smiled. "Rumour has it you sing as well, Dr. Von Dietz, much like Dietrich."

"Ach, nein, I'm just an amateur," said Victoria.

"I'll send you a few of the best pictures," Leni said, the closed the door behind her. Out the window Victoria saw a Gestapo member in a long black leather coat open the door of a limousine for the not yet famous Leni Riefenstahl.

Chapter Thirty-Eight
Victoria Cries

Time and the bell have buried the day
The black cloud carries the sun away
— T.S. Elliot, "Burnt Norton" from *Four Quartets*

The next week, Victoria sat at her desk in their spacious apartment at Charlottenberg. She looked out the window at the vast courtyard, where an SS guard paced back and forth, a rifle jutting up from his shoulder. She was working the last chapters of the theory of time, spelling out the ramifications of time travel.

She wrote: "If the technical aspects of time travel were exploited, they could be used for war. A general could jump ahead in time, see the course of the battle. But so could the opposing general. Perhaps seeing outcomes ahead of time would lead to the end of war." She laid her pen down, her thoughts racing ahead of her hand. But we've always known that the purpose of war is death and destruction and this did not stop us. And what if everyone switched to an earlier time to avoid certain death? She trembled, her thoughts moving to her own situation. Now it's almost too late to reach home before the baby arrives. If she could refine her techniques she would go back to before she got pregnant. She put her palms, now wet with anxiety, on her belly. "No, my little ones, I must bring you into being. You have your own destinies, and I know it is mine to give you birth. Oh my divided heart, my torn self. Time-spanning hurts. I feel like I'm going mad."

The phone rang. It was Martin, his voice deep, breathless. "I ache for you, Meine Schoenen. I can't break away. If I miss even a day at the university, I will loose ground. The old ground is crumbling under us like quicksand."

She could say nothing, choking back her tears.

"What's the matter, Victoria," he said to her silence, his voice gentle now, yet she noticed a distance in the tone. She swallowed her sobs, pretending to cough. She must control herself.

"Victoria!"

She interrupted. She couldn't put more burden on him. "I'm fine, Martin, please don't worry. It's just a bit of a cold.

"I know you, Liebschen. Tell me!"

If anything, their relationship rested on honesty and deep intuitive knowing. How could she have thought to dissimulate? "I care for you, deeply. I am so torn. I need to go to Chicago, to have the babies. You understand more than anyone about the meaning of place, of home. I lost this basic sense by leaving my daughter Kathy, then coming to Germany. But now you are also my deep home. I feel like a chameleon placed on plaid with too many colors to match and bursting open from the strain." She again coughed to disguise her tears.

"Nonsense, darling. Nonsense. Your home is here. You are German. Please, darling, please, for the sake of the baby, our child, you must stay here in Deutschland. I'll come as soon as I can. I'll send Guy when he is finished with our mission. I must go. I preside over a meeting with party officials. Procedures of faculty dismissal. Wiedersehen." She heard voices in the background. Heidegger hung up.

She felt like she was drowning. Waves of tears came like a rip tide. She let them come until she fell asleep.

A loud knock on the door woke her. She sat up wearily, looked into the mirror. She pushed her hair back from her face revealing red eyes. She called out, "Who is it?"

"Hello, Dr. Von Dietz. Are you all right? The desk clerk couldn't ring you. It's Fetzer."

Victoria called to him to wait a minute. Perhaps she should have accepted the offer of a maid. She would have to handle this herself. She wished Guy were here. She went into the bathroom, splashed water onto her face, powdered her nose, put on lipstick, sprinkled on some lavender oil.

"Herr Fetzer, I'm afraid you may have come at an inopportune time. My husband is not home, and Mr. Guy, my assistant, is away."

Fetzer made appropriate and charming excuses.

Minutes later they sat face to face having tea. Fetzer had ordered sandwiches, fruit salad, small chocolate cakes. Victoria ate heartily.

"I love the egg salad. It has lots of paprika," she said.

"My good friend Martin Heidegger remarked on your love for paprika," said Fetzer, handsome in a well-tailored suit with a vest. A faint hint of expensive spices mixed with fresh wool surrounded him.

She felt exposed, angered that Martin would have shared such an intimate detail about her. But Fetzer was perhaps their only hope for securing safe passage home.

"What brings you here, Herr Fetzer?" She smoothed her linen napkin on over her belly.

"Martin asked me to look after you." He ate several small ham sandwiches, took a sip of tea. "Ah, zehr gut. I see you like your tea hot and strong." His blue eyes penetrated her face, then quickly flicked down at her breast and up again.

Victoria normally glared back at such impertinence. She restrained herself. It would not do to alienate their best ally. Instead she lowered an eyebrow slightly and remained silent.

Fetzer reached across the table, laid his warm palm over her hand, picked it up and kissed it. "I find you very attractive, and even more so with your belly filled with new life."

She pulled her hand back. Hesitated, then said "Herr Fetzer, I . . .I ."

He raised his hand reassuringly to her shoulder. "Bitte, no offense please. Even if I should be fortunate to achieve your affection, I would never cuckold a friend." His wide smile revealed bright even teeth, one of them gold.

The aura in the room changed as sunlight coming into a clearing. "I am a man of principle. As such, I am in a bind. To look after you I must help you leave Germany, leave my friend, with his child. Tell me what should I do?" he looked heavy, his face sagged ten years in two sentences, yet his eyes were pools, reflecting warmth, concern.

Unable to suppress her emotions, she put her face in her hands and sobbed. Fetzer stood up, and standing behind her, gently touched her shoulders. Then he poured her another cup of tea, adding lots of cream. Victoria said, "Excuse me Herr Fetzer, my emotions are all over the place. I think it is the effect of being pregnant. Please, you must help us."

"You need no excuse. It is good that you could show your vulnerability. That makes for a true heroine. German heroines don't cry. Screaming is O.K. for them but never tears, never do they show weakness. Perhaps this is the American part of you."

"It's just the human part, Herr Fetzer. And we have just as many "Mother Courage" types in America as Bertold Brecht found in Germany."

"If it is all right with you, please call me Ernst."

"Certainly, and "Victoria" for you. Crying does break down barriers," she said.

I haven't heard of such a work by Brecht, 'Mother Courage' did you say?" said Fetzer.

"Well, perhaps I was just thinking of an article he wrote. But the idea is a woman becomes a heroine by being pleased to send her sons off to war," said Victoria, recalling that Brecht may have not written this novel yet.

"Ach yah, this is a way for women to be honored here," said Fetzer. Used to be "mother of the bride" was a coveted role. Now its "mother of a dead soldier."

The warmth of the hot tea was comforting. A baby kicked in what felt like a celebration of the inner warmth. Victoria was getting impatient. "Please, tell me, have you any hope to offer me as to returning home," she said.

"Yes! I was so distracted that I forgot to tell you. I spoke with Herr Goebbels, asking him to grant you a visa. I suggested that bad publicity now in American would not be in the Reich's interest. Retaining a revered professor and his pregnant wife would not be good propaganda. The results were not what I had hoped. He said even if you were not already pregnant, you would need to be kept here for breeding for you are so pure Aryan heritage."

Victoria's heart pounded. Her despair turned quickly to anger. "How disgusting! As if women were cows!"

Fetzer clicked his tongue. "Yah and in your case there is double jeopardy. The theory of time you and Martin have been working on has security

286

implications, especially now that England has entered the war. Goebbels is well aware of this."

"What do we do now?" Victoria's voice resonated with despair.

"We must go directly to the Fuhrer. We'll use our trump card. The pictures of you taken by Fraulein Reifenstahl.

"How am I going to get the pictures to The Fuhrer?" asked Victoria.

"Leave it to me. I'm invited to a dinner party there tomorrow night. I'll be sure he sees them. He's been in ill humor, almost crazed, since his niece, Geli, was killed. And you do look like her," said Fetzer.

"What do you think Hitler will say?"

"He will send for you."

Chapter Thirty-Nine
Hitler and Fetzer

"No, this cannot be, she was never pregnant! Oh, this woman is nicht so young—but could be her sister. Wo ist Sie?" said Hitler, looking at the photographs of Victoria that Fetzer had handed him. His moustache twitched. Fetzer was pleased. Adolph's reaction to the photos of Victoria was immediate.

A lavish display of meats and fruit adorned a table at the opposite side of the ballroom. Men in officer's uniforms or tuxedos danced with women in sleek satin ball gowns. The strains of a Viennese waltz filled the room with a sense of grace and gaiety. Fetzer thrived on the energy and excitement of such events. They reassured him that German life and culture were alive and well, even though he knew better.

Hitler's eyes wandered to the ceiling, then around the room. His cheeks lost their color. Fetzer grabbed his arm, guided him towards a chair. "Nichts zu fenster—not by the window" said Hitler. The Third Reich had so many business dealings with American corporate executives that Hitler frequently spoke English phrases. Fetzer recalled meetings where he was present with suppliers of munitions, fuel, power supply, and communications equipment. Among them were the American contracts with Becktell, Inc., manufacturer of gas ovens and with Heilburton, a munitions company.

Two uniformed SS men followed and stood on either side as Hitler held one of the photographs close to his face. Fetzer returned the remaining ones to the envelope.

"Wo ist Sie?" Hitler said. Fetzer felt Adolphs' finger nails digging into his arm like crab claws.

"She's an American, a professor, Frau Dr. Victoria Von Dietz Mead. Here at the request of Professor Heidegger. Working together on the theory of time overlapping time." Finally Adolph released his grip. They both sunk down into the elegantly upholstered chairs.

"Ah, zo. Goerring told me about her work. He didn't tell me she is also an Aryan beauty," said Hitler. He held the picture to his nostrils and sniffed. One side of his moustache curled upwards.

"Ah, aber Herr Goering has not met her. Sie ist mere schoen auf dem Leben. She is more beautiful in life than in the photos," said Fetzer. His eyes looked up as if he could see her. Looking now at Adolph, he saw the color rush to his sallow cheeks.

"You know, for a moment I thought it was Geli, that she was somehow still alive," said Hitler. His faced washed pale. A subtle tic began under his left eye. He slid the picture into his pants pocket.

A waiter, dressed as a royal footman, bowed, offering cognac. Hitler took a large gold embossed glass from the silver tray. He held it to his nose, drew in the aroma, his nostrils quivering.

"I don't need to drink any of this, just sniff. My mother told me men only drink when they feel weak or frightened. She called them 'silly boys' who didn't know that drinking merely made them weak. Beer doesn't count as drinking, of course, but it is not served at these high state functions," said Hitler. Fetzer had come to recognize that Hitler, from a working class background tried to emulate upper class ways, not always successfully.

Fetzer swirled his cognac around and took a sip. He licked his lips and smiled, "Very delicious, smooth. But Mein Fuhrer I also would prefer a stein of Guten Duestchen Bier. I think most of the men in this room would. Why not ask for beer to be served in historic German steins at special occasions. It is folkish. Soon it will become the fashion at elegant events as everyone wants to emulate you."

Hitler snapped his fingers. He asked the attendant to request two large ornate steins of beer immediately—the best. He pulled the picture from his pocket. "Where is the lady professor now?" He held the picture in his left hand, stroking it with his right.

"Frau Dr. Von Dietz is here, at Charlottenberg. Her husband, Professor George Mead is lecturing at the university. She is trying to get a visa back to America."

"That is not possible. Especially as she is pregnant. She will remain in Duestchland, her home!" Hitler held up the picture, snapped his finger at it and returned it to his pocket.

A waiter arrived with two steins of beer. Ernest Fetzer and Adolph Hitler reached for a frothy stein. Heads turned throughout the hall. Fetzer and Hitler held their steins up saluting the guests. The orchestra played the Horst Wessel song. Hitler said, "Gute bier for Guten Duestches—Good Beer for Good Germans," lifting his stein high. Soon waiters scurried through the room with trays of frothy beer.

Hitler stood. "I will keep the picture, Herr Fetzer. Good Day Mein Freund."

"Of course, it is yours, Mein Fuhrer."

Hitler stood up sharply, on his way from the room leaving Fetzer standing in salute.

Chapter Forty
Hitler Summons Victoria

The next week, while Victoria was working at her desk on the treatise on time, the desk clerk rang their buzzer. She rushed to hit the listen button, as George was napping. While he never complained, the fatigue and stress were evident. He was showing his age. The crackling voice of the desk clerk said, "Excuse me Madam. An SS officer is here. He insists on delivering his message in person. The officer spoke in spitting low German. "I am under strict orders to deliver this message in person to Frau Dr. Professor Victoria Von Dietz Mead."

Victoria instructed the desk clerk to allow the officer up. She opened the door when he knocked. He pulled a black leather wallet case from an inner pocket and flashed an I.D. card. "Secret Service, Supreme High Command, Executive Messenger." Victoria was struck by the statuesque visage of the young officer. He smiled almost imperceptibly as his blue eyes glanced quickly over her protruding belly.

"Frau Dr. Von Dietz Mead?" he asked.

She swallowed her fear, looking him in the eye. "I am Dr. Von Dietz. We have no maid." She didn't explain that she dispatched the maid to help Annabelle. Victoria preferred her privacy.

A glance of surprise swept over his face. He handed her the letter.

"Die Fuhrer has instructed me to bring you to him at once. Please get your coat. I will escort you. The car waits."

Victoria's heart raced. Her feelings jumped, bounded like a nervous rabbit, between exhilaration, terror, excitement, anger. How can I influence Hitler? Everyone has a kernel of good, of reason within. Hitler loves power, adoration. Perhaps he can be moved to see how he may be remembered with honor, a hero for all humanity, not one of the most destructive demons in history. Or, at least, perhaps he will grant our safe passage home.

She broke the letter's thickly waxed gold swastika seal. The stationery had a wreath and a rose embossed at the top. It read:

"Dear Frau Dr. Professor Von Dietz,

I have heard much of you and your important work that has implications for the future of our Fatherland. Please come at once and have tea with me.

Adolph Hitler, Fuhrer."

There are moments, Victoria thought, when one realizes ones life has changed in a deep and irrevocable way. She felt an earthquake had opened the world and if she survived everything would be unrecognizable thereafter.

Mead appeared at the door, blinking his eyes. "Hitler wants to see you, my dear? Why would he want to see you?"

"This is not your business," said the officer.

"I am her husband," said Mead, "so above all it is my business."

"Not above our leader. Nothing is above our Fuhrer and to say so is high treason. I shall report you."

"You will not," said Victoria. "If you insist, I shall tell Herr Hitler that you were insolent and abusive. Do you care to gamble on who he will believe?"

"No, Frau Dr. Von Dietz. My apologies!" He stood ram rod straight, staring at the far wall, his hands stiff as hatchets along the satin outer seams of his black uniform pants.

"A wise choice," said Victoria. "I am ready. Let's go Captain."

"I am only a lieutenant," said the young man, still as stiff as the wall he stared at.

"I have just promoted you to captain," she said, "but I could just as easily demote you."

"Ya wohl," he said, going through much of a salute before abandoning it and turning toward the door.

"What's this about a car? The Fuhrer's offices are at Charlottenberg, just around the corner," Mead said.

"The Fuhrer will meet with Dr. Von Dietz in his private residence," said the lieutenant.

"I'll get our coats," said George.

"Nein! Dr. Von Dietz must come alone. Bring her wrap only," said the lieutenant.

"I can't allow my wife to go unaccompanied. You can see by her condition, she is due to deliver. The stress could be dangerous for her."

"No, Dr. Mead. I am sorry. But I must follow orders. It is a great honor to have company with the Fuhrer and, as you must know, is highly guarded. You need not worry about your wife. The Fuhrer has a private physician on hand at all times."

Mead put his arm in front of Victoria and was about to speak again. Victoria pushed it gently aside. Victoria took his hand, looked him in the eyes. "My time is coming. I must go." Then she added more lightly, "It's all right dear, please bring my coat."

"Dr. Von Dietz, the Fuhrer has also requested that you bring the most recent copy of your manuscript. He would like to read it."

Victoria thought quickly about the two versions, and that Guy hadn't yet adapted the current version for the Nazis. Since she did not include the crucial aspect of Kundalini yoga, the theory was in any case incomplete.

"The manuscript is far from complete, I'll bring what I have." She almost slipped and told him her assistant, Guy, had the most current version but caught herself. This could cause them to search for Guy, interfering with his mission with Schutz and Wagner.

"As you will Madam."

Victoria went to her desk, picked an earlier disguised version of the manuscript out of a drawer, and put it in her brief case that was under the desk.

"When will you be back?" said Mead.

Victoria looked at the officer, her eyebrows raised, "Captain?"

"Herr Dr. Mead, since the Fuhrer's plans may change even at the last minute, I cannot say precisely when your wife will return. Most likely, it will be before nightfall. We will keep you informed."

Mead helped Victoria into her long coat and scarf. Mead led him to the door and opened it motioning for the lieutenant to exit. He held Victoria close and kissed her on both cheeks. "Good luck my dear." She walked out the door. Mead closed it behind them.

Chapter Forty-One
Guy and Kolya on the Train

The sun was setting as the train slowed down in a valley, casting an orange glow on the mountainside. Kolya sat next to Guy, stroking his forehead with a damp piece of her linen tablecloth. From time to time she lay her head on his shoulder, her hair caressing his neck.

Kolya loved the feel of Guy's shoulders, the hint of rum aftershave on his shirt. She adored the challenge of a man whose heart was elsewhere, which makes him even more exciting. Once I get him in bed he'll forget about this Victoria he keeps calling for in his sleep. I can make men forget about their wives, at least while they are with me. Some have offered to leave. It is the reluctant ones I like. Yet, there is something else about Guy. I've got wrinkles. I can't do this much longer. I'd like to have another husband, a different kind, like Guy, glamorous, a man of action, not just a man of thought and that incessant manuscript writing, editing, proofing, typing, thinking, thinking, thinking.

When Guy opened his eyes they met Kolya's sad and fiery ambers. She wants me, he thought. She's warm and lovely. Then Victoria's image came to him. Victoria, why can't I shake her aura, Victoria, married to an esteemed philosopher. Pregnant, most likely from Heidegger, another philosopher whose ideas she fell in love with. Victoria, I love you, always will, but there are so many other men surrounding you. I'll never stand to be anything more than your assistant, your butler, your former student.

"Darling, you have a fever," Kolya said, wiping Guy's brow.

Guy looked her in the eyes. Darling? This is quick. "Where's Schutz?" he asked. He felt relieved that the excruciating pain had subsided.

"He tries to find out what is happening," said Kolya.

"And to pay off more Nazis," said Guy. There was deep sorrow in the lines of her face, making her vulnerable. Dangerous for a rescuer type like me.

She placed her hand on his thigh, caressing it with her long red nails.

"How did you manage to keep a manicure while trying to escape the Nazi's hiking in the snow?" asked Guy.

"It's the force of habit. I can't imagine not doing my nails and make-up in any situation. It is like brushing my teeth, which I would be more likely to forget," she said, shaking her auburn hair off her lovely face, placing her head back down on his good shoulder.

Guy reflected on her effect on him. Surely I'm immune to feminine seductiveness by now? I don't want to feel this way about her. I've turned lots of them away, many sexy, beautiful. They can be sickeningly disgusting. Most of them don't have anything else to offer but beauty, sensuality, and their version of love. Love that is sticky and clinging and demanding, engulfing, boring. But Kolya's interesting. She has a brain. She's also dangerous. He recalled reading about her in a biography of Hullerst, in this time zone not yet written. She had a reputation with his students.

"Thank you for lending me your shoulder," she said, interrupting his thoughts.

He wondered at her composure. "Of course. You just had a great loss, a shock." The death of her husband and son are probably not even real to her yet he thought, placing his hand lightly on her back. He started to be uncomfortable with her leaning on him, but how to get her off without offending her?

"Yah. The past months are like at extended nightmare from which I can't wake up. I havn't caught up with the other losses. Etzie's professorship, our home, having to crowd in with both sets of parents in my parents' small house."

"Etzie?" said Guy. He took his hand off her back and straightened up in the seat, hoping she would do likewise.

"Edmund, my Etzie," she sat up straight now, her voice tense, her speech rapid. "They took Etzie to the work camp, along with Crannach, Schwartz, so many others. Then there came some hope, with Dr. Schutz and his friend Wagner, then poof, he's gone and our little son as well."

Her litany seemed more angry than grief-stricken. What was really there?

She trembled, reaching into her bag. "My boy being shot." She sobbed in waves. He held her hand and said nothing.

After a while she regained her composure. "I, I'm sorry. I've been holding on for so long for the sake of the children."

Streams of mascara ran down her cheeks. Guy gently pulled his hand out from under her reaching into his pocket for a handkerchief. She wiped her face.

She took a cigarette out of a silver case, put one in her holder with quivering hands. Guy reached for the lighter in his pocket.

"Guy, don't." She put her hand on top of his and placed it back on his lap. "I'll look forward to your lighting my cigarettes when your arm is healed."

The sound of the train seemed to echo, "Victoria, Victoria, Victoria." I must learn to put Victoria out of my mind, thought Guy. She lit her cigarette then put his lighter back in his pocket. As she drew on the cigarette with her curvaceous lips, her knees trembled. Victoria, Victoria, echoed the train. He felt himself falling asleep, probably from the pills Schutz gave him as the train rocked and Kolya blew smoke up and down his body.

"Frau Dr. Von Dietz is quite friendly with Professor Heidegger, I understand," he thought he heard Kolya ask him, as in a dream. Guy's vision was blurred. He looked up and saw her standing next to him, swaying back and forth with the train. The bandages pinched his left arm. It felt the size of a beach ball, but one that weighed a ton. It was throbbing but not nearly so painful. If it did not get infected, he would be well.

"Why did she bring Mead back to life, anyway?" he thought he heard Kolya say, then he awoke.

"He's coming back awake," repeated Kolya to Frau Crannach, sitting across the aisle.

"Ah, Frau Hullerst, sorry, I must have dozed off again," Guy said and smiled up at her.

"Kolya, please."

As she said her name her tongue seemed to touch a thousand places on the inside of his mouth.

Kolya said. "At least now that he's gone, my Etzie can't fall prey to Dr. Von Dietz. Frau Heidegger complained to me of how she has enchanted her husband."

Guy stiffened. She's trying to discredit her rival. With his right hand he smoothed his hair back.

"She's completing an important book on the theory of time and Professor Heidegger is working on it with her. That's why she came to Germany," said Guy, feeling defensive on Victoria's behalf.

"She should instead worship at the feet of a feminist philosopher, such as Simone de Beauvoir. Simone propped up her husband's work, helped him hone his thinking, supported his ego, and yet she is the superior thinker," said Kolya.

"Victoria's work far transcends both her husband's and Heidegger's. She not only writes theories but realizes them in practice," said Guy.

"I always felt that somehow I was doing this same thing with Etzie's work. I fell in love with his ideas, as a student in his class. Oh how disgustingly typical. Young googly-eyed coed in love with the dazzling genius professor. You worship his ways of speaking, his ideas. You want his recognition."

She was agitated, her mouth crinkling as she drew deeply on her cigarette. "You feel flattered when he shows personal interest and give him your all. You soon cannot separate your own thinking from his. You realize soon that although he married you, there will always be a succession of young adoring girls ready to jump in bed with him." All this she said with smoke puffing out around her words.

Guy mused that perhaps this explained her anger.

"Oh, but I was determined that this would not be my role. The long-suffering, adoring Frau. I insisted that he meet his graduate seminars in the home, where I could watch over, intimidate any young thing who may get ideas. At the same time, I had the pick of the ardent young men," she laughed.

"This sounds like a game which could be dangerous, and self-defeating, Kolya," said Guy.

"Nonesense. That is something you would never say to a man," she retorted, taking another long drag on her cigarette.

Frau Crannach came down the aisle and handed Kolya a cup of water.

"It is too much what has happened," she said. Her face was pale, her eyelids red. Wiping tears with a scarf, she returned to her seat several rows back.

Guy said, "I'm sorry for your great loss as well, Frau Crannach."

Guy drew his hand over his chin now shadowed by whiskers. "I need a shave. I must look a mess."

"No more so than Humphrey Bogart in Casablanca," said Kolya. "Do you need some help?" she said, as Guy attempted to remove a leather pouch from his bag.

"I can manage, Kolya, thank you," he said.

Nevertheless she followed him through the next car and down the stairs. When he opened the bathroom door to go in she said, "I thought you may need my help after all. She smiled at him and brushed her hand down his cheek.

Guy felt a surge of desire. Then disgust. "No, I can manage." Guy gentley nudged her away and started to close the door.

Kolya kissed Guy on the cheek and went upstairs.

Guy began his shave. "There is something about these desperate times," he reflected on how he almost succumbed to her. "But I am a man of true heart, and it is with Victoria, regardless of her circumstances. Maybe someday she'll realize that a real man from her real time can be more to her than a philosopher hero from the past," he thought.

The train slowed down. Guy went upstairs and back to the car and sat down next to Schutz, breathing a sigh of relief that this seat was vacant and Kolya was seated across the aisle with her mother, Frau Eckstein.

The train shook as another trained passed. They could look into it, see glimpses of shoulders and heads. It was going to Switzerland and freedom. "That was the train you were to have been on," said Schutz. "Perhaps Fragenzimmer has arranged for us to get on the other train."

Several cargo cars passed. Metal brakes squealed and both trains came to a halt.

Schutz' had put his coat on. He stood up and it hung heavy down his arms, a shroud. He pulled his shoulders back. The cut of the coat became again that of the successful banker. Schutz would continue to carry the load, whatever it took, thought Guy.

Guy offered his condolences to Frau Eckstein. Her face looked beneficent, though weary. Her white hair was braided with the two braids pinned over her head, peasant style.

"And thank you for your family's heirloom table cloth that is now wrapped around my arm," Guy said.

"Your shoulder is more important," she said. I'm pleased my daughter is taking good care of you." He noticed that she too was beautiful, an older version of Kolya.

"How is Daddy?" asked Kolya.

"Why do you even ask? He tries to be strong, for my sake and yours. And the Hullersts are bags of anguish," said the Frau Mutter.

The train jostled and screeched as if a car were being added or removed.

"Are we being left out here in this car? Deserted?" asked Kolya.

The door opened and the rest of their party came into the car, led by a conductor.

The engine sounds started up again, the sound moving off.

"I must get out to see what has happened," said Schutz.

"I'll come along, try to get us some coffee, milk for the children," said Guy.

"No, Guy, you are suspicious and don't speak good German," said Schutz.

Guy felt jolted by his comment, but Schutz was right.

After some time Schutz came back, carrying a basket with a pot of soup in it, mugs, milk and coffee. Kolya and Frau Crannach distributed this.

"This is thanks to Frau Konigstein, here in Clabenz," said Schutz. He looked pale.

"What happened?" asked Guy.

Schutz stood. "No one here is in danger. This car will be hooked to the train next to us and be taken into Switzerland. You are all safe. To Guy he whispered. "Get ready to jump off at the first slow down. You and I must get back to Berlin.

Chapter Forty-Two
Victoria Meets Hitler

Victoria stepped into the large black Mercedes that stood at the curb. The SS man closed the door, got in the front seat and issued the driver orders in clipped German. She hadn't taken Fetzer's offer to intercede seriously until Reifenstahl showed up with her camera. But even so, Hitler did not have to search for women admirers. And what about his mistress, Eva Braun? Or hadn't he met her yet? Oh, if only she had had a better memory for such details which in her high school history classes she had thought to be trivial.

Victoria shuddered at the thought of being in Hitler's presence. The arche villain of the twentieth century. Always pictured in uniform, raising his arms and yelling, his strange little mustache. Was he really worse than Stalin, Mao? Even the U.S. had cold-blooded murdered millions with atom bombs in Japan, napalm in Vietnam.

How could she hope to convince Hitler to alter his course? Perhaps she could appeal to his ego. Share secrets of time travel to let him know he will be universally despised if he does not change his plans. Maybe he does not have plans, but acts in the moment. Perhaps he is really crazy, he surely was abused by a stern father, a weak mother, had post-traumatic stress disorder from WW1. Could she be a therapist to heal his wounds?

The Mercedes drove on smoothly and quietly, like a stingray. They crossed an elegant bridge with gargantuan white marble statues of horses on either side. They drove down Friedrichstrasse then along the shore of the Wansee to a lovely stone mansion. A high brick wall surrounded it with coils of barbed wire at the top.

As the car came to a stop, she took a deep breath and connected herself to the divine feminine energy that she visualized in the form of Quan Yin. Two guards stood in front armed with rifles. Looking like the granite statues, the guards did not blink as Victoria and the officer walked between them.

Once inside, a short middle-aged officer greeted Victoria and led her to wait in a spacious library. Victoria barely had a chance to peruse the titles, which ranged from philosophy to myth to architecture, when a guant elderly woman opened one double door and hobbled inside, her back bent forward from arthritis. She left the door ajar.

"Frau Mutter Hitler sends her regards and regrets she cannot come down to meet you," said the woman. The gaunt lady's eyes narrowed, carefully scrutinizing Victoria.

Through an awkward silence, Victoria wondered what was wrong and what to say when the woman spoke.

"Entshultegensie, Madame. You bear a resemblance to someone. But, no, excuse me. Is there anything I can get for you?"

Thinking of her babies' teeth and bones, she asked for milk.

"Of course, Madame. Important for you and the little one." The woman nodded, pirouetted and left, leaving the door partially open.

Precise, harsh footsteps echoed in the hallway.

A group of uniformed officers walked past. High officers by their bearing and medals. They argued in hushed tones, interrupting each other.

"You know what happens when we tell him bad news. We must break this to him piece by piece," said one.

"You act like a woman," said another. "He can't make a good decision if he doesn't know what's going on."

"Remember, he can see way ahead," said the first.

"Nonsense, he can only see as far as his . . .," The footsteps and voices faded.

The old woman came back with a tray, a small pot and a china mug with a Bavarian emblem.

"I thought you might want your milk warm, Madame. And there is honey in the pot." A plate of apple cakes and slices of schtollen were also on the tray.

Victoria ate greedily. She spooned honey into the milk. It soothed her throat and eased the tension in her belly.

The old woman stood by, watching. "She liked honey in her milk too."
Victoria looked up at her. "Who did?"

"Oh, I'm sorry. Fraulein Geli, Adolph's niece and my grandniece by marriage. She called me Auntie Inge. You resemble her so. We miss her terribly. She used to sing and play the piano for us every evening."

"Oh yes," said Victoria, surprised that Hitler would allow his great aunt to work as his parlor maid. "I heard of her tragic death. I'm so sorry."

As if she read Victoria's mind Inge said, "I'm grateful that Adolph allows me to live and work here. I can see all the comings and goings. I never liked sitting around and being waited on." She nodded and left.

Victoria took a forkful of Apfelkuchen. It was tart in places with bursts of sweetness from the lumps of brown sugar streusel topping. She hadn't had any this good since her childhood in Germantown, Chicago.

A short time later, Auntie Inge returned. "Grosse Frau Hitler has requested that you please stop in to see her when you are finished speaking with the Fuhrer," she said.

Victoria raised an eyebrow before she could catch herself. "That will be my pleasure," Victoria smiled hoping to cover the effect of her raised eyebrow. She recalled a picture of Hitler's mother when he was a child. The account of Erik Erikson which portrayed her as weak and manipulative, cowed and self-effacing in relation to her tyrannical husband. Erikson never met her, of course, but speculated based upon historical records and his psychoanalytic training.

"Grosse Mutter Hitler has heard of your work with Professor Heidegger. She has an interest in philosophy," said the old woman, picking up the tray. Hmm, a woman interested in philosophy hardly seems to fit Erikson's portrayal. Victoria looked forward to meeting her. It caused her to think that if time travel caught on there would have to be a whole new academic discipline of scholars to set the historical record straight.

Inge began to pick up the tray. "It would be wonderful also if you would sing and play for us."

They know so much about me, Victoria thought. She found this at once pleasing and disconcerting.

A tall man in sergeant's clothes came to the doorway, said something in German to the old woman as she was leaving the room.

"Here is your escort," she said.

Victoria blotted her mouth with her handkerchief and brushed a wisk of hair from her face.

She followed the sergeant up a flight of marble steps. The sun was high in the sky behind the large windows at the landing. Two men in SS uniforms stood at attention by the double doors into Hitler's office. They saluted Victoria, clicking their heels. She wasn't sure what the protocol was for women, but simply nodded. They opened both doors saluting her again as she passed through.

The sight before her took her breath away. It was like being in a movie, or a dream. Hitler sat at a large onyx desk with a silver swastika medallion on the front. The sky behind him was alternatively dark and light as before a storm.

"Please come in Frau Dr. Von Dietz." He looked at her without blinking. The whites of his eyes were more a bluish grey, the pupils black and cavernous. His face mirrored the sky, as his emotions shifted with each breath.

He stood slowly, staring at her. His lips opened as if about to speak, but he remained silent. He flicked his wrist at the uniformed man standing behind him. The man walked to the side of the room and disappeared via a wall panel.

"Greetings, Herr Hitler," she said, her heart racing, her legs weak. The air in the room was dead, like a mausoleum. As he returned her greeting he reached across the desk and took her hand, lifting it to his lips. She felt the brush of his mustache sweep down the length of her fingers.

His narrow moustache was odd, repulsive, but she tried not to show it. His lips were moist. He possessed her hand as he escorted her to a large leather sofa. He smelled of new wool and freshly ironed shirts. He walked with a slight tilt to one side, as if weighed down by a heavy sword. Facing her in a leather chair with large carved armrests, his dark eyes opened wide then closed as if savoring a grape, then opened again and rested on her. She turned to liquid, as if she were melting from intense heat.

"Herr Fetzer has spoken most highly of you, your beauty, your charm. He has greatly underestimated." His voice was rich, resonant. His expression switched from that of a baby looking at his mother's breast to desiring to cut her in half. He was like a needy little boy, then a tower of energy. She wanted to hold him. Then she wanted to run out of the room. His aura of strength and mystery was hypnotic and intoxicating. It was as if she were in a secret smoking den, yet the air was clear. She realized that she was smiling at him, despite herself. He stiffened like a toreador facing the toughest bull, who knows his own skill and who faces one who might gore him to death.

She took a breath, "I appreciate this opportunity to meet with you, Herr Hitler. You are surely the most significant person in Germany today, with enormous effect in the world." Her insides trembled. Should she let him take the lead, bringing up her request later? After all, he summoned her. She remembered Annabelle's and even George's emphasis on trying to get close to him in order to murder him. She would not think of this, she instead would try to change him.

His eyes slithered beneath her skin, momentarily immobilizing her. She wanted most to be safe at home with her babies. To her surprise she thought of Guy as well. Shaking off this thought she cleared her throat, deciding to step in with her request.

Herr Hitler, "Please grant me a visa so that I may return home to have my babies." She glanced at her belly and folded her hands in her lap.

He stared at her, seemed to be unaware of her words. "You are important to me, to the world as well, Dr. Von Dietz. I must request that you stay in Germany, for a little while yet. We will take very good care of you."

"Herr Fuhrer, I'm flattered at what you say. However, I must return home. I have another daughter there, a little girl, and I also would like to have my child at home."

"We have no knowledge of your other child. You may send for her," he said. He leaned forward in his chair and took both her hands in his. "We have the best gynecologists in the world here, and midwives too. There is nowhere you can get better care. We have the most advanced knowledge here of breeding and have modern nurseries and kindergartens. You know kindergartens were invented in Deutschland."

His hands were sweaty. He squeezed her hands tightly together. She felt a rush of heat sweeping up her spine.

She took her hands from his and placed them on top of his. He started to pull back, then relaxed.

"Herr Hitler, we also have kindergartens and nurseries in Chicago. It would be wonderful if you could arrange to come and visit. I know you are very busy, of course. But there are lots of Germans in Chicago." He raised one eyebrow. She continued. "You are interested in architecture. The great Louis Sullivan and his student, Frank Lloyd Wright, have designed wonderful theatres, department stores, homes." She hoped to get him interested in friendly travel a new way of life. At least it was worth a try.

He smiled, sat up straight. He pulled his hands out from under hers, placed them on top of hers. They were hot and smooth. To her this felt like a playground game, the seductive male-female version of boys exchanging punches.

"Ah, I've heard of the Chicago architects. They do think more like me about architecture, its being organic. Some of our schools of what is called 'modern' architecture are responsible for destroying true German cities, making them into soulless boxes." His voice had risen in volume and pitch, his mouth twitched. Victoria recalled reading that Hitler had been denied admission to architecture school. Why did it seem that so many rejects and failures became powerful politicians and business leaders, where their personal failure, ineptitude and injured pride hurt the entire society?

He squeezed her hands, let go of them, sat back in his chair and put his own hands on his knees. He looked her in the eyes. "I wish I had the time to get away, to travel."

"I have heard that those who are most powerful often have the least amount of personal freedom," she said.

"The Fatherland takes my all, these days, it has ever since the war." His eyes fired red. She was anticipating a violent tirade about the betrayal of Germany. He swept his head from side to side, got up, turned toward the window with his hands folded behind his back. After waiting a few minutes in cold silence, she stood up, thinking perhaps he was dismissing her.

He turned to face her, radiating heat. "Frau Dr. Von Dietz, please sit down. I want to hear about your work." As she sat back down, she felt like she was falling into a tunnel.

"Speaking of time, tell me more about your theory." He descended into his chair. "Herr Fetzer said you would bring your latest manuscript. I am interested in your work." He looked at her brief case.

"It's kind of you. My work is still far from finished. I seem to be stuck. I'm so preoccupied with the need to get home."

"Show me vas you haf!"

Victoria reached into her briefcase and pulled out the manuscript. "This is my latest chapter."

He read the title aloud: " 'Psychological and Social Issues Involved in Time Spanning'. Was sprechts Sie in this chapter?"

"We, Professor Heidegger and I, were grappling with possible dangers for the mental health of those who travel back to earlier times. We also examine some possible unintended consequences. It seems like every time we humans augment our powers, awful things happen to a lot of people and animals while a very few of us get richer and more powerful," she said.

"What do you mean, 'time spanning? Does this mean I could go ahead to the future, see what is to become of me? of Germany?"

She swallowed. Had there been a leak? Possibly through Frau Elfriede Heidegger? She'd have to cover. "No, Herr Hitler. We havn't yet worked a way for us to leap forward in time. However, we are working on the possibility of some backward time movement."

Hitler raised his eyes to his forehead. "Zo, I could go back to being a child again. Danke nein. We were so poor. My father beat me and my mother. This is common practice in many Duetsche homes. Then I became a soldier. I saw the blood, the senseless carnage, and then the betrayal of my country in the treaty, German children starving in the streets. Nein Danke! I have no wish to live through it again, and as I see it I could do nothing differently. Nein! Nein! Nein!" He pounded a fist into his other palm with each "no," the pitch of his voice rising then falling.

She once again had mixed emotions, first pity, then fear. She wanted to hold him to heal his pain. But she also wanted to run out of the room. How could she feel motherly to a man she had learned to think of as the devil incarnate?

She drew inwardly upon her years of learning to become a professor in a male dominated academy. She had to learn to discuss highly emotional topics, such as the lives of the poor, as if she were counting cans of beans. Otherwise her professors (all men) would have deemed her too emotional and incapable of functioning in academia.

"Herr Hitler, please don't be concerned. We aren't able to relive the past, Herr Hitler. But under special conditions, as our work progresses, some day we may be able to move to other space-times, as we are, as adults."

His face turned red. Was he about to have a tirade? He laughed. It was melodious, captivating. She was stunned. She had never seen or even imagined that he could laugh. "Please, Dr. Von Dietz, this is an absurdity. For then you would be able to be a child and an adult at the same time."

"It doesn't work that way. But we have not eliminated all the bugs yet," she said.

"Bugs? This thing has filthy bugs in it?"

"I beg your pardon, Herr Hitler. Simply a word we use to mean problems."

"This is important work. It would have been good to influence the allies toward a real treaty, one that would not guarantee economic slavery, starvation, depression and additional war." Hitler stood, walked up to his desk and rang a bell. "There's someone I want you to meet."

The door opened. In walked a beautiful German shepherd. "This is my Blondi, fifth generation, from Germany's best stock." He tapped his thigh. The dog walked to Hitler and sat next to him. Her belly was distended. "Blondi will also give birth in a few weeks." He looked at Victoria's belly. "You are both alive with Prussia's heritage. Please don't take the comparison the wrong way," he said, smiling.

Victoria laughed, "Oh, I don't. I actually believe dogs and other animals are more highly evolved then humans. In many respects, they are the angels." Victoria reached towards Blondi's head. Blondi looked warily at Victoria but held still until Hitler opened his hand toward Victoria. Blondi got up and nuzzled Victoria, licking her hand.

"She reminds me of my dog back in Chicago, 'Snuggles', who is part German Shepherd and part Labrador retriever," Tears came to Victoria's eyes. "Excuse me, but I miss Snuggles."

"Ah, when you send for your daughter she can come along. This Snuggles is a mongrel, but our immigration restrictions against the racially mixed don't apply to dogs. You see, left alone, there would be no more German Shepherds, only mongrels, like the Jews with the Negroes at their tail," Hitler said. "Blondi Sizts Du!" Blondi sat, raised her paw for a handshake and barked twice. Hitler patted her on the head and said," Gute Madchen."

He extended one finger towards the floor. Blondi lay down at his feet. He wiggled his finger. She rolled over to one side, then the other. He reached into his pocket and gave her a small biscuit.

"A bitch, like a woman, must understand her place," he said, smiling.

Victoria stifled her reflexive anger. "My Snuggles is not so well trained. But she is loyal, courageous and loving."

Victoria stroked Blondi's head and continued, "I don't believe so much in blood, and I know I am capable of thinking and doing more than 90% of men, with the exception, of course, of pure muscle power. Besides, knowing exactly what a particular woman's place is would be a challenging question, Herr Hitler. I am thinking of Fräuleins Dietrich and Reifenstahl."

"Ach, don't mention Dietrich to me." His speech became rapid and rose in volume. "She has gone to England. Betrayed her homeland. Our heroine singer now is Fraulein Lamhecht," Hitler's cheeks flushed red.

Victoria realized that may have been why Dietrich did not show up that night in the Inn to sing. She also sensed more to the story between Hitler and Dietrich. Judging from Hitler's change of mood, she realized she might have little time left with him. She must press her point.

"I respect and value my Prussian ancestors. But now I am American. Please allow me to return home," she said.

Hitler rose quickly from his chair. Blondi sat up, pointing her ears forward. Hitler paced with hands clasped behind, then walked back to her and knelt next to her chair, taking both her hands.

"You will return to America in due course. For now you are to remain here in Germany. I must go away in a few days, matters of crucial importance. I'll send again for you so we can continue our conversation." He kissed her hands and stood, helping her stand. He looked again at her face and almost seemed about to cry. He led her to the door. "For now, Auf Wiedersehen," he said.

"Auf Wiedersehen, Herr Hitler," she said. She felt strangely pleased and at the same time frightened by her pleasure.

Chapter Forty-Three
Where is Home?

The tall sergeant escorted her to the end of the hallway and opened the door to a dimly light room with a high ceiling. Victoria's eyes accommodated to the soft lamps. The furnishings were ornately carved and upholstered with rich patterns. Aunt Inge stood just inside the doorway and led her with an air of excitement to an elderly woman perched among pillows in a high backed lounge chair. The woman's silvery hair was piled upward in a style reminiscent of the 1890s. Her veined hand stroked a small lap dog. The gaunt woman announced, "Frau Mutter, this is Dr. Victoria Von Dietz." Frau Hitler looked shocked, perplexed. Her mouth hung open.

One corner of Inge's mouth curled up and she raised an eyebrow. Then she continued, "Frau Dr. Von Dietz, this is my sister-in-law, Frau Mutter Hitler. Frau Hitler nodded, "My son, Adolph, called me Frau Mutter as a term of endearment and somehow it stuck."

Victoria nodded and stepped forward. She felt herself sinking back in time to childhood, a yellowish image in a carved frame on her grandmother's mantle. A photo of her great-grandmother in Prussia.

Color rose in the Frau Mutter's cheeks as she lifted her hand to Victoria, welcoming her in a warm voice. Victoria's eyes moistened as her accent was so similar to those she heard at home as a child. Victoria trembled as she took the Grossfrau's hand, so like her dear grandmother's and expressed her pleasure at their meeting.

Still clinging to Victoria's hand, Frau Mutter looked into her eyes.

"Ach, mein Liebschen, you look so much like my grandneice, whom we lost. My dear little angel, Geli. She was tall and blond like you with a wonderful sweet and wise face." Frau Mutter Hitler's sad eyes were layered with wrinkles. Aunt Inge reached behind the Frau Mutter and plumped her pillows.

"Frau Von Dietz, may I introduce my sister-in-law, Frau Inge Krempien. She insisted on taking the roles of parlor maid and lady's maid. And I can't blame her. I'd prefer to do something useful instead of sitting around acting like a lady were I well enough to do so. I'm from peasant stock and used to working."

"I understand," Victoria said, nodding to Inge. "Women in my family were always hard working."

"Grossfrau Hitler and I are companions since childhood. Oh it was so good in our village in Austria back then. But our Adolph will also bring this back," said Inge.

Inge hobbled to a side cabinet, pulled out a bottle of Liebfraumilch and three glasses. She filled each glass and passed one to the Frau Mutter, one to Victoria. Inge downed her wine in one swallow, walked back and poured herself another.

"Adolph does not approve of alcohol but allows us our small pleasures. Geli's family on the other side came from Prussia," said the Frau Mutter taking a sip. "Not much remained of Prussia after the last war, but now they are recovering with my Adolph's help."

"I'd hoped to visit there, try to find some relatives," said Victoria. "Now I just wish to go back to Chicago, to have my babies at home."

The Frau Mutter sat up straight in her chair. "My dear Maedchen, surely Germany is your true home!"

Victoria lost her breath.

The Grossfrau continued. "At a time like this, a woman needs to be home." She moved her head from side to side. "Ach nein, Chicago. People from all over Europe, all living in the same city. Judging from your American movies, Chicago is run by those Italian gangsters, Al Capone, and a mob. Certainly not a good place to raise a child."

Victoria's heart pounded. She must get these women on her side. "I so much appreciate your worries, but my life in Chicago is safe. And besides, I have a daughter back there in school, and my work. We had only intended to stay a month or so. Please help me and my husband obtain an exit visa."

Victoria looked up at the Frau Mutter who shifted in her chair, took another sip from her glass.

"Ah, I see, another kinder back home in school," said Auntie Inge. "Perhaps you can bring her here."

Victoria sighed, how could she answer this? "Dear Grossfrau Hitler, this is a good thought, however, the U.S. authorities would never let a child come to Germany during a war. Can you not help me, talk to your son?"

The Grossfrau shifted in her seat. "Ah, my dear, it is such a dilemma. There is much attention being paid by the Reich to what should be private business. Aber, Bitte, I have no influence on Adolph. He is always off in his own thoughts." She finished her wine, put her glass down on a crocheted doily on the side table.

She continued. "But he is a good son. He sees after me, stops in to visit me three times a day whenever he is here. But he doesn't think I can advise him about anything so I don't try." She looked away from Victoria to Inge, picked up her glass for more wine.

Victoria said, "I mustn't tire you, and my husband will be waiting for me." She stood and placed her glass on the tray.

"Surely your husband must know you are safer here than anywhere else in Germany," said Inge.

"Well, men worry anyway," said Victoria.

The Frau Mutter looked at Inge, frowning. "I used to think like Inge that we are safe here," she said. "Since that bomb went off at the front steps last month, I always feel afraid for Adolph, and for those of us who may get in the way of desperate people," said the Grossfrau.

Victoria felt she may have gained some ground with this admission of terrorism nearby. "Yah, these are dangerous times, even here," she said. There was silence for a second, as if all three women shared the same inner fear and dread of war and what was to come.

Victoria wanted to ease the tension. She looked at the large Duesenberg piano sitting in front of the windows. "Such a beautiful instrument," she said.

"Do you play?" asked Inge.

"Yes, but not so much here, due to my travels, staying at Inns and work. Everyone would like you to play but no one especially appreciates hearing you practice," said Victoria.

"Please try. Play something for us before you go," said the Frau Mutter.

Victoria sat down on the padded bench and ran several arpeggios, a few scales, rich mellow tone filling the room. She played a Brahms Intermezzo, feeling the wave-like motion and the rich bass notes reverberate in her entire body. The babies inside her kicked in time. "My little ones like it. They are dancing in my belly," said Victoria, ending the piece in several lush chords.

"Two of them?" said the Grossfrau.

"So my midwife says and I am certainly large enough for two! I have to use my arms differently playing with such a big belly in front of me. Brahms must have composed on a Duesenberg. My Steinway at home is wonderful, but doesn't do Brahms justice like this piano.

She played a song by Schumann and sang. As she sang, the side door opened. She felt a rush of cold air. She glanced over her shoulder and saw Hitler standing in the doorway, as if frozen. One side of his moustache crept up toward his eye. Then, intense heat seemed to radiate from him towards Victoria.

"Adolph, comst du hier bitte," said the Frau Mutter.

"Nein, Mutter. Ich mochte gehen. Wiedersehen, Mutter, Frau Von Dietz, Tanta Inge," he said, turned, and closed the door.

Chapter Forty-Four
Wounded Warrior

"That's Annabelle's knock," said Mead, early the next morning. "Why don't you tell that woman not to come unannounced?" A sliver of light came in between the drapes. He didn't wake Victoria late last night. Her need for rest in the final weeks of her pregnancy outweighed his anxiety over her meeting with Hitler. Mead kissed Victoria on the forehead, got up slowly feeling his aches and pains, put on his dressing gown. He wondered if he could sustain himself, if he would even survive the trip back. He darn't say this to Victoria.

Victoria stirred, barely opened her eyelids. "I didn't hear you come in last night."

"I didn't want to disturb you." He sat on the bed.

Pounding on the door. "Only Annabelle gets to do that. Shall I tell her to come back later?" he said.

"African culture has doors open to friends," said Victoria.

"Does that mean I have to act like an African?" said Mead.

The knock came again. "You alive in there?" Annabelle hollored.

"Coming Annabelle," he hollered back.

"How did your lecture go last night?" said Victoria, sitting up and rubbing her eyes.

"Fine, no tomatoes this time, but pickets outside saying "Germans in America komst gut Heim," he said.

"Do they want us to go back to America or to bring German-Americans to Germany," she said.

"That I don't know, I think the later. I'll tell you more, after you tell me what happened last night." He went to the living room leaving the bedroom door ajar.

"I've got breakfast here!" yelled Annabelle.

Mead opened the door wide, stood aside and bowed dramatically. "Good morning Queen!"

Annabelle swished in, her colorful caftan billowing behind. Her hair was bound high on her head. A sweep of her arm brought the in the waiter, rolling a kart.

As annoyed as Mead was with Annabelle's intrusions, he enjoyed her bombastic sense of assurance, and he was hungry.

"Ummmhmmm can you smell those links? Took negotiating to get something adequate," she said in a voice that would carry across a street. Catching herself, she added at normal volume. "Opps forgot I'm not in the hallway or on the Serenghetti." Then in a whisper. "Oh, is Victoria still sleeping?"

Bleary eyed, Victoria shuffled into the large sitting room, her green dressing gown flowing over her belly. She dropped into the lush sofa. The waiter nodded and set up a table. He looked around the room, his eyes shifting rapidly to every detail. He set out silver-covered plates, three place settings poured coffee, bowed and left.

"He'll no doubt report on every detail to someone," said Annabelle, sinking into the sofa.

Mead sat in the chair across from them. Victoria looked distant, blurry. What had happened last night? He kept silent. She was already exhausted and did not need to be pressured.

"Ah, Vicky, did the Fuhrer turn you into a mindless zombee?" Annabelle said. "Why didn't you call me when you got in? I was awake most of the night wondering if he had abducted you, taken you to his Wolf's lair in the Alps."

"Annabelle, let Victoria drink her coffee. We havn't spoken either since before she was swepted away last night. "She was deeply asleep when I got home."

Annabelle reached for the serving platter filled with sausages, stabbed one with her fork followed by another. "Sure beats the German version of continental, with those rock hard rolls, jam and cocoa. A body can't live on that stuff." Her eyes darted to Victoria, who silently sipped her coffee.

Mead reflected on his own situation, his sense of unease. Being in Nazi Germany with a young pregnant philosopher wife and an African Queen both transplanted from the 1970s stretched his capacity to its limits. Schutz had written about multiple realities, but living them simultaneously was a challenge he had not fathomed. But he must stay focused. Whatever it takes.

Victoria stared at the cup in her palms, caressing it as if to warm her palms. How beautiful she looked. He wanted so much to bring her home safely to Chicago. What a joy it would be to raise a family with her. Yet, he said to himself, 'I am very old to be a father again. I feel my strength failing each day. I'm already way beyond my time'.

Glancing at Mead, Annabelle said, "Looks like The Fuhrer cast a spell over the lady, and George over you as well. " She leaned closer to Victoria, stared, and said, "All right, gal, tell us the real scoop. What's the bastard like? Bad as we've been led to believe, or worse?"

Victoria placed her cup back in the saucer. She served herself some eggs and a small ham hock. "I felt my emotions pulled, fear, awe, romance, danger. He was really nice to me. Yet there was more. He was like a little child, needing to be reassured. Unpredictable, as if he could suddenly turn on me. Yet his energy was magnetic, hypnotic. At times I was afraid and wanted to leave, but could not move." Her usually soft voice was now almost inaudible.

"Please, Vicky, speak up so I can hear you above my own chewing," said Annabelle.

"I'm sorry, it seems so unreal to me I first had to realize that I wasn't in a dream," said Victoria. She recounted her experience from the night before in detail from first seeing Hitler to the brush of his mustache on the back of her hand when they parted, to his intense stare at the doorway as she played piano for the Frau Mutter.

"You've charmed the man, Vicki. Now you have to take the next step— kill the bastard," said Annabelle.

"Nonesense, Annabelle. She's risking her life and the babies'. We can't ask this of her!" Mead snapped.

Victoria's face twisted in dismay. "Please lets not quarrel." She took a deep breath. "We are here for a reason."

Mead took strength in her strength. "I can see Adolph, if I may call him that, appealed to you in many ways—the lonely, misunderstood hero, the lover of animals," said Mead. He took a forkful of scrambled eggs. Picked up his coffee.

"Darling, that's true and at the same time I saw him as a devoted son, and a lost child," said Victoria.

Annabelle took a large bite of sausage, shifted the meat to one side of her mouth. "It's deeper than that. The man is a wounded warrior, an ancient archetype. Sees himself as a Messiah. Very powerful magic. I'll call it 'white' magic."

"Aren't wounded warriors and messiahs essentially the same?" said Victoria. She spread butter on a roll. "I've always liked these Kaiser rolls. They may have been named after Kaiser Wilhelm. Perhaps my great-great-grandfather, General Von Dietz carried them in his saddle bag to battle Napoleon."

"They probably defeated Napoleon by throwing these rolls at him," said Annabelle. "And they wouldn't spoil or crumble when carried on horseback to battle."

"The Kaiser's rolls are something else perhaps we should scrutinize through Jungian psychology," said Mead. "You know, I consulted with Carl Jung when I was here as a student. But our subject is Hitler, not the Kaiser. Annabelle's right. The wounded hero appeals to your heart, Victoria. He's suffered and continues to suffer on your behalf, but needs you to take care of him. A messiah also suffers for you, but wants you to obey him, fight for him. Yes, I can see the the appeal of their combination.

"That ain't all," muttered Annabelle as she took a bite of a large cruller. She licked a sliver of glazed sugar off her lower lip.

"I didn't know you were analyzed by Jung!" Victoria poured herself more coffee.

Mead held up his cup. He was pleased Victoria seemed to be waking up, acting more like herself.

The two archetypes combined, wounded hero and messiah, are irresistible for any woman with maternal instincts," said Annabelle. "He is both father and son, protector and in need of nurturance. The woman who rejects him makes herself rootless and fruitless. This one happens to be flesh and blood, not a fairytale myth. I wish it were the other way around. "

"I'm proud of you, my darling, Vicky, and impressed," said Mead. "I'm also frightened."

Victoria picked up her coffee cup, gazed into it again, as if reading from it. She looked up at Mead, "I frightened too. I made no headway with him on getting our visas. In fact, my visiting him may have made it less likely that he'll let me go, especially with my being pregnant. And while my likeness to his niece and his vague interest in my work got me in, it is those same qualities that may keep him from letting me go. I must make a separate appeal for you to return."

Mead's stomach churned as he wrestled with conflicting emotions. He was jealous of her strange attraction to Hitler. Yet he agreed with Annabelle. Victoria may be able to get close enough to the monster and assassinate him. But most of all he wanted to protect her. "Nonsense, I will not leave without you," said Mead. "Absolute nonsense!"

"Perhaps if you put on a little weight and some heavy make up, you could leave disguised as me. I doubt I'm a high priority keep, for them, except maybe a ballast on one of their U-boats," said Annabelle. She poured herself a second cup of coffee from the large carafe on the table.

They all chuckled.

"We sure are drowning in our coffee this morning," said Victoria. She continued to recount and analyze her evening with Hitler.

"Sounds like the Grossfrau would like to adopt you," said Annabelle. "What a wonderful chance. When you are asked back, dump something in his tea."

"He drank nothing," said Victoria." What if I could change his poisoned thinking instead?"

"You've been too influenced by *Beauty and the Beast*. Those sorts of changes only happen in fairy tales. By knocking him off you'll give him a chance at a reincarnation in some form above a dung beetle," said Annabelle.

Mead held back his urge to tell her to shut up. Instead he sat back, pulled out his pipe, loaded it with rum tobacco, tapped it down in the bowl, tilted the lighter flame, and puffed it to life. The fragrance of it circled the air above the table as he exhaled.

"Human beings who create murder and mayhem are the lowest rung in the evolutionary ladder," said Mead. "Their only chance to avoid an endless abyss of their soul is to somehow, even if it is in an instant, to see a glimmer of light, to repent, before they die."

"Don't lower the status of the dung beetle," said Victoria. "The dear creatures work tirelessly converting waste into soil. In cases of evil and cruel persons, there can be no lower incarnation for them to work their karma. Perhaps that is why we need the Western notion of hell."

Annabelle sighed, putting her roll down on her plate with emphasis. "You two always get lost in philosophy. She's got to do him because otherwise millions will die. It's just that simple. Girl if you can get me in there for thirty seconds, you wouldn't have to think about it any more." She picked up the cruller again and took a deep bite.

Mead leaned back, frowning at Annabelle. He puffed and blew out a column of smoke. "Ethically and psychologically it is still wrong. If she murders him, she is doing wrong to make right. That's what he's doing, and it would destroy her, even if there were a slim chance she wasn't discovered and killed. Victoria, if ever you listened to me, do it now in this matter."

"I've always listened to you, Darling, but obeying is another thing entirely," said Victoria. "But I've been swayed by your way of thinking for twenty years. George, you know there is a reason why we're here. We didn't just come for a vacation."

Mead shuddered inside but had to admit she was right. "You're so wise," he said. "It's just very hard for one who loves you to bear." He admired her courage and the clarity of her thought as much as her beauty.

Annabelle got up and stood behind Victoria, rubbing her neck. "You need to take it easy, let it go, girl." Annabelle began to hum and sing. Her lovely voice resonated in the high-ceilinged room. Mead found it as soothing as his pipe. "Lu bae catalae, Lu lae Caceae, Manei tomanu, romout Katab."

"That is so comforting. What does it mean?" said Victoria.

"The ways of the world and the songs of the gods, bring them together. I learned that in Africa."

"Just the opposite of Wagner's Gotterdammerung, The Twilight of the Gods," said Mead.

"Hitler loves Wagner, or so I heard," said Annabelle.

"He also likes lots of other music," said Victoria describing her playing Brahms, and Hitler listening by the door.

"Well, lets' not condemn the composers for the sins of the listeners," said Mead.

∾

Hitler sent the car for Victoria a few days later, then every day until he suddenly left Berlin. Each visit followed the same pattern. Inge, who somehow seemed perkier, greeted her. Inge led her always to Adolph's office.

After a few minutes of emotionally confusing conversation, Hitler would call for Blondi, his dog, to come in and would show Victoria Blondi's latest tricks. They discussed the theory of time.

At each visit Victoria brought up the work camps, the war, trying to plant reassurances that there were better ways for Germany to reach its goals. Hitler countered adamantly.

"We must make bold moves as we are facing dangerous times," Hitler's voice rose in pitch and passion. "When you find yourself burdened--called— to be at the center of destiny, you must act! We must be harsh as well as decisive. Resistance must be crushed immediately before it breeds."

Victoria continued to request exit visas. He denied or evaded, but offered hints of hope for after the babies were born.

Each visit before leaving, she was invited to visit the Frau Mutter, play piano, sing. Each time Hitler walked by, stared at her from the door, listened, walked away.

The last visit things were different. After Blondi performed her new tricks and they had discussed time and the war, he took her hands as usual but then knelt next to her.

"May I, may I, Oh, please hold me, Victoria," Hitler said with tears in his eyes. He put his head between her breasts and sobbed for what seemed like an hour. Then, just as suddenly, he got up, filled with tension, fists at his sides, a sense of urgency.

"It is terrible what a woman will make of you. Oh how beautiful you are, how you've bewitched me. Now get out! I'm very very busy. I've spent too much time, time, time with your milk already." He strode stiffly out the back door of his office.

Downstairs, the Grossfrau asked asked why Victoria was upset. When she explained what had happened, the Frau Mutter said, "Never mind. He's temperamental. Always was. Play something sweet and soothing. It will help him if he comes down."

Victoria played the second movement of Beethoven's Sonata in E. He didn't come to the door that evening to listen.

Chapter Forty-Five
Victoria in Labor

E eeeygghhhh! EEEuyaaaaaghhh! Got in Himmel, Holy Mary Mother of Godddddaaarrrrgh! Momman, Sister, Aaarrrgh! Victoria screamed. Stomach bursting, backbone splitting, going to die, she thought. Her skin stuck to the mattress. AAAARGth! The cracked white ceiling circled. Her throat burned. Aaugh! Pain racked through her entire body. Her backbone retracted into one large cramp.

Clump, clump, clump, the footsteps of the large bosomed nurse. "Shshsshsddskup" "Schloossen Sit–Shut up, shut up, you are disturbing the other patients," she yelled. "They're soldiers fresh wounded! High heroes of Germany. Du bist ein Worthless Whore." The name on her badge "Beektoff" stood out boldly.

She's going to let me die, thought Victoria. "Bitteschoen, Nurse Beektoff, please, get me a doctor. I've lost my water, the baby is stuck," she said in German. "Please, Nurse, send for Dr. Mead, Mein Mann. We are residents here in Charlottenberg Manor!"

Beektoff ignored her. She was Fuhrer of this ward. "No visitors allowed!" shouted the large nurse.

"I'm here at Herr Hitler's request."

"So are the soldiers."

"Aaaghh, Euaggh. My baby will die!" Victoria had no arms or legs, only voice and pain. The scream was coming from deep within the earth. "Eauugh!"

"Shut up!" Beektoff said, smacking Victoria across the face.

Nurse Beektoff stomped off, yelling orders.

She is going to kill me, Victoria thought, and continued to wail.

Thank heaven they had been able to get to Berlin in time, thought Guy at the door to the hospital wing of the Charlottenberg castle. If only he could have been here sooner. Once in the hallway he heard Victoria's screams. "Emergency, Das Ist Mein Frau screaming!" He shouted to the guards at the door. He had called her his wife without thinking. Anyway, they were more likely to let him through if they thought he was her husband. The guards locked their arms together in front of the doorway. Guy thrust himself against them with all his force. They easily thwarted him. He pulled out the diplomatic immunity papers Schutz obtained for him. He put on a poker face so as not to reveal his fear that they would recognize them as forged. Her cries got louder as he ran up the stairs. His heart pounding, Guy pushed past the next set of guards at the folding doors. He could not loose her.

Through the veil of agony, Victoria saw a hand reaching for Beektoff's shoulder. She looked up. "Guy!" Was she hallucinating? No, it was Guy, his other arm in a sling. Beektoff, a full six foot one, grabbed his injured and pushed him away. "Rouse mit dich! Out! Varoom! No one is allowed hier!" Beektoff pulled his good arm behind his back and spun him around. Ummph! She socked him in the jaw, knocking the breath out of him.

"Wine-breathed Schweinhund. Just like my no good boyfriend." Beektoff kneed him in the stomach. "Guards! Kommst Sie Hier! Machts Schnell!"

Screams coming from her own throat horrified Victoria. Pain surged through her with such force that it seemed to come from outside as well as within, becoming her entire world.

"Get her a doctor," said Guy. "She must have help immediately, or she and her baby will die."

"A doctor, a doctor. Wir haben nicht Drs. for Americanishe Frauen vilst our German soldiers bleed to death," said Beektoff. "Guards, Guards, come at once!" she yelled.

"She is a special friend of the Fuhrer," said Guy.

"The Fuhrer does not sleep with foreign women." She caught Guy's arm as he moved towards Victoria, and wrenched his arm behind his back.

"Sie is einen Freunden nichts Lover auf den Fuhrer!" said Guy.

Two uniformed young men ran into the room, their boots leaving marks on the white marble floor. They grabbed Guy and dragged him towards the door.

"Victoria, I'll get help!" yelled Guy. "Ihren Kinder sind Deutsche! Ihren Baby ist Deutsch. A son or daughter of Herr Dr. Professor Heidegger, Rector of Freiburg University."

One of the guards snickered. "First he is the husband then a Professor is the father. Let's get this nutcase out of here." Beektoff hovered over Victoria " "Pushen Sie auf, Pusche, Pusche" she yelled.

"Guy, Call Annabelle!" shouted Victoria.

"I did. She's waiting for us! We'll be back!" Guy called over his shoulders as the guards dragged him out the large wooden doors. As she had another contraction, Victoria heard her own screams echoe like a crash of thunder across a deep valley.

"I've got to get out, get up, get out of here." Victoria pushed herself to a sitting position. The wounded and dying were carried in on stretchers, crowding the ward, moaning in waves. The pain roared through her again. Her head fell back onto the pillow. Two white-coated men with military hats rushed in.

Beektoff issued orders. "We must quiet her down. More wounded are coming from the Eastern front. Use the spinal injection." One of the men held her arms up over her head and the other held her legs together. Nurse Beektoff took a long needle from the table next to the bed and injected Victoria in the back of her spine just above her coccyx. The pain was so intense she could not scream. Yet she heard herself screaming anyway, as if it were the voice of Brunhilde in exile, calling alone on the mountaintop. A blue haze filled in the light from the window. Then a shower of light filled her body. She thought she was dead.

Guy's boots scuffed down the stairs as the guards pulled him, each one holding an arm. Where would they take him? They were tall, with shoulders like oak beams. They shoved open two sets of folding doors then dropped him. One at each arm, they escorted him down KonigFrederickStrasse. Guy cried out from the wrenching of his wounded shoulder as one of them twisted his arm behind his back. The other stepped to the call box. "Yah, carried him out. Er ist nicht important, just a Americanisher whose Frau is having a baby. He says she is a special friend of the Fuhrer's. Yahvol, they all say that, but who knows? . . .O.K. we vill let him go . . .Nein, he won't be let back in."

The guard continued to hold Guy while the other guard punched him in the gut.

Guy sat, doubled-over, on the curb, his head swirling. Cars, trucks and pedestrians went by, looking past him. He groped in his torn and dusty sports jacket for coins. He struggled to his feet and hobbled to a phone booth on the corner. I must look like a bum or a displaced person, but this is a good disguise for an American resistance worker, he thought. A couple of women wearing babushkas passed him in the street, looked sympathetically at him, but kept on walking.

He dialed Annabelle, hung up waiting for an answer. After a few tense moments the phone rang. "We must get Victoria out of Charlottenberg. She's in the East wing, they're using as a military hospital. Second floor, second room from the end. In advanced labor. Can't make it much longer, sadistic nurse wants her dead.

Annabelle's contralto boomed into the earpiece. "I'll take care of it. You go to MannheimStrasse number Three. Give the code and tell them to get ready for the delivery—deep water. Then go back to the castle and wait with the car until Schutz and Wagner arrive."

Guy already held Annabelle in high esteem from being her administrative assistant back in Chicago (or should he say 'ahead' in Chicago, since that is or thirty years forward. Here he admired her even more as she was able to muster support from the Pan-African embassy as well as the U.S. and British intelligence. What a gal!

"High command, SS, special orders." Helmut hoped to impress the guards at the gate of Charlottenburg using a Berliner accent. "Dr. Schutz is here for an emergency transport."

The golden yellow of the castle gleamed in the spring sunlight. Troops goose-stepped on the east lawn, the sun reflecting off their helmets and bayonets.

Helmut Wagner knew presenting Schutz as a military doctor would carry weight. He was frantic with worry. He could not explain why he felt such a deep connection to Victoria, someone he had barely met, yet somehow it seemed as if he was in labor with her.

The Guard opened the gate, held out his hand. Schutz, in a German officer's uniform, carried a black medical bag. He reached into his jacket and pulled out papers. Helmut and Guy stood behind, wearing white medic's garb. By combing his hair forward under the white cap and walking slumped over, Guy had changed his appearance. He carried a folded stretcher under his good arm, keeping his slinged side under his coat. The guard lifted his arm, "Heil Hitler," clicked his heels and stood aside. The guard was several inches taller than Schutz, about 6'4".

A large nurse stomped to the doorway, two male nurses on each side. Schutz said: "Nurse Beektoff, Bitte. I am here at the special order of the High Command. He pulled a paper from his inner pocket. Release Frau Dr. Von Dietz Mead to my custody immediately."

"Why was I not notified directly?" she glared. Her beady eyes, magnified by her thick glasses, peered over the document. Her face reddened and her posture sagged.

"This IS your direct notification. The command has much more important things to do than worry about delivery wards! Step aside Madam," said Schutz.

Schutz sure knows how to handle officious bureaucrats, thought Wagner. Schutz was one of those intellectuals, like Max Weber, who also could act powerfully in the political world.

She stepped back slightly, her face sullen. "All right. Help, Dr. Schutz get her out."

"That's impossible. She's in advanced labor," said a young nurse.

"This is not your affair, nurse, step aside," hollered Beektoff regaining some of her height.

Wagner took this as a favorable turn. Asserting her power in the ward may divert Beektoff's aggressive energies. He knew the type, women too large or homely to attract a man, overcompensating, and especially despise beautiful women, such as Victoria.

As Schutz and the two men in white pushed past her into the ward nurse Beektoff said, "Das machts nichts. She has been nothing but trouble for us. Do what I say."

Schutz placed a hand on Victoria's forehead. "Kalt." He felt her belly. "Put her on the stretcher on her left side," said Schutz. "The baby is twisting toward one side, this will release the pressure," he said to Victoria.

Guy and Helmut unfolded the stretcher and gently moved Victoria onto it.

Opening her eyes, Victoria looked at Guy, who was doing all his lifting with one arm, the other tied in a sling to his chest. "Bayrum," she said, recognizing Guy's aftershave.

Helmut Wagner wanted to lighten the mood. "How he can carry the stuff around is beyond me. I just use cold water," he said.

"My boss likes it," Guy retorted with a smile. Wagner was pleased to see the corners of Victoria's mouth turn up.

"You are safe now, Frau Professor," Wagner said. She had joked with him about his use of Germanic academic titles.

Once out the front doors and on their way to the car Helmut attempted to continue with lighthearted banter: "This is Dr. Schutz."

"Dr. Schutz," she said, "but I thought you were a doctor of philosophy, not of medicine." She looked up. "Nice uniform," she added.

"Yes, my German friends, like Helmut here, continue to help me. But don't worry. I was a medic on the Italian front, and delivered lots of babies in a war zone. Guy said they gave you a shot in the spine," he said.

"Yes, Beektoff with a long needle. It was agonizing, they held my legs together. I've lost my water." She shivered.

"Don't worry. The injection slows down labor," said Schutz. "We'll get you to a safe house."

They guided her off the stretcher and into the back seat of a large black Mercedes.

Guy opened the door of the driver's seat to get in.

"Your arm. It may get rough," said Wagner, nudging Guy aside.

"No, I'll drive," said Guy.

"Do as Helmut says, Guy," said Schutz. "Helmut knows the route." Guy slid over and Wagner got behind the wheel. He started Mercedes, reassured by the deep purring of the engine.

Guy turned around in his seat. "You'll be fine, Dr. Von Dietz, don't you worry."

"Guy's a hero," said Schutz. "As you can see by his sling, he took fire on our last mission."

"Some hero. We lost three," said Guy, now looking out the window.

"I was hoping you'd spare her that right now," said Wagner.

"Guy knows me. I require the truth," said Victoria.

In the rear view, Wagner noticed a car following close behind them, almost hitting their bumper a couple of times. "A tail, got to loose them," he said.

"Turn right, then left twice down the alleys ahead," said Schutz.

Wagner pushed on the gas pedal and swerved suddenly to the right in front of a car then just got out of the path of a bus. The alley was brick paved, making the ride bouncy. They knocked over two garbage cans and scared a man sitting on a ledge with a brown bag around a bottle. As Wagner turned left again he saw the car that was behind way ahead and turning right in the opposite direction.

"Whew, we lost them," said Wagner. "Sorry Victoria."

Despite the bumpy ride, Victoria felt secure, cradled by Schutz. "Spread your knees apart," he said. "with your water broken and the sedation, I doubt you will have contractions."

How wrong Schutz was. Her belly cramped. She moaned with excruciating pain. "I can't push," she said.

"Do not try," said Schutz. "It's the worst thing to do in a dry birth," He put his right hand on her lower belly and gently massaged it. He reached his left hand up under her buttocks. She couldn't feel anything except the ride was smoother now that they were back on the road.

"The baby's heart is beating, no actually two hearts!" said Schutz. "Your having twins, Victoria! Keep breathing deeply."

"Yes I know, Annabelle actually was the first to suspect," said Victoria.

Schutz took a large flask from the pocket behind the seat and held it to her lips. She drank the water greedily. Then he pulled a small silver flask out of his coat pocket, offered her a drink.

The liquid was aromatic and thick. Victoria coughed. "Cognac," Schutz said. "The doctor prescribed it."

"Which Dr.?" Victoria took another generous slug. She felt the warmth going down to her stomach. She looked up at Schutz. "You write about the structures of the lifeworld when you spent so much time in the war, around those pursuing death," she said.

"War does not just destroy lives. It destroys the lifeworlds that sustain them. When I went back home after the war I found that lifeworlds had disintegrated. I write about lifeworlds so that we can appreciate more of what is lost," he said. "The interlocking worlds of relationships over generations is more intricate than a spider's web."

"Spiderwebs are so beautiful," she said. "Human lifeworlds are unfathomable."

"You, Victoria, have made what Schutz calls 'predecessors' and 'successors' into contemporaries by putting Mead and Heidegger's theories of time into practice!" said Guy.

"A most astute point, Guy. Gentlemen, not many people would believe we could have such a conversation in this situation. It's wonderful. I hope I can remember it to write about later!"

"Schutz is writing about the we-relationship," said Wagner, "so important when relationships are torn apart."

"And built in an instant" interjected Schutz. "What Heidegger called "authenticity" comes much more readily to the forefront during war. But perhaps we tend to write about what troubles us, otherwise why write."

"There is little possibility to deny death at such times," said Guy, "and Heidegger says one can only be authentic when one faces one's mortality."

"I don't fear death so much but fear for my little ones." Victoria moaned. "The anesthesia is wearing off," she said, feeling a contraction coming on.

Victoria felt soothing relief as Schutz placed a hand on her sacrum and the other over her belly. "Helmut, how are we doing," he asked.

"We're almost there," Wagner said turning a corner nearly on two wheels.

A two-way radio on the dashboard hissed. Guy picked it up. "Hello, Annabelle. Can you hear? Over."

"Yes, is Victoria with you? Is she all right? Over."

"She's O.K.," said Guy. "Dr. Schutz is holding her. They gave her a spinal. It's wearing off now. She lost her water. Over."

A wave of pain burst inside Victoria. Her scream sounded as if it were coming from the sky. Was she dying now?

"Why the hell didn't you tell me about the water? Over." Annabelle's scratchy voice boomed over the speaker.

"I thought I did tell you! Over."

"How far away are you? I have a water immersion ready! Over."

"About a five kilometers. Water immersion? Sounds really new."

"Midwives were doing this in 600 B.C. It is only male dominated Western medicine that took it away. Now get the hell over here! Over and out," said Annabelle.

Victoria panted to relieve her cramp as a wave of pain rolled through her body. "Martin emphasizes acceptance of death as important to authentic living. But he says nothing about pain and birth, which are close to life as well as death."

"It is worth your writing a book about," said Schutz.

"Let her finish the one she is already working on first," said Helmut."

"Jesus H. Christ!" said Guy. "Why do you pressure her about writing books when she is about to have a baby, for God's sake!"

Victoria puffed and moaned as they pulled into the driveway of a stone mansion. Wagner opened the window. "Its Dr. Schutz with Dr. Von Dietz," he said. The gate opened and they went through to a lush garden. Wagner pulled around a graveled circle, got out of the car, and opened the back door. Guy assembled the stretcher, helped Wagner slide Victoria onto it.

With halting breath, she said: "in eastern thinking . . . death leads to rebirth . . . in other forms . . .endless circle of life . . .until one enters Nirvana . . .need not be reborn . . . Martin's thought reaches . . . towards east . . .through pre-Socratics. . .yet does not . . . mention such things." Everything whirled around. Victoria felt drunk and dreamy. The setting sun shimmered through tall pines.

Schutz cleared his throat as he walked ahead of the stretcher towards the huge dark door.

"Yes, his questioning towards the presence of Being leads in that direction," he said.

Guy glared at Schutz.

"I started it, Guy," said Victoria. Two crows flew overhead, cawing before flying off to the large oak grove to the left. A white owl hooted from high in one of the trees.

Was there a struggle of souls waiting to incarnate in human form? Yet Victoria's outward question was mundane. "Where are we?" her voice was weak, echoing pain.

"A secure house that Annabelle found with the help of Herr Fetzer. The American embassy is being evacuated and is heavily guarded," said Wagner.

Helmut and Guy carried Victoria into the mansion.

"It's one of the manors of the Von Humboldt family. They are in favor with Nazis party officials. But they have relatives in America and are disconcerted about recent developments," said Schutz.

A middle-aged woman came to the door. She wore a black dress with a white starched collar and cuffs, apron and cap.

"Hello, Katie, is everything ready? said Schutz.

"Yes, Dr. Schutz. Her Highness, Queen Ogubiko, is up waiting in the spa." Katie looked down at Victoria, her lips pursed. "Don't be fearful, Frau Dr. Von Dietz. We'll look after you. Lady Von Humboldt has discovered that you may be distant relatives," said Katie.

Guy and Helmut carried Victoria down a long hallway. Looking sideways, Victoria noticed a polished walnut floor. Through an arched doorway, she saw a large sitting room with a huge fireplace ablaze. A picture of General Von Humboldt on his white stallion hung above it.

"There is a park named after him in Chicago," said Victoria, "with a large statue of the general and his horse."

"Lady Von Humboldt will be pleased to know," said Katie.

They took Victoria to a large room with several spas and bathing pools at the back of the house. Wagner was summoned by a butler to see after the car.

Chapter Forty-Six
Deep Water Birth

In the beginning was the word . . . and the word was made flesh
I John 1

"Push, Girl, Push," hollered Annabelle Carter Jackson. She sat beside Victoria in a spa made of tiles painted with water lilies and swans. Her large hands reached around Victoria under the water to support her back and sooth her belly. Victoria felt as if she were an infant cradled in her mother's arms.

Annabelle wore a red-skirted bathing suit. Her hair was bundled in a flowered turban. "Glad I was able to pop over to Lane Bryant's before leaving for Germany. Didn't know if there'd be anyplace around here where a large gal could get a swim suit." she said.

Annabelle ordered Schutz, Wagner and Guy to sit behind a curtained screen back near the doorway, twenty feet from the spa. Through a doorway on the other side, Victoria saw a bedroom suite. She longed to be there, the birthing completed, resting with her infants.

The mist from the spa provided an additional curtain between Victoria and the men. She saw only their heads above the screen and the shadow of their seated forms on the bench, their hands folded. This made the situation seem even more unreal, dreamlike. Until she had another cramp. Yikes, this is real. "Holy mother help me!" She screamed.

"I'm here, Vicky, and the Holy Mothers are here too. I can feel them," said Annabelle.

Victoria's shoulders were draped with a warm towel, brought by Hilda, Lady Von Humbolt's personal maid. "Hilda was present when I had my babies," Lady Von Humbolt had said as they rushed in. She looked more like a maid than a nurse with a grey dress, white apron and cap. Her presence was calming assured, non-intrusive. Her face was wrinkled, her grey hair pulled up under her cap.

"I'm going to lift your bottom up under the water, so the water can get inside you to ease the little ones' way." Annabelle scooped Victoria's bottom higher under the water and rested it on a soft pillow. The warm water felt soothing on her sore perineum.

Her belly cramped. Above, the ceiling was sky blue with a mural of clouds and birds. The fine cracks in the ceiling transversed each other like life and heart lines on the palm of a wise man. The pain subsided. Phew! Got through that one.

Looking down, Victoria noticed a white cloth in the water between her knees. She lie suspended now in this huge basin, her feet hooked over the edge, her head on a large water pillow. Hilda wrapped Victoria's ankles and anchored them to ceramic loops at the side of the spa. Her legs were spread wide.

"You must keep your knees open now, Miss Victoria," said Hilda.

"Nice color on your toenails," said Annabelle.

Victoria laughed. "My version of heeding my grandmother's warning never to wear torn underwear or a safely pin on my skirt in case of an accident." Then she frowned. "Won't my babies drown?"

"Water is what you and the babies need right now. Whatever made male doctors think they could or should deliver babies in the dry air is beyond me. Remember, girl, they are used to swimming around in the womb like little fish. Warm water is home for babies, darling, and soothing to you."

The painful burning sensation in her belly began to blurred into a feeling of gentle warmth as the water entered her.

"It's actually saline solution, just the same as what is in the belly, and as your tears," said Hilda.

From back behind the screen, Schutz said, "May I assist? I delivered many infants on the front."

"We're doing fine in here, Dr. Schutz. But Victoria, do you want the gentleman in here?" asked Annabelle.

Victoria moved her head from side to side in a gentle "no". She didn't want to hurt Schutz' feelings. After a bit of silence she thought of a way to decline. "Thank you, but, I feel more comfortable so exposed with just the women here," she said.

"Of course, we'll stay back," said Schutz.

"It's wonderful to share this moment with you," said Guy, "and to see how birthing was done by midwives," said Guy.

A shiver of pain wracked through Victoria's guts, as she contracted.

"Breathe, darling, breathe and push," said Annabelle.

"I'm trying but I still feel like my belly is not connected to my brain," said Victoria.

"I could kill that Nazi bitch nurse for giving you that epidural in the middle of labor," said Annabelle.

Annabelle Carter Jackson slid her right arm and shoulder under Victoria's left shoulder. Her right hand reached up between the crack of her buttocks. Victoria felt a soothing sensation as the pain subsided. Annabelle's lefthand held Victoria's lower belly and pushed down gently.

From behind the curtain Schutz said, "Spinal injections were tested by the German doctors for situations when soldiers are in pain from large wounds."

"Hmms, using it on women in labor may also help rid them of 'undesireables'," added Wagner.

"Or, maybe Eva Braun is jealous of me and set me up with Beektoof," said Victoria.

"Yeah but Braun is childless. Maybe she wanted you to go down so she could get the babies," said Annabelle. "But don't you mind about that now, darling."

Annabelle palpated Victoria's back and belly. "Relax and breathe. Your babies are tired of being cooped up in there. Breathe with me, Vicky, Breathe!" They both inhaled, pulling the air into their lower bellies. Annabelle smelled of salt, musk and baked caramel apples. "Breathe, hold, hold, Vicky, hold."

Victoria said, "This is just like holding at the end of breath of fire in Kundalini yoga."

"Yes, where do you think those male yogis got the idea in the first place—from watching their mothers and their midwives give birth!" said Annabelle.

Victoria felt like she was inside a giant brightly colored pleasure balloon, floating over a white sandy beach.

"Hold, hold, now relax completely, and blow, blow all of the air out," said Annabelle.

The room was still for what felt like an eternity. Then both women blew out air. Annabelle Carter Jackson gently shook Victoria, her fingers spread wide on her sacrum and belly.

Victoria wailed.

Guy rushed toward the spa, then fell silent. His eye was black and swollen. Hilda held him back.

"I thought something awful was happening to Victoria."

"No, ist wonderbar," said Hilda. "Sit down, Guy."

Guy returned to the bench.

Annabelle joined in the wailing. The two earth-mother voices cried up to the heavens, becoming a song. They were two Valkyries, singing from Valhalla, for all below to see the glory of beings coming forward.

The three men behind the screen stood.

Schutz said, "It's wonderful to hear the cries become a singing. I read that women used to gather around the one in labor and all of them would sing together, usually on top of a hill in the moon light, all night long before each birth. Then there were no such things as labor pains."

"That's why village women in Vietnam squat while they work," said Guy. "It kept their inner thighs stretched and their spinal columns long. Over the nine months of pregnancy the baby could come into position to just arrive when he's ready."

Victoria felt like this may be her last moment of life and also her first. A rush of relief and joy and hope, then a stream of hot fluid gushed out between her thighs. Annabelle held an infant upsidedown over the water. "Here she is, Victoria, I mean, he is. A lovely boy!"

Beads of sweat broke out on Annabelle's forehead. Annabelle pulled her right arm from beneath Victoria and gently rubbed his little behind with her large white palm. He cried and Victoria and Annabelle cried with him. The boy had blue eyes and wisps of curly blond hair. his nose was short and slight.

"He's light like George and me," said Victoria.

"Hilda, hold this little one here, next to Victoria. Keep him in the warm water, except for his head," said Annabelle.

"I wish George were here," said Victoria, also wishing that Martin could be there, but perhaps not both at the same time.

"Where is George, darling," said Annabelle. "We can send Guy to pick him up."

"George and Martin had a debate today at the university in Freiburg, on the merits of world government and the rising forces of technology."

"Wouldn't you know it!" said Annabelle. "Meanwhile, back at the ranch Victoria gives birth!"

"Heidegger with his anti-technology stance must feel betrayed by the direction Hitler has taken things," said Helmut from behind.

Victoria could not help but chime in, even though a stabbing cramp wrenched through her body. "Martin must not anger the party. That way he can continue to teach."

"His inside support has been essential to our work," said Schutz.

Annabelle held Victoria's back and lower belly between her two hands and gently massaged. "No more political or philosophical comments, guys. You are in a sacred setting, and she is not finished!"

"To Victoria philosophy is sacred," said Guy, laughing.

"But then words were made flesh," said Annabelle.

Victoria cried out, wracked with pain. "And hence politics," she said between yells.

"Here comes the other one," said Annabelle. "Push once again like before, Girl. Breathe with me breathe."

Victoria took a deep breath and held and blew and soon there was a second baby boy in Annabelle's palm.

"Holy Divine Mother." cried Annabelle. Cheers came from behind the screen. "This little guy looks very different from the other, a bit smaller, with dark hair and chestnut eyes." Annabelle patted this one until he started to wail. She handed him, then the blond boy to Victoria, helping to raise her higher in the water so they could lie on her breasts.

"Looks like a little George and a little Martin," said Annabelle.

"Very rare in humans, yet the evidence is before you," said Schutz.

Victoria felt a sense of astonishment, but yet they were right. The two boys each looked like George and Martin.

Hilda dipped a knife from a sterile solution and handed it to Annabelle, who cut the umbilical cords.

The blond baby opened his eyes and looked up at Annabelle, then shuddered and fell asleep. The dark haired boy gurgled and drooled.

"Dr. Schutz, is this what you call "growing older together ?" asked Victoria. She thought of the point Helmut had made about Schutz saying this to him after they had an engaging moment together.

"Actually," said Schutz, "this is not a foregone conclusion. The babies do not converse and are not even aware of themselves as separate beings."

"Therefore, you could not have a 'we-relationship' with them or a conversation in the strict sense," said Schutz.

"This is an outrage," said Annabelle. "what a barbaric discrepancy between philosophy and actual life. Philosophers have discounted the actual world and can't relate their ideas to birth!"

"You're all wrong," said Victoria. "I would say all wet, except I'm the one in the hot water."

"Even now she is witty," said Wagner.

"I see what she means," said Guy. We are thinking dualistically. It's not mind or body. It's bodymind, mindbody. Its 'being'."

"Word made flesh and flesh made word," said Schutz.

"Flesh and Mind!" said Victoria.

Hilda brought undergarments, kotex, a gown and a robe for Victoria. She dried and wrapped the infants while Annabelle helped Victoria out of the water, holding a towel up to shield her from view by the men. Victoria sponged off, dressed. Hilda wrapped her in the robe, and handed her the babies. They babbled and gurgled, seemingly enthralled with their voices. "They are going to be little singers," said Victoria.

"Or maybe professors," said Annabelle.

"Heaven forbid," said Victoria.

"See fellas, the babies are dominating the conversation that you said they could not take part in," said Annabelle. When she stood up the water level in the spa sank. She sponged off and put on a red bathrobe.

Hilda pushed a switch and drained the water, pink now from the birth blood. Annabelle handed Hilda a covered ceramic pot that was on a side table. "Put the afterbirth in this jar. In Africa we bury it to nourish the crops.

Hilda said something in German. Schutz translated. "She said her grandmother, who was a midwife, did the same."

Guy offered. "I could bury it under a tall pine tree. They are sacred too."

"Yes!" said Victoria. She felt like she was sacred, already in heaven, then the babies started to wail.

"It may be sacred but we aren't in heaven yet. Guess what Victoria. Now it begins, feeding and diapers, feeding and diapers." Annabelle led her to a four poster bed in the adjoining suite.

All three men remained silent following to the door of the suite. "Maybe being in a matriarchal culture wouldn't be so bad," said Wagner.

"Come in, gentleman, but please only for a few moments. Victoria must rest," said Annabelle. Annabelle dried herself off, wrapped herself up with a large robe.

Cars engines sounded from below. Guy walked to the window.

Victoria felt grateful and moved by his presence. "Guy, you really should put an ice pack on your eye," she said.

"Later, it'll be all right," he said.

A voice from the outer door and a knock. "Victoria, are you in there?"

Victoria was relieved. It was George. Guy opened the door. Mead rushed to the bed and kissed Victoria on the forehead. "I went to Charlottenberg hospital where they said you were. They would tell me nothing about you, not even that you were there. I was beside myself. But Schutz was able to get me on his radiophone. Oh my, such beautiful babies. And you are so lovely, darling."

The babies whined.

Victoria said to herself, "I'm alive, I'm whole. I have two sons." The babies nursed contently again. Victoria wondered if George noticed the striking difference between the two boys. She had planned to name the baby, if there were one and a boy, "George" and if a girl, "Annabelle". Now that there are two, as Annabelle had predicted, dare she suggest that the second boy be named "Martin"? Inspired by the miracle of their birth, she braved it.

"George, darling, I wish as planned to name the firstborn of the two, the blond boy, after you.

"I'm delighted, dear, delighted. And the second boy? Perhaps as you worked so closely with Heidegger during your pregnancy, we should name him after Martin."

Victoria could not have been happier, the suggestion she feared to make coming from Mead himself. She must not show too much enthusiasm. "Well as my father's name was also George and I grew up Lutheran, George and Martin also have double meanings for me. What a lovely suggestion." She looked at each boy again. "Yes, we have our names then, little George and little Martin it is."

Cheers from came from the three men in the doorway as well as Annabelle and Katie. "To little George and little Martin!" they said raising their hands as if they held champaign glasses. Victoria felt gloriously happy and fulfilled.

Chapter Forty-Seven
Afterbirth

Victoria's blissful moment as the mother of twin sons was soon interrupted by a loudspeaker from outside the window. A sharp voice said:

"All persons must register with the official party of the Third Reich. All persons must register . . .No one who is not registered is allowed on the streets."

Victoria's mind flashed forward to the curfew at the university during the anti-Vietnam war demonstrations. Police came to the campus, tear-gassed the dorms, arrested the students for violating curfew and took them to large holding tanks that had been made for the occasion. America was not immune to fascism; she had seen it. And American bombs and soldiers killed thirteen million Vietnamese. But that was a time and place yet to be. Maybe if things could be changed the Vietnam war and those that followed could be prevented.

"Anyone harboring an unregistered person must report to the authorities at once or be subject to arrest," the blaring voice continued."

Schutz said, "We must let Victoria rest and make plans. She cannot stay here."

Planes flew close to the rooftops. "Lady Von Humbolt must be in danger for keeping us here," said Victoria.

"No, she has her connections. But they just want to keep us all nervous, fearful," said Schutz.

"And they are successful in this," said Wagner.

Schutz said, "Seeing the babies born renewed my energy. No matter the circumstances, birth is always a miracle. Don't worry. We will get you out as soon as you and the babies can make the trip. There's a lot of money in the transfer of persons to France and elsewhere." Looking at Mead, he added. "If there was really what you called the 'Generalized Other', there would not be war."

Mead cleared his throat. 'The point is, there is a long historical trend, for the 'Generalized Other' to encompass an ever more universal perspective. We started the League of Nations for this purpose, to increase the scope of the Generalized Other. But the forces for money and power are very persistent and powerful."

"For God's sake, let Victoria rest. You all look exhausted. You must take care to rest yourselves so you have the strength to get us out of this hellhole country," said Annabelle.

Helmut, Alfred and Guy put on their coats. Just as they started towards the door there was a loud knock. Guy opened the door and whispered to someone, left the room for a short time, and came back with two envelopes. He stepped forward, holding them with a fist. "Both are marked urgent. One is addressed to Herr Dr. Professor George Herbert Mead, from the office of the Fuhrer, Herr Hitler." He held up the letter, so all could see the gold swastika with the words 'Fuhrer, Soil, Nation, The Third Reich'.

Guy handed this letter to Mead.

Victoria hoped for word from Martin. But the excitement in the room kept her feeling exhalted despite his absence.

Mead opened the letter and read:

The Fuhrer regrets that Frau Dr. Victoria Mead did not find the accommodations at our special military hospital at Charlatenberg Castle satisfactory. He wishes you and your infant health. He welcomes you back to your suite at the Charlantenberg manor where every means will be provided for the comfort of mother and baby. A guard is assigned to you and your entourage to escort you.

With heartfelt wishes,

Adolph Hitler

P.S. Die Frau Mutter also sends her good wishes."

His face turned grey, "We have no choice but to go back for a while," he said.

Schutz interceded, "That Hitler cares enough to write this letter is a good sign that you will be safe at least for now."

Guy added, "Victoria and the babies should not take such an arduous journey at this time in any case."

Victoria did not wish to appear too anxious about the other letter. "The other letter, Guy?"

"It is addressed to Frau Dr. Victoria Von Dietz Mead," from Professor Martin Heidegger." Guy held it up for all to see the seal of the rector of Freiburg university on the back of the envelope.

"Shall I read it for you, Victoria?" said Guy.

Annabelle snatched the letter from him and handed it to Victoria. How she wished Martin were here to hold her, see his son. Victoria's mind raced back to her best times with Martin. Yet upon reflection, their time together was always about his words and their powerful aura.

"Heidegger is sure able to keep track of you," said Mead. His voice was tense, strained.

Schutz came to the rescue. "Mead, come downstairs, Wagner and I need to discuss some arrangements with you."

They started towards the door. Guy stood by the bedside waiting for Victoria to open the letter.

"Guy, we need you too. Come," said Schutz.

Annabelle added, "and take care of that black eye of yours." She turned to Katie and asked her to prepare broth for Victoria.

They all left the room. Victoria let go a sigh of relief. She pulled out the letter from Martin and read:

"Mein Schoene Frau:

Excuse me for addressing you in this way. You are the wife of my deepest heart. I heard you were in labor in Berlin and was on my way there but there was an emergency at the university. Then I could make no connection until Fragenzimmer told me you were at the Lady Von Humbolt's estate.

This is a sacred moment when our essential oneness revealed itself to the world for everyone to see for all time. Do not worry about the obstacles. We will overcome all, one way or another, and be together.

No, this is not the truth. The truth is that we are together even at this moment, now and through eternity. Given the situation, I can assure your safety and the little ones only if I remain here, in the background. Otherwise we are all in danger.

My heart is with you always.

Martin"

Tears streamed down her face. She folded the note carefully and put it in the drawer next to the bed. And yet there was a nagging doubt in her mind. Was Martin better at lofty words than actual deeds?

- The babies slept peaceably like little angels.

The door opened. Hilda came in with a cart with broth and fruit and a bouquet of white roses. They were the largest she had ever seen. They reminded her of Picasso's last painting, which of course he had not yet rendered. She basked in their sweet smell as Hilda placed them on the bedside table.

Victoria read the card:

"In deep appreciation, schoene Deutsche Frau und Mutter, Adolph Hitler."

Victoria was astonished. A surge of hope that she could yet influence him and alter the course of history moved through her. But then she sighed, as she was exhausted and also fearful. So much could go wrong.

Chapter Forty-Eight
Heidegger vs. Mead

Thinking is not inactivity, but that very action
which is in dialog with the world's destiny.
Martin Heidegger, *Was Heist Denken*

The test of intelligence is found in action.
George Herbert Mead, *Movements of Thought in the Nineteenth Century*

A few weeks later, back at Charlottenberg manor, Victoria was wakened from an afternoon nap by a knock at the door. It was Katie, her maid she had loaned to Annabelle. After the birth of the twins, Victoria appreciated having assistance, so she could take naps.

"Frau Dr. Von Dietz, so sorry to disturb you. There is a gentleman to see you downstairs, Herr Professor Heidegger. He is most impatient and insists on coming up. What shall I do?"

Victoria just finished nursing the babies and put them to sleep. Her heart trembled, she felt weak. Somehow things seemed simpler, more normal, with Martin miles away. She felt angry and abandoned that he had not been there when the babies were born nor visited in the weeks since their birth.

Victoria asked Katie to bring Martin into the nursery where she would meet him, but to ask him to please be quiet so as not to wake the babies.

She stood at the window, the afternoon sun glowing softly through the curtains. The boys looked angelic in their cradle. The large cradle for two was hand carved and hand painted Bavarian style. It was a gift from the Frau Mutter Hitler.

The sun struck Heidegger on his face as he entered. He wore a twead jacket and brown wool trousers, with a hand knit sweater. He stood transfixed, looking like Hermes, the gods' messenger. Her anger towards him melted away. "Now you have come," she said.

"My darling, I could not break away. As you know the party is seeking every excuse to take the university completely under their control. They could destroy all of the best of German culture if they succeed. Fragenzimmer reads all of my mail. . ." His voice shook.

He ran to Victoria and held her close. "You are so beautiful," he said, running his hand through her hair. A hairpin came loose and a lock of hair fell over her forehead.

She took his hand and pulled him to the cradle. Heidegger's face beamed with delight.

"Oh, my sons, my darling sons." he said in excited voice. Victoria held a finger to her lips. She hoped Katie didn't hear this, but then if she did maids working at Charlottenberg manor would keep privacy. "They are so fine, so sweet. How glorious," he whispered. He touched each gently on the cheek.

Victoria led him out of the room into the adjoining sitting room.

"Where's Mead?" asked Heidegger.

Victoria wanted to spare his feelings about her and George's continued hope and plans to return to Chicago. But Martin would see through any subterfuge. "He's with Guy and Annabelle, to the Lord Mayor's office, to look into our return home. He'll be back in a half hour or so," she said, trying unsuccessfully to hide the disappointment in her voice.

His face shifted from mellow to troubled. "America is aligning itself with the Bolsheviks! How can you even imagine going back there!"

Victoria raised her chin towards the babies' room. He switched to an emphatic whisper. "The U.S. was never your homeland anyway. Your own great-grandfather's blood saved this land, fighting Napoleon. Now you are going to help America destroy Germany?" Martin's voice was strained, high in his throat. He held her at arms' length; his hands placed on her shoulders. His eyes penetrated her as if her body were a shadow.

"Martin, please, you'll wake the little ones." She gripped his arms. "I'm frightened about what may happen, what is happening. Once you no longer hope that Hitler will change his course, what then?" Victoria said.

She looked into his eyes as they stood facing each other. Victoria took a deep breath and Martin followed. She realized that Kundalini breathing together had become second nature for them. She adored this man who had so changed her life.

Shadows of nightfall crept into the room which became cool as the sun set. She pulled the lapels of her gray wool jacket together over her soft white sweater.

"Here, darling, I'll keep you warm." He pulled her close to him on the sofa. He whispered into her ear. "The most important thing is that we be together. Du bist Deutsch."

She pulled away slightly, put her hands on his knees. "Together, yes, that would be wonderful but in America!' she countered. "Professors, scientists are emigrating to the U.S. Your work would have a big impact there. You can't stay and become a part of what is to come. Please, come with us. Please," she said.

"I'd be deserting the university, my country, my family. I'd be mixing with the displaced hoards from all over the world. Do you think Germany will be any better if ruled by the Russians?"

This was not the time to challenge Martin on his elitism. "The point is to save us, our children," said Victoria.

"You're necessary here. You could help influence Hitler to change the course of things," said Martin.

She directly looked into his rich hazel eyes. "I had hoped so, Martin, really. Hitler felt something for me, welcomed me into his home. But he's driven by forces out of my reach," she said, then doubting her own words, recalling the card, the white roses.

"Nonsense. He's busy making a world war. You could go to him any time, bring him into the sway of your benign yogic goddesses," Martin said.

"There's no getting through to someone as stubborn as you," she turned away from him.

"Or you, thus proving you are a real German," he said pulling her close. He reached behind her and rubbed her back.

He opened her jacket, then unbuttoned her sweater his fingertips gentley caressing her breasts. "Your breasts are lovely, laden with mother's milk. My mother didn't nurse me. She was not well. She found a wet nurse for me but did not like her. She reluctantly accepted Gerda, a Lutheran woman although she had hoped to find a practicing Catholic. It was as if religion went right into the milk." Martin laughed. "'At least she is a devout Christian,' my mother told me. But when she discovered that Gerda's husband was Jewish, she asked her to feed me sterilized goat's milk from a bottle instead. Gerda had become pregnant from a Jew, she said, as if this meant her milk was Jewish, like blood." Martin's eyes were deep and warm and rested on her face.

"We are all sons and daughters of Yahweh. Yet for Christians only Jesus is incarnate. Lots of work for one Jewish boy. There's evidence that Jesus of Nazareth journeyed to Kashmir and Tibet and was inspired by the Vedas of the Hindus," said Martin.

"Jesus' message in the Sermon on the Mount certainly fits Ancient Indian wisdom. For the Hindus, the innermost self of each of us, our Atman, is one with Brahman. We must just recognize this," said Victoria.

His hands still near her breasts he said, "I want to taste your lovely nectar." He bent forward to kiss her breasts. She pulled away, pulled her sweater together over her breasts.

Martin persisted to try to nuzzle her breasts. She stood up. Somehow they were sacred to her and meant only for her sons' nourishment.

"Martin, please," she said.

"They are filled with milk because of me," he said.

"But only for them," she said looking towards the nursery, then into his eyes. His energy softened from desire to acceptance.

"Yeah, I was dense," Martin said. "I of all people should understand the pure and sacred connections between mother and infants. Yet I feel such connection only with you. You are my Goddess," said Martin. They sat together peacefully, holding hands. That part of Victoria still in love with Martin Heidegger let herself fall asleep in his arms.

❧

They woke with a start a while later as they heard footsteps coming down the hallway. "It's George," said Victoria.

Heidegger got up, smoothed his trousers, put his jacket on. Victoria went through to the nursery to check on the babies. She left the door ajar so she could peak out at them and hear their discussion. She hoped George finding Martin here unexpectedly did not rouse his jealousy.

"Herr Heidegger, what brings you to Berlin?" said Mead as he took off his coat, handing it to Katie.

"I have business at the Reich ministry. I've been arranging for all of you to extend your stay. Victoria and I must continue our work together," said Martin. He would find someway to keep her here.

"Humph! Don't be disingenuous. You could have asked us first. I just returned from the Lord Mayor's office to arrange for our return to Chicago." Mead put his hands on his hips. He felt heat rise in his neck. But he resolved to keep his temper for Victoria's sake. He motioned to a chair opposite one he was about to take. This would be a good opportunity to challenge Martin on issues of real importance—their philosophies.

They sat facing each other.

Katie brought them tea and sandwiches. "Dr. Von Dietz asked me to bring you some refreshments, gentleman." Mead was grateful for the relief. How smart of Victoria, he thought. She poured them each a cup. Each took a liverwurst sandwich off the tray. "Dr. Victoria said she would join you after she feeds the infants." She left for the nursery.

Martin took a sip of tea. "Nice and strong. We Germans boil our tea."

Mead lifted his cup. "Victoria and I always make our tea strong, Chicago style," he said. "By the way, Herr Heidegger, your entire hullabaloo about Being." What an egotistical little shrimp head he is, thought Mead.

"What is this 'hullabaloo'?" asked Martin, thinking how to pin this would-be philosopher to the ground.

"Just an American idiom," laughed George, "should we switch to Duetsch?"

"Nein, it makes no difference to me, although philosophy and English are like oil and water." Martin felt one up already.

"Back to my point, about your concept of Being. It is about nothing, Nothing!" Mead said with dramatic emphasis, feeling he had made sharp blow.

Turgid Asshole! thought Martin. "Of course Being is about Nothing—Das Nichts. Being emerges from deep nothing. A French philosophy student, Sartre, made his name by stealing my concept of 'The Nothing' from my *Being and Time*, and calling his book *Being and Nothingness*. Physicists will find these pockets of concentrated Nothing to contain intense power." This academic pipsqueak has nowhere near my influence. Martin knew he won this round. A debate with Prof. Mead will be a piece of kuchen (cake).

Mead needed a pipe to endure more of this pompous son of a bitch. Stuffing and lighting his pipe always gave him time to regroup. This guy knows something about modern science, he thought. Still he acts like a Swinehund.

Martin shifted in his chair, quickly finished his sandwich. Mead is enjoying this, he mused. Rumour has it his students write his books for him based on classroom dialogues. A Jackass, but an interesting fellow. I'll let him dig his own philosophical grave. He took a sip of tea, waiting for Mead's next statement, like a boxer dancing around, waiting for his opponent to swing so he could knock him out from below.

Mead struck a light blow. "Haven't you heard of Occam's razor? Why invent a concept like 'Being' just to explain what we can observe about the human self, mind, the social situation? No wonder you have no concept like my 'Significant Other' You should have called your book Being and Me." he said. He stood up and took a deep drag on his pipe, pacing a bit as if he were about to lecture. Heidegger's speculations are as overblown as his ego.

Peeking through the curtain, Victoria enjoyed her two philosophical loves struggle with each other.

Heidegger's back stiffened. Arrogant Dumkoph! he thought, but controlled his words through gritted teeth. "I'm not trying to explain the human self. I dig into the archeology of knowledge to uncover the nature of Being. When civilizations wax and wane, much of what was known is lost. Being was concealed in the West since 500 BC. Your blindness to Being is symptomatic. 'Man' as a subject arose to prominence only in the 18th century. Then science became so arrogant it decided to kill God and put Man in His place. It is pure unadulterated arrogance to think we are the ultimate end of creation." Heidegger reached under his jacket to where his suspenders would have been and flicked his fingers as if he were snapping them, making a gestural emphasis for his words.

Heidegger's glared at Mead. What could Victoria see in him? Mead drew on his pipe. He felt the heat of anger in his face. "To a point, I agree within you. Spurred on by Watson and his 'behaviorism,' social scientists in American deny there are such things as 'understanding' or even 'meaning'. To them there is only 'behaving'," said George.

Martin gritted his teeth. The man is a goat, an old arrogant goat, and his color pasty. How could Victoria marry him? He spit his words. "Behaviorists were right in moving us toward looking at what is really there, what we can actually see, hear and touch," he said. "But the language they use to describe their observations, takes the emotion and meaning out of life. They replace 'desire' and 'anger' with 'stimulus-response', and 'negative reinforcment'."

George interrupted. "Then we agree on that point! But at least the behaviorists present clear arguments. No philosopher has a reputation for obscurity so much as you, Professor Heidegger." Inside, Mead felt a weakening. He was too old for such an intense encounter. Thinking of Martin pushing his filthy cock on his sweet angel, Victoria, he built up steam. "Yes, there are still actual and real lives involved. Are all lives worthy? What if your Nazi blond beasts like the machine speed worshipers in Italy, convince the world that the more cold and machine-like we humans become, the more evolved we are," said Mead. "Victoria tells me there are (or will be in time ahead) researchers called 'trans-humanists' who seek to 'download' brain wave contents into mind machines so that all is retained, and nothing dies except the body. Like a mechanical brain," said George.

Martin stood up, walked around the tea table and looked out the window at the street below. A cat ran through the courtyard, then jumped on the stone fence and looked up at him. "The Katz down there is an essential manifestation of being," said Heidegger. "Animals are pure. They are simply life. They seek only to eat and play and rest, and when the time comes, they accept death." I despise this Mead for coming into Victoria's world. He clenched his fist and his teeth, looking at Mead.

Mead's hand in his coat pocket opened and closed in a fist. "Nonesense. We have language, animals don't. You've said, 'Language is the house of being," said George. I hate his guts. I hate the thought of Victoria in bed with him.

"Yes we are DASEINs. Dasein is a being who is for, with, from, to, against, with, by, other beings and things. A being thrown into the world is all these relationships. A being whose destiny it is to know about other beings, to uncover Being, or to make a clearing, open up spaces so beings may appear," said Martin.

George bristled. Now the creep is really over the edge. "Sounds like magic," said Mead. He pulled out his pipe and filled it. "We discover what exists through conversation. A gesture calls out the same response in the sender as in the receiver. We create objects by naming them. The meaning of an object is how it is used," said Mead.

Martin interrupted. "Simple everyday events rest upon the presence of Being. We forget about this, or rather, cover it over with concepts, idle chatter," said Martin.

George paced back and forth, his arm held rigidly in his coat pocket, as if he'd smack Martin with it if it were free. What a fucked up guy, he thought. I won't have him raising my sons. "Heidegger, where do you go with all this stuff? What do you have to say about science, ethics, about the nature of the mind?" said Mead.

Heidegger was also pacing, they were like two boxers in a ring. "You draw a parallel between democracy and the way scientific discoveries are made. It should be blatantly clear that democratic processes seldom, if ever, lead to truth. The risk is that the masses can be misled. The risk is rule by the worst or mob tyranny," said Martin.

"To the contrary, only by taking a broad perspective on the situation, taking into account as many perspectives as possible, can we approximate truth. Science takes such a universal perspective," said Mead.

They both stopped short, glaring at each other.

Dumbkoph! "Science is already resting on a fundamental deception or distortion of Being, for it rules out all other forms of reasoning," said Martin. He took hold of Mead's collar.

Katie came in. Mead and Heidegger froze in place. "Please Gentlemen, sit down. Frau Von Dietz has asked the two of you soften your voices. You are disturbing the little ones." They looked at each other sheepishly.

Martin dropped his hand from Mead's throat. "I'm so sorry," he said.

"Just like a dog fight," said Mead, recalling using this example it a lecture on communication. "Tell her we are sorry and we'll be good," said Mead, with a wry smile. "Please, bring coffee and brandy."

Katie left kert nod and a "yes sir," as the two men sat back in their chairs checkmated.

"You must let Victoria and the babies stay here with me. She and they are German and Germany is their home," said Heidegger softly but emphatically.

"How can you even suggest that I leave my wife and children here," whispered George, glaring at Martin. He paused and puffed his pipe. "Legally, I am their father," he added.

"Wrong. All Aryan children born in the Reich belong to the Fuhrer," said Heidegger.

"Our home is in Chicago. Interesting the way 'home' as a significant symbol calls out the same emotions in both of us," said George.

Katie returned with fragrant coffee, brandy, and Apfelkuchen. "If I may say so gentlemen, it is good to see philosophers of such reknown settle their differences amiably. Dr. Von Dietz will be joining you shortly."

Mead and Heidegger relaxed. Mead smiled slightly, amused at the scene they had created. Heidegger took a sip of brandy.

"We both have good taste in women, after all," said Mead. After saying this he realized too late it was not a topic that would promote congeniality with his rival.

Before Martin could offer a rejoinder, Victoria walked in from the adjacent room. She held the two smiling babies. "I just hope the twins don't fight with each other as vehemently as you men do," she said. "By the way, neither of your philosophies make much of the birth process, or for that matter, observations of real children. Martin, you emphasize death and nothingness as the basis of human experience all the while surrounded by women and children, life and fullness. And you take things so seriously. There is no room in either of your philosophies for the most unique aspect of human nature, the sense of humor. And you, George, saying that there is no self until after the child communicates in language. You haven't changed enough diapers to realize what kinds of personalities infants have!" She was proud of herself for saying this.

"Perhaps in my next book I'll assert that the human identity emerges as diapers are changed," said Mead.

"I agree with you on that," said Martin. "Besides it is a good way to address the Scheis in your theories." He sipped again, triumphantly.

'Ah, the missing humor. Thank you. And just to seal our friendship one of the twins are named after each of you. Martin, the dark eyed one, and George, the blue eyed one," said Victoria.

"I like one of the names but not the other," said Mead, smiling.

"We agree on that!" said Heidegger. "And what last name will they carry?"

"Hmmmm. Perhaps Von Dietz," said Victoria.

"As long as it isn't 'Hitler' I'm O.K. with it," said Mead.

Chapter Forty-Nine
Midnight Diaper Madness

G eorge rubbed his eyes as he walked to the cabinet in the hall, pulling out two fresh diapers. The clock on the mantel chimed half past something. Looking up, he saw it was three.

"No need to get up, darling, I'm on my way," he said, somewhat regretting he had said he would handle the babies tonight. Never expected to be doing this at the age of seventy-something, or whatever I am, he thought. Depends if you count the years leaping forward to 1940 something.

The babies whined and gurgled, in a way that meant they soiled their diapers and were hungry. The past weeks of sleeping in three to four hour segments were taking their toll. Until this morning, Victoria or Annabelle were the ones to get up. Today the door to Annabelle's adjacent room was closed. Katie's day didn't begin until 7.A.M. breakfast.

"I've observed this procedure a hundred times. I can manage dear," Mead said to the bleary-eyed Victoria. Light from a small opening in the drapes lit her face. She rubbed her eyes. Mead walked into the bathroom and filled a small basin with warm water, washcloth and towel.

"Dr. Mead," she called, "once you finally get a point you learn fast. Bring them to me for their breakfast when you're done." Mead heard the coverlets swish as Victoria settled back for more rest.

In the bathroom he appreciated that hot water came almost immediately from the wall-mounted gas heater connected to the sink and tub. Germans made things to run much more efficiently than Americans. The water was run on demand through yards of very thin piping, coiled like intestines, reminding him of his irregularity over the past weeks. Stress.

The babies howled.

"So much for sleep," said Victoria. She got up and stood by the cradle, rocking it as Mead filled the basin with water. "I'm sorry, dear, I'm just not very efficient at this." He returned and picked one of them up, carried him into the bathroom and placed him gently on the bassinette table. He removed the soiled diaper and swished it in the toilet bowl, and put it in a pail. He washed the boy's pink bottom, sprinkled him with talcum powder, and reached for a clean diaper on the shelf. He worked the little night shirt over the baby's arms and head, bounced him, and rocked as his cries changed to squeals of delight. "This could be fun if it weren't the middle of the night," he said.

"Don't worry, dear, there are plenty of such opportunities during the day as well," said Victoria, sleepily.

He handed the baby to Victoria, who took him back to bed to nurse. He picked up the other. The baby opened his eyes and looked up at him. "This little one's eyes are going to be brown, to match his hair," Mead said. "Your grandma, Ida, had hazel eyes, did she not, Vicky? Everyone on my side is blue or green eyed like you and me. " The boy smiled up at George and curled his tiny hand around Mead's finger.

Mead felt his heart pound. Am I really up for this, a father again at my age? I snapped into the jealous husband role. I don't need another round of grief. He was always jealous of Helen, his first wife—the attention other men gave her, especially the ones with means he did not have as a professor from a family of clergy and teachers. Yet he was reliving it. The dark-eyed boy must be Martin's. Why did I grill Victoria about whether her grandmother had brown eyes? It's not like this is real time. She is acting out her passion for both Heidegger and me. She doesn't love us for ourselves, but for our ideas, perhaps even our prestige. As a man I could come back at her and say, "You don't really love me, all you care about is my mind." He chuckled to himself. Like all such accusations, it is only part of the truth.

Victoria lives our philosophical struggles, our identity conflicts, limitations as male members of the human race. She embodies our struggles then gave birth, bringing it all to a head. What could be a better setting, situation for this? She gives birth to twin boys in Berlin, with philosopher Alfred Schutz as physician and Annabelle Carter Jackson, a black lesbian feminist, as midwife. She has time traveled. One of the babies is mine, blond and blue eyed, the other Martin's. I know it. It happens with other animals, why not human? One egg fertilized in Chicago, the other after time traveling when she arrived, met by Heidegger's passionate mind and swarthy cock.

"Did you hear me? I said, yes, my Grandma did have brown eyes and brown hair," said Victoria.

Mead did not seem to hear her, absorbed in his thoughts and the diapering process. I'm tired, my life weighs on me. I should be already dead even in this time frame. I crave resolution. I look at Victoria and I want to stay with her forever. It's been over two months since we last made love. Now there are the two boys to share her delicious breasts, brimming with milk. It was never like that with Helen, or any of the others. They always made it seem like they were submitting to me, doing something for me. With Victoria it is beyond that. When we unite it is like the universe returns to the course it fell away from, eons ago, a black eternal tumble into dark space.

Mead laughed sardonically. And all these thoughts I have while handling very real shit. He finished changing the dark eyed boy's diaper and handed him to Victoria.

"You surely don't still think babies don't have a self until they speak, do you George? Little George and Little Martin each have such distinct personalities already." Her disheveled hair fell over her eyes as she kissed the babies.

"Caring for the babies takes the utmost concentration for me. I never was involved with my children in my previous life. If I had been, it would have profoundly changed my theories of the development of self. It does appear that the self begins before birth and intensifies as we look and hold and touch the little ones, respond to cries, diaper them." He had succeeded in hiding his self-doubts and jealousy, drowning them once again in the swamp of theory.

"Mead, darling, it's the music in language that we all respond to, even before birth," she purred, as the babies nursed contently on each breast.

"How I could have been so oblivious is amazing," said Mead. I was so busy philosophizing about the development of consciousness and the self that I missed it happening."

"The damming nature of academic life," said Victoria.

Victoria and the babies were asleep. Mead gently put one child, then the other, back in the cradle. He crawled to bed, held Victoria close. Her body quivered, then she relaxed into a quiet snore. Let her rest, he thought. She used to tell me she had orgasms just being in my presence. It seems she has just had one, judging from that look on her face, like she used to get straddling me in bed, rising and falling on my hard cock, then suddenly moaning. Or should I say singing, her body begging me to penetrate her more deeply.

Was it like that with Heidegger? Perhaps he could keep it up for days, stocked with food on a bedside table, intermittently discussing his next lecture on the destruction of philosophy. It must have happened the night she arrived. He met her in London, she said, and they took the boat over the channel that night. One of her eggs was already fertilized with my son. The other waiting, slightly delayed in her womb, got fertilized that night on the boat from Dover. Oh, those white cliffs. I can see her wearing her long burgundy jumper, silk scarf draped over her neck, wearing the diamond earrings, my mother's. Perhaps Martin pressed her from behind, standing on the deck of the boat, her eyes still dreamy from our love making the night before, her labia oozing last remnants of my milk. Martin would have stood behind her looking out at the channel, the moonlight shining. She would have gasped for air as she felt his large swarthy cock press against the small of her back. He would spin her around and kiss her and they would walk hand in hand down to his compartment, adulterers, swollen with thoughtless passion, because if it were not unthinkable, how could she fall sway to him while barely out of our bed? Stop, stop, my awful mind. This is the madness of Othello, he thought. "Madness!"

Victoria heard him, woke up, said "Darling, what's wrong? You're drenched in sweat."

He couldn't show her his crazy jealousy. "Only having a bad dream, dearest, that's all," he said, striving for a calm voice.

"As if the reality of being in Berlin under Hitler isn't already a nightmare, my love," she said sleepily.

Chapter Fifty
Kirschflasse

A messenger arrived with a note for Victoria. It had a faint aroma of Guy's Bayrum aftershave. He had been away this past month, continuing the underground work with Schutz and Wagner.

"Meet me at 3 P.M. at the Kirschflasse restaurant on Klabberstrasse. Only if you can, of course. Yours as always, Guy."

The words "yours as always" cheered her. Victoria missed Guy more than she had thought she would. 'Hmmm, Kirschflasse. It jingled in her mind with kiss. It's a cherry liquor. Victoria loved the sweet taste of it.

She had been housebound since the babies were born, nearly two months ago. Her emotions swirled the last couple of days. The situation for Americans in Germany was getting more precarious by the day. Victoria had convinced Annabelle that, dressed as a German matron, she could walk inconspicuously a few blocks around the town. They were back in their Charlottenberg suite and well guarded. But then who could trust the allegiance of the guards? There was great unrest. Every person was called upon to be on the lookout for enemies within, as well as foreign "terrorists."

As she opened the door the mid-afternoon sun shone through the maple trees. The limbs were still bare, icicles heavy on the boughs dropping off, becoming slush in the streets, a precursor of spring. She recalled the opening of the third act of Beethoven's *Fidelio*, the glorious song of the prisoners emerging from years in dark dungeons.

A large orange tomcat meowed and brushed between her ankles. She reached down and petted his soft fur. He was plump indicating he had lots of human admirers and was most likely a good hunter. "Poor Tommy, got into a scrap." She noticed the chips out of his left ear.

Turning the corner she saw a man half a block behind her. Perhaps it was just Annabelle having her followed. Still it felt good to walk around the city a bit, like a normal person, returned post-partum to her normal size and weight. Only the constant flow of military vehicles and men in uni-form reminded her of where and when she walked. She longed to be back in Chicago with Kathy. She knew Kathy would have been a wonderful big sister and a willing helper with the babies. She had figured out how to bring Kathy to her, but she did not know that Kathy would fare well with the shock of time travel at her age. She had to make due with the occasional phone calls that she could get to work. She had spoken with Kathy last time about psychic connections as she could also always tune in to Kathy, sending her love and support. Kathy had learned meditation and yogic breath as a young child. She did not share this aspect of the time travel with her. No way did she want her to experiment and end up who knows where, especially here in Nazi Germany.

A man with wonderful shoulders stood next to a large black Mercedes on the winding street about fifty feet ahead of Victoria. She felt a warm rush. It was Guy. He held open the car door. A slight woman got out. She had auburn hair, about shoulder length. He placed his hand on the woman's back and the two of them walked up the street. The woman wore a fitted black coat of soft fabric, which tied at her waist. Who is she? Guy hadn't said anything about a woman.

Guy and the woman walked on another fifty feet. The woman looked up at him several times. Each time the wind blew her hair back under her black beret. They stopped under a sign with a large cherry tree painted on it, saying "Kirschflasse". Guy opened the door and waited for the woman to enter. He glanced to his left and right and saw Victoria coming. He smiled and motioned to her to come with his right hand. His coat was not buttoned. It hung loosely over his left arm, still wrapped from the bullet wound.

Victoria's stomach shot up into her throat. She knew her jealousy was totally unreasonable. Guy needed to find someone, to fall in love. It would be better for him. He has been obsessed with me for so long. But, what would she do without him, now? What if he decided to stay in Europe? She hated her, whoever she is. And wouldn't you know it, a petite brunette. Probably one of those clingy housefrau types. Victoria's heart pounded as she entered the Kirschflasse.

The air was thick with cigarette smoke and the smell of Turkish coffee. Murals on the wall featured cherry trees in all seasons, with little elfin figures enjoying them. The elves danced on one wall under the blossoming trees in spring, climbed ladders to harvest them in summer, squeezed them into Kirschflasse bottles in fall, and looked out from a cozy cottage window at cherry trees covered with snow in winter, holding their liquor glasses high. The atmosphere alluded to a time when all was right with the world, but when could this time have been? Victoria wondered.

There were small ornate lamp scones on the wall. Beneath them hung several coats and scarves, smelling of dampness, drooping on long hooks. A small hearth warmed the room.

Victoria saw Guy and the woman seated at a table to the right of the hearth. The woman had her back to the door, her hair hanging down over a red cashmere dress. Guy stood, erect and handsome despite his bandaged left arm. Had his smile changed? Was the same sparkle in his eyes?

When Victoria arrived at the table he kissed her hand, then kissed both her cheeks, Hungarian fashion. The woman remained seated, looked her up and down.

"You are being followed," Guy whispered. "A man down the street stopped when you came in."

She felt a century younger being near him. The situation did not allow for the long hug she needed. "One of Annabelle's, I hope," she said.

"I thought I had met all her agents," he said.

"I doubt if Annabelle or her compadres would let this happen," said Victoria as Guy pulled out a chair for her.

"Victoria, this is Frau Kolya Hullerst." Frau Hullerst, Dr. Von Dietz."

"Just Kolya is best for me," said Frau Hullerst, brushing her silky hair back behind her ear.

"Vielen Danke, Kolya. Do call me Victoria. And please, I'm so very sorry about your loss," said Victoria. Remembering this she felt shame for her jealous thoughts. Guy was doing the right thing to befriend her, the widow of a great thinker of the time.

Kolya was a fading beauty, which somehow made her more intriguing. There were gray streaks around her temples and forehead. Her face was chiseled, expressive, with high cheek bones. When she raised her eyebrows, deep furrows marked her forehead. Her hand quivered slightly as she took a silver cigarette case out of her black handbag, flicked it open and held it out to share. Both Victoria and Guy refused. She pulled out a cigarette with long white fingernails and placed it in a short ivory carved filter. Victoria reminded herself that this was a time before widespread concern for depletion of the elephant population.

"You both surprise me with your austerities," said Kolya. Guy reached for matches on the table and lit her cigarette. She put her palm gently over his when he held the match to her. As she sucked in the smoke, creases like sunrays on a child's drawing, marked her face.

"At a time like this, it is best if you don't deprive yourself of small satisfactions," said Guy.

"Yes, that's what I told myself while pregnant and drinking sherry," said Victoria, smiling. When Kolya looked puzzled, Victoria said, "Oh, nutritionists in America believe pregnant women should not drink alcohol for the sake of their babies."

"Nonesense," said Kolya. "Pregancy requires fortification." She blew her smoke over Victoria's head.

The door of the cafe opened. A man of medium height with a grey hat came in, put a hand in his overcoat pocket, walked to the bar.

"That's the man," said Victoria, trying to appear uninterested.

"All this intrigue is so exhausting," said Kolya. She placed her left hand over Guy's, as if to balance herself. She does a good 'Fragile Woman', thought Victoria. Something irresistible to Guy, a Rescuer.

An old waiter with a limp came to the booth, smiling. "Hello, Herr Guy. What will I bring you and the two charming ladies?" he winked at Victoria, then Kolya. "At mid-afternoon we have only drinks and snacks. For a meal you must come back after five."

"Ya, Harry, I know, but your snacks are wunderbar," said Guy.

"Not so gut now, we are short on sausages, food is rationed for the soldiers Aber today I have cheeses and cherry Kuchen Mein Frau made fresh this morning," said Harry.

"We'll have the cheeses and Kuchen by all means, along with coffee for three," said Guy. "Oh, and some brandy as well, Bitte."

"Bitteschein," said Harry as he turned.

Looking at Kolya, Victoria said, "I thought you were to have gone on to Geneva with the others."

"They were making a fuss about the numbers," said Kolya. "It was safer for my in-laws to go without me, and less risky in the long run for me to take on a new identity before I leave. Or so says Dr. Schutz and his tall handsome skier friend, Wagner." She rose from the table, lifted her handbag. Touching Guy on the knee lightly she said, "Powder my nose, darling," and swept to the back of the room.

Guy reached across the table and grabbed Victoria's hands. He pulled them to his mouth and kissed them. "I love you," he said.

Stunned by what he said, she talked past it. "What is she doing here?" she said.

"As Frau Hullerst said. We're hoping to get passage for her with a new group. Less conspicuous."

"Why didn't she go on with her parents and family?" Victoria was breathing deeply, a tear in the corner of her eye. I didn't realize I love him this much. Guy is real. Mead, Martin, even the babies are a dream, she thought.

"What's the matter, Victoria," said Guy.

"I'm jealous of her and you. I know its absurd."

Guy moved his chair toward Victoria, put his arm around her and held her close. "That's such good news, Victoria. But do you know your own heart? Even your marriage, your affair, are not enough to keep me away. You are my dearest. That's why I'm here, following you through time, back to this hellhole." Guy looked down, then up at her.

Tears ran down her cheeks. "But that woman!" she said nodding towards the ladies' room.

"Like you, I'm pulled into a boiling pot of destiny. You of all people should understand."

"I do understand, but it still is so difficult. Oh, to have one life again in one time." She looked up and squeezed his hand. She could not press back her tears.

"There are reasons beyond ourselves, pulling us forward," he said. "Whatever time or space, I'll always love and protect you. You'll understand someday that I'm real. The others loves of the head, I'm of the heart." Guy moved his chair back into place.

Harry returned with a tray. He placed coffee mugs and a small glass on the table for each of them, then bowls of sugar and cream. He put a decanter of brandy on the table and a pot of coffee. He poured each of them brandy, then coffee. "First things first," he said. "Madam, is everything all right? he said, looking at Victoria.

Victoria assumed a cough behind her handkerchief. "Ah, yes, I'm just catching a cold. The coffee and brandy are just what I need," she said, she sniffled, then wiped her eyes.

"I'll be back with the cheese and kirsche kuchen," he said.

Kolya returned, her face freshly powdered, smelling of flowers. "I hope you two havn't been plotting to run off together, at least not without me."

Victoria tried to soften her glare into a chortle. "There's much that must be done. I wanted to tell you, I personally regret your husband's death. I've been in awe of his work for some time."

"Vielen Danke." She took a quick sip of brandy, then changed the subject. "Did you know I had met your husband, Professor Mead, years back when he was a student?" She took out another cigarette, waited for Guy to light it. Blowing the smoke over Guy's head, she continued. 'George Mead came to study with Wundt. I met him first in Heidelberg at Max Weber's gathering. There were wonderful musical evenings attended by philosophers, scientists, students, politicians. Wundt came a few times, but he was always nervous, restless. We all delighted in the intriguing charm of the aging Professor Dilthey and his philosophy. He was quite involved with the arts, espousing the 'lived experience' ".

Guy snickered, "As if there could be any other kind."

"George was quite influenced by Wundt's methods of building theory from minute observations," said Victoria.

"Maybe that's why he was so restless," laughed Guy. "He thought you always had to be doing something to be real. But isn't that where Hullerst said Wundt went wrong?

"I don't know, since my husband was obsessed with describing the obvious in infinite detail," said Kolya, blowing a column of smoke in Victoria's face.

"He was called in America, 'the philosopher of unending tasks'," said Victoria, waving the smoke back toward her, "but he described the details of how consciousness constitutes objects, all objects. Whereas Wundt paid little attention to consciousness."

"Philosopher of Unending Tasks. That does describe Edmund. Who in the world came up with that?" said Kolya.

Realizing that Fratensen's book on Hullerst had not been written yet, Victoria said, "some American journalist, can't remember his name."

Noticing Guy's rapt attention as he stared at Kolya, Victoria felt her heart quicken.

"'Unending tasks', sounds like you are talking about me," said Harry. He arrived at the table with a plate of sliced cheese and rye bread, and three slices of kirsche kuchen oozing with juice. He placed a small plate, fork and napkin in front of each of them.

"This is lovely, Harry," said Victoria, "and may your time off be coming soon."

"Ah, nicht until after dinner," said Harry. He poured each of them more coffee and brandy. "By the way, Herr Guy, the gentleman over across the way, when I asked him want he wanted, he said to give him the same thing I gave you. Then he asked how often I've seen Dr. Victoria here."

Guy turned pale. "I hope you said, "never before." The man in grey was studiously looking down at a newspaper, while eating bread and sausage.

"These days, I never know anything, never recognize anyone," said Harry.

Guy reached in his pocket and slipped a ten-mark note under a napkin on Harry's tray. "I'm glad you understand," said Guy.

"Anything else, ladies?" said Harry.

"It wouldn't be right to come here without having a Kirschflasse," said Kolya. "Please bring one for each of us."

"Certainly my lady, perhaps that is where you get the auburn tint in your hair," said Harry.

"No, at my age the color is also from a bottle, but in a beauty parlor, not a bar," said Kolya.

"However you get it, the color is becoming," said Guy.

Victoria felt another cramp. What is he doing? He professes enduring love for me, yet compliments her on her hair color.

Kolya brushed her fingers down Guy's arm, left them there. "Now, tell me this plan for getting us to freedom."

Wagner and Schutz and I will escort you with the next group by car out of Berlin, then by train to Geneva. Victoria, Mead, Annabelle and the babies will stay here until we come back for them. Fragenzimmer will probably try to extort more money. Helmut is arranging for his colleagues in the underground to be on border patrol to prevent what happened last time," said Guy.

"Annabelle wants us out, but also wants us to complete our work here first," said Victoria.

Harry returned with the cherry liquor on a small silver tray and placed it before Kolya with a crocked bow. "Harry serves with the flair of a waiter at Berghoff's in Chicago," said Victoria. "Although now that I think of it, Hitler's villa is called 'The Berghoff'', just coincidence, I'm sure."

"I wish we were at the Chicago Berghoff's now," said Guy.

"I look forward so much to seeing your country," said Kolya gazing at Guy.

Victoria was disgusted. "I struggle to know what my true country is," she said. "Germany is where I have the deepest roots, but I grew up in Chicago. My family will be fighting against itself. And my babies are claimed by the Reich."

Speaking of your babies, Victoria, I know you were working closely with Martin Heidegger. I ran into him the other day," said Kolya. "He was once a student of Edmund's you know. Hard to tell what side he's on. His own, I suppose. You know he signed a paper reassigning Jewish professors, which meant to the camps. Even Edmund, who helped him get his professorship, was taken." She swallowed, looked down, then at Victoria. "Martin seemed to be obsessed with you, your work together. He even mentioned your babies, going on and on about them being German, born in Germany. He is so deep, intense."

"Of course, Martin wants us all to stay," said Victoria. She wondered if Kolya had been more than friendly with Martin. "You know, Kolya, that Martin was under great pressure to sign those papers. Had he refused he would have lost his position as Rector. And worse things would then have been possible.

"Hmm, well there is much discussion about this. We shall see," said Kolya.

"Martin did believe in Hitler for a while," said Victoria. "He saw Hitler as someone who would lead Germany out of the quagmire it was in after world war one. He didn't want to see Germany sink, become part of Russia. Now he just wants to hold things together at the university as long as he can, keep them from getting worse until the war ends."

"I know that's what he tells you," said Guy. "If Heidegger is deep, I'm unfathomable. I grew up in England of Italian immigrant parents and we all moved to Chicago when I was a teenager." He took a sip of Kirscheflasse and licked his lips.

"That's where you get the exotic combination of swarthy handsomeness and British refinement," said Kolya smiling. She slid her hand off Guy's arm.

A cuckoo clock on the wall clucked as a little Tyrolean man and lady emerged.

"Does that clock remind you of him, in his lederhosen?" said Kolya.

"I saw him in them only once, with his friend Fetzer," said Victoria. "But the little Bavarian dancers remind me I must be getting back. My little ones will be hungry. Guy, when shall we see you and Schutz?" She wanted to ask him when she could see him, alone. She added. "I am seriously behind on my manuscript work without your assistance."

Guy's forehead creased. "Vicky, it is best for us to stay apart. Now that Hitler himself has forbidden your passage, for anyone to see you with Schutz would put you both in danger. Annabelle will know when and where you should go next."

Victoria felt a deep emptiness without Guy nearby. "I do hate having my freedom impinged upon," she said, sipping the last drops of her Kirscheflasse. "This liquor is wonderful. How can a culture that makes this make fascism as well," she said.

"The Nazis don't make it, the elves do. And you haven't seen too many of them around anymore," said Kolya. She held up her Kirschflasse glass and twirled it around in her fingers, then finished it. "No one here knows who I am. I'll come by and see you tomorrow," Kolya said to Victoria.

What did this manipulative little vamp want of her? Victoria wondered. Guy raised his eyebrows.

"I want to see new life, perhaps my last chance to see babies." Kolya answered their unasked question with what seemed a subtrafuge. But Victoria would find out tomorrow.

"Till tomorrow, then Kolya, about 2 PM?" said Victoria, standing. "I must go, time for the little ones' feeding soon."

Guy helped with her coat. He hugged and kissed her. The two women shook hands, staring coldly at each other. Victoria strode out, feeling like she left the tenderest part of her behind.

The man at the bar tossed down his cherry liquor and left a few seconds later.

Chapter Fifty-One
Guy's No Woman

Victoria was surprised to see Kolya at the door to their suite at Charlottenberg manor promptly at 2 P.M. the next afternoon. She half expected Kolya to cancel, in order to focus her energy on Guy. But then, maybe this was Kolya's way to do just that.

The twins were fed and cradled for their afternoon nap, in the parlor with Annabelle and Victoria. Katie had just brought in tea.

Victoria stood, motioning Kolya to a chair. Annabelle stayed sunk in the sofa. Victoria introduced her to Annabelle, as Queen Okubiko as well as head of a U.S. Office of Research.

"There's a third cup there, Madam," said Katie, still holding Kolya Hullerst's coat. " I thought Professor Mead may be coming."

Victoria dismissed Katie, saying she'd pour. "Kolya, do you take lemon, cream?" asked Victoria. Kolya looked sexy in a red tailored suit that fit her slender frame perfectly. She pictured Kolya sleeping with George when he was a student, then with Martin, and now with Guy. The thought of Kolya with Guy stung the most.

"Straight, please. I like it straight and strong," said Kolya.

Victoria wondered if the double meaning was intended. Her hand shook slightly as she placed Kolya's cup on the table beside her.

"And you know me, Girl," interjected Annabelle. "I like it soft and sweet. Three lumps, one-third cream and no lemon." She looked at Victoria on the "cream" and Kolya on the "lemon".

Victoria poured Annabelle's tea, then her own. She reflected on her own character. Was she no better than Kolya, who wore men like notches on a belt? No, this was not it at all for her. Victoria was no vamp. She was living as authentically as she could amidst these warped temporal worlds.

Annabelle took a sip of tea, licked her lips. "Perfect, just as I like it." She looked at Kolya. "Frau Hullerst, I'm sorry about your loss. Your husband was a great philosophical pioneer. Frankly, I could never get through more than a few pages at a time."

Kolya replied with surprising energy. "Edsey tried to turn Western thinking around, but his students, some who you know well, Schutz, and Heidegger, took my husband's work in different directions."

Annabelle snapped back. "Both, like most of the philosophical patriarchy leave women out of the picture."

Victoria chimed in, happy that the conversation had shifted from personal tragedy to feminist ideas. "Not all of them. Karl Jung believed men could not fully realize themselves until they recovered the feminine within— their anima, as he called it.

"Ah," said Kolya. "But the anima, the feminine for Jung is like God making Eve out of Adam's rib in Genesis, making woman imaginary from men's psyche's."

"Only as a part of himself, from within, could women be powerful, goddesslike," said Victoria.

"Yes, and not a real goddess, a mythological one," said Kolya, taking the cup and saucer in her long fingers, sipping the tea and finding it too hot.

"Meanwhile popular culture reduced young women to Barbies or Playboy Bunnies or older women to cow-bitch-mother-wives." Annabelle frowned. Victoria realized her temporal error, too late.

Kolya wrinkled her brow. "Bunnies? Barbies?"

"Ah, these are cartoon personalities in U.S. movies," said Victoria, casting a quick glance at Annabelle.

Victoria realized that although she and Kolya were very different outwardly, they bore a strange resemblance. Always excited by such realizations, she decided to bring it out. "Kolya, you are like me, turned inside out," Victoria said. "I loved George Mead's philosophy, worshipped his ideas. I used philosophy as a shield from real life relationships. You came from the opposite direction, inwardly despising their ideas, but using their bodies. Both of us lost ourselves."

Kolya glared at Victoria with eyes and mouth wide open. Victoria's candor had caught her off guard.

"You speak straight and strong, just like your tea," Kolya said. "But surely, being married to Mead has healed the gap for you?"

Was Kolya testing her out, clearing the path to Guy?

Kolya looked down at the babies in the cradle. "The little boys are darling," she said, rocking the cradle gently. She sat down on the soft sofa, took a sip of her tea. "Have you named them yet?"

Victoria was tempted to lie and say no, but this was not her nature. "Martin and George, of course, after my two favorite philosophers," said Victoria, grinning broadly.

Kolya raised her eyebrows, then laughed. "Yes, and like their namesakes, one is dark the other light—I like that."

"Kolya at least had a good time with the guys," said Annabelle, reaching for a piece of streusel coffee cake. She took a bite, licked her lips, looked Kolya up and down, sipped her tea.

Kolya gripped her cup so tight her hand went white. She was gaunt in a Vogue-anorexic way, hipbones distinct in her tight skirt, ribs showing under small breasts.

"Brilliant, fascinating men came in droves to visit Edmund seeking to become part of his circle. But how awful to be 'Frau Hullerst'. You're right, Victoria, like a cow," said Kolya.

Annabelle's eyes opened wide.

Kolya continued. "Yes! I enjoyed seducing them. Disgusting how Edmund's best friends and most devoted followers loved to go to bed with me upon the slightest suggestion on my part. It gave vent to their secret envy, even hatred for the power of the 'great man'. It made them outdo themselves in bed, striving to be better than Edmund. I ran Edmund's social life, invited all guests, screened all company. They justified their behavior by speaking of Edmund not being able to get into his body enough to satisfy me. One of them told me they counted how many invitations they got to our home for soirees. If a graduate student got several of them, he would boast of being on my hot-list. Of course I did not invite any of the ugly, boring or uncharming ones more than once."

"Reminds me of the bachelor elephant seals on the West coast of California," said Annabelle, "assaulting the king bull's harem while he is sleeping."

"Speaking of young bulls, I thought you and Professor Mead kept Guy around to assist you," said Kolya looking towards the doorway to the dining and kitchen areas.

'Sorry to disappoint,' said Annabelle. "We keep him busy in necessary assignments helping escapees."

Victoria reached for the jar of honey, white porcelain with a border of a green vine and blue daisies. She opened it and with the silver spoon put a small amount into her tea. Who was this woman, Kolya, anyway? And what did she want from Guy? Could it be that we have both finally cured ourselves, Kolya by flooding herself with their sex, me by devoting myself to the ideas of the great men whose minds I worshiped? Could it be that now as we are maturing to a truer self, we both need the same man, Guy?

Kolya, it seemed was having parallel thoughts. She brushed her hair back over her left ear. "I gave them my body for a few hours, or a night if Edmund was away." She looked directly at Victoria. "But you gave them your entire work, your mind, your ambition, your soul." Kolya's voice was harsh and hollow, like a kettle beaten by a dried wooden spoon. She looked into her teacup. "My life was otherwise boring, non-consequential," she added.

Partly to deflect her own pain, Victoria asked, "Who was the man in Berlin, who gave all those marvelous lectures?" interjected Victoria.

"Simmel, Georg Simmel," said Kolya. He was also Jewish, never got a tenured professorship, though hundreds poured into his lectures. Oh, Georg, yes quite a character, and raconteur, he was. After I heard him lecture once on romantic love and saw the hundreds of fashionable women hounding him, I sent him an invitation. He came. We met. And we had a few wonderful hours. But he had sipped the poison of male arrogance. It blinds men. They can't ever see actual women once they've ingested it." Kolya took a cigarette from her little silver case, and a gold lighter.

"Girl, you just needed some recognition, some power of your own," said Annabelle.

"Until lately I thought I could never really be in love," said Kolya.

Victoria's heart raced. Kolya is really in love with Guy and he's young enough to be her son, protective enough to be her father and he came around her right at the time of her loss. Powerful for her, she mused.

"Such a sexy smoking apparatus!" said Annabelle.

Kolya struck the lighter, pulled on the filter with puckered lips, then blew a thick cloud over their heads. "I never get the lighter out when men are around. They seem to enjoy lighting me so much, and it gives me a chance to see how much I can make them squirm."

Victoria flashed back to the restaurant when Kolya stroked Guy's wrist as he lit her cigarette. She felt a cold shiver in her stomach. She forced herself to deflect the feeling. "I remember reading Simmel's work on romantic love," said Victoria. "Speaking of desire, Simmel believed men and women bore innate differences. He said that when a man has sex, he has sex, whereas when a woman gives her body to a man, she also gives her soul."

"Hmmph!" Kolya took a deep drag. 'Obviously not true in my case," she said.

"Simmel was an unadulterated ass to say such nonesense," said Annabelle. "Actually it's only when a woman gives her body to a woman that she can give her soul." She sat up from her lazy comfort in the large stuffed chair. The coffee cake on the tea table in front of her was half gone, crumbs having tumbled from the plate onto the black lacquered table. Annabelle reached for another piece and engulfed it with her mouth.

Kolya raised her eyebrows as if evaluating the possible truth of this assertion. "No one should give away her soul. See what happened to Faust?" She took a drag, blew smoke in the air, then put it out in the ashtray beside her.

"On the other hand, Simmel was half right," said Victoria. "It's natural to adore the man or woman you make love with. False teaching, and narrow research monographs, such as Masters and Johnson's, have distorted sex, separating it from the truly erotic. They have taught men to recklessly throw their own genes into places of thorny sorrow, sewers of Angst and perfumed pits of despair." She lifted her cup to her lips and emptied it. This honey tea is just what I need, she thought. I also need strong arms to hold me and help to raise my boys. But whose?

"Watch out how you characterize your sister's pussies," said Annabelle. "I'd love to hear you two compare notes on what they were like as lovers, Mead, Heidegger." She smiled as she stuffed another piece of streusel into her mouth.

"Annabelle, don't get too nosey. I'd rather compare this streusel with Gastreich's in Chicago, with their brown sugar crumb topping about half as thick as the entire cake," said Victoria pouring herself a second cup of tea and breathing in the aroma.

"Actually, I wouldn't mind comparing their performance. But honestly, between the sheets they all feel pretty much the same," said Kolya, helping herself to a piece of coffee cake.

"All equally hopeless," said Annabelle.

"Dichotomous thinking in regards to men and women gets us nowhere, as we can see from Simmel's mistakes," said Victoria. She smoothed her burgundy wool and silk blend skirt. Kolya's gaunt figure made her feel huge, her stomach still not back to normal.

"Your figure is remarkable considering you gave birth to twins recently," said Kolya.

"Its nice to have a lap again," said Victoria.

"The only time men can't see their laps is from weight lifting—heavy beer steins," said Annabelle.

"There you go male bashing again," said Victoria.

"Girl, remember how heavy the yoke of oppression has been and still is for women. It can't hurt to be biased in the other direction for a while to help bring back the balance," said Annabelle. "When women owned land and property, the economies they built took care of children, of the earth and all the creatures."

"Annabelle is so right," said Kolya. "Back in pre-ancient Europe, under matriarchal culture, even men were happier because they could devote themselves to hunting, war games, fishing and telling tall tales."

"Correct," said Victoria. But my direct experience says women also can be tyrannical, abuse power. Take for example Nurse Beektoff, who nearly killed me."

Annabelle interrupted, "I never meant to imply that there are no filthy, despicable, disgusting women!"

Kolya stood, her face red, " I know you're talking about me. I am a soulless slut." Tear flowed down her cheeks. "Well, you are right, you are right."

"Hold on there, Kolya. We all have our flaws. I'm a tyrant and Victoria an adulteress," said Annabelle. "We each of us is coping the best we can with the cards that we were dealt."

Kolya sobbed. Annabelle walked over to her and put her arms around her. "That's all right, Girl. We all do things at times we don't know why," Annabelle said.

Kolya held onto Annabelle and continued to cry. Annabelle patted her back gently.

"Kolya, you are a beautiful and brilliant. Yes, still, at your age. I should say, <u>especially</u> at your age. You don't have to prove it to anyone." She put her hands on Kolya's cheeks, turned her face up. She looked Kolya straight in the eye and smiled.

The babies stirred. Victoria went to them and rocked the cradle.

"Oh, I've got to change their diapers," she said. Victoria thought about her own ethical challenges, leaving a daughter behind, giving birth to two babies from different fathers, flirting with Hitler and contemplating whether to murder him.

Kolya rested her head on Annabelle's breast. Annabelle's face shone with pleasure.

Kolya's sobbing subsided she said, "It goes back to my mother. She had no time for me. She was cold, always involved with her charity affairs or with men," she said.

Annabelle stroked Kolya's back. "You need more mothering, Girl," she said. "Just soak it up, there's plenty more where this comes from."

"It seems there must be more to it than that," said Victoria, as she changed baby George's diaper.

"Don't badger her, Vicky," said Annabelle.

"That's O.K.," said Kolya, drying her eyes on Annabelle's flowing purple kurta. "She's right. One day I was left in the care of my elder brother when I was about twelve years old. My father was a doctor, my mother a nurse, the stereotypical bourgeois family. My brother, then sixteen, had invited a couple of friends over. My brother and Carl went out to get some bread and cheese, and to the music store. The third boy, Jeremy, stayed behind. He said he wanted to look over my brother's library. He was tall and dark-haired, with hazel eyes. He came into my room, took a knife out of his jacket, and told me he'd kill me if I didn't undress. After it was over, he told me he'd deny everything and kill me and my dog if I told anyone. I was ashamed. Frightened. My father sensed something was wrong the next day when they returned. I told my girlfriend Shelley, who insisted we must tell my mother. She said she would come with me. We told mother. Mother sat silent for a minute. Then she laughed. She shouted that Judge Bloomberg's boy would never do anything like that. She slapped my face for lying and warned me not to speak of such things again. I didn't. A week later my dog was missing. I got a call from Jeremy saying the dog was a warning to me not to talk. Next day Sheffie's body was found in the street. My father said it looked like his throat had been slit before he was run over. Most mysterious, he said."

"It angers me so much to think of someone raping and terrifying a child and abusing an innocent animal. I hate such people," said Victoria.

Kolya sobbed on Annabelle's chest. Victoria, still holding little George in one arm, walked back to the cradle to pick up little Martin.

"That's O.K., Girl, That's O.K.," said Annabelle continuing to stroke Kolya's back and hair.

"I only feel good with women, that is until I met Guy. He's brilliant but it doesn't stop there. He listens. He takes action. I've been hanging around with men who live in their heads most of my life," said Kolya.

"Guy's wonderful, but he sure is no woman," said Annabelle.

Victoria's stomach churned. She made playful faces at little Martin.

Kolya got up, walked to the mirror, took a compact from her bag and powdered her nose. "I must be getting back," she said. She put on her long camel coat and black beret. "Don't know when I'll see you again. Or if. We're off to Geneva anytime, hopefully tonight," she said.

"Aufwedersehen," said Victoria.

"You can call on me should you need anything. Guy knows how to contact me," said Annabelle. "We are friends now, and 'Freunden' in Germany means for life."

Chapter Fifty-Two
Annabelle's Undercover Story

"Guy, oh Guy" she said. He kissed her and held her in his arms. She put her leg over his thigh as they lie side to side. She opened her eyes slightly. No Guy under her thigh. She had been dreaming of Guy, the only man in her life who was real. In her dream, Mead and Heidegger faded back into the pages of their books. She dozed off again.

After a while Victoria opened her eyes as a ray of sunlight, refracted into its rainbow colors, came through the beveled glass windowpane. A soft eiderdown floated over her. She closed her eyelids. Lord Krishna, blue skinned and playing his flute, danced. "Beloved Guru, there are no living mortals who can bring me the ecstasy I feel when you come close to me," she said to him silently. The sun on her face drove away the image. She loved this space between sleep and awake, one of the "multiple realities" Schutz wrote about. "Am I dreaming or awake? If dreaming, will I wake up back in Chicago with Kathy? Is all of the stuff with Mead and Heidegger and the Nazis just a long dream turned into a nightmare?"

A wave in the mattress told her she was not alone. The body next to her was big. Interesting the way the weight of another felt in a bed. This body was heavy, but not tall, like George. If it was Martin she would feel more, already be sharing her reveries on Krishna. Besides, she had never slept the night with Martin. Guy could not be here. He was helping George, Schutz and Wagner arrange their escape.

It was clear. She was more deeply anchored to Guy than George. She depended more on Guy for her daily flow of energy, for keeping everything together. Besides, George had had a life, living now by some warp of time beyond his lifespan. Guy was in his prime, first time around. Were these thoughts of Guy inflamed by jealousy, competition with Kolya? No, this was not her nature . . .or was it? She had been intensely angry at Tom's betrayal as well as jealous of George's affection for his Chicago friend and colleague, the esteemed Jane Addams.

The lump stirred. A large brown arm emerged and reached over Victoria.

"Annabelle!" she was shocked, repulsed.

"It's all right Honeygirl, nothin happened. You're not ready for it, in more ways than one." Annabelle licked her lips revealing her perfect white teeth, except for the gold crown, shining when Annabelle smiled.

Victoria shook her head. Waking up in bed with Annabelle was bazaar. Perhaps she was still asleep. The pain in her neck and shoulders told her she was indeed awake. "Where are we? Where are the babies?" she asked, sitting up.

"They're fine, asleep in their cradle. Here, darlin, rest a bit more." Annabelle stuffed a large pillow behind Victoria's head.

"Where are we, where's George? said Victoria, brushing her hair off her forehead.

"Remember? We're at a house of Fetzer's. In Steinmertz. Schutz brought us here in the middle of the night. That's all you need to know. George left with them to make arrangements for our journey home. You were fearful and agitated. I gave you a strong herbal tea once we arrived."

"Oh, yes," Victoria sighed. She was so weary from the intensity of her lives in several time zones that at times she was not quite sure which was real and which was a fantasy. Compound this with Annabelle's tribal tea and her sense of reality was shaky.

Annabelle reached under the covers and put her hand on Victoria's belly. "You're belly's almost back to normal."

Victoria pushed Annabelle's hand away. "Annabelle, you know I care for you, as a friend, colleague, advisor, guide. But I don't have romantic leanings towards women."

"Girl, I'm sorry. I just can't seem to keep my hands off you. I could make you feel so good. But don't worry, it's too soon after the birth anyway." Annabelle pulled back, folded her hands above the eiderdown.

"Annabelle, I feel invaded, with you in bed with me like this," said Victoria. She got up and covered her bronze pajamas with her white cashmere robe. "Please call down for tea, I still feel so weary."

"All right, Vicky. But you cried out for help, screamed out, in the middle of the night. Some man was out to get you in your dream. You yelled, "get away, go away, leave me alone!" Remember my holding you? You were shaking all over, in a cold sweat."

Annabelle got up, put on a black robe over her white flannel nightgown, opened the door and called down the stairs: "Katie, bring tea and fresh juice, sausage, eggs and toast."

"Yes, Madame, anything else?" came Katie's small voice.

"Yes, plum jam!" Annabelle came back into the room.

"I'm glad Katie is still here. Schutz and Wagner are arranging for her to leave, but not with us. She'll be a lot less conspicuous that way," said Annabelle.

"Yes, you know her brother has already been taken to a work camp with her father who is Jewish," said Victoria. "Her mother who is not Jewish escaped under an assumed name to Paris last month."

Annabelle sat on the bed. "Vicky, you're a brave woman. You gotta face the male demons inside of you sooner or later. Why not now?"

Inexplicable, how both soothed and energized I feel, Victoria mused. Annabelle's touch felt so warm, so opening. "Men don't know some things, can't know them," Victoria said. "The basic need for comfort in a relationship. The need to be held close." Feeling the lingering effects of Annabelle's herbs, Victoria sat back down on the bed.

"Here, girl, let's rest a little while before breakfast comes, and talk." Annabelle lifted the Eiderdown and sheet so Victoria could climb under. Victoria took her robe off and threw it on the loveseat and slid back in bed.

They faced each other in the bed. Annabelle seemed mellow, calm, as she had never seemed before. The sun came in through the sheer curtains and lit her forehead. "I never had no comfort from a man, is all I can tell you," said Annabelle.

Annabelle lapsed into Black grammar with a hint of her Georgian roots when she was relaxed. Victoria found the sound of her colloquial voice like a lullaby. It was as if a top layer lifted from her, a painted sarcophagus, and all the layers of clothing, sometimes expensive and formal, such as she wore on business lunches, sometimes layered and flowing, like she wore in Germany lately.

In her African queen flowing robes in bright colors, Annabelle looked lovely. She was earth, sky, looked as if light ran through her veins. She looked like the dark veiled woman who appeared repeatedly in Victoria's dreams, who she had later identified as the image of mother Kali, the goddess who brings the comfort of death at the right time.

Annabelle took Victoria's hand, which was resting between the pillows. Victoria put her hand on top of Annabelle's and Annabelle in turn put her hand on top of Victoria's. "This reminds me of the hands-pile-up game we used to play as children," said Victoria. She pulled her bottom hand out and put it on top, Annabelle did the same.

"And they got faster and faster until you both gave up," said Annabelle as they moved arm over arm slapping faster down on top of each other's hands. Then they both began to giggle like little girls.

Annabelle radiated warmth. Victoria thought is a good time to learn more about this brilliant woman who had been her benefactor, protector and now her midwife. "Did you ever love a man?" she asked.

Annabelle heaved a deep sigh. Sat in silence for a minute. "Here's my story. I've told no one but a few therapists along the way. They never did me any good, just took notes and my money and nodded."

"Annabelle, you don't have to tell me. It must be painful," said Victoria, putting her hand on Annabelle's broad shoulder.

Annabelle grasped Victoria's hand and squeezed it.

"Oh yes I do," she said, looking intently at Victoria, "I really do." She released Victoria's hand. Victoria placed her hand back on her own hip.

"Here goes . . . ," Annabelle said. "I was married once, married to Charlie Lee Johnston, of Rover Grange Georgia. Rover Grange or as we called it, R-G, is where I was born. It's on the eastern border between Georgia and South Carolina. Don't even show up on no map, 'cept for ones you git at Sam's Fillups just at the edge of town. Sam drew up and printed a map, Sal, his wife used them for placements in their diner up behind the Fillup. Actually the place is called "Sam and Sal's Fillup—Gas and Home Cooking." "They lived right behind the station in a two story place, unusual in those parts. And on the bottom of the placemat it said 'Sam and Sal's put Rover Grange on the map.' "

"Anyways, I did luv Charlie Lee, I mean L U V, Luv. He was a star baseball player in Rover Grange High School, a pitcher and home run hitter, and batted 580+ from his sophomore year on. And I used to be, believe it or not, cheerleader and was home coming queen of RVHS." Annabelle's collar bone rose up and she smiled.

Victoria now could see Annabelle under the poundage, a raven beauty. She had good cheekbones, nicely shaped lips. At the top of her broad based nostrils was an aquiline North African nose and silky glossy skin.

"You too?" said Vicky. "I was queen of Boys Country Prep High in North Chicago. My boyfriend was the star quarterback."

"That's somethin, to git to be queen fa all those guys. Charlie Lee and I got married right after graduation, and we was both virgins. I got pregnant right away. He was restless, came home drunk one night, said he had enlisted to go to Nam, cause it was better than facing spending the rest of his life in Rover Grange. He left the next day and never came back. I went to see Grandmaw Barger the following week who fixed me a gut-wrenching potion caused me to bleed. I bled so bad I had to be taken to the emergency unit in Savanah to get transfusions. And they had to cut me and sew me up. I'm fixed. And let me tell you, girl, it was like when he loved me, a part of him was never there. If he had ever been there, he would not have wanted to leave me and go off to Nam.

But now that I think about it, there was always a way that I didn't feel real close to him, it was partly what I learned I was supposed to feel, you know. I really always felt attractions to some of my girlfriends. . ."

They lay looking in each other's eyes. Victoria placed her hand on Annabelle's forehead. Annabelle gently placed her hand on Victoria's shoulder and stroked it.

Victoria felt there must be more to Annabelle's story. "That's a story of doomed young love. Youthful love, with few exceptions, is love for the image of the other, love for the other's love, proving oneself. Not truly loving the other," said Victoria.

Annabelle took her hand off Victoria's shoulder, took a deep breath and swallowed. "You're right. Course the deeper stuff goes back to my Daddy. I tried a few mens after that, but always, always found they were not there, not with me. They just screwed me. If you ask me, those books about women's sexual response did more harm then good. They always seemed to be doing things mechanically, like it was a contest with a winner and a loser, only when you make it a contest you kill the heart of it, which means you've lost from the start." She looked at Victoria with her deep brown eyes. "What's your story, girl?"

Victoria's heart felt heavy, like a stone. "The search for the right man is like a search for God. He's everywhere. He's nowhere. Really he's within you." Victoria's heart felt heavy as a stone. "I had an abusive boyfriend, Giovanni, scared the hell out of me. When he smoked pot and felt paranoia, he would rant and rave, once he threw me against the wall. I was so gullible. He kept saying he didn't smoke or he would quit. He was 6'4" and had the psyche of a raging bull with the mind of a computer programmer who hated himself because he wasn't bright enough to do pure math," Victoria said.

"I knew you must have been through junk with men. Poor baby. Otherwise you wouldn't have been so engrossed in the dead white guys with grand ideas," said Annabelle.

Victoria tucked the eiderdown between her and Annabelle. She was uncomfortable without a protective physical barrier as she readied herself to reveal more of her self. "I used to think when my man hollered, coming inside me; it was only for me, no one else, that it was so special between us it could not be any better. Now I know this was for him just sex. I could have been anyone else and he would have bellowed just as loud."

"If a man could just lie with me like this, and talk to me, and if we could just find peace together." Victoria's heart raced. Time to focus back on Annabelle. "But I'm getting carried away. Annabelle, tell me, if you wish, what happened with your Daddy," said Victoria.

Annabelle looked her in the eyes. "It's hard to bring this up, but it is something a good friend should know." She took a deep breath. "Here goes. Papa did not spare the rod. He beat me, my sister and my Mom every night. It's an old story. Ancient. Men beating wives, children. So old and boring. Why does a man live with a woman if he wants to beat her, have chillens only to chastise and hit 'em up? I believe such a thing only happens so much among humans, and we are 'God's chillen' the preachers say? Where? Where is this God? What my Daddy had was demons. Yes he could be charming. He was a very handsome man. No drinks he was cranky. One drink charming. Two, amorous and corny. Three drinks and he beat up anyone in sight." Annabelle sobbed and shook.

Victoria held her. "It's O.K. dear, your Daddy's not here, not going to get you now," said Victoria. In a moment she was crying too, for herself as well as for Annabelle. They held each other until the bed was soaked in sweat and tears.

Almost abruptly, Annabelle stiffered. She sat up and shouted. "God, how I hate mens. How I hate the mo-fuckers. How the hell can you seek them out with such passionate devotion? How can you? George and Martin, they's mens too. And I'll tell you what. I helped the first black man get to be mayor. Nice bright guy from South Chicago. And he gets there and what does he do? nothing! little or nothing but talk good and go on with cut backs to the schools and cuts to Head Start and other inner city endeavors–and screw the poor! Mens are so far from grown up. Like big adolescents," said Annabelle. She threw on her black robe over her white nightgown and tied it around her waist.

"Not that different from any politician I know," said Victoria. "I wanted so badly to believe in a man. The work of these men, George and Martin is the work of the gods, or so I thought. The search for truth, justice. I needed a god-man, I mean, needed. George and Martin's ideas about time and being were–are so powerful deciphering them allowed me, then you and Guy to enter their time zones."

With her robe on Annabelle became her powerful persona again. She opened the door to the hall and asked Katie where breakfast was. Her tone was imperial, her voice resonated: "Please bring a pot of tea, and our breakfasts. Don't forget lemon and milk for the tea. We're famished."

Katie answered, "Yes Madam. I was waiting until it sounded like you were really getting up so as not to disturb your rest," she said.

Annabelle sat down at the window. "You are an amazing creature, Vicky. I thought you went to too much trouble just to write a philosophy book. All this time travel. I knew your passion for these guys ran deep. Now I understand. You were looking for true love. And you sure as hell were not able to find it among those deadbeat living guys."

"Yeah, as you know, the heroes of the civil rights and peace movements of our time, the 60s and 70s, like the other Martin—Martin Luther King, and Daniel Elsberg, were MCPs," said Victoria.

Annabelle laughed. "I'd forgotten about that acronym, Male Chauvinist Pig! God the world is full of them."

Victoria joined in the laughter. She got up and covered her bronze-colored silk pajamas with her white cashmere robe. She brushed her hair back over her ears. Her blonde hair seemed to glow above the reddish bronze. In the mirror the two of them looked like a figure-and-ground Rorschach, black and white.

"You've gone to an awful lot of trouble to support one of your NIL grant principle researchers," said Victoria, smiling.

"Well there's special passion in this project for me, too. And now the project gives me an outlet for another's life's project: Helping folks escape oppression. Cracking the mo-fuckers oppression here in their archetypical form—German Nazis."

Annabelle got up, went into the bedroom and returned wearing a black pants suit, her hair into a colored turban. "In case we get unexpected visitors," she said. Her forhead wrinkled. "Vicky, you must be ready to take the babies and hide up in the attic on a moment's notice."

Victoria surmised that Annabelle's contacts with the secret service were keeping her informed of movements of in their direction. She looked at Annabelle hoping for more information.

"Don't worry, Vicky, I can handle them. And there are blankets, food and water, and even a porta potty. Trying to keep the babies quiet is most important. The attic is sound proofed, but they are very savvy," said Annabelle.

Knock on the door. Katie entered with a tray cart, seeming to carry the warmth of the hearth in with her, rosie cheeks glowing. "May I pour for you, Madam?" said Katie.

"No thank you, Katie," said Victoria. "I'll gladly pour for us. It looks lovely."

"Very well, Madam. Is there anything else?" Katie looked at Victoria and over at Annabelle, who was seated at the bay window, across the room.

"Please check on the babies. If they are restless, bring them in," said Annabelle.

"Of course, Madam," said Katie, hesitating by the door.

"Katie, is there something wrong?" asked Victoria.

"I just wanted to thank you for helping me," said Katie.

"Sorry about your father and brother," said Victoria.

"We'll get them out, Katie, we havn't given up on them," said Annabelle.

Tears fell silently down Katie's cheek. She got a handkerchief out of her apron pocket and wiped her eyes. "Thank you both," she said.

"Any news of Dr. Mead, or from Professor Heidegger?" said Victoria.

"No, Madam, but Herr Guy has been calling. He asked that you call him. He said not to tell you until you are up and dressed. He wanted to make sure you were well rested. He left a number." Katie reached into her apron pocket and handed Victoria a piece of heavy linen notepaper, neatly folded.

Victoria was excited to hear from Guy and wanted to call him at once. She thanked Katie and told her she was free to attend to her other duties.

Annabelle got up from the bay window and picked up her tea.

Victoria looked at Annabelle's black pants suit and laughed. "You know, Annabelle, you are wearing the color white folks wear at funerals. Victoria uncovered her eggs and put jam on her toast.

"Your white robe, Girl, does remind me of a funeral," said Annabelle.

Victoria found this intriguing. Blacks wear white at their funerals and whites wear black as the color of mourning. "I once went to a Black Baptist church for the funeral of one of my students who died of a heart attack. "It was the most moving funeral, alive with music and passion. All the women and some of the men wore white!" said Victoria.

Annabelle took a forkful of eggs and a bit of sausage. She licked her lips. "That's when you get the spirit, and spirit comes to you more likely when

wear white," said Annabelle. Spirits to us Black folks are light. Live folks is dark. Dead folks is white, got no blood, no color, don't even know how to wail when they Momma dies."

"And death to us is shrouded in darkness," said Victoria. "I didn't tell you how after that the preacher came forward, speaking powerfully he worked us up into a faster and faster pace, into joy, joy, joy, he kept saying, until we all walked out after the body on our way to the cemetery clapping our hands and singing."

"Singing can heal the soul," said Annabelle. "Sometimes things get so hard ya just want ta give up. In my tradition, a midwife is called Elay Mama. Earth mother, home mother. In my triba; language Elay means home, community and earth, depending upon if you sing or speak it high, medium or low in your throat. The midwife brings the baby home to the earth from the spirit land, brings the baby to its birth Mama and Daddy's home, and presents the baby to the community.

"Young men and women grow up with a special bond to their earth mothers or midwives as well as their birth mothers. Vicky, I delivered your babies to the earth, now I must deliver them home."

"But where is their home?' Victoria got up and gazed out of the window. Just then she heard babies crying. "Bring the boys in, please, Katie. My bursting nipples remind me I need to feed them."

"Thanks to Mama Erda," said Annabelle. She opened her palms wide at each side as if she were drawing the energy up from the earth. Victoria took the boys from Katie and sat down on the bed and opened her soft white robe and unbuttoned her bronze silk pajamas. Putting them to her breasts she felt comforted.

This momentary peace was harshly interrupted by pounding on the downstairs' door.

"Katie, don't answer it!" shouted Annabelle. The pounding got louder. A German man's voice shouted: "We are here under orders from the Fuhrer. Open up at once."

Annabelle pointed towards the attic ceiling in the bedroom.

"No, I'm not criminal. I won't run," said Victoria.

"Shut up and do what I say, Vicky." Annabelle put a chair in front of the mantle. She stood on it and slid a white ceiling panel over. She pulled down a hanging ladder. Victoria handed her the babies and climbed up.

Victoria lay on her stomach on the floor of the attic, which was covered by an old threadbare Oriental rug.

Annabelle held little George over her head. Then she handed little Martin up: "Ironic, he is Martin's son, but George looks more Aryan," she added.

One of the boys started to gurgle. "Hush, Hush," said Victoria. "Momma's here, Momma's here."

Annabelle whispered. "Victoria, you must stay up here and keep them quiet until I come for you. It may not be until after dark. We leave tonight."

Footsteps clumped in crescendo up the stairs. "Germans make good boots," said Annabelle. She shut the ceiling panel and moved the chair back to its place by the table. She quickly took the second plate and teacup off the table and slid them under the table.

She signaled Katie to open the door. With the door open the two uniformed officers charged past.

Annabelle stepped forward with queenly dignity. Her voice rang with outrage. "What brings this invasion? Why this interruption of my work?" she said sharply in impeccable German.

"The Fuhrer demand the German, Dr. Von Dietz, and the two German babies," said a tall young man with a red nose.

"We are here for Dr. Victoria Von Dietz. She must come with the Fuhrer's babies," said the other officer. His uniform was a bit large. He puffed up his chest as if to try to fill it.

He stomped around the room, tapping on the walls, looking under pictures. He opened the closet and sorted through the hangers. He pulled out a gray suit with a long skirt and fitted jacket. "This is about a woman's size eight or ten. Obviously it is not yours, you are too well fed." He looked at Annabelle and grinned.

"Frau Fetzer will be outraged at you invading her wardrobe." Annabelle glared at him. "My tribe values the benefits of storing your reserves in case your fortunes change. You may want to put on a few liters yourself, in case things change for you." She patted him on the rear end, then on the tummy. He blushed and his face melted. Suddenly he looked like a scrawny boy of fourteen, grown too fast. Then, catching himself, he stood tall again. The other officer said, "an awfully friendly wench. I have heard stories of negro women's charms." He leered at Annabelle.

"They are all true. But I don't have time to show you boys anything about that now. I've got work to do. You both better leave before Frau Fetzer returns and complains to Herr Fetzer." She pointed toward the stairs. "Katie show these men out." The two officers walked down the stairs and out the door.

Chapter Fifty-Three
Escape

I don't know whether you're frightened. I am when I see TV
transmission of the earth from the moon. We don't need an
atom bomb. Man has already been uprooted from the earth.
Martin Heidegger, *Only a God Can Save Us Now*

All day Annabelle remained watchful, in touch with her allies from the underground. Herr Fetzer helped diffuse the situation from behind the scene. We may make it out of Germany yet, she mused.

Annabelle never felt so entranced by anyone, man or woman, as she was by Victoria. She reflected on where this involvement had taken her–she had supported Victoria's time travel research back to 1930s Chicago. She marveled at Victoria's accounts of arriving there married to the reknowned George Herbert Mead and visiting Jane Addams at her famous Hull House. Annabelle also supported Victoria's trip to Germany, in pursuit of world acclaimed philosopher, Martin Heidegger, and his deeper philosophy of time! At first she had seen Victoria and her work as a way to turn back the clock, change the course of history. Victoria may be able not only to develop a theory and means of time travel, but to use it to some good ends. Why not slit the throat of Adolph Hitler if she could get close to him, why not cut off the head of the Holocaust before it got fully underway!

No point in musing about this plan anymore. She did not expect twin infants to enter the picture, or her love for Victoria and desire to bring her safely home. Their sole purpose now must be to get out for the sake of the babies and their own hides.

Just after sunset, Annabelle opened the ceiling roof ladder in the bed-room closet. She hoisted up the ladder, stuck her head in. "Phew! Stuffy." She pushed herself up a couple more rungs. She was able to shove her huge bosom through the opening, one breast at a time, but could budge no more.

"Girl, are you all right? It's me, Annabelle. We've got to get out, tonight. I couldn't squeeze my butt up this hole if someone had buckshot behind me!"

"Annabelle!" said Victoria, her voice vague, sleepy. "I was afraid we'd die stuck up here." Victoria looked pale. The babies blinked their eyes, whined.

"How are my little darlings?" said Annabelle cooing at them. They cooed and gurgled back. "You were such good boys when the police came. No sounds out of you. I think you two are avatars, know why you're here and what's going on. Isn't that right?"

Two little blue eyes and two tiny brown eyes flashed back at Annabelle Victoria stroked them. Her face had a luminescent glow.

Annabelle felt a panic. "Victoria, come down, I've got a plan. Hand me George and Martin." Once down a couple of rungs, Victoria handed her one baby at a time, climbed down herself. Strands from her upswept hairdo fell into her face.

"We're going to leave early morning. Before dawn," said Annabelle. "George will meet us five miles out of the station. We'll get there by car. The train will stop for us. George and I are cleared to leave."

"The babies won't be easy to disguise or smuggle on a train," said Victoria.

"I've got you a special ID. You are one of the Von Humboldt's, returning to your Geneva residence with your sons. I'd hoped we could clear things up over here, like you could slit Hitler's throat or something and end this mess. But now I'm afraid for our hides. Hard to keep your priorities straight in this time warp thing."

"The boys do complicate things, you little darlings," said Victoria bend-ing forward and kissing each one as she put them on a blanket on the floor to exercise. "But it's a different story with Hitler claiming them."

"Adolph can't tolerate disobedience," said Annabelle. "He's hoping you'll see the light and stay." Annabelle recalled what happened to his neice, Geli, when she tried to leave Hitler's household. Found shot dead the next day.

Victoria looked up, then at her sons, smiling. There was something else Annabelle detected not only in her face but in her countenance. It was almost as if her whole body was beginning to vanish. Ah, this must be her own fears clouding her vision.

Victoria looked earnestly at Annabelle. "Eva Braun wants my babies, to keep them, get rid of me."

"There are no motherly bones in that Babe's body," said Annabelle. "She may put on a motherly guise, to impress her boyfriend, but soon as you'd be out of the picture so would they. She wants old Adolph to marry her and give her one of his. Saw films, her in the background, hovering around Adolph. I bet he has trouble getting it up. Otherwise, with an ego like that he'd probably have dozens of kids."

"Yet even he has a human side. He would become like a tender child, sobbing deeply. I'd feel then I could reach him, change him, if only I knew the key," said Victoria. "Then suddenly he'd become mad, his color turn grey. He'd withdraw inside a plate of armor."

Victoria's eyes were cloudy, her skin silvery pale.

"Whew! Scary guy. We've got to get you away from him. I pushed you into this. Now I just want you home and safe," said Annabelle.

"Safe has little meaning to me. But I'll go for the sake of my little ones, and my daughter, Kathy." Victoria picked baby Martin up, held him over her head and brought him down to her face and kissed him. He smiled and laughed. She put him down and picked up little George, who drooled on his nighty. "Help me give them baths."

Annabelle headed toward the bathroom. "I'll get some water ready, and towels. We'll try to catch a couple hours sleep, then in full darkness we'll walk out the back, climb the fence and a car will take us to the train," said Annabelle, as she ran water into the bathtub. The changes she saw in Victoria were alarming, yet compelling. She was at once more ethereal and more resolute. Like an angel.

∿

Later, Victoria and Annabelle, each carrying one baby, slipped out the back door. They whispered farewell to a tearful Katie. "See you soon in Chicago,"

Katie said. Schutz thought it best if Katie go later, she'd be safer and less conspicuous on her own.

A man jumped out of the car parked in the alley behind the house. He opened the doors. "Rouse!" he said. Victoria's heart sunk. She had seen this driver somewhere before, but he was not Guy. Dear Guy. And because of her stay in the attic, she had not returned his call. The driver nodded at Annabelle, said nothing.

"Where's Guy? said Victoria as they settled into the large black car, and as an afterthought added, "Why are these cars always black?" she added.

"Vicki, they didn't make them any other color in these times, or very few, remember?" Annabelle's broad mouth turned up at the corners. "They had the good sense to know black is the power color."

"I'm concerned about Guy, now that he also has to deal with Kolya, a fugitive," said Victoria.

"He can handle himself," said Annabelle. "I think you're jealous of that woman."

"He's been shot once. I fear for his safety."

Victoria still felt jealous of Kolya, a powerful and highly intelligent beauty. Kolya may pull Guy into her life line out of Victoria's. . . But then perhaps that is his destiny. . .

The car pulled off the road onto a dirt pathway through the woods. Ahead the train engine snorted and puffed. They got out of the car and walked toward the train.

Victoria was relieved to see Mead standing at the door next to a porter. He looked much like he did in the picture she used to have on her desk, from which he had emerged. This seemed so long ago now. His skin was papery, cracked. It was one thing for Victoria in her prime to come back in time to the heart of this war, another for Mead, already old before they came together back in Chicago. His proper place now was not as a father of infants, but as a philosophical prominence in the world through the pages of his books.

Yet, when he held her close for a moment, kissed her cheeks, took hold of little George, she breathed easier. The porter, wearing a gun belt, greeted them and escorted them to a compartment. There was a large basket on the shelf.

Annabelle looked up at the basket. "Looks like whoever got paid for this thought of everything."

"Schutz paid the transportation minister and the conductor as well. They're probably hoping for a good recommendation," quipped Mead.

Annabelle reached up and pulled the basket down on the seat. She sat next to it. George and Victoria sat across from her, riding backwards, holding the babies.

"The babies are sleeping through the night, despite all the travel," said Victoria.

Mead smiled, "After all, they were traveling a lot while they were cooking," he said.

Annabelle opened the basket and pulled out a checkered cloth. She rummaged through the sundries. "Schutz is wonderful. We have ham hocks and chicken, hot coffee, boiled eggs," she said. A note fell out. Annabelle said, "We have Guy to thank! It says, 'Wish I could have enjoyed this with you. See you in Geneva, Guy.'"

He probably didn't have time to write me a private note, thought Victoria. Why didn't he say anything about going home to Chicago? Meet us in Geneva . . .

The train whistled and chugged off. The babies whined. Victoria opened her long fur coat and her sweater and blouse and put one child to each breast.

"You nurse them with that fur on, Girl, and they're gonna fixate on 'She-Wolves,'" said Annabelle. She grabbed a chicken leg, took a bite, then tucked it back in the basket.

"There are much worse things they could fixate on," said Victoria.

"Venus-in-Furs Nursing"—you combine de Sade with Melanie Klein's breast fetish. We'd better be awfully careful with their weaning and toilet training," said George smiling."

"George, it's hard enough nursing with the train jiggling like it is, but if you get me laughing, too, it will be impossible," said Victoria.

"O. K., Don't laugh. It may frustrate them at the breast, making woman haters out of them," said George raising his eyes and the corners of his mouth.

"Lord knows we have enough of them already!" snapped Annabelle.

"George, cut it out! I know you have no respect for Freudian theory or the criticism of it by feminists," said Victoria. "I'm just glad there are no anti-fur-coat activists around. I sympathize with their cause and would never buy a fur coat, but in a Berlin winter, my mothers' hand-me-down has been a life saver."

"At last we're on our way home, darling," said Mead, a loving expression in his deep blue eyes.

"Great Spirit willing, we make it," said Victoria. She felt the steady vibration of the train, soothing her sensitive bottom, wet with blood now beginning to saturate the cotton padding. "The way I'm bleeding it's like having three of us in diapers," she added.

"Are you sure you're not hemorrhaging? You've not had time to recover," said George. The sun was coming up over the mountains on the right side of the train.

"Your bleeding should be tapering off by now," said Annabelle.

"It is, but then suddenly it flows again. But that's normal, I think, especially with twins," said Victoria. She didn't want to alarm them by revealing how many kotex and diapers she was using.

The train slowed down to a crawling speed as it approached a train coming from the opposite direction. The car rocked back and forth. A green flowered canvas bag, filled with diapers and baby clothes fell on Mead's lap. He got up to rearrange the bags. Annabelle turned out the light so they could not be seen from the other train. The other train became a jagged succession of still photographs in a silent film.

There were two cars of uniformed men. Those in the first car wore officers' peaked hats. A smokey haze dimmed the light in the car. The car had tables with white linen cloths and small lanterns. Some of the men held large beer steins and lamb ribs to their lips. Rosie cheeked young women stood by the table where two men sat, sucking large cigars, one of them with his hand on the back of a woman's skirt.

"Those Nazi officers are having a party. First time I've seem rack of lamb in Germany," said Annabelle.

The next car flashed rows of uniformed men in blue-grey jackets. They all faced forward under glaring lights. Victoria caught the eyes of one high cheek boned young man, who looked like her sixteen-year-old cousin Freddie.

He was holding up a newspaper. Victoria caught the front page: "Frankfurter Zeitung. Gains on the Front: Fuhrer Predicts Rapid Victory!"

Three more cars packed with soldiers followed. Victoria looked down at little Martin and George who were asleep after their meal. She shifted one away from her breast, wiped his mouth with an embroidered handkerchief and handed him to Annabelle then cleaned and held the other. She looked up and was startled to see familiar faces in the car creeping past them.

"Oh my God, It's Schutz and Wagner" she exclaimed. She saw several sleepy children, then recognized the frozen grief on a woman's face, an elderly couple, a couple of women and a seat full of children, their faces taut and dreary. A little girl with braids looked out the window trying to see into their train. A soldier stood at the end of the car, holding an automatic rifle with a bullet belt hanging from his chest.

Then Victoria saw them, Guy and Kolya, her auburn hair spread across his chest, her head bobbing on his shoulder. Victoria felt a rush of blood gushing out of her vagina. "It's O.K., she said to herself. You have George, your babies, and yes, your dear friend Annabelle."

"That group is being brought into Germany," said Annabelle. They are going the wrong way. Looks like Fragenzimmer may be up to his tricks again.

"We get some out, but many more are brought into the camps," said Mead.

Victoria felt her stomach sink into her knees.

"Guy and Schutz are with them. They'll make it. Here George, hold your son" said Annabelle as she lifted the little brown eyed baby from Victoria's breast.

Mead took the baby, smiled and rocked him. His eyebrows crinkled and he turned pale. His jealousy and antagonism towards Heidegger is evident, but he's curbing it well Victoria observed.

"Now that you've fed the little ones, its time for us. Let's eat!" Annabelle pulled herself loose from her long skirts and scarves. She faltered as the train speeded up. She got her balance, then up again and pulled the checkered cloth from inside the basket. She set up the little fold out table and distributed the victuals. "Can't have you going hungry with those two hungry little devils to feed. She pulled out a thermos and cups and poured each some coffee, found some goats' milk and put some in Victoria's. "George, why don't you get out the bottle of brandy I saw in there and open it for us.

Mead handed little Martin to Victoria and gave Victoria a peck on the cheek. He stood up, and pulled out the bottle. He took a knife out of his vest pocket, and loosened the cork. He poured brandy some into each coffee. "Schutz knew we would need something to warm us up," he said.

Victoria looked at Mead. "You do need some brandy, my dear, you look tired," she said.

"I'm glad not to be ahead in the 1970s, when nursing women are not supposed to drink, at all," said Victoria. "When my first baby, Kathy, was born, the doctor actually prescribed a glass of sherry for me each night while pregnant. But better go light on the brandy in my cup." She took a sip of the coffee and began to eat.

"George, you're not looking too ginger, what gives?" said Annabelle.

"I'm exhausted. And I've got deep problems with my philosophy," said Mead, taking a slug of brandied coffee.

Annabelle bellowed. "I should have known. Its not enough we are trying to escape from Nazi Germany in the middle of the night. It's your philosophy!" Annabelle took a mammoth bite of a ham hock sandwich she put together for herself.

"I wonder what I can do to resolve things. Should I rewrite my philosophy to include Being? Can Heidegger rewrite his to include birth as a basis as well as death?" said Mead. He picked a piece of bread off his paper napkin, took a bite.

"That's all beyond you and Heidegger now," said Annabelle. "Its up to younger folk, like Victoria, who I think, given where we are, has made her case."

"So I'm just a Has Been," said Mead.

"Shaw, your work and Heidegger's together made an enormous difference to issues in the twentieth century, dealing with issues of war, technology, loss of meaning and being. Max Weber saw it coming and called it 'technology without spirit, sensuality without heart—a nullity calling itself civilization', or something like that," said Annabelle. She took a bite of chicken leg.

"Thanks, Annabelle. Nice to hear such an interesting conversation in the middle of the night," said Victoria.

"Annabelle, that's the first time I've heard you say anything good about my work," said George, looking at Annabelle. "I'll forgive you for including me in the same sentence with Martin." Having finished eating, George took out his pipe.

"George, you already brought Martin in. Besides, he's almost part of the family now," said Annabelle.

Victoria looked cautiously at George and smiled, hoping to smooth over old wounds. Why was Annabelle so insensitive to George's feelings, stirring things up like this? But George smiled.

"Satisfying snack," said Annabelle, putting the leftovers into the basket. George put his arm around Victoria and took a long drag off his pipe. Victoria felt comforted in his arms, holding the babies with the train rocking them gently along. And yet, she thought of what it may have been like if these were Guy's arms . . .then feel asleep.

Chapter Fifty-Four
Fragenzimmer Shows Up

The brakes of the train screeched, augmented by the wails of little Martin and little George. "Where are we?" Victoria woke thinking perhaps she was dreaming. But no, the nightmare was real. They were on a German train in the middle of the night, hoping to make it to Geneva. She rocked and soothed the twins. Mead was already standing by the door.

Annabelle opened the shade on the compartment window. "Looks like nowhere." It was black out the window. Annabelle's turban fell off. Her hair was wild, framing her head like Medussa's snakes.

The train ground to a halt. Scuffling on the gravel outside the window, clipped German, flashlights bobbing. Boots stomping up the steps, the heavy door clattered open. A tense, clipped voice, "We are here to speak with Dr. Von Dietz. Frau Professor Victoria Von Dietz und her husband Dr. George Mead." This voice was high pitched, strained, like an out of tune viola. It was all too familiar.

"It's Fraggy," said Annabelle, tucking her tresses under her turban and smoothing out her tunic. "He may have been forced to come after us and have a back-up plan in mind. Be careful not to give away our agreements with him, " she whispered and snapped the shade down.

The conductor protested. "Nicht hier, we cannot stop this train." There was a dull thud, then clunking like someone had fallen.

"Hell," said Mead. "The conductor was one of us, in the underground, a friend of Schutz."

Heavy footsteps through the hallway, pounding on the compartment window. "Riechsminister's office, open at once."

Fragenzimmer tromped in. His bloodshot eyes gazed at Victoria, the babies. Two uniformed gorillas stood behind in the hallway.

"Good evening, Frau Professor Mead, Herr Professor Mead, Queen Okubiko. May I trust you and Die Kinder gehts well?" He smiled with one side of his mouth, somehow managing to raise the opposite eyebrow.

"Herr Fragenzimmer! What do you want? Why have we stopped?" said George. "We must get on to Geneva. We have special embassy transport documents."

Fragenzimmer ignored Mead. He repeated his question directed at Victoria. "I trust you and the babies are well, Madam?" he asked.

She decided politeness would serve them best. "Veile Dunke, Herr Fragenzimmer. The little ones are doing fine, given all of the turmoil. I am fine also. Und Sie?" said Victoria.

Fragenzimmer gazed down at her, his eyes hazy. "Ah Sehr Gut. But too many duties to perform, and so many edicts to enforce." He focused on the babies. "Dieser Kinder were born in Deutschland were they not? Nearly so in Charlottenberg castle." His uniform coat hung in folds over his gaunt frame. He reached inside his pocket, pulled out a piece of paper. "Read this." He handed the paper to Victoria.

Her heart sank as she read: "Edict Number 352 of the Third Reich. All babies born on German soil or born of persons of German Aryan blood are legally citizens of the third Reich. As they are all children of the Fuhrer and under the control of the Reich." She handed the paper to Mead, her hand shakey.

"The babies cannot leave the Reich without the Fuhrer's permission," said Fragenzimmer. "Each of you must have special authorization as well. Please show me each of your passports."

Victoria's mind raced. If Hitler had wind of their leaving, he would be furious, and as with Geli, probably have them all shot. So this must either be some ploy of Fragenzimmer's or someone higher up, perhaps Fetzer. Or was Martin somehow behind this?

"We've already been through this," said Mead. "We have our tickets and visas approved. The American embassy will not look happily upon our being detained. Furthermore, there is a dispensation for all German citizens in the

U.S. and all U.S. citizens in Germany to be allowed to return home. Holding us up will cause Germans in America to be detained."

Annabelle stood, her face inches from Fragenzimmer's. "Herr Fragenzimmer has risen in power very quickly. But going down can be even quicker than rising."

Fragenzimmer shoved her into her seat, pulled out a gun and held it to her belly. "Any more such nonesense and you're finished. Verstehen Sie?" The two guards in the hallway drew their weapons.

Mead put up his arm. "Easy, easy. We will be able to clear all this up."

Fragenzimmer put his gun back and so did the guards.

"Thank you Dr. Mead. The documents, please." Fragenzimmer held out his gloved hand.

Mead reached into his jacket pocket and pulled out a brown leather pouch, removing papers from inside. Fragenzimmer snatched them from him. He read them slowly, moving his head from side to side and wrinkling his nose. He looked up at Victoria. As he had provided the documents initially through Schutz, he was a good actor.

"Frau Dr. Mead, you were born in Chicago, were you not? Your parents were born there, but their parents were from Prussia. This makes you also a citizen of the Reich." He opened the next one. "Herr Mead, your parents are of questionable stock, but mostly English. You will no doubt want to return to America as soon as you can."

"Not without my wife and children. Not without my colleagues on the other train," he added.

"Should you choose to stay in Deutschland, we have lots of work for you to do," said Fragenzimmer. Our universities are in need of good Aryan professors to replace the Jews." Looking down at Annabelle Carter Jackson scornfully and then back at Mead he added: "Your servant will of course be sent back at once. In Deustchland we have no use for inferior types."

Annabelle sat up and starred him in the eye. "I am Dr. Annabelle Carter Jackson here on a research assignment for the National Institute of Human Learning, United States government. I am also a member of the Nigerian royal family with a diplomatic passport. I am a non-combatant and will be exchanged for a non-combatant of equal status. However, I refuse to return without my colleague, Dr. Victoria Von Dietz." Her voice was full and rich and resonated through the whole car. The babies began to whine.

"I must nurse them," Victoria looked at Mead and Annabelle, hoping they would not mention that the babies were just fed a short time ago. Their agitation, Victoria sensed, was due to the malice and tension they picked up from Fragenzimmer and the fear they sensed in the room.

"Of course. We in the Third Reich give highest priority to our Aryan mothers and their infants who are the future of the German world. Please go ahead. There is no shame but only glorious beauty seen in nursing mothers for the Fuhrer," said Fragenzimmer. By now the babies were wailing.

"I need privacy. They must be nursed in peace or they can't digest," said Victoria. "Or do you presume to know a mother's business?"

Fragenzimmer bent over, lifted the blond baby, held him high. For a moment, Victoria feared for the child. But Fragenzimmer smiled and said "Don't cry, little one, you are born into a great civilization. You will be a noble master some day." Little George seemed to wink at her, stopped crying. He grinned, drooling on Fragenzimmer's face. Victoria stuffed her laughter, handed the officer a handkerchief. Fragenzimmer took the dark haired one and held him up. "They look very different, no? This one is not the true twin of the other. This one can go back to America."

Victoria thought that should this happen, ironically it would be the son of the German father, Heidegger who would be sent to Chicago, and Mead's son who would stay in Germany.

The baby grunted, shat in his diapers. Annabelle reached for him, stifling her laughter. She reached into the diaper bag for a change.

"Nurse them both here. You cannot leave this compartment right now." He told the guards to stay back in the hallway.

Victoria opened her blouse carefully under her coat and put one infant to each breast. Annabelle tucked a shawl around them.

The officer demanded her papers. "Hmmmmm, very interesting. No wonder your German is so good. Your mother was actually the bastard daughter of a German soldier! This explains your intelligence and your spunk. You are a lucky nigger. You may stay in the Reich as well. We are not prejudiced against any persons of good blood who have dark skin, as long as they are good workers."

Annabelle stood up, started to raise her arm. Mead put his hand on it, stepped forward toward Fragenzimmer. "Please, Herr Fragenzimmer, let my wife nurse the infants in peace before we proceed with these matters," said Mead. Victoria caught Annabelle's eye. She sat down.

Fragenzimmer hesitated, enjoying the control he had over their emotions. "Of course, the next generation must be served first," said Fragenzimmer. As Fragenzimmer turned around Victoria smelled the damp wool of his heavy overcoat and the sharp odor of his leather gloves, with which he whipped his right thigh. He stepped out and closed the compartment door.

"He's evil," said Annabelle.

In the hallway the porter argued with him that the train must proceed or it will be late. "We are Germans, not Italians or French!" the porter shouted. There was a shot, a clunk to the floor. Victoria wondered if he and the conductor were still alive. There was shuffling and the sound of something or someone being dragged across the floor then down the stairs and out the door.

Annabelle reached over to caress the babies, now sleeping on Victoria's breast. Victoria felt soothing comfort from the energy in her large black hands. She is the Great Mother, the Black Mother in my dreams, the Kali. I've come to depend on her. None of this could have happened without her, Victoria thought.

"Fragenzimmer must be fearful of exposure for his racket," said Mead. "I have mixed feelings about this. On the one hand I want him to be exposed as a traitor, on the other hand I want him to continue to facilitate escapes."

Victoria held both sleeping babies with her right arm as she buttoned up her sweater with her left hand. Her diamond ring caught the rays of the rising sun coming in the window. Tiny reflections moved around the ceiling and walls.

Fragenzimmer slapped on the door, pushed it open. "I see the little ones are well satisfied. That is good." He cleared his throat. "So then Dr. Mead, Dr. Von Dietz, we have come to an agreement," said Fragenzimmer. "A compromise. This is the American way, is it not? We take the blond boy, who is obviously a true German. The Mutter Victoria must stay at least until the little one is weaned. You may take the dark haired one back to the United States. Dr. George Mead and Fraulein Jackson, you also may decide if you want to stay or return to America."

Victoria's mind raced. Should I tell him the dark haired one must be Martin's? Victoria breathed deeply. What does it mean that both of their fathers were already dead before they were conceived in the first time zone of their mother? Does this place a new meaning on death? Ahead in my time, scientists have transmitted particles faster than the speed of light. This means objects can come into presence in space before they can be seen. I love my babies, but who are they? Monstrous for me to entertain such a question. They are both my sons. They are not symbolic surrogates for a philosophical resolution which I must accomplish. She felt the sweat on her forehead.

"I will not be separated from either of my babies. And, as a United States citizen, I must be allowed to return home," said Victoria.

"Am I to take it that you decided to stay as long as one or both of your infants remains here?" said Fragenzimmer.

"That is correct, Herr Fragenzimmer," said Mead. "We all go, or we all stay."

"As you wish," said Fragenzimmer. He spoke to his assistants in rapid fire German.

The whistle on the train sounded. The conductor with a welt on his head and accompanied by three trainmen carrying large wrenches came through the door bringing in a gust of cold air and a cloud of steam. "The engineer says the train must move on, immediately," he said to Fragenzimmer. "You will get off at once unless you are going through."

"Herr Fragenzimmer," said Mead in a courteous but no-nonsense tone of voice, "let me remind you that the funds we have promised are in Geneva and are to be released only upon the safe passage of all."

"You know, Professor Mead, the situation has changed entirely since the United States supports the Bolsheviks," said Fragenzimmer. He reached inside his jacket, pulled out a large black pistol. "Enough is enough. All of you, off the train, or must I prove I mean business," said Fragenzimmer.

The five of them followed Fragenzimmer down the hallway, out the door of the train. The two goons followed. The early morning air was cold and damp. It smelled of grease and coal burning from the engine. The rising sun was barely visible behind the winter clouds and the smoke of the train as it left for Geneva without them.

Chapter Fifty-Five
On the Way to Hitler's Chamber

The marble halls of Charlottenberg castle glistened in the morning sun-shine. Victoria's footsteps echoed in the long, hollow corridor toward Hitler's chambers. Little Martin and little George bounced in her arms. Her slim bias cut skirt brushed her thighs. Between her breasts, she felt the blade of the dagger. Would she find the means, the resolve to murder him?

They were in house arrest now, back in Charlottenberg manor, under constant guard. Annabelle felt certain Schutz would find a way to negotiate or bribe their way out. In the meantime, Victoria sent a note to Hitler, asking for immediate audience. She was ordered to come immediately, but with only the babies.

Marble busts lined the hallway, set on white pillars. She noticed a bust of Kaiser Wilhelm, and several generals. Had she missed the one of her great grandfather, a general under the Kaiser? Hitler was obsessed with pure German blood. He had documented her bloodline.

The boots of the two young guards behind her pounded like a timpani drum in her ears, an afterbeat to her own. George and Martin. Martin and George. George and Martin, their footsteps said. George: Her father's name was George, sure of himself, sure of the difference between right and wrong, good and evil. She flashed ahead to his painful death of pancreatic cancer. How he would have loved the twin boys . . . but that was another world.

Martin: The ever-present shadow of Martin Luther, like a great grand-father, looming over everything. There was Luther's *Small Catechism*, the daily memory work. Luther had something to say about each commandment. After repeating the edicts passed down by Moses, he dictated the meaning.

He was sure of himself. Thou shalt not kill, thou shalt not steal, thou shalt not commit adultery . . .and yet she was determined. Was it worse to kill one man in order to perhaps prevent the deaths of millions . . .? Martin Luther did not address this question . . .

The footsteps of the two guards clicked behind, afterbeats, as if they knew that being called into the Fuhrer's presence, into his private quarters, as a 'guest' meant she was extremely important. She relied on this and her past visits to Adolph's home to protect her from search, and discovery of the knife. Her footsteps set the tempo. George and Martin, Martin and George.

George Mead and Martin Heidegger brought new understandings to life, of time and being. Because of her love for their philosophies, she was here, with their sons and on her way to try to change history for the better.

A gust of wind rattled the tall windowpanes. The babies whimpered at the sounds. "Hush, little ones, your mother is here, hush." Oh how could she think of doing anything that may endanger them? But what was the greater danger?

A sharp blade of sun hit her cheeks. Why is he, The Fuhrer, Adolph, so interested in my babies?

Annabelle had insisted on coming along, but was compelled to wait in the front parlor. When Victoria protested this on the grounds that she needed her assistance with the babies, she was summarily told, "Nein. Both Nurse Beektoph and Fraulein Braun would be there to assist if needed."

"But they are strangers to the babies," Victoria protested. "The babies are used to Dr. Carter Jackson since birth." These comments went unacknowledged. Her insides quivered at the thought that Beektoph and Braun may be planning to abduct her babies.

As to Eva Braun's abilities to care for infants, she had no idea. She could get no image of what Eva was like from the pictures where she wore a dress with an A-line skirt, which always seemed to be blowing around her thighs, and a simple hat, shaped sort of like WAC's (Women's Army Corps) hats. She seemed deeply lonely, detached, out of touch, raised Catholic, perhaps plagued with guilt and shame that she was "living in sin".

Eva, like many women, seemed hypnotically in awe of her powerful paramour, Adolph Hitler, this intense man, a man of conviction, passion, action. He spoke as a prophet in a flow of German at a pitch reminiscent of passages of Beethoven. *Sturm und Drang*—storm and stress, is what musicians called the style. Victoria could feel it herself. Whether or not he is a good lover, his aura circles around the eros and thanatos connection, sex and violence, love and death. It was not just his animal magnetism, but the strength of his message, the conviction, the drive to take power in order to act.

The worst thing a man can be is a drone, a slug, like so many were; so many more were becoming. Did most men need a battle to rouse them from their sofas? TVs?

Her thoughts spun forward. If I didn't know what Hitler will do, I too would feel him to be a hero. Heroes are usually not kind to enemies. He is a Messiah, lifting his people out of financial slavery, captivity to the cruel taxation and reparations demanded by the allies after World War One. He answered the cry for help of his people, for all future generations of Germans.

The Fuhrer also carried that dark appeal of thanatos, the death wish that Freud thought governed us as much as the force of eros. Hitler made dire predictions that all would be lost if Germany goes down. Women love a man who is a protector, who attempts to take care of his people, who will fight, die for the good of all. This was his appeal.

With each footstep she got closer to Hitler. Understandable that Eva would fall in love with him. Eva, Eve, like a first woman. Maybe he picked her for her name, first woman. Eva didn't know what would happen. Many women have been wives and mothers of warriors. All the way from Good Soldier Schweck's wife to Mother Courage.

I have no such excuse. I know what is to come. I am still excited by him. I am aroused in the circumstance of the horrors, the camps now just beginning to happen. I know what will happen. I have no excuse. Can the power of death be just as appealing as the power of life?

Little Martin clung to her right shoulder. Little George to her left. They bounced on her hips as she walked, smiling and pulling at her hair and cheeks. I love them dearly. Their countenances are so pure, noble, light. They are innocent yet wise, essential. They are necessary. Their fathers, Martin and George, are jousting, dueling, fighting with words, ideas, in the background. I am fighting for their lives.

Little Martin and George's coos sound like songs of doves against the steady pounding of my footsteps echoed by the guards'–a funeral march.

They did not search me. Adolph wouldn't have wanted them to touch me. I am hot, heavy with a dagger in my nursing bra, nearly cutting my breasts.

I know what will happen if he continues. I know the millions who will die. I have already lived a rich, full life. More than one. But what of my babies? They are cheerful sweet beings. Maybe Adolph and Eva will change if I give them my babies. No, that is not the history. Hitler is crazy.

I want to go home with my babies, back to my time, my home by Lake Michigan, to my daughter, Kathy. I could take the babies with Guy and Annabelle to the beach, place them on a blanket, let them crawl along the shore, dig in the sand with little shovels, wade into the gentle waves, collect buckets of shells. Small and cone-shaped on Lake Michigan's beaches, with pink and blue reflections in the shells. Do these creatures still live in the Lake which some say is dying?

And Annabelle. I want her to be in our lives, my friend, earth mother. I want the sun to shine on us, and Guy and I would go hear B. B. King, make love every night, and go hear B.B. King.

The long corridor was striped with light and shadow, the sun shining in from towering windows, turning the floor and wall opposite yellow. The faces of every other statue were radiant in these spotlights. The busts in between were shrouded in shadow, seemed to be whispering dark messages to her.

Light: The bust of Immanuel Kant. Author of the categorical imperative: "Act in such a way that if all others acted as you, you would want to live in such a world. Treat each being as an end, not a means." Are we all capable of monstrous acts? If we can justify them? If we can project our fears, anxieties, short comings onto the enemy, the other? Can I know this, move away, deny, overcome my compassion?

I have compassion only for the innocent. Eva must have read *Mein Kampf*. No, perhaps not. Few of my friends and lovers have actually read my books. Yet Eva must know of the concentration camps. She must know of and share Hitler's intentions. But she does not know, as I do, what he will do. She is not privy to the wisdom of hindsight. Hitler illegally wrested the power away from the legislature. He used raw intimidation, threat, violence. He feels righteous in his violence. His SA is a pack of bullies and murderers. They think they are righteous, correcting the wrongs of the past, making right with might, as all loyal warriors.

Dark: The bust of Friedrich Nietzsche. No one is really kind. Only some pretend to be. The nobles and the pueriles. Nobles move forward, push ahead into creative acts. Pueriles grasp and claw, and out of resentment pull others down into illness and despair. The German people are poor, stomped on by arrogant American and French capitalists and fortune hunters.

Germany is the land of music. Mozart, Beethoven, Wagner, Mahler, writing away the time, and great philosophy. Americans do not recognize or remember their great philosophers, such as Mead and James. Instead, they revere Benjamin Franklin's with his law of material accumulation.

War and rape, murder, all are integral to human history. Is it coming to that time again, with overpopulation? The eleven million killed because of Hitler's regime, the sixteen million murdered by Stalin, the nine million murdered in Vietnam by the United States, the million in Hiroshima. Multiply them out by two generations and there would be another ten billion on an already stressed planet. Are we like overcrowded rats eating each other, but because we are plagued with morality, we must find reasons, explanations, justifications, lies.

We lie to ourselves, to our gods. But the gods are indifferent.

Light. The noble face of Kaiser Ferdinand with his long, aquiline nose. He welcomed all into his castle and strengthened the bonds with neighbors. His aim was power. The weak-minded masses need one enemy to focus on. Only then can they focus their energies, said Hitler in *Mein Kampf*. His focal point was the Jew. Hitler is a social monster.

Will the guards follow me into his room? If Eva held the babies, can I stab Hitler and get away? It is better, more real to think of him as Adolph, crazy Adolph, rather than as Der Fuhrer.

Dark: the cool shadow falls on another philosopher's bust. Schopenhauer. *The World as Will and Representation.* Everything that happens does so because of the force of will. The will of most is stupid and limited. The world is over-run with the lazy and the stupid. Germany after loosing world war one was a "dehorned Siegfried." The Alpha male gets the drones moving, masculinizes them. He woos them and all women into devotion, submission. The same feeling I have for George and Martin, only Hitler is a knight, a man of action. Hitler is singular. A knight able and willing to fight and die for all German women. The drones must hide.

411

Victoria walked forward into a missing bar of light on the floor. A place between light and shadow. She glanced up. The drapes were closed over the window behind a bust of Fichte. His was a compassionate face. Could she feel compassion even for Adolph, crazy Adolph? He was destitute in Vienna. He was hungry. He suffered. He lived among the poor. Disturbed to see the alcoholism, broken families, the hunger. Schutz, a wealthy Jewish banker, was in Vienna at the time. He was not suffering. Hitler preached for German dignity. He knew the dangers of Bolshevism, developed by Marx, promulgated by Jews. He also knew the perils of democracy, distorted by bribery, beset with argumentation, unable to act.

Dark: He is destroying Germany in the name of saving it. The defeated, bewildered, frozen faces of Jewish scholars in lines in the camps, Hullerst's body in the snow, surrounded with blood. Anne Frank. I must use the dagger. This is why I am here. This is my destiny. But what of little George and Martin?

Chapter Fifty-Six
The Final Solution

For there will be an end
to the dogfaced gods in wingtip shoes or Gucci slippers
in Texas boots and tin hats
in bunkers pressing buttons
Lawrence Ferlinghetti, *Endless Life*

A t last she reached the steps to Hitler's chambers. Victoria's body was soaked in sweat. The back of her neck tingled as she reached the tall doors with the elongated handles. Little George patted her gently on her face in the rhythm of the guard's footsteps. Then Martin joined in and laughed with delight. She kissed each of them on the cheeks and laughed herself. Her hair was piled on top of her head, ringlets dangling in front of her ears.

She walked up the two broad stairs toward the doors and waited for the guards to catch up. Click–click, click–click. One of them walked up behind each side of her. They smelled of rich wool, leather and rum. They wore full dress uniforms, Cavalry, with long swords hanging from their left hips, augmented by pistol holsters over their right hips, looking like aristocratic versions of two-gun cowboys. "Enschultigen Sie Bitte Frau Dr. Von Dietz," said the one on her left. He spoke the spicy inflection of Berliner Deutsch. The other looked identical, both a head taller than Victoria.

"Bitte. Are you twins like my boys?" asked Victoria as they moved toward the door.

"Yes, Madam/Yes Madam," they said, one echoing the other.

"Do you know the Fuhrer well?" She hoped to distract them, get them to trust her, make them less watchful.

"Yah, he knew us as small boys," said the one on her right.

The one on her left chimed in. "We were orphaned during the great war, just boys. He found us on the streets and took us to a military school. He has been the closest we have had to a father. Such a warm heart." They beamed. George and Martin beamed back at them.

The one on her left knocked three times on the door, stepped aside.

"Machen Siet Auf!" It was Hitler's rich baritone.

Victoria's mind raced. Little Martin kicked her as he squirmed in her arm. She felt the cold dagger against her breast. "Calm down, little ones." They looked good in their little blue knit sweater suits. Above all she wanted them to be safe. But she had a mission to perform. Like Lady MacBeth she must steel herself with resolve to use the dagger. She rehearsed in her mind how reaching behind him she could slice his jugular. It would be over quickly. But she had to be in the right position. He must not suspect her.

Hitler stood at the center—in front of the desk with his two beautiful German shepherds on either side. Behind stood Nurse Beektoph and Eva Braun.

The room was paneled in sky blue and snow white, with gilded edges. There was a Louis XIV desk beside the fireplace. Victoria walked past a mural of the Prussian Cavalry defeating Napoleon. On her other side a forest scene depicting Sigfried, sword in hand with one foot on a dragon. Smoke flowed from the beast's nostrils, torch-like flames coming from its mouth. A painting behind Hitler depicted Brunhilde on a white horse, leaping through a Ring of Fire on her way to Valhalla. She wished to have the courage of Brunhilde.

Then Hitler smiled at her, beamed at the babies.

She bowed her head, "Herr Hitler."

"Frau Victoria," he said, smiling. His using her first name with the polite "Frau" was disarming.

Hitler looked at the babies and said: "So these are my little sons." Victoria's stomach quivered at these words, but she simply raised her eyebrows slightly. She must not create an argument.

The Fuhrer hesitated, then came to her eagerly, put his hands over hers to support the babies, kissed each on the cheek. He bent towards her right hand holding little Martin and kissed the back of it. He smelled of pine and leather.

"Come, sitzen Sie sich." The German shepherds came to her, their tails wagging. One was Blondi, the other Adolph introduced as Rolf, the best of her most recent liter. Blondi licked Victoria's hand, Rolf followed suit. Would they attack her should she succeed?

As if to answer her question, Hitler raised his eyebrows at them and they sat back down, one each side of a large leather covered chair with a lion and an eagle carved across the back. The lion had a crown on its head with a swastika embedded in it. Victoria's heart pounded. The German shepherds had the majestic bearing of royal wolves, keen, fearless, loyal, alert, fast, powerful. Hitler's animal magnetism was stronger.

Most women die without feeling such masculine intensity as Hitler exuded, and such disarming warmth. Yet knowing of his deeper depravity churned her stomach. How could one man be so personally charming yet conjure, design, and command such heinous acts before and during the war to come? But the, she reminded herself, this is what soldiers were trained to do.

Lights flickered from behind Hitler's dark eyes, mirroring passing thoughts. For a moment they burned like full rage or deep desire, then melted to tenderness. Suddenly the light went out to nothing, like the empty eyes of Charles Manson or Ed Guine. Just as quickly the soft light returned. The rapid change in texture was fascinating, disconcerting. Did she imagine the flash of emptiness? No, she had seen it, felt it before. Yet her earlier visits lacked this rapture. Hitler put his hand gently on the small of her back guiding her to the sofa with his other hand. The infants gurgled at him as he smiled.

Victoria sat, placing George and Martin on her knees. Eva, across the room standing next to a red velvet covered chair, stepped forward, then stopped and looked at Adolph.

"Eva, mein Schotze, Professor Frau Dr. Von Dietz," said Hitler.

"I'm delighted you have come and brought the little ones," Eva spoke a low-colloquial form of German. Her smile reached more broadly on one side of her face than the other as she walked over to the sofa. She smelled of fresh parsley and lemon. Her complexion was clear, her nose small. Her lips were painted a light raspberry color. She wore an expensively tailored gray viyella dress, a string of pearls and pearl drop earrings. She was beautiful. Yet her slender body seemed weightless, stagnant. Eva hummed at the babies, who smiled and sung back, grabbing for her pearls.

Nurse Beektoph, standing beside Eva, cleared her throat, shattering the lovely fragile cordiality among them. The guards stood by the open door like wooden soldiers waiting orders.

Hitler flipped his hand towards the door. "Stand by at the outer door, as usual," Hitler said. They smiled without showing teeth, clicked their heels simultaneously saluting and barking: "Heil Hitler." They walked out the doors and closed them. Their footsteps once again sounded in the corridor, in a gradual decrescendo.

"Nurse Beektoph says you and the boys gave her quite a scare during your labor," said Eva. "I would have come to be with you, except the Fuhrer and I were away, in Munich. We had to visit my ill father for his 80th birthday. I'm sure you understand." She stared coldly at Victoria.

Victoria was bewildered. Braun had not even been introduced to her at that time. It was as if Victoria was her sister.

Victoria looked at Nurse Beektoph who nodded and smiled, occasionally looking Victoria in the eye as if to warn her to "watch what you say." Victoria felt as if she would regurgitate.

Beektoph cleared her gravelly throat, pre-empting any comments from Victoria.

"Yes, Frau Dr. Von Dietz had a very difficult labor. She had lost her water," said Nurse Beektoph. "Ones like that scream unnecessarily; she was scaring the other patients, upsetting the brave injured soldiers from the front."

Hitler raised his eyebrows, looked at Victoria.

"Dr. Schutz took me to my private midwife, Dr. Annabelle Carter Jackson," said Victoria. "She is trained in ancient African ways, which relax and comfort the mother. She put me under water. The babies were born relaxed and contented."

"We must learn how to do those things," said Adolph. "The ancient ways were often better. For such events there is a natural wisdom from the untainted nobility of native women."

This man does not sound like a racist, thought Victoria. But then even American slave owners put their babies in the care of Negro nannies. Eva was ogling the babies. Adolph said, "May I pick them up? Or will they cry?"

"Yes, pick them up." Victoria handed George and Martin to him. "These boys are remarkable. At birth they squealed with delight," she said.

True little warriors! The joy of freedom overcomes fear!" said Adolph.

He knelt on one knee, his black leather boots squeaked. He wore brown riding pants and a jacket with a belted waist and epaulets. His front pocket was adorned with a silver swastika and a golden eagle. He sat little Martin on his knee and held little George on his other arm.

"Dr. Victoria, thank you for bringing my little boys to us. May Fraulein Eva also hold them?" Not giving Victoria a chance to refuse, he signaled Eva to come with a swish of his neck.

Eva blushed and eagerly approached. Another woman living to adore a man. They both understood ultimate devotion. Adolph handed her little George. "He is blond like you," he said to Eva.

Victoria did not want to let things go to far in the direction Eva was taking them. "Herr Fragenzimmer has asked that I leave him, little George, here when I go home," said Victoria. She thought now she would make one more attempt for all of them to return home. "Of course I could not agree. The twins belong together. You can see. I can't be separated from them, I am nursing them. And I must go home."

Hitler looked her in the eyes, his hand holding little Martin on his knee, bouncing him slightly, as baby Martin smiled and babbled.

Hitler looked into Victoria's eyes. "You are a good and beautiful German woman, of the Prussian nobility. The Prussians, above all, know the sacred honor of Germany. Your Grandfather helped defeat Napoleon. These boys belong to Germany. They are my sons. Their true father alone will determine their fate. I can see now that you are correct, they belong together, but here in their homeland, in Deutschland."

Little George and little Martin whined and reached towards Victoria. She gathered them first from Ava, than Adolph back into her arms, then next to her on the large sofa.

"Fragenzimmer picked the wrong boy as German, Herr Hitler. The blond boy, little George, is the son of my American husband, philosopher

George Mead. Little Martin, here is Professor Heidegger's son. You can see the likenesses," said Victoria.

Nurse Beektoph stepped forward toward them. Eva continued to look softly at the boys and said, "Could this not be so, Adolph? I have met Professor Heidegger and there is a resemblance to the dark haired one."

Hitler cleared his throat and stood. "Such things happen in liters with more than one sire, why not with us as well?" He walked around the room with his hands folded behind his back.

Picking up on the change in mood, the infants began to fuss.

Beektoph stepped forward. "I'll take them to be fed. We have a formula ready, scientifically much superior to mother's milk." She thrust little George up from the sofa next to Victoria onto her large bosom, which seemed to be supported by an iron breastplate under her crisp gray uniform. George howled! Beektoph patted him on the bottom and reached down for little Martin who was already halfway on Victoria's lap. As she did, Victoria swiftly took George back before the nurse could think to resist.

"No. They have never yet been bottle fed," said Victoria, pulling little Martin to her. Now both infants were crying.

The two massive dogs stood up, their ears twitching. I wonder if they would eat the babies if left alone with them, thought Victoria. The dogs' eyes and countenances were blank, waiting. They were trained for violence. She remembered an article she read about a dog eating a baby. They will kill me if I raise a hand to Hitler, or if I shoot him, she now could sense.

"Sitzs Du" said Hitler. The dogs sat.

"There are only three of us he refers to by the familiar, Du," said Eva. "I'm the third." She smiled with her mouth, but her eyes remained neutral. She walked over to the two dogs and stroked the scruff of their necks. The dogs laid down sphinx style.

Nurse Beektoph said, "I will call a wet nurse. A good healthy woman of strong Aryan stock, daughter of an officer. She gave birth last year to an SS officer's child. Many young German women are stepping forward this way for love of the Fuhrer and for love of the fatherland. There is nothing more noble a woman can do then to deliver a child to the Fuhrer."

Eva added, "All men in the SS must be physically and mentally perfect with two centuries of pure German stock behind them."

"I see," said Victoria. "That reminds me of the cows in my homeland. The breed goes back to seventeenth century Schleswig-Holstein stock." No one caught the irony in her voice. "Even so, it will take too long for this wet nurse to arrive," Victoria added.

Now both babies were crying wildly. Victoria held them close. "Excuse me Herr Hitler. I need to nurse my boys. If not for their sakes, for mine, or I will be in pain. May I be excused for a brief time, please?"

Hitler's eyes scanned Victoria's bosom. His eyes are so intense I am forgetting where I am. I must remember the faces in the line of men at the camp.

"Please, stay here and nurse them. We will leave if you like." He lifted his chin and flicked his fingers toward the door looking at Beektoph, then Eva. They immediately turned and went out the side door. There was pain in Eva's "Aufvedersehen" and anger in Beektoph's silence.

At the door, Eva looked back, smoothing down the sides of her dress over her slender hips. "Adolph, I'll be in my parlor," she said. "Frau Von Dietz, please don't worry, I will personally see to it that the babies are well taken care of here in Duetschland." She shut the door behind her.

Hitler walked toward a door on the other side of the room behind his desk. I must act quickly, Victoria said to herself. She pulled the dagger out of her bra and slid it under her right thigh. She unbuttoned her gray suit jacket and her white lace blouse. She pulled the now frantic boys to each breast. The cacophony of the hungry infants became sweet peace.

Hitler turned and looked back at Victoria, standing perfectly still, as if stunned.

"I have never seen anything so beautiful." His eyes were moist.

"They are truly wondrous," Victoria said. The babies made soft sucking sounds. I must play this just right. I may have no more moments alone with him. He may leave at any time and not come back, leaving Beektoph or Fragenzimmer to handle the situation. Eva clearly wants them for her own. Maybe she can't get pregnant. Maybe Hitler is sterile or impotent. Maybe that is what is behind the virulence of his ranting.

"You may stay with us, if you like," she said. She pushed her thigh down on the daggar securing it in place. The handle dug into her flesh.

He stood for what seemed like an hour in silence, watching her. Her mind's music played excerpts from Parsifal, Tristan, and Siegfried. If Germany, as he said in *Mein Kamph*, was a "dehorned Siegfried," here he stood.

Finally he spoke. "I saw babies, orphaned, crying for milk and there was none to give them, back in Vienna, after the war. Now no German baby goes hungry." He strode to the sofa and knelt on a knee as if he were going to propose.

"May I?" he asked, a hand lifted up behind George's little back as if to pet him. Victoria nodded yes. Hitler's hand was gentle and soft. He put his left hand on Martin's back. After stroking them, he put his hands on the sides of her breasts. He put his head down between them, kissing her cleavage, a baby on each side of his head. Perhaps fathering the babies would sweeten his mind. Perhaps she should leave the babies with him and Eva. Her body stirred. He is warm and gentle at this moment. This is my direct experience of him.

No! I must do whatever I can to stop him. If nothing else, this would prevent the 1941 Edict which resulted in the SS killing 1,400,000 Russian Jews. The daggar was digging into her right side. Her heart pounded with fear. What if he finds the dagger? I could tell him it was for self-defense. He would understand this.

No! This is my only chance. Her mind raced through all the arguments of the past months. He is one of the most powerful men in the world. Who else would have stood up to German's enemies? But no! What about the Jews and other victims? Her mind flashed to newsreels she saw as a child. Auschwitch, Buchenwald, then the Nuremberg trials. But he was not the instigator of anti-Semitism, or blind hatred. It will go on without him. Maybe I could influence him if we stayed, change the course of history for the good. But that would be risky. I may not have the chance to convince him, the time it would take. His death would change history. What of my babies? Guy? George? Martin? Annabelle? No! I must act now. It's up to me.

She reached her left arm up and stroked the back of Hitler's head. She put her right hand over his and moved his more solidly up over little Martin. She slowly reached under her thigh and grabbed the dagger. Tears streamed down her cheeks. The babies were falling asleep. She raised the dagger around the side of Hitler's neck reaching for his jugular. From the corner of an eye she saw the dogs' heads rise in unison. We change history in each moment, she thought. Forgive me Great Spirit. As Hitler called out his eyes gazed at her in surprise, then recognition. Fangs exposed, the dogs leaped towards Victoria.

Biographies

For the sake of the stories I wanted to tell, I took license with the lives and events around them of some persons who were real. Here I set the record straight.

Jane Addams (1860-1935) was the founder of Hull House, the second settlement house in the United States. She was a founder of the Women's International League for Peace and Freedom, a social critic and reformer, and the first woman to win the Nobel Prize (1931). She authored of eleven books, which show insight and offer new theories of human individual, social and political development. She wrote in language not only accessible to the lay reader, but filled with moving stories and anecdotes from her life and work. She was born September 6, 1860 in Cedarville, Illinois, to John Huy Addams and Sarah Weber Alleton. Jane's mother died in 1863. John Addams was a prominent miller, active in state and national politics and friend and supporter of Abraham Lincoln. When Jane was eight her father married Alice Halderman. She graduated in 1881 from Rockford Female Seminary and received a bachelor's degree in 1883. After graduation she toured Europe. She suffered from a debilitating illness and recovered. In 1889 she purchased Hull House on Chicago's near west side.

At Hull House Addams fostered the self-esteem and well-being of immigrants and others in the community guided by her principle of extending the principles of good housekeeping, democracy and the inherent worth of all persons from the local neighborhood to the international level. Hull House expanded over the years including components such as a day care center, language classes, cultural events, a little theatre, music classes, vocational training, and a residence for young workingwomen.

Community leaders such as philosophers George Herbert Mead, Florence Kelly, Dr. Alice Hamilton, Julia Lathropp and Ellen Gates Starr served as residents and participated in the work of Hull House. Jane was a leading internationalist and Pacifist before and through world war one. Her books are accessible to the general public through the way in which they connect stories and dilemmas from the lives of people with astute analysis of the causes of suffering and workable means to alleviate problems. The topics of her writings range from exploitation of labor, child labor, adolescence and the causes of juvenile delinquency, the importance of education for all and respect for all cultures, women's suffrage. Her work resulted in the enactment of compulsory education laws for children, (1903) and child labor laws. She died of cancer May 21, 1935.

Hannah Arendt (1906-1975), was a German political theorist. She has often been described as a philosopher, although she always refused that label on the grounds that philosophy is concerned with "man in the singular." She described herself instead as a political theorist because her work centers on the fact that "men, not Man, live on the earth and inhabit the world."

Arendt was born of secular Jewish parents in the then- independent city of Linden in Lower Saxony and was raised in Konigsberg (the hometown of her admired precursor, Immanual Kant) and Berlin.

She studied philosophy with Martin Heidegger at the University of Marburg, and had a romantic relationship with him. Arendt moved to Heidelberg to write a dissertation on the concept of love in the thought Saint Augustine, under the direction of the existentialist philosopher-psychologist, Karl Jaspers. The dissertation was published in 1929, but Arendt was prevented from teaching in German universities in 1933 because she was Jewish, and thereupon fled Germany for Paris, where she met and befriended the literary critic and Marxist mystic Walter Benjamin. While in France, Arendt worked to support and aid Jewish refugees.

However, with the German military occupation of parts of France following the French declaration of war during World War II, and the deportation of Jews to concentration camps, Arendt had to flee from France. In 1940, she married the German poet and philosopher Heinrich Blucher.

In 1941, Arendt escaped with her husband and her mother to the United States. She then became active in the German-Jewish community in New York. After World War II she resumed relations with Heidegger, and testified on his behalf in a German denazification hearing. In 1950, she became a naturalized citizen of the United States, and in 1959 became the first woman appointed a full professorship at Princeton. She also taught at The New School in New York City and served as a visiting scholar on The Committee of Social Thought at The University of Chicago. Arendt maintained her friendship with Heidegger until his death with yearly visits. On her death at age 69 in 1975, Arendt was buried at Bard College in Annandale-on-Hudson, New York, where her husband taught for many years.

Marlene Dietrich (1901-1992) was the daughter of a Prussian Calvary general. Both her father and her stepfather died in world war one. She became a nightclub singer in Berlin, then a movie star with a unique blend of vivacity and melancholy, with special appeal at the times of war and upheaval. Hitler welcomed her to Berlin in 1931. She later abandoned Nazi Germany and during world war two entertained allied troops. She became a U.S. citizen in March 1937.

Eva Anna Braun (1912-1945) was born in Munich to a schoolteacher and dressmaker. She was raised Catholic, the middle of three daughters. Despite being encouraged by her parents in the arts through music and dancing lessons, Eva turned her attentions instead to sports and fashions. She met Adolph Hitler while employed by the Nazi party photographer in 1930. They became lovers in 1932, marrying only shortly before they committed suicide together April 28, 1945.

Martin Heidegger (1889-1976) was born in Messkirch, Germany, the eldest of two sons of hard working, respected Catholic parents. Martin attended Gymnasium in Constance on a scholarship at the age of fourteen, preparing for a clerical career. He continued clerical training in Freiburg, then studied theology and philosophy, writing anti-modernist articles in Catholic journals.

In 1911-1913, having discontinued clerical training, but still on scholarship to study Catholic philosophy, Heidegger studied natural sciences, philosophy and humanities at Freiburg. He assisted Edmund Husserl, father of the phenomenological movement. Heidegger completed his doctorate in 1913 and habilitation in 1915 both at Freiburg.

He enlisted for military service in W.W. I., in 1915. Due to heart trouble he was assigned to the postal censorship service and later the meteorological service.

In 1917 Heidegger married Elfride Petri a young Protestant idealist he met in the youth movement. She was a student of economics and supporter of the woman's movement. She was also reputedly anti-Semitic and a Nazi party member. The Heideggers had two sons, Jorg, (1919) and Hermann (1920). Elfride remained dedicated to providing him a stable home environment to pursue his work until his death.

From 1918 until 1923 Heidegger served as Privatdozent (lecturer) and assistant to Husserl in Freiburg. He took a professorship of philosophy at Marburg in 1923 where his ontological lectures gain him a reputation as an outstanding philosopher. Hannah Arendt became his student and his lover (1924) *Being and Time* was published in 1927, and was rapidly recognized as one of the masterpieces of twentieth century philosophy. Reputedly Hannah Arendt was a muse for this work. *Being and Time* was dedicated to Edmund Husserl who retired from the professorship at Freiburg in 1928, with Heidegger appointed as his successor.

In 1933 Heidegger reluctantly accepted the Rectorship of Freiburg University, and joined the National Socialist (Nazi) party. He was hoping that Hitler would help reassert the mission of the Western Universities and the nation. He had disputes with the party and resigned the rectorship in April 1934. Between 1936 and 1940 Heidegger presented lectures on Nietzsche, which were critical of National Socialism. The Gestapo put Heidegger under surveillance. Having been categorized by the Nazi leadership as "very dispensable", in 1944-45 Heidegger was forced to dig trenches.

After the war, (1945) Heidegger was brought before the deNazification committee and banned from teaching until 1949. In 1950 Hannah Arendt visited and they resumed their friendship, which continued with yearly visits until his death. Heidegger resumed his university lectures in 1951. Heidegger continued to write and lecture, producing his famous "Essay Concerning Technology", his work with the students of Medard Boss, and his collected writings. Heidegger died in 1976.

Adolph Hitler (1889-1945) was born in Braunau am Inn, Austria. His father, Alois Schicklgruber, the illegitimate son of Maria Anna Schicklgruber, was legally adopted at age thirty-nine by his stepfather Johann George Heidler, who changed the spelling at that time to Hitler. Alois had succeeded beyond all expectations given his impoverished peasant origins He obtained a post as a civil servant, and became a customs inspector in 1875. Alois Hitler married Klara Polzl in 1885. She gave birth three times before having Adolph, but all three of his older siblings died prior to Adolph's birth.

The family lived a solid middle class life style, with an overbearing father who had fits of bad temper. His mother, Klara, was kindly, neat, submissive and pious. She gave birth to two more children after Hitler, Clara and Paul. Paul died at age six, leaving Adolph to be her pampered only son. Adolph adored his mother throughout his life, carrying her picture with him into his bunker at the time of his suicide in 1945. According to his sister, Clara, Alois beat Adolph daily in a drunken rage. Alois retired from civil service at age fifty-eight, when Adolph was six years old. The family moved frequently to satisfy Alois' desire for the ideal location for his bee-hiving hobby. For two years Adolph attended classes at a Benedictine monastery at Lambach. He sang in the choir, took singing lessons and dreamed of one day taking holy orders. Hitler attended high school at Linz, but did poorly in school, perhaps because he rejected the idea of following in his father's footsteps as a civil servant. Adolph wanted instead to become an artist. He was known as a ringleader on the school playground, delighting in war games. Adolph was deeply critical of all of his teachers except for one, Dr. Leopold Poetsch, his high school history teacher, a fanatical German nationalist.

Alois died of a lung hemorrhage at age sixty-five, leaving his much younger widow and two children. Adolph was a mediocre to poor student in all of his classes except for free hand drawing, in which he excelled. He relished his years from age16 to19, when he played the role of the carefree artist. Not making it into the Vienna Academy of Fine Arts after two attempts was a crushing blow to Adolph. He decided then to become an architect but could not succeed in being admitted to architecture school, as he had not finished high school.

Adolph Hitler's mother died of breast cancer on December 21, 1908 when he was nineteen. He left for Vienna where he lived in the midst of this golden age of the city in poverty and hunger eking out a living selling drawings on the streets. Hitler had already given up drinking and was a vegetarian. He was reputedly shy with women.

Hitler left Vienna for Germany in 1913. He reported for service at age 24, in 1914. From 1914 until 1918 he fought bravely and with distinction, being twice decorated. His fellow soldiers found him intolerable in that he never complained or condemned the war. He felt betrayed and angry, as most Germans' did, by the Versailles treaty. From that time on he decided to go into politics. Adolph Hitler despised the Weimar Republic and blamed the social and economic ills on the "illegitimate power of Jews and Bolsheviks."

By July 1921, Hitler had become the leader of the National Socialist Democratic Party, the "Nazis". In 1923 he failed in an attempt to take over the government in Munich through what became known as the "beer hall putsch". He was sentenced to five years in prison, but was released after nine months. He used his time in prison to dictate a book to Rudolph Hess. In *Mein Kamph* (My Life) Hitler portrayed himself as the Messiah come to rescue Germany from the ruthless schemes of Jews and Bolsheviks.

In 1925 Hitler again began to speak in public, supported by his SS (body guards) and SA(Storm Troopers) who physically removed any protesting voices.

Due to the collapse of the world economy in 1919 Hitler's violent predictions and dramatic speeches gained world notoriety. The Nazi party in 1930 gained 107 seats in the Reichstag. Hitler ran for President in 1932, receiving over 13 million votes, narrowly defeated by Von Hindenburg. However Von Hindenburg appointed Hitler as Reich's chancellor.

Hitler won a majority in the last German election of the Nazi era, in 1933. In June 1934, after a purge of the SA, Hitler was confirmed as dictator of the Third Reich, merging the roles of president and chancellor on the death of Von Hindenburg.

In 1935 Hitler abandoned the Versailles treaty and built a war economy achieving full employment by 1936. In March 1936 Hitler occupied the demilitarized Rhineland without opposition. In 1938 his troops marched into Austria, greeted with open arms by most Austrians who were tired of the corruption and chaos there. He also liberated the Sudetan Germans. Hitler further consolidated his dictatorial powers by firing sixteen generals and appointing himself commander and chief of all the armed forces.

In 1939 Hitler dismantled Czechoslovakia. The Nuremberg racial laws were enacted and concentration camps expanded. Dissidents were persecuted along with Jews. In September, 1939, Hitler invaded Poland to secure "Lebensraum", living space. By June 1940 Germany occupied Denmark, Norway, Holland, Belgium, Luxemburg and France.

In 1940-1941 Hitler took over Greece, Yugoslavia, and Crete. He continued the bombing raids in England. On June 22, 1941 he invaded the Soviet Union. That same year the United States entered the war. In July 1943 the allies captured Sicily moving to Rome by June 1944. Continued attempts on the part of high military officials to assassinate Hitler failed including the German generals' attempt in July 1944. Finally accepting that Germany was defeated, on March 19, 1945 Hitler ordered the destruction of remaining German industries, communications and transportation. On April 29, 1945 he married his mistress, Eva Braun. On April 30, 1945 Adolph Hitler and Eva Braun Hitler committed suicide together in his bunker.

Thirty million persons died as a result of Hitler's extermination camps and because World War II.

Edmund Husserl (1859-1938) was born in Pursnitz, Moravia (now Czechoslovakia) on April 8, 1859 in a Jewish section of town, but his family had assimilated following the March 1848 revolution when Jews gained full rights as citizens. His father ran a textile business. Husserl attended the German Gymnasium in Olomouc. He studied astronomy at the University of Leipzig (1876-1978) as well as math, physic and philosophy. In 1878 he studied mathematics in Berlin. He completed his Ph.D. in Vienna in 1883. From 1884-1886 he studied philosophy in Vienna with Franz Brentano and wrote a Habilitationschrift on psychological analysis in 1887. He taught at the University of Halle until 1901. His studies of the underpinnings of mathematics and science in direct experience of consciousness resulted in the publication of his *Logical Investigations* in 1901.

Husserl became known as the father of phenomenology, publishing the Yearbook for Philosophy and Phenomenology while a professor at Gottingen. In 1916 he was appointed to the philosophy faculty at the University of Freiburg. That year his younger son was killed as a volunteer soldier in World War I. The war and the subsequent development of National Socialism were signs for Husserl of deep disturbance in European culture with a narrow rationality and bankruptcy of spirit, which he criticized in *The Crisis of the European Sciences.*

Although Heidegger worked with Husserl who promoted his success at Freiburg, Husserl saw after reading Heidegger's *Being and Time*, that Heidegger had taken another direction.

The National Socialists suspended Husserl's status as emeritus professor on April 6, 1933 (but reinstated July 20 as race laws made exceptions for academic non-Aryans appointed prior to 1914). The Nuremberg race laws of 1935 excluded Husserl from academic life and forced him to vacate his home of over twenty years. Despite these dire circumstances, Husserl continued his philosophical work until his death in Freiburg, April 27, 1938. Husserl believed that relativism, objectivism and skepticism were undermining the life of enlightened rationality which alone gave human life its purpose.

George Herbert Mead (1863-1931) was an American philosopher, sociologist and psychologist, primarily affiliated with the University of Chicago, where he was one of several distinguished pragmatists. He is regarded as one of the founders of social psychology.

Mead was born in South Hadley, Massachusetts. He studied at Oberlin College from 1879–1883 and spent several years as a railroad surveyor prior to his enrollment in Harvard in 1887. At Oberlin, Mead developed a close friendship with Henry Castle, which continued through a rich correspondence until Castle's death in 1895. At Harvard, Mead studied with Josiah Royce, a major influence upon his thought, and William James, whose children he tutored. In 1888, Mead moved to Germany to study with psychologist Wilhelm Wundt, from whom he learned the concept of "the gesture", a concept central to his latter work. Mead married Helen Castle, his friend Henry's sister, in 1891. The Castle family had a primary residence in Honolulu, Hawaii, where they owned a plantation. George and Helen Mead had a son, Henry, in 1892.

Mead took a position on the faculty at the University of Michigan in 1891, under John Dewey as department chair, leaving his dissertation unfinished. In 1894 Mead moved, along with John Dewey, to the University of Chicago, where he taught until his death. Mead was active in Chicago's social and political affairs; among his many activities include his work for the City Club of Chicago Mead was also active as a speaker, supporter and board member of Hull House, a settlement house founded by Jane Addams and affiliated with the university. Mead died of heart failure, April 26, 1931.

Mead is a major American philosopher by virtue of being, along with Charles Pierce, William James, and John Dewey, one of the founders of pragmatism. Mead is also an important figure in 20th century social philosophy. His theory of how the mind and self emerge from the social process of communication by signs founded the symbolic interactionist school of sociology and social psychology. He also made significant contributions to the philosophies of nature, science, and history, to the theory of democratic society, to process philosophy, and to a theory of temporality.

Mead the social psychologist argued that the individual is a product of society, the *self* arising out of social experience as an object of socially symbolic gestures and interactions. In his lifetime, Mead published about 100 scholarly articles, reviews, and incidental pieces. At the moment of death, he was correcting the galleys to what would have been his first book *Essays in Social Psychology*, published only in 2001. His students and colleagues, especially Charles W. Morris, subsequently put together five books from his unpublished manuscripts and from stenographic records of his lectures. *Mind, Self and Society*, is his most widely recognized work. In the *Philosophy of the Present*, Mead posits a theory of time as a series of "presents" which contain the past and the future.

Leni Riefenstahl (1902-) was born in Berlin. Her career as a professional dancer ended prematurely as she was injured at age twenty-one. She was a film star, director and photographer. She became famous for her propaganda films, which portrayed Nazi rallies with artistry and glamour. She celebrated her 100th birthday in California plagued by accusations of being a Nazi sympathizer. She claimed that during the Third Reich she was simply "apolitical."

Alfred Schutz (1899-1959) was born April 13, 1899 to Johanna Schutz nee Faille and Alfred Schutz (who died prior to his son's birth). Johanna married Otto Schutz, Alfred's brother in 1901. Johanna did not tell Alfred that Otto was not his biological father but his uncle until Alfred was seventeen. Otto raised Alfred as his son and worked for forty-five years as a bank executive.

Alfred Schutz was talented as a musician and poet, and also had an interest in science. He graduated summa cum laude from Gymnasium in 1918, a course that included eight years of Latin and Greek.

Schutz served in the army, joining the artillery, and performed dangerous tasks such as poison gas protection. After serving in World War I Schutz earned a doctorate in law in 1921, then became secretary for the Austrian Banker's Association. He joined the banking firm of Reitler and Co. in 1929 and continued with the company for eleven years. Schutz was of Jewish heritage but assimilationist in orientation, embracing some Christian customs, such as Christmas cards and presents.

Schutz studied economics with Hans Kelsen, Ludwig von Mises and Felix Kaufman. He began his extensive studies of Edmund Husserl's work in 1929.

Schutz married (Ilse) and had two children, George and Evelyn (Lang).

Schutz critically engaged Husserl's work, particularly developing the sociology of the lifeworld. He also critically engaged Max Weber's sociology of understanding and Henri Bergson's phenomenology of time consciousness. He became engaged in helping Jewish persons and their families leave Nazi Germany, emigrating himself to the U. S. in 1939. In New York he taught part time at the New School for Social Research, still holding a full time position in the banking business. Throughout this period he continued to write scholarly works. In the U. S. he became acquainted with the work of William James, John Dewey, Alfred North Whitehead and George Herbert Mead and became editor of the journal, *Philosophy and Phenomenological Research*. In 1952 he was appointed full time professor of philosophy and sociology at the New School at a salary of $3000 a year and chair in 1956-1957 with a salary of $8500. At that time he stopped outside work. In 1955-1956 he taught a course on signs and symbols, which included the work of George Herbert Mead, Husserl and others. While at New School he taught Maurice Natanson (who later wrote a book on Mead), Lester Embree, Fred Kersten and Helmut Wagner.

Schutz contended that to study the lifeworld, as it actually is experienced, requires a different methodology from Husserl's eidetic phenomenology. Schutz consequently developed a sociology of the lifeworld. Schutz developed a model for the informed citizen, which focused on speaking out in small groups as opposed to through the anonymity of opinion polls. He believed that each single individual had a unique viewpoint, and a unique responsibility to the whole.

Alfred Schutz died May 20, 1959.

Helmut R. Wagner (1904-1989) was born in Dresden, Germany. He attended public schools in Dresden, graduating in 1924 from a college level technical school where he studied engineering, economics and social sciences. He was a freelance writer and lecturer (1924-1929) and lecturer at the Volkshockschule in Thuringer (1929-1932). He immigrated to Switzerland in 1934 continuing studies in economics and social science and worked in the camera industry in urich (1939-1941). From the late 1930s until his emigration to the United States in 1941 he worked in the anti-Nazi movement.

Helmut Wager was an outstanding skier and long distance runner. He married Hannelore Joseph in 1951 and had one daughter, Claire.

In 1950 he began graduate work at the New School for Social Research, studying sociology with Alfred Schutz. He completed his Master's degree in 1952 with a thesis on Mannheim. He completed his PhD. in 1955 with a study of young labor elites. He taught at the New School (1952-1956), at Bucknell University (1956-1963) and Hobart and William Smith colleges (1963-1975). He was research professor of sociology until his death in 1989. He served as visiting professor at Texas Woman's University and the University of Alberta.

Wagner is the author of a monograph on early Lutheranism in Germany, religious authority and Max Weber. His books include: *Alfred Schutz: On Phenomenology and Social Relations*; *Phenomenology of Consciousness and Sociology of the Lifeworld*; and *Alfred Schutz, An Intellectual Biography*; and *Life-forms and Meaning Structures*.

Sources of Biographies

Barber, Michael D. (2004) *The Participating Citizen: A Biography of Alfred Schutz*. Albany: State University of New York.

Cook, Gary A. (1993) *George Herbert Mead: The Making of a Social Pragmatist*. (1993) Urbana: University of Illinois.

Elshtain, Jean Bethke (2002) *Jane Addams and the Dream of American Democracy*. New York: Basic Books.

Encyclopedia of Phenomenology (1997) London: Kluwer.

Heidegger, Martin (1976) in "Only a God Can Save Us: Der Spiegel's Interview with Martin Heidegger," published in *Philosophy Today*, Winter, 1976: 267-284, p.275.

Kershaw, Ian (1998) *Hitler, 1889-1936*. New York: Knoph.

Knopp, Guido (2001) *Hitler's Women*. New York: Routledge.

Safranski, Rudiger (1998) *Martin Heidegger: Between Good and Evil*. trans. by Ewald Osers (Cambridge, Ma., Harvard University Press.)

Wagner, Helmut R. (1983) Alfred Schutz: An Intellectual Biography. Chicago: University of Chicago Press.

Wikipedia.org

Growing up in a German-American family during World War II gave Valerie Bentz a love-hate relationship with her heritage. She loved Germany's music and philosophy, but despised its connection with Nazism. She made it her life mission to work for peace and justice and the fight for women's rights.

Bentz, professor of human and organization development at Fielding Graduate University, has written numerous articles about philosophers George Herbert Mead, Martin Heidegger, Alfred Schutz, and Helmut Wagner; all of whom she cleverly fictionalizes in her novel, *Flesh and Mind: The Time Travels of Dr. Victoria Von Dietz*. Also a psychotherapist for twenty years, she is additionally a certified yoga teacher and massage therapist.

Bentz won the first prize novel award in the Lillian Dean Writing Competition for *Flesh and Mind*. She lives in California with her husband and pets, where she is currently working on *Spank Me with a Wooden Tie*, a book of fictionalized memoirs.

Questions explored in *Flesh and Mind*

1. Is love more about the imagined than the real?

2. Is it possible to love a philosopher or writer you don't know, who may be already dead, more than a live man?

3. Is the attraction to a philosopher's work only intellectual, a matter for the mind, or is it deeply emotional as well?

4. If we could travel back in time, could we prevent man-made disasters, such as the holocaust?

5. Are persons who are recognized as world-class villains, such as Adolph Hitler, amenable to change? Could the right person in the right circumstances move them to transform their thinking and action for the better?

6. Is it possible for persons to mix philosophical/intellectual debates with everyday life events, such as birth, war, escape from tyranny, betrayal, real or imagined? Is it even possible that this ability is necessarily humorous and that this in itself ameliorates and changes the circumstances?

7. Can a normal heterosexual woman find that her most profound relationship may be with a lesbian?

8. Is it possible that rather than being a Nazi sympathizer, Martin Heidegger was in fact working behind the scenes to help in the resistance?

9. What is the strange kind of sexual/erotic attraction that Adolph Hitler, and other villainous men have on women, even highly intelligent women? What are the Jungian archetypes involved?

10. Under what circumstances could an ethical upstanding women be involved with more than one man while being true to herself and her utmost values?

27927168R00261

Made in the USA
Lexington, KY
29 November 2013